9-12

D0046555

HERON'S
COVE

HERON'S COVE

CARLA NEGGERS

HARLEQUIN®
entertain, enrich, inspire™

ISBN-13: 978-0-7783-1375-5

HERON'S COVE

Printed in U.S.A.

First printing: August 2012
10 9 8 7 6 5 4 3 2 1

To Jodi Reamer

1

WITH THREE DONOVAN BROTHERS AND AN Irish priest watching her, Emma Sharpe choked back her sample of the smoky single-malt Scotch—her sixth and last tasting of the night. "Intense," she said, managing not to slam the tulip-shaped nosing glass on the table and grab the pitcher of water. *Give it a few seconds.* She was an FBI agent, after all. Tough as nails. She smiled at the four men. "People pay to drink this one, huh?"

"Dearly," Finian Bracken, the Irish priest, said. "You're not one for a heavily peated whiskey, I see."

Emma tried to distinguish the other flavors of the sample— spices, fruits, whatever—but only tasted the peat. "I don't know if I'm one for a lightly peated whiskey, either."

A cold wind penetrated Hurley's thin walls and sprayed the old windows with salt water and rain. The restaurant, a fixture on the Rock Point harbor, was basically a shack that jutted out over the water. Now only a few lights penetrated the dark night and fog. Finian had organized the impromptu tasting, setting up on a back table away from what few diners were there on a windy, rainy late-October Friday. He and

Michael, Andy and Kevin Donovan were already gathered over a half-dozen bottles of high-end whiskey when Emma had arrived in southern Maine an hour ago, up from Boston and her job with a small, specialized FBI unit.

Only Colin, the second-born Donovan, wasn't in Rock Point. Mike was a Maine guide, Andy a lobsterman and Kevin a state marine patrol officer, but, like Emma, Colin was an FBI agent.

Not like me, she thought.

She specialized in art crimes. Colin was a deep-cover agent. He'd left his hometown a month ago, pretending to return to FBI headquarters in Washington. The true nature of his work was known to only a few even within the FBI, but his brothers had guessed that he didn't sit at a desk. Initially he'd kept in touch at least intermittently with his family and friends—and Emma—but for the past three weeks, no one had heard from him.

The silence was far too long, not just for his family and friends but for the FBI.

And for Emma.

She felt the draft at her feet. She had come prepared for the conditions, dressed in jeans, black merino wool sweater, raincoat, wool socks and Frye boots. The Donovans were in a mix of flannel, canvas and denim, no sign they even noticed the cold and the damp. Finian had opted against his usual black suit and Roman collar and instead wore a dark gray Irish-knit sweater and black corduroy trousers. He was a sharp-featured, handsome Irishman in his late thirties who had arrived in the small Maine fishing village in June. He had run into Colin, home for a few days in the midst of a difficult, dangerous mission, and they quickly became un-expected friends.

Emma hadn't met Colin until September. She suspected

his friendship with the Irish priest was less of a mystery to her than to his brothers. Finian Bracken was a fish out of water in Rock Point. He had no history with the town and little familiarity with the FBI. He also had a ready Irish wit, and he knew whiskey. He was objective, intelligent, tolerant—a safe friend for a federal agent with secrets.

Andy Donovan held his small glass to the light and examined the Scotch's deep caramel color, then swirled it and brought it to his nose. He raised his eyes—the same shade of gray as Colin's—to Finian. "Do you want me to tell you what I smell?"

"If you like," Finian said. "Just sniff. Don't inhale deeply. It's not a yoga class."

"As if you'd ever find one of us in a yoga class," Andy said, then shrugged. "It smells like peat."

Finian observed him with interest. "What else? Do you smell spices, fruit—chocolate, maybe?"

"Nope. It smells like an expensive Scotch to me."

"Have a taste, then," the priest said with a sigh, his Irish Kerry accent more pronounced than usual.

"No problem." Andy tossed back the Scotch and made a face. "I'm with Emma. Too smoky for me."

It was the final whiskey of the evening. The Donovan brothers hadn't left so much as a drop in any of the specially designed glasses, one for each whiskey. The glasses all had little hats, like Scottish tams, that concentrated the aromas of each sample. Finian had brought them from the rectory; Hurley's didn't have whiskey nosing glasses. Before turning to the priesthood six years ago, Finian and his twin brother, Declan, had founded and operated Bracken Distillers on the southwest Irish coast. Bracken 15 year old, an award-winning single malt and rare peated Irish whiskey, was one

of the night's offerings—or "expressions," as Finian called
his lineup of bottles.

Emma noticed Mike, the eldest Donovan, eyeing her from
across the round table. He was down from the remote Bold
Coast where he worked as an independent wilderness guide.
"Special Agent Sharpe's a wine drinker. Aren't you, Emma?"

She couldn't detect any hint of criticism or sarcasm in his
tone, but he still was looking at her as if she had done something wrong. "I like wine." She kept any defensiveness out
of her voice. "How about you, Mike? Do you pack a nice
Central Coast red in your canoe when you take tourists on
moose-sighting excursions?"

Kevin and Andy both grinned. Mike ignored them and
settled back in his chair. "I took a couple out on the river in
August. They had a wicker picnic hamper stocked with real
wineglasses, cloth napkins, silver cutlery, French cheese, a
baguette, apples and pears and two bottles of fancy wine."

"Must have weighed down the canoe," Kevin, the marine
patrol officer, said.

"Oh, yeah. They insisted on having a picnic on the river-
bank but they didn't count on Maine mosquitoes. They lasted
three minutes before we had to throw everything back in the
canoe. We paddled straight back to their car."

"Don't tell me," Andy said, amused. "The next stop on
their Maine tour was Heron's Cove."

"Couldn't wait to get there. I'm sure they enjoyed the
quaint shops and fancy restaurants."

"Everyone does," Emma said.

"I don't care." Mike raised his as-yet untouched glass of
the heavily peated Scotch; his eyes were lighter than those
of his three younger brothers but no less intense. *"Sláinte."*

Finian winked at Emma but said nothing. She reached
for the Inish Turk Beg, a clear, triple-distilled whiskey from

an independent distillery on a small island off the west coast of Ireland. She splashed a little into a fresh glass, set down the distinctive tilted bottle, then held up her glass to Mike. *"Sláinte."*

He swallowed the Scotch and she sipped the Inish Turk Beg, one of Finian's favorites. He had explained that it was gentle on the palate, clean and fresh on the nose, with fruity aromas, flavors of apple and orange zest and a dry finish. Emma wasn't discriminating enough to go much beyond whether she could get a taste down with or without choking.

"Colin would have enjoyed tonight," said his eldest brother, still watching her.

Emma nodded. "He'll have that chance soon. Lots of whiskey left."

"Are you and your FBI friends any closer to finding him?"

"You're assuming he's missing—"

"That's right. I am."

Her head spun and she wished she had skipped the extra taste of the Inish Turk Beg. "I can't discuss your brother's work with you."

Andy and Kevin were as serious now as Mike was. Even Kevin, a law enforcement officer himself, didn't have any information on his older brother's work as one of the FBI's most valuable ghosts. Emma had only a few details on his latest mission herself. It wasn't as if Colin couldn't handle himself in a dangerous situation. He was bold, aggressive and tough.

He was also sexy, she thought.

Incredibly sexy, in fact.

She kept that assessment to herself. "I'm sorry. I don't know why Colin hasn't been in touch."

"He's not a desk jockey in Washington." Mike got up abruptly, grabbed his jacket off the back of his chair. "You don't have to confirm or deny. We all know. He's always

stuck his nose in dangerous situations. Even as kids, he'd be
the one jumping into cold water and waves, chasing sharks.
It's his way."

"I understand that," Emma said.

"Is it your way, Emma?"

She didn't respond at once. Aware of the four men watching her, she picked up one of the tiny tam-style hats and set
it atop a glass. "Maybe Colin and I have more in common
than you realize."

"You're a Sharpe," Mike said. "You were a nun."

"A novice. I never made my final vows." Emma kept her
voice even, neutral. "I studied art history and art conservation
during my time with the sisters. I come from a family of art
detectives. That background helps in my work with the FBI."

Mike shrugged on his jacket. "I just think you have a knack
for attracting trouble."

"And you're worried about your brother."

"Maybe I'm worried about you, too."

She let his comment slide. She had already said too much.
"When do you go home?"

He grinned. "Not soon enough for you, I expect." The
seriousness returned to his eyes as he looked down at her. "If
you hear from Colin, you'll let us know, okay?"

It was more of an order than a request but Emma nodded.
"I will, Mike."

He leaned over and kissed her on the cheek. "Take care
of yourself." He shifted his gaze to Finian. "Thanks for the
whiskey and the whiskey education, Father. *Uisce beatha*. 'The
water of life.' I like that."

"We'll do it again when Colin's in town," Finian said.

"Yeah. We will." The eldest Donovan grinned suddenly.
"I think I tasted chocolate in that last Scotch."

Kevin and Andy thanked Finian and said good-night to

him and to Emma as they followed Mike out of the nearly empty restaurant. The late–October weather wouldn't faze them. They would take whatever weather northern New England threw at them in stride. Rain, snow, sleet, fog, wind. Wouldn't matter.

Once the brothers disappeared through the outer door, Finian sighed as he corked the Inish Turk Beg. "If you had information that could ease their worry, Emma, would you give it to them? Could you?"

"If I'd heard from Colin, I'd have said so."

"His story of an intense schedule in Washington has worn thin. I assume the FBI will be in touch with his family if need be."

Emma felt the whiskey burning in her throat. "The safety of an agent—any agent—is of paramount importance to the FBI. Colin's brothers know that."

"But you don't know where he is, do you?"

The look he gave her told her she didn't need to answer.

A strong gust of wind whistled, whipped more rain against the windows. The small, protected working harbor was lost in the dense, swirling fog. In September, Emma had gone on a boat ride with Colin, kayaked with him, picked apples with him. Laughed, made love. They had met over the horrific murder of a nun at the Sisters of the Joyful Heart, Emma's former convent. Until then, she hadn't realized another FBI agent had grown up just a few miles from her own home in Heron's Cove. They'd had a short time together before Colin was gone again, chasing illegal arms merchants.

He had the FBI behind him but, ultimately, he was alone. Emma understood he could go dark, but not like this. Not with no word for weeks.

His Irish friend's midnight eyes narrowed on her. "Colin's in trouble, isn't he, Emma? It's all right. You don't have to answer. I watched you tonight. I could see the answer for myself."

"He's independent."

"He's good at working alone. All the Donovans are."

She watched raindrops slide down the window. "Do you ever feel alone here?"

"I'm here for a reason. I have a purpose."

She glanced back at Finian. "That doesn't answer the question, does it?"

"It does for me."

She thought she understood what he meant. After the deaths of his wife and their two young daughters in a sailing accident, he had walked away from Bracken Distillers to enter the priesthood and follow his calling wherever it took him. In June, he had landed in Rock Point to serve struggling St. Patrick's parish while its priest, Father Callaghan, was in Ireland for a year.

Emma touched the elegant, distinctive gold label of the Bracken 15 year old. "Do you miss Ireland?"

"Every day. That doesn't mean I'm unhappy here. What about you, Emma? Are you happy?"

His question caught her off guard. "Right now?"

"In your life. In what you do. In where you are, at this moment."

A cold draft came through the thin walls and worn floorboards. "I don't miss the convent, Father, if that's what you're asking."

He smiled. "You only call me 'Father' when you think I'm speaking about your life as a religious sister."

"I suppose you're right," she said with a small laugh. "Yes, Fin, I'm happy. In my work, in my private life. I haven't known Colin long but our relationship feels like the real thing. I understand that I'm a new addition to his life, and that his brothers regard me as impermanent."

"Is that how you feel, Emma? Impermanent?"

"Colin and I are very different. I know that much."

"You're worried about him, too. And you miss him."

"Yes."

She helped herself to a couple of the Simple White Stonewall Kitchen crackers Finian had provided, and his Donovan tasters hadn't touched, then poured water from one of Hurley's plastic pitchers. Finian disapproved of adding ice or water to whiskey but he encouraged having water on the side to help counter the dehydrating effects of the alcohol. Only during a tasting did he tolerate, if reluctantly, adding a bit of room-temperature water to the whiskey, which arguably helped with "nosing" the aromas, but there'd been no takers tonight. Mike, Andy and Kevin had all stuck to whiskey, period. Emma had followed their lead, if, admittedly, in part because of their scrutiny.

Her head spun with whiskey, fatigue and tension—with the uncertainty and frustration she felt at not knowing where Colin was, if he was safe. "He'll be back, Fin," she said in a half whisper.

Finian transferred the tasting glasses to a tray and took them to the empty bar. Hurley's would wash them and he would pick them up tomorrow. Emma ate the crackers and took a few sips of the water, thinking now that she should have stayed in Boston for the weekend instead of making the two-hour drive to southern Maine. She had become adept at avoiding lonely evenings, but tonight, she suspected, would be very lonely indeed.

Finian returned to the table and lined up bottles of Glenfiddich, Inish Turk Beg, Midleton, Lavagulin, Connemara and Talisker. Most of his choices for the evening were from his private stock. "No one over imbibed," he said.

"I'm still not fit to drive." Emma got to her feet and pulled on her raincoat, skipping buttons and just tying the belt loosely around her. "I can help carry stuff to your car."

"I walked here from the rectory. I'll come with the car to pick up everything in the morning."

"I left mine at Colin's house and walked down here, too. I made it before the rain started, but it looks as if it's letting up. We can walk back together if you'd like."

"That'd be good. Emma…" Finian touched her shoulder, none of his usual spark or humor in his eyes. "You must find Colin."

She nodded. "I know, Fin."

They headed out into the cool evening air, the fog breaking up, the breeze steady off the water, smelling of salt, sand and seaweed. She had enjoyed the evening, listening to Finian describe the different "expressions" of whiskey—or whisky, if it were Scotch—and how each was made, dispelling myths and preconceptions in his Irish brogue. She had enjoyed being with Mike, Andy and Kevin as they had teased Finian Bracken, her, each other.

Even so, ultimately, she knew, her presence had reminded Colin's brothers and his Irish priest friend of what they were trying so hard not to think about—that Colin was an FBI agent who hadn't been in touch in far too long, and was likely in trouble.

Emma entered Colin's small Craftsman-style house through the back, using the key he had given her before his abrupt departure a month ago. He didn't pop out of the shadows, and he wasn't in his kitchen, drinking one of the bottles of Smithwick's he had left in the stainless-steel refrigerator.

The house was quiet and cold, masculine with its dark woods and neutral colors.

His refuge, she thought, heading to the front room.

He wasn't there, either, sitting by the fireplace in the dark with a glass of Bracken's finest.

Not that she had expected him to be. Technically they worked on the same team. She would know if he were back in Maine.

As she went up the stairs, she noticed a light, undisturbed film of dust on the wood rail, a tangible reminder of his absence.

She made her way down a short hall to the back bedroom he had chosen for himself.

No Colin Donovan there, either.

Emma turned on a lamp on the nightstand. She remembered him sweeping her into his arms a few short weeks ago, as if she were a fairy princess. He'd carried her upstairs and laid her on the soft duvet atop his bed.

They had fallen for each other so fast, so hard.

Madness, really.

And perfect.

She stood at his oak dresser and ran her fingertips over the stack of books, sports watch and a few coins that Colin had left. She caught her reflection in the mirror and stared at herself, as if somehow it would help her see answers that so far had eluded her. She had moved to Boston in March to join a small, specialized team. Her area of expertise was art crimes and their intersection with other major crimes. In early June, she had discovered that Vladimir Bulgov, a wealthy Russian citizen and the kingpin of a transnational network of illegal arms traffickers, had a passion—a perfectly legal passion—for Picasso and would be in Los Angeles for an auction.

At the time, Emma had suspected a deep-cover operative was chasing Bulgov but had no idea who it was. When she met Colin in Maine in September, she thought he was a lobsterman.

Well, for a minute, anyway.

She had learned that his friend and former contact agent was Matt Yankowski, the same senior agent who had encouraged her to join the FBI as a young novice and then handpicked her for his new Boston-based team.

Colin had done the hard, dangerous, often solitary work to investigate and build the case against Vladimir Bulgov. The Los Angeles auction was a way to lure Bulgov onto U.S. soil and arrest him.

Emma had no illusions that Matt Yankowski—Yank—had recruited her solely because of her expertise in art and art crimes. She was also a Sharpe. Her grandfather was Wendell Sharpe, a renowned art detective who had started Sharpe Fine Art Recovery out of his home in Heron's Cove. He had six decades of experience working with the FBI, Interpol, Scotland Yard and countless other law enforcement agencies, as well as embassies, insurance companies and individuals—celebrities, princes, heiresses, CEOs, new money, old money. Fifteen years ago, he had opened an office in his native Dublin and had worked there ever since. Now in his early eighties, he was semi-retired and Emma's older brother, Lucas, was running the family business.

Yank had known from the moment he met her at the Sisters of the Joyful Heart convent and decided he wanted her in the FBI that as a Sharpe, she had her own sources, her own contacts.

Emma noticed her cheeks were pink from the wind and cold. As Finian Bracken had wished her a simple good-night, continuing on his way to St. Patrick's rectory, she had felt his deep concern for his friend. She understood. She was worried about Colin, too.

She turned from the mirror and sat on the edge of the bed, tugged off her boots, her wool socks. She had come up to Rock Point several times during Colin's absence but never stayed overnight at his house. She had always gone back to her apartment in Boston or the Sharpe house in Heron's Cove.

She flopped back onto the soft duvet and gazed up at the ceiling, knowing it wasn't just the whiskey that was keeping her in Rock Point. It was being here, in Colin's house. In his bed.

"Colin, Colin. Where are you?"

Her whisper sounded hollow, even bewildered. She sat up straight, shivered in the chilly room. The sheets would be cold. And no Colin there to help warm them.

Her cell phone rang and she realized she still had on her raincoat and dug her phone out of the outer pocket.

A private number.

She answered without giving her name. "Hello, who is this?"

"Hello, Emma Sharpe. It's good to hear your voice."

Her breath caught in her throat at the Russian-accented voice of the man on the other end. He would never identify himself over the phone, and she would never ask, or guess, or say who she thought—knew—he was.

"And yours," she said.

A half beat's pause. "Your man is in danger."

Colin.

Emma stood up from the bed, the floor cold on her bare feet. "Do you know where he is?"

"Yes."

He gave her an address in Fort Lauderdale, and disconnected before she could thank him or ask any questions.

Another ghost, she thought, and dialed Matt Yankowski.

2

THE TWO RUSSIANS WANTED TO KILL HIM NOW.
Pete Horner, the American, wanted to wait. Then kill him if
he didn't produce the weapons they wanted. In their shoes,
Colin Donovan would have sided with the Russians. Time to
cut their losses. Too many risks doing business with a turncoat FBI agent.

They were out by the pool behind the pale yellow stucco
house that Horner had rented on a finger of the intricate web
of canals that had given Fort Lauderdale its nickname as the
Venice of America. It was a hot, humid night, even for South
Florida in late October.

A cabin cruiser was tied to a private dock in the dark, quiet
Intracoastal water. Colin had the feeling the boat was in his
immediate future. He was already sore from a few warning
blows back at the marina where he had tried to persuade his
new friends to let him be the one to take them to the weapons they wanted, but they weren't doing this his way. They
were doing it their way.

Horner and the two Russians were armed. Colin wasn't.

"Watch this guy," Yuri, the older of the two Russians, said.

He had short, thinning gray hair and a scar under his left eye, his English excellent but heavily accented. "He's like cat. He has nine lives. Maybe more. First he's alive, then he's dead. Now he's alive again."

The younger Russian, Boris, who was especially eager to kill Colin now, stood at the edge of the pool, the water turquoise in the light from the house. Boris was good-looking, with wavy brown hair, pale brown eyes and no visible scars. Colin didn't know their last names and doubted their first names were Yuri and Boris. The American, however, really was Pete Horner, a private pilot in his mid-forties who had flown one of Vladimir Bulgov's arms-smuggling cargo planes.

A good thing for Colin, Horner was the leader of the armed trio and still held out hope that their FBI agent could help them. "We give him this one chance to deliver," Horner said. "If he does, he gets to live. That's the deal."

That clearly wasn't the deal but Colin wasn't offended at being lied to by a sandy-haired, blue-eyed, amoral thug who wanted to procure illegal weapons and then sell them to anyone who would give him his price—drug cartels, warlords, guerrilla groups, terrorist cells, paramilitary organizations, mass murderers. Horner didn't care provided he got paid, and he would get paid more selling weapons—picking up the pieces of Vladimir Bulgov's network—than he ever had flying planes.

The house behind them was an expensive furnished rental walled off from its upscale neighborhood of currently absent snowbirds. Horner lived above his means, and the lure of easy money was obviously too much for him to resist.

"I'll take you to the arms," Colin said. "I stashed them myself."

"When?" Horner asked.

"I told you. Two days after Bulgov's arrest in June. My

buyer got cold feet and bolted. I had to disappear for a while and let the dust settle."

Yuri narrowed his gaze on Colin. "Does FBI think you are dead?"

Colin shook his head. "I couldn't fake my death with them. I'm an undercover agent. Turning up dead would have drawn too much attention to me. You boys might keep that in mind. The FBI thinks I'm on their side. If you kill me, they won't rest until they catch you."

Boris smirked. "Or FBI thanks us for killing a traitor."

"The weapons he promises are a fiction," Yuri said.

"They're not a fiction," Horner said. "He bought them with FBI money for a fake buyer but he was running his own game. He had his own buyer waiting in the wings. A real buyer."

"I like how you talk about me as if I'm not standing here," Colin said. "We've been through this. I put the weapons in a safe place and told the FBI that Bulgov had them. Then I let everyone in Bulgov's world think I was dead and bided my time until I could find another buyer. That would be you three budding arms merchants."

The younger Russian looked disdainful. "He double-crossed the FBI."

Honor among thugs, Colin thought. "I don't want a career doing this," he said. "I want to unload my stash and disappear. I'll take you to enough weapons to prove I'm legitimate. Then we do business. My price is a third of what your buyer is willing to pay. You'll make a tidy profit. It's a risk worth taking."

Horner gave him a cool look. "I didn't say we had a buyer."

Colin didn't argue but he knew they had a buyer.

Yuri jumped into the aft deck of the boat. "I still say we kill him now. We can find other weapons."

"We don't have time," Horner said.

Colin rubbed a bruise on his forearm where he had blocked Boris's first hit. "Your buyer's impatient."

"Everyone is impatient," Boris said with a short, disgusted laugh.

Horner shrugged. "You and Yuri have a point but your way, we know we get nothing. My way, we have a chance."

From the boat, Yuri pointed a thick finger at Colin. "And if our deep-cover agent here leads us straight to the FBI instead of to weapons? What chance do we have then?"

Horner didn't answer. He motioned with his gun for Colin to climb into the boat. "Let's go."

As Colin got in the boat, pretending to be in more pain than he was, he noticed the light from the patio catch Horner's face, and he knew. The Russians had finally persuaded him that the risk of walking into an FBI trap was too great. The promise of fast, easy weapons was a mirage. They would have to find another source.

Kill the FBI agent now. Move on.

Only Horner wouldn't kill Colin here by his pool. He would get out to the ocean first, then kill him and throw his body overboard.

Colin had expected that resurfacing as his undercover alter ego would be tricky, suspicious, but sometimes it just wasn't any fun to be right.

Faking a limp, he sat in a corner of the aft deck. Horner and his two Russian thugs had no respect for a turncoat FBI agent; even one they had hoped would lead them to an easy cache of orphaned illicit arms and their start as arms merchants. They knew Colin was an undercover federal agent because he had told them so, just before they shoved him into the back of Horner's Mercedes and drove to Horner's rented Fort Lauderdale house. Colin had offered them a reasonable explanation for what he had been up to the past few months and what he wanted now, and he had set conditions for his continued cooperation.

He hadn't bought himself as much time as he'd hoped but he wasn't dead yet, either.

Yuri and Boris went inside, up to the helm to pilot the boat.

Colin breathed in the thick, stifling air. He didn't like hot weather, but he was a former Maine lobsterman and Maine state marine patrol officer and knew his way around boats and the water.

It was something his captors didn't know about him.

The boat cruised up the narrow canal toward the main Intracoastal Waterway. Horner was watching a party aboard a luxury yacht, lit up against the black night. Boris and Yuri were navigating the turn out of the canal into the main Intracoastal.

Without a second thought, Colin eased himself over the side and dropped into the dark water.

He didn't make a sound.

The water was warm, certainly by Maine standards, but he figured it had snakes. Maybe an alligator. It'd be a hell of a thing to escape armed thugs only to be bitten by a poisonous snake or eaten by an alligator.

He liked Florida well enough but really wasn't one for the subtropics.

He swam back to the rented house and climbed up onto the dock, then ducked onto the patio, the pool still glistening in the light through the French doors. Once Horner and his Russian friends realized he was gone, they would come straight back and kill him on the spot. No waiting this time.

Colin planned to be gone by then.

Then he would find them, and he would find their buyer.

"Scary bastards," he said under his breath.

The warm canal water dripped off him. His head pounded. His bruises ached. Dehydration blurred his vision.

He wanted to be back on the rocky coast of Maine.

Back with Emma.

He noticed a movement by the far corner of the pool.

He saw two black-clad figures by some tropical shrub.

Not the bad guys. Not this time. Colin grinned, and he felt the tension ease out of him.

The cavalry was here.

Two hours later, Matt Yankowski was frowning at a large painting of black, red and white splotches on a stark white wall of the rented house. He had on a medium gray suit that looked crisp despite the South Florida heat. Colin watched the senior FBI agent from his position on a soft, white leather couch. He had changed into fresh clothes from his pack, still in the back of Horner's Mercedes. The tactical team had almost finished going through the car, the house, the three-car garage, the yard and patio.

So far, they hadn't found the name of Pete Horner's buyer or a little note saying where he, Boris and Yuri would be if the FBI swarmed the house.

Yank moved to another painting, almost identical to the first one. "I don't like them," he said. "Emma knows art. Do you think she'd like them?"

Colin hid his impatience. "I don't know, Yank. I'm not thinking about art right now."

"If I ever buy a house down here, I'd want flamingos on the walls. Not splotches. Looks like somebody got shot." Yank turned and took in the large, airy room. "This place is sterile. More like a hotel than a home. How long were you here?"

"Minutes. I was staying at a fleabag hotel a few blocks

off the beach. Horner, Boris and Yuri met me at a marina where I had a boat rented. The plan was for me to take them to weapons. Instead they tossed me in the Mercedes at gunpoint and drove here. We parked, walked through the house out to the pool, got in the boat and left. I waited until they were distracted and went overboard. For all I know, they still don't miss me."

"Unlikely."

Colin agreed. "Any sign of them?"

"Not yet."

"How did you find me?" Then he saw Yank's grimace and knew. "Emma."

"She got a tip and gave us this address. I alerted the team and flew straight down here."

"Where is she?"

"Heron's Cove. She went up there to bake pies and drink whiskey with Father Bracken and your brothers."

"My family?"

"She'll get them word you're safe."

"No more lying to them, Yank."

He nodded. "They've guessed what you do, anyway. I should have known telling them you worked in D.C. wouldn't fly."

Colin looked out through the tall windows at the patio and the canal, quiet in the morning haze. He volunteered for his first undercover mission four years ago. Matt Yankowski had ventured up to the Maine coast to talk to him about the mission and being his contact agent. As of a month ago, Colin was technically the newest member of Yank's Boston-based team and Yank was his contact agent on this mission.

"I had to go dark," Colin said. "It still didn't work. I don't have Horner's buyer. I don't know who's bankrolling him. He and Boris and Yuri are in the wind. This stinks, Yank."

"You got a toehold with them. It's a start." Yank sat on another white leather couch opposite Colin. "Are you sure you don't need a hospital?"

"I have three brothers. I can take a punch."

The senior agent's dark eyes were steady, serious. He had been a legendary field agent, but he had never strayed too far from the book. He had never gone deep undercover to chase a transnational threat like Vladimir Bulgov and his complex arms pipeline.

"You do like to go it alone," Yank said heavily.

"I didn't have much choice this time."

"Well, you're no good to us dead."

"That's why I decided to jump off that boat, Yank. So I could be an FBI asset."

"You know what I meant." Yank drummed his fingers on his thigh. "Your luck saved you this time."

"Not luck. Skill."

Yank didn't crack a smile.

Colin worked a tight muscle in his jaw. He thought he would be sleepy by now, but he wasn't. He was wide-awake, thinking about how Yank had found him. "What Russians does Emma know?"

"Between her and her family, I imagine she knows quite a few."

"Vladimir Bulgov's Russian. Horner flew planes for him. His pals Boris and Yuri are Russian."

"Emma's contacts are one of the reasons she's on my team," Yank said, his tone cool, measured.

Colin leaned forward. "What else?"

"Nothing else. She's every bit the asset I thought she'd be when I recruited her. That hasn't changed in the past month."

Colin watched a small boat cruise past the house on the

picturesque waterway. "Any reason to think whoever tipped off Emma knows my real name?"

"She wouldn't do anything to compromise you."

"Not intentionally, maybe."

"You've had a rough few weeks. You need a break. We'll find these guys."

"Their buyer? Whoever it is won't like a delay. Horner knows that."

Yank didn't look as confident but nodded. "We'll find Horner and the Russians and stop them from procuring more weapons. We'll find their buyer. You laid the groundwork."

"I knew a blown cover was a possibility going into this thing, turning up alive after three months. I told Horner myself that I was a federal agent." Colin touched a bruise on his wrist. "But having one of your people get a tip about me isn't sitting well."

"One of my people?" Yank raised an eyebrow. "Emma got the tip about this place while she was sleeping in your bed in Maine."

Colin pictured her honey hair, her green eyes, and sighed. "Hell, Yank."

He draped an arm on the back of the couch and stretched out his long legs on the white-tile floor. "You two complicate my life."

Colin didn't argue. His relationship with Emma complicated his life, too. He had never expected to fall for a woman like Emma Sharpe, granddaughter of a renowned art detective, ex-nun and FBI art crimes expert, but he had. Thinking about her over the past few weeks had been both a comfort as well as a potentially dangerous distraction. Any contact with her—with his family, his real life, even Yank—had become too risky given the stakes and the scrutiny he was under.

"You're nothing if not pragmatic, Yank," Colin said. "It's

easier not to ask tough questions if Emma got this tip from a Sharpe source."

"Let me worry about that."

"You know who it is, don't you?"

The dark eyes didn't waver. "Informants are a tricky business. We have strict rules, but they include reasonable room to maneuver. Are you going back to Maine?"

"I always go back to Maine." Colin drank some water from a bottle one of the agents had handed him. His lips were dry, burning from his salty swim in the canal. "Are you worried Emma got in over her head to find me?"

Yank got to his feet and stood by the French doors. "I don't know yet. Maybe."

"You've been known to hold back pertinent information," Colin said. "For instance, you didn't mention Emma had been a nun when you asked me to keep an eye on her in September. I had no idea that this pretty FBI agent used to be Sister Brigid of the Sisters of the Joyful Heart."

"She'd just found a nun from her former convent murdered. I needed your fresh eyes on the situation. I wasn't thinking you two would end up...you know. Together."

Maybe so, but Colin wondered how he would have responded to Emma if he had known from the start she had once been a postulant and novice. "What are you not telling me now?"

"Her brother's in Dublin with her grandfather."

"Is that relevant to the tip she got on my whereabouts?"

"I don't know."

Colin shifted on the couch, the Florida sun burning through the haze and hitting him in the eye, as if to remind him he hadn't had any sleep. "You've never met Vladimir Bulgov, have you?"

"Not in person, no."

"He's this likable, chain-smoking former Soviet helicopter pilot who cobbled together a small fleet of aging planes and made a fortune hauling cargo. Most of the cargo was legitimate, but he also had access to stockpiles of Soviet-era weapons, from Kalashnikov rifles to shoulder-fired missiles. He tucked them in with the legitimate cargo. No problem finding buyers."

Yank turned from the French doors. "Your point?"

"Along the way, Bulgov developed a taste for modern art. Emma found out and we finally had him in the U.S. and arrested him. That's the only tie I can see between him and the Sharpes. Peter Horner and his two Russian friends aren't interested in art." Colin noticed that Yank was all but pacing now. "If you asked Emma for her source, would she tell you?"

"I'm not asking."

"Because you want to trust her?"

"I do trust her. She's analytical, intelligent. She's not a black-and-white thinker. She sees the shades of gray in a situation."

"She's not like anyone else on your team."

"That's not a negative."

Colin stood, ignoring a twinge of pain in his lower back. A bruise had blossomed on his forearm, and when he had changed clothes, he had noticed a nick on his right temple. "What's your best guess, Yank? Did Emma put herself in danger to find me?"

"I don't like to guess, but I get nervous when emotion enters into a decision. You operate on instinct and experience. You're good at reading people. Emma…"

"Emma gives people a lot of rope, and she was worried about me."

"Your whole family was worried." Yank seemed to give

himself a mental shake. "Emma can handle herself. Come on. We have a flight to catch."

"Where are we going?"

"Washington. The Director wants to see you."

Colin wasn't surprised but had no desire to board a flight to Washington. "I'm not finished, Yank."

"Don't start second-guessing yourself. We have more than we had a month ago. If you hadn't gone overboard when you did, you'd be dead now."

"No kidding." Colin grinned. "Why do you think I braved the snakes and gators?"

Yank sighed. "What was I thinking? You never second-guess yourself."

They crossed the bright, elegant living room and went up three steps to a wide front door. "Is Lucy in Washington?" Colin asked.

"Paris. She's shopping with her sister."

"You didn't want to go?"

"No, but it doesn't matter because I wasn't invited." Yank opened the door with more force than was needed. "I don't see me in Hermès, do you?"

Colin followed him out into the South Florida heat and humidity. "What happens when Lucy and her sister get back from Paris? Is Lucy moving up to Boston with you?"

Yank's expression was unreadable. "I'm on a need-to-know basis, and I guess I don't need to know."

They walked over to a black sedan idling in the driveway. Colin glanced at the lush, professionally landscaped yard, vines curling over a tall fence, a stone fountain bubbling amid colorful flowers. Suddenly he couldn't wait to be out of there. He would go to D.C. with Yank and talk to the Director of the FBI, but he wanted to be back in Maine. He wanted to enjoy a glass of whiskey with his brothers and Finian Bracken, and he wanted Emma.

Not in that order, he realized.

Emma was first.

3

EMMA BROUGHT HER RED SABLE BRUSH, saturated with cerulean-blue watercolor paint, to the dampened paper she had clipped to the easel on the back porch of the Sharpe house in Heron's Cove. She pulled the brush across the paper, right to left, practicing a simple flat wash and, out of the corner of her eye, watching the woman down on the docks. She had looked up at the house several times. She was small, with long, straight dark hair, and she wore a pumpkin-colored barn jacket that, even at a distance, was obviously too big for her.

A Sharpe Fine Art Recovery client? A sightseer who had wandered down to the waterfront and now was trying to figure out how to get back out to the street with its attractive houses, shops and restaurants?

Emma noticed her cerulean-blue was leaking down the page into her burnt-sienna. Probably should have stuck to one color. Perfecting a flat wash wasn't as easy as it looked. In the weeks since Colin had gone after his arms traffickers, she had started taking painting lessons with Sister Cecilia, a young novice with the Sisters of the Joyful Heart. She and

Emma had become friends since their encounter with a crazed
killer in September. The lessons at the sisters' shop in the village were therapeutic for both of them, and always followed
by a walk, tea or just a good chat. Sister Cecilia especially
loved hearing the latest about Rock Point and the Donovans.

Yank had called an hour ago. He and Colin had arrived in
Boston and were on their way to Maine. Yank would drop
Colin off in Rock Point. Then he was on his own.

No handing over the phone to Colin to say hello. Not
Yank's style.

Colin, Emma knew, would want to know about her source.
He would have figured out the tip about the Fort Lauderdale house had come from her, or Yank would have told him
outright.

She stood back from her painting, her brush in hand. Not
her best effort.

A lobster boat drifted from the open ocean through the
channel into the tidal river. It was late on a still, cool autumn afternoon. Several pleasure boats had passed by, heading to the marina and adjacent yacht club, but there were
fewer boats now, with the colder weather and the foliage
past peak. In midsummer, Heron's Cove would be bustling
with boats and people.

Colin had been a lobsterman in his teens, before joining
the Maine state marine patrol. Emma didn't know why he
had decided to become an FBI agent. Boredom? Ambition?
A precipitating incident? An unsolved case?

How could she have fallen for a man about whom she ultimately knew so little?

She had showered and changed in Colin's house that morning, putting on fresh jeans and a sweater she had brought up
from Boston. She'd had little sleep, dozing in his bed. When
she got word that he was safe, she called Mike Donovan, then

Finian Bracken, and let them know all was well and Colin would return to Rock Point later today.

She had stopped at Hurley's for coffee and a cider doughnut and took them with her to Heron's Cove. A run on the beach, a visit to a local apple orchard, a stop at her brother Lucas's house to check on his cats while he was away—it had been a long day. She had known she wouldn't hear from Colin until he was fully debriefed and back home.

The woman in the pumpkin-colored jacket had circled up to the retaining wall and was squeezing past tall hydrangeas, their white blossoms turned burgundy with autumn, into the Sharpe yard.

Emma set her brush in a jar of water on a small dresser against the back wall of the covered porch and stood at the rail. "Hi, there," she called down to the woman. "It's a beautiful afternoon, isn't it?"

"It is. And it's a beautiful place." The woman spoke with an accent that Emma couldn't immediately place. "You're Emma Sharpe, yes?"

"That's right. What's your name?"

"Tatiana," she said, crossing the yard to the porch. "Tatiana Pavlova."

Emma stiffened at the Russian name, what she now realized was a Russian accent with a British undercurrent, as if Tatiana Pavlova had learned English on the streets of London. "What can I do for you, Tatiana?"

She started up the porch steps. "You mind?"

"Just keep your hands where I can see them, okay?"

"Yes. Yes, of course. You're an FBI agent. You must worry about villains."

Villains? "Are you a Sharpe client?" Emma asked.

Tatiana joined her on the small porch of the gray-shingled house where Wendell Sharpe had started Sharpe Fine Art

Recovery in a front room. "A friend was," she said. "I'm a jewelry designer in London. One of my clients once hired your grandfather. But that's not important. It's not why I'm here. Your grandfather is retired now, yes?"

"He's semi-retired."

"Ah. I can see that. I want to work until I can no longer lift a pencil." Tatiana tightened her oversize jacket around her slim frame. "It's colder here than I expected but I'm used to the cold."

Emma leaned back against the rail. Tatiana wore black leggings and black flats more suited to London than a walk on the docks of Heron's Cove, but no makeup or jewelry. Her nails were blunt, unpolished. Stylishly unstylish, Emma thought. "You're Russian?" she asked.

Tatiana nodded. "But I left Russia years ago."

"Years? You must have been a child. You're young—"

"Twenty-five. I was twenty when I left the country for good. It's a long story." Her dark eyes gleamed with emotion. "Are there any short Russian stories? Some of our fables and folktales, perhaps. Do you know the fable of the cat and the nightingale?"

"I don't think so," Emma said.

"It's very short. Of course, since it's a fable." Tatiana stood at the porch rail and watched a great blue heron swoop low to the water. "A cat catches a nightingale and taunts the poor bird to sing for her. The terrified nightingale can only manage pitiful squeaks, which remind the cat of annoying kittens. Disgusted, the cat eats the nightingale."

"Charming," Emma said with a smile. "What made you think of this particular fable?"

"My walk, maybe. Seeing all the birds here." Tatiana sighed as the heron dipped past a sailboat, then out of sight. "The cat and the nightingale remind us that we can't expect beautiful songs from a bird trapped in the clutches of a creature that can devour it. Their story tells us that fear isn't always the best instrument to get us what we want."

"Are you describing yourself, Tatiana?"

She turned, smiling enigmatically. "But am I the scary cat, or am I the terrified nightingale?" She waved a slender hand in dismissal. "It's just a fable. It's best in Russian, of course. Do you speak any Russian?"

"A few words," Emma said truthfully.

"Heron's Cove is very beautiful. I knew it would be, but I hoped to get here for peak leaves—that's what you say?"

"Peak foliage."

"That's it." Tatiana's smile brightened. "There are still many orange and yellow leaves, but the reds are all on the ground. But I'm not here as tourist." She spied the easel and frowned at Emma's attempt at a watercolor wash. "Such a pretty blue, but watercolor is not so easy, yes?"

Emma groaned. "Watercolor isn't easy at all."

"A painter and an FBI agent. I suppose that's not such a surprise since you're a Sharpe." Tatiana lifted the brush out of the jar and blotted it on a sheet of paper on the small chest of drawers that held Emma's painting supplies. "My English is better when I concentrate, have you noticed?"

"Your English is fine. When did you arrive in Heron's Cove?"

"This afternoon. I have a cottage just on the other side of the yacht club. I have it for a week but the owner said I can stay longer if I wish. It's very small. Adorable. It's one room on legs—stilts. We're neighbors."

"Why Heron's Cove?" Emma asked.

Tatiana laid the rinsed brush on the dresser, so that its natural bristles hung over the edge. "You shouldn't leave your brushes in water. They will last longer." She picked up the tube of cerulean-blue watercolor paint and screwed the top back on, then set it back on the dresser. "A rare, valuable collection of Russian Art Nouveau jewelry and decorative arts is arriving in Heron's Cove soon. Perhaps as soon as tomorrow. I'm afraid it's another long, sad Russian story, but I don't need to tell it, do I, Emma Sharpe? This one you already know."

"I've learned in my work not to make assumptions." Emma kept her voice neutral, despite her shock at mention of the collection. "Why don't you tell me what you know?"

Tatiana sighed at the practice painting. "You didn't wait for one color to dry before you tried another color. They bled together, and now you have mud." She glanced disapprovingly at Emma. "You must not give in to the excitement of creative inspiration at the expense of craft. You must make the tension between the two work for you. That's true mastery."

"Tatiana…"

"You grow impatient," she said lightly. "It's the Rusakov collection. A dozen works of great beauty and artistry crafted during the last days of the Romanovs. You know it, yes?"

Emma nodded. "I know it, yes."

"Twenty years ago, Dmitri Rusakov discovered the collection hidden in the walls of his Moscow mansion and hired your grandfather to help him understand it. Its history, its provenance, its value. We were just small girls then, you and I."

Emma remembered her grandfather coming home from Moscow and reading Russian fairy tales to her and Lucas. Later—four years ago, when she dealt with Dmitri Rusakov herself—she had learned that each of the dozen works in the collection was inspired by some aspect of Russian folk tradition. Dmitri was a former army officer who had made a fortune in oil and gas in post–Soviet Russia.

He was also the trusted friend of the man who had called Emma last night with the Fort Lauderdale address.

"Dmitri Rusakov has never publicized his discovery of the collection," Emma said. "How do you know about it?"

Tatiana pulled open the top dresser drawer and helped herself to a soft lead pencil, her dark hair hanging in her face as she continued. "Everyone in Russia knows about Dmitri Rusakov. I hear things in my work. Fabergé, Tiffany, Gaillard, Lalique—I study all the great designers of the late nineteenth century. It was a time when art met life, when an object as simple and ordinary as a cane knob, a picture frame or a cigarette case could become an artistic creation." Tatiana smiled, a dimple showing in her left cheek. "I especially love Art Nouveau."

"I do, too. Who is bringing the collection to Heron's Cove?"

"Natalie Warren, the daughter of Rusakov's American ex-wife." Tatiana checked the tip of the pencil with her thumb. "Her mother died earlier this year in Tucson. I don't think Natalie realized her mother had the collection, or perhaps even of its existence. That's why she's coming here. She wants to talk to the Sharpes."

"My brother and grandfather are both in Dublin."

"Ah. Well. Perhaps Natalie wants to talk to you."

Emma noticed streaks of pale lavender high in the sky. It was dusk. Colin would be back in Rock Point soon after weeks of dangerous undercover work, after escaping certain death just hours ago. How could she tell him about Dmitri Rusakov?

About his connection to last night's call?

She turned back to Tatiana. "Do you and Natalie know each other?"

"No, no. We've never met. She lives in Phoenix. I'm rel-

atively invisible at my studio. I listen. I hear things. I heard
about the collection."

"That's not all there is to it," Emma said. "Why are you
really here?"

Tatiana looked out at the water, gray now in the fading
late-afternoon light. "I believe someone will steal the collection."

"Who?"

"A villain," she said, half under her breath.

"Tatiana, if you have specific information about an immi-
nent crime, then you need tell the local police. I'll put you
in touch."

She shook her head. "I have no proof of anything. I know
you're not with Sharpe Fine Art Recovery any longer, but
can you help, Emma—Agent Sharpe?"

Emma considered her response, then said, "If the Rusakov
collection arrives in Heron's Cove, I'll see what I can do."

"Good." With a few swift strokes of the pencil, Tatiana
sketched a graceful great blue heron, incorporating Emma's
washes and muddy drips, so that suddenly they didn't look
amateurish and awkward. She stood back from the easel and
appraised her handiwork. "You can go from here. I love
grand blue herons."

Emma smiled. "Great blue herons."

The young Russian laughed. "Yes, just so. Thank you,
Emma Sharpe. I appreciate your help."

She skipped down the porch steps and back across the yard,
her hair flying in the wind as she jumped from the retaining
wall down to the pier.

Emma abandoned her painting and went back inside. Although she had been to the house a number of times since
renovations had started, she still felt a tug of nostalgia when
she entered the kitchen and saw the counters were now home

to carpenters' tools, rags, cabinet brochures, paint chips and an empty box of Hurley's cider doughnuts. Most of the guys working on the place were from Rock Point. She had promised them she would clear out the rest of the kitchen over the weekend.

She stepped past a roll of insulation. Renovations had been a long time in coming and a joint family decision, but Lucas was in charge. The idea was to transform the small house into a modern base for Sharpe Fine Art Recovery while still retaining its Victorian charm and character. Lucas, who had his own house in the village, had asked the architect to include a guest suite for family and friends, or for their grandfather should he eventually return to Heron's Cove.

Getting Lucas to acquiesce to preserving the porch had taken some doing. He had envisioned taking over that space for the interior and adding a stone terrace out back, but Emma had reminded him how much of their family life had centered on the porch, especially before their grandmother's death, the fall on the ice that had relegated their father to a restless life of chronic pain and their grandfather's relocation to Dublin.

Emma rinsed dried watercolor paint off her hands and saw she had a text message.

It was from Colin: I'm home.

She smiled as she typed her response: I'll come to you.

She headed out through the front and got his message back: Yank just left. I'll be at Hurley's.

Emma got in her car. She would be in Rock Point in twenty minutes. That gave her at least a little more time to consider how to handle his questions about how she had found him in Florida, and what to tell him about Tatiana Pavlova.

★ ★ ★

Colin was alone at Hurley's bar, a bowl of steaming fish chowder in front of him. He patted the stool next to him. "Have a seat, Special Agent Sharpe."

Emma climbed onto the stool, taking in his broad shoulders, the thick muscles in his legs, the smoky gray of his eyes as they settled on her. He was so damn sexy, she thought. So incredibly physical and down to earth. He could handle deep-cover work because he was focused, decisive and independent. Yet he wasn't a man easy to get to know. Maybe that made him good at what he did, too.

She noticed a purple bruise on his forearm, then met his eyes with a smile. "Welcome home."

He winked at her. "Nothing says home like a bowl of Hurley's fish chowder."

"Your brothers aren't here yet, I see."

"On their way. Finian, too. Word travels fast in Rock Point." He touched a hand to her cheek. "How are you, Emma?"

"Glad to see you back in one piece."

"I came close to being eaten by alligators." He tucked a few stray strands of hair behind her ear. "Yank says you saved my ass."

"We all help each other."

"Did he tell you to say that?" Colin turned back to his chowder. "As I pointed out to him, I had already escaped when the cavalry arrived. I do allow that if they hadn't swooped in when they did, my new friends could have doubled back and thrown me to the gators."

"That wouldn't have been good," Emma said.

"It would not. Then where would you be?" He picked up his spoon, dipped it into the milky chowder. "Sleeping alone in my bed again."

She helped herself to an oyster cracker. She knew what
he was getting at, had suspected it was coming. How much
would she tell him about her source? How much *could* she
tell him? She'd had a good chunk of last night and all day to
prepare her response, but Tatiana Pavlova's arrival in Heron's
Cove, with her talk of Dmitri Rusakov, had further mud-
dled the situation.

"The call came to my cell phone. Not to your house
phone." Emma kept her tone even, without a hint of defensiveness. "Yank knew I was at your house because he asked
and I told him. Father Bracken had organized a whiskey
tasting."

"What was your favorite?"

"I just know I don't like the heavily peated ones."

"An acquired taste."

"Colin—"

"It's okay, Emma." His eyes softened. "It's been a long
month. You can sleep in my bed anytime."

In other words, his questions about last night could wait.

"Were my brothers good to you while I was away?" he
asked.

She nodded. "Mike's not a big fan but we do all right."

"Mike's not a big fan of anyone."

"He's been down here more because of your family's concern for you."

Finian Bracken arrived, wearing his black suit and Roman
collar today. He stopped short when he saw Emma. "Am I
interrupting?"

"Not at all," Emma said with a smile.

Colin eased off his stool. "It's good to see you, Fin." He
clapped the priest on the shoulder in a warm greeting. "Mike,
Andy and Kevin will be here in a few minutes."

"They're outside now," Finian said.

"Then grab some glasses and pour the Bracken 15 year old."

Finian glanced past him at Emma. "Wine for you tonight?"

"Nothing for me, thanks," she said, standing up. "I'll let you gentlemen enjoy your evening."

"Good to see you, as always," Finian said, then headed to his favorite table by the window.

Emma buttoned her jacket, aware of Colin's gaze on her. His questions about the past twenty-four hours wouldn't wait forever. He wanted answers. But she saw the cut on his right temple, the fatigue in his eyes and the stiffness with which he moved, and she knew this wasn't the time or the place for a serious conversation.

He needed tonight with his brothers and his Irish priest friend.

He seemed to guess what she was thinking and slipped an arm around her waist. "Missed you, babe."

"I missed you, too. Be with your family and friends." She leaned into him, just for an instant. "I'll see you soon."

He patted her hip. "Real soon."

Emma managed to get out of there without running into his brothers. It was colder, clearer than last night. She listened to the tide wash in on the sand and smooth stones. A bright star had come out above the harbor. She took in a deep breath. She could still feel Colin's strength and warmth—as well as his questions, his doubts.

If Natalie Warren was bringing the Rusakov collection to Heron's Cove, would Dmitri Rusakov be right behind her?

Would Ivan Alexander be with him?

"Your man is in danger."

Emma put her own doubts and questions out of her mind as she watched Mike, Andy and Kevin Donovan walk up the stairs to Hurley's. They were one reason Colin could bounce back from the dangers he faced. His resilience wasn't just due to his training and experience, or even his nature. It was also due to his family and friends, the solid foundation he had in Rock Point.

A gust of cold wind propelled her into her car. She debated what to do. She could stay at her parents' house in Heron's Cove, Lucas's house, with friends. At the Sharpe house. The state of renovations meant it wasn't as comfortable as in the past, but she'd manage.

She could check on Tatiana Pavlova and see if she was in her rented cottage, working on sketches.

Emma started her car. She needed to get in touch with Lucas and her grandfather in Dublin.

Would her grandfather remember Dmitri Rusakov?

"Of course he would," she said aloud.

Wendell Sharpe remembered everything.

She noticed the bag of Northern Spy apples on her front passenger seat. She'd bought them at her visit to the orchard that afternoon, before her attempt at a flat wash. They were perfect for pies.

Tough to bake a pie in the Sharpe kitchen.

Emma smiled and decided she might as well head up to Colin's house after all.

4

FINIAN BRACKEN MARVELED AT THE CAMARADERIE
of the Donovans and the obvious, if unstated, relief and pleasure they shared at being together after the fear and worry of
recent days. He had poured Bracken 15 year old for all four
brothers and even a *taoscán* for himself.

"Did we run Emma off?" Mike asked, tasting his whiskey.
"I think she peeled rubber getting out of the parking lot."

Colin shook his head. "She would have stayed if she wanted
to."

"She's as bullheaded in her own way as you are," Kevin
said.

Andy grinned but was quiet as the eldest Donovan swirled
the whiskey in his glass. "What did you call this, Father?"
Mike asked. "Not a dram. Some unpronounceable Irish
word."

"Taoscán," Finian said.

Mike gave a mock shudder. "I'll never get it right." He
set his glass down on the worn table. "The Sharpe house is
torn up for renovations. Emma's not driving back to Boston, is she?"

"She's not picky," Colin said. "She'll sleep on the floor if she has to."

Kevin reached for the water pitcher. "I have to remember she's an ex-nun. She can tolerate spare conditions. Right, Father Bracken?"

Finian wasn't getting into the middle of this particular discussion. "The Sisters of the Joyful Heart have a lovely convent. As a matter of fact, I just came from there. A young woman stopped me at the gate to ask about the sisters' work in the arts and art conservation. She's an artist herself. A jeweler in London."

"Maybe she's an ex-nun, too," Mike said.

Finian suspected Colin's brothers were ambivalent about his relationship with Emma less because she was an FBI agent and a Sharpe than because she had once come close to professing her final vows as a religious sister. Chastity, obedience, poverty. The profession of vows wasn't as simple as it might seem and involved deep thought, study, prayer and reflection. Emma had come to the right decision for her.

All that was for her and the Donovans to sort out among themselves.

Finian continued with his story. "I don't think the woman who spoke to me was a nun, or even considering the convent. She lives in London but she's Russian. She has the most charming accent."

Colin raised his eyes over the rim of his glass as he tried his whiskey.

Finian saw that Kevin, also a law enforcement officer, had noticed Colin's alert expression, too. "A Russian jeweler in Heron's Cove," Kevin said. "Imagine that. What else did she say?"

"It was a casual conversation. I asked her name, and she told me it's Tatiana and she had heard about the sisters' work."

"Did she mention Emma?" Colin asked.

Finian felt as if he had unknowingly just dived into shark-infested waters. "Not by name, no."

Colin's gaze narrowed on him. Next to him, Kevin had one hand on his glass on the table and his gray eyes likewise narrowed. Andy looked as surprised by their intense reaction as Finian was. Only Mike's expression was impassive, impossible to read.

"What do you mean, not by name?" Colin asked.

"Well." Finian now regretted having brought her up. "She said she'd run into an FBI agent in Heron's Cove who used to be a nun."

"That's true," Kevin said. "Where in Heron's Cove did this Tatiana run into Emma?"

"She didn't say, and I didn't ask." Finian wished he didn't sound so defensive. "It wouldn't occur to me to interrogate a young woman—a tourist—enjoying an autumn afternoon out at a convent gate."

Kevin picked up his glass. "If that's what she was doing. Sounds more like she was checking out Emma."

"Or the convent itself," Finian said. "The sisters tell me they've had a marked increase in visitors and curiosity seekers since Sister Joan's death and the subsequent discovery of a Rembrandt in the attic."

Colin drank some of his water. "Did this Tatiana give you her last name?"

"Not that I recall, no. Dear heaven, I'm starting to sweat. Did I do something wrong?"

"Not a thing." Colin seemed to make an effort to smile. "You're a good man, Fin. Bringing Bracken 15 tonight instead of leaving us to Hurley's rotgut. I don't know what arrangements you and John Hurley have made but I'm all for it." He raised his glass. *"Sláinte."*

Finian splashed more Bracken 15 year old into his own glass and raised it. *"Sláinte."*

Mike finished his whiskey in one last swallow and stood, reaching for his canvas jacket as he glanced down at Colin. "One night we'll break open another bottle of Bracken's finest and you can tell us about the real nature of your work. I'm guessing it involves Russians. It's good you're back. Our sweet mother worried about you."

That she had, Finian thought. He'd had more than one conversation himself with Rosemary Donovan about her fears for Colin—for all four of her sons.

"I warned her I'd be difficult to reach," Colin said.

Mike grunted. "You couldn't have sent her a postcard, put up something on Facebook? Sent a carrier pigeon telling her you were alive and well?"

"You know Washington. Crazy place."

"Right. See you tomorrow." Mike shifted to the youngest Donovan. "Come on, Kev. I'll drive you home. We can talk about Russians."

"There are millions of Russians, Mike," Kevin said, getting to his feet.

"Only one showed up at the Sisters of the Joyful Heart this afternoon. Forget it. I should go back to the woods."

Andy rose, too. "I have an early start. See you all later." He gave Colin a curt nod. "Good to have you back." Then he smiled. "You can help Father Bracken dig bean holes for his first-ever bean-hole supper."

"Better than getting the shit beat out of you by Russians," Mike muttered, then exited with Andy and Kevin on his flanks.

With his brothers gone, Colin eyed the Bracken 15. "I could empty this bottle but I'm not going to."

"All things in moderation," Finian said, appreciating the

long finish of the whiskey he had overseen from distillation to laying down in the cask. "It's good to be back with your brothers, isn't it?"

"It is," Colin said with a heavy sigh.

Finian pushed back an unexpected memory of hiking in Ireland with his brother on a sparkling autumn morning. He and Declan had just turned twenty and were filled with hopes and dreams. They had paused to appreciate the view of the Atlantic and the surrounding countryside and decided then and there they would do it; they would find a way to start their own distillery.

"Brothers are to be cherished," Finian said. "Mike especially has good instincts about people."

"Mike hates people."

"'Hate' is too strong. He's a loner. An observer. That's why he lives the way he does. Being here in Rock Point helping your parents with their inn, with their worries, has worn his patience."

"Have you been out to the Bold Coast where he lives?"

"Not yet, no."

"It's way down east on the Bay of Fundy. Strong tides, huge rock cliffs. Remote. Stunning scenery. Mike deals with people just enough to make a living, then spends the rest of his time on his own. He's always been like that, even before he joined the army."

"He came home from the military a different man?"

Colin shook his head. "Same Mike, just more so. What's going on with him and Emma?"

"My assessment? She looks at him and wonders if she can fit in among the Donovans. He looks at her and wonders if he really knows his brother, perhaps wonders if he'll ever have a relationship in his own life such as the one you and Emma have."

Colin frowned, then grinned suddenly. "I think I actually understand what you just said."

"This Russian woman, Colin…"

"Not your problem. Worry about your bean-hole supper. I'll worry about Emma's Russian."

"She's making pies for the supper."

"The Russian?"

Finian sighed. Colin, of course, knew better. "Emma."

Colin hesitated, just for a fraction of a second, but it was enough. Finian could see that his friend wasn't so sure about his new love inserting herself into his life in Rock Point, perhaps less sure than he had been a few weeks ago in the heat of their first days together. It was only natural, Finian thought.

"I'll clean up here," he said. "You've had very little to drink. You'll be fine to drive."

"I walked down here."

"But you'll be driving to Emma in Heron's Cove."

"So I will." Colin rose, a spark in his gray eyes. "Thanks for the whiskey. It's good to be back."

Finian studied his friend, noted the clear pain he was in, the depth of his fatigue. "How bad was it, Colin?"

"I'm here drinking whiskey with you, so it could have been worse."

"Your brothers know you didn't get your cuts and bruises in Washington."

Colin grinned. "You don't think I can convince them I tripped on my way to a cocktail party?"

Finian gave up and smiled. "Go, my friend. Be with your woman."

"An excellent plan." But as Colin pulled on his jacket, he pointed a finger at Finian. "If this Russian jeweler shows up again, you call me. Got that, Father Bracken?"

Colin left without waiting for an answer, and Finian corked

the Bracken 15 year old, then poured himself a glass of water. He had to remember to keep a clear head when dealing with a Donovan. He put the uncomfortable conversation out of his mind and looked around the quiet restaurant. An elderly couple was sharing a piece of wild blueberry pie—a local favorite—and two young sisters he recognized from the church were talking themselves out of ice-cream sundaes.

His previous life in Ireland seemed so long ago, so far away.

He shook off his melancholy before it could get him in its grip. A woman on Hurley's staff edged over to his table with a plastic tray. She was slender and shapely, with deep gold-flecked hazel eyes and a thick golden-brown braid hanging down her back. "I'll get these glasses, Father," she said, anchoring the tray on one hip.

He thanked her. "What's your name?"

"Julianne Maroney. My grandmother is helping with the bean-hole supper at the church this next weekend—that is, if she's able."

"Is she ill?"

Julianne grabbed Mike's and Colin's empty whiskey glasses. "I don't know if you'd call it ill. More like thoroughly pissed off at God." She blushed. "Sorry, Father."

Finian leaned back in his chair. "I understand being pissed off at God. I was for a time myself."

"Were you? Really? And you're not now?"

"I'm not now. In fact, I never was. I just thought I was."

"Misdirected anger," Julianne said thoughtfully. "That's Granny. She loves the bean-hole supper but she says she's mad at God for taking Grandpa away from her. He died last year, before you arrived at St. Patrick's. We all miss him, but it's not good for her to be so mad all the time. I think it's making her sick."

"Physically sick?"

Her eyes shone with sudden tears. "I think she wants to die, too. Join Grandpa in the great beyond. Heaven. What-ever." Julianne added the water pitcher to her tray. "Do you think you could talk to her?"

"Of course."

"Don't tell her I said anything. Her name is Fran. Franny Maroney. Her grandmother was from Ireland. Sligo, I think. Do you know where that is?"

Finian smiled. "I do, indeed."

"Granny likes your Irish accent. I want to go to Ireland someday. Working on it, in fact." Julianne snatched up Andy Donovan's whiskey glass with more force than was necessary and banged it onto her tray. "It's nice to see Colin back in town. He does come and go. He and Kevin are my favorite Donovans. I don't know Mike that well."

Given the way she grabbed Andy's water glass and banged it onto the tray with the same force as she had his whiskey glass, Finian had an idea of her opinion of the third-born Donovan.

"Andy Donovan's a rake," Julianne said matter-of-factly. "You know that, right, Father?"

"I haven't heard a man called a 'rake' in an age."

"It's fitting." She glared out the window at the dark har-bor where Andy had his lobster boat moored. "I'm working my way through school. I'm finishing my master's in marine biology. I don't know what I was thinking...Andy and I..." She sighed. "That son of a bitch broke my heart." Her cheek color deepened. "Sorry, Father."

"Not at all."

She seemed to regret having said anything. "I told Granny I'd go with her to the supper. She says she doesn't want to go without Grandpa, but I think it'd be good for her."

"Thank you for letting me know," Finian said.

Julianne spun back across the restaurant with her tray and through the swinging door into Hurley's kitchen. Finian returned the Bracken 15 to the bar, where it would be safe until his next visit, said good-night and headed outside, the wood door creaking as it shut hard behind him.

He crossed the quiet parking lot, a sharpness in the air he hadn't noticed earlier. He was just barely warm enough in his suit coat. He continued onto the narrow streets above the harbor, lined with modest homes lit up against the dark night. He passed a large shade tree, bright yellow leaves clinging to its sweeping branches and scattered on the pavement, a reminder that the long Maine winter was soon upon them. He had heard tales of brutal New England winters. This would be his first.

At least by winter the blasted bean-hole supper would be behind him.

A man in a black fleece jacket and baseball cap walked across the street from Hurley's. Finian didn't recognize him but the man approached him as if they knew each other. "Evening, Father. Nice night. Chilly." The stranger hunched his shoulders. He looked fit, with fair skin and fine lines at the corners of his eyes. "Didn't I just see you at Hurley's with the Donovan brothers?"

Finian hadn't noticed him. "Are you a friend of theirs?"

"Nah. I've never stepped foot in Rock Point until today. A kid sweeping the floors told me. Four brothers altogether. FBI, marine patrol, lobsterman, Maine guide. Tough guys. Their folks own an inn on the waterfront. The father's a retired cop."

"Are you asking me?"

"Just shooting the breeze. I needed to stretch my legs." He ambled a few more steps up the street, his hands shoved deep into his jacket pockets. "Colin Donovan's the FBI agent brother, right, Father?"

"If you'd like, I can give him a quick ring—"

"Thanks, but I'm on my way to Heron's Cove. It'll be my first time there, too. I should let you get back to your walk. You serve a church here in Rock Point?"

"St. Patrick's. We're having a bean-hole supper next weekend. You're welcome to join us."

The man grinned. "I can't remember the last time I was at a church supper."

He said good-night, turned and walked back toward the harbor. Finian stood still, watching the man cross the street back to Hurley's.

At least he hadn't spoken with a Russian accent.

It was a fair guess that Colin's secret work with the FBI involved Russians, Finian thought as he navigated the maze of now-familiar streets to the simple, stone-faced church and rectory that would be his home for at least a year. St. Patrick's Church was a small parish, struggling more than some and less than others. A gnarled maple in front of the church had dropped all its leaves, but a river birch by the back steps—or what Colin had told Finian was a river birch—held on to its vibrant yellow leaves. The New England fall foliage season was as spectacular and festive as he had hoped and anticipated. St. Patrick's bean-hole supper marked the last of the popular autumn suppers among the local churches.

Finian had no illusions that Rock Point and the people of St. Patrick's had fully embraced him since his arrival in June. That was all right. His presence was deliberately temporary, and he was Irish and a different sort of priest—a widower who had lost his wife and two young daughters before turning to the priesthood.

He entered the rectory kitchen and pulled off his clerical

garb, then slipped into a hand-knit Irish sweater. He went still, his pulse quickening as he noticed several envelopes on the floor by the old stove. All the windows were closed. Had he brushed them with his arm before he had left and simply hadn't noticed?

He thought of the man who had intercepted him. Could he have sneaked in here before heading to the waterfront?

Why would anyone sneak into a rectory?

Finian started for the telephone to call Colin but stopped himself. The poor man was just back home after what had obviously been a difficult ordeal. Finian shook off his uneasiness. He hadn't observed any sign of a break-in at the back door.

To further reassure himself, he checked the threadbare living room and dining room, but nothing was out of place, broken or disturbed. He had let his imagination run wild.

His gaze rested on a framed photograph on the china cupboard of his beautiful wife, Sally, and their sweet daughters, Kathleen and Mary, together on a sunlit Irish morning at their home above Kenmare Bay. They were smiling, and he could hear their laughter as he took the picture, only a few weeks before he lost them forever.

He didn't come into this room every day, but when he did, he would see them. The pain of his grief was still there and he recognized—accepted—that it always would be.

But he hadn't lost his girls forever. He'd lost them in this life.

They had gone to God and were at peace.

He left the dining room and checked the front door, discovering to his surprise that it was unlocked. Perhaps that oversight explained his sense of intrusion. With no evidence of a break-in, he had no reason to call Colin or the local police. He would feel ridiculous.

He returned to the kitchen and made tea as he opened St. Patrick's well-worn file on the bean-hole supper. The menu was tried-and-true, unchanged in decades. Homemade baked beans, roast pork, coleslaw, applesauce, pickles, rolls and pies. The folder included handwritten recipes and instructions on digging the bean holes, building the fire inside them and burying the pots for the slow baking of the beans.

Well. Why not?

Finian settled back in his chair, reading the recipes and dismissing his stubborn sense of uneasiness as the result of having just enjoyed a bit of Irish whiskey with four intense Donovans.

5

EMMA WAS SURPRISED TO FIND A ROLLING PIN in one of Colin's kitchen drawers. It had a worn, broken-in feel that suggested he had inherited it from someone else's kitchen. She didn't find a pastry cutter, but she used her fingers to work in the shortening and flour that a cupboard had yielded, another surprise. She managed to put together a respectable pie while Colin was drinking whiskey with his brothers and Father Bracken.

She leaned back against the sink and forced herself to focus on her surroundings and practice the kind of mindfulness she had during her days with the Sisters of the Joyful Heart. They had shared all the routine chores of convent life, hiring out only what they couldn't do themselves. She had discovered purpose and comfort in preparing meals, cleaning, doing laundry, gardening—daily work that didn't directly involve the sisters' mission in art conservation, education and history.

A different life, and yet she still could draw on what she had learned during her time as Sister Brigid.

She smelled the apples bubbling in the oven and felt the warmth of the kitchen, noticed the reflection of the overhead lights in the windows. Colin didn't have drapes or curtains, only natural-fiber shades. There were no plants or knick-knacks on the windowsills, although he had left a small, rounded gray stone on the sill above the sink. He must have picked it up on a Maine beach. It was smooth, polished by the sea.

She heard footsteps outside and saw him in the back door window.

"I see you didn't lock the door behind you," he said, entering the kitchen. "I guess you're not worried about intruders."

"I guess not." She smiled through her sudden, inexplicable tension. She had just been with him at Hurley's, but his presence still was a shock to her system. She pointed at the gas stove. "I have a pie in the oven."

"Smells good. Apple, right?"

"I had some Northern Spies in the car. I bought them at the orchard where we went apple-picking before you took off to parts unknown."

He shut the door behind him, a stiffness to his movements that reminded her it had been only hours, not days, since his escape from killers. "That was a good afternoon."

"One of those afternoons you never want to end."

"You enjoy baking."

"Most of the time. Baking helps me think."

His smoky eyes narrowed on her. "What were you thinking about, Special Agent Sharpe?"

Dmitri Rusakov, a Russian billionaire. Ivan Alexander, a private security consultant who had started out as Dmitri's bodyguard. Her week in London four years ago when she had met them, shortly after the disappearance of the Russian Art Nouveau collection Dmitri had discovered in the walls of his Moscow house sixteen years earlier.

She hadn't heard from Dmitri since London, but she had heard from Ivan.

Three times, she thought. The third was last night.

All three times his information was valuable, provided with the understanding that she would utter his name to no one.

She stood straight, noticed the shadows on Colin's face. "You must be exhausted."

"Emma, Emma." He took a dish towel she had forgotten about off her shoulder and set it on the counter. "You have a lot on your mind. Calls from confidential informants in the middle of the night. Russians in Heron's Cove."

Emma covered her surprise that he knew about Tatiana by turning on the faucet at the sink, washing a stray apple seed down the drain. "One call, and one Russian. I assume Yank told you about the call. Who told you about Tatiana Pavlova?"

"That's her name—Tatiana Pavlova?"

"She's a jewelry designer in London. She's renting a cottage in Heron's Cove."

"Finian ran into her at the Sisters of the Joyful Heart. Why would she go all the way out there to check you out?"

"Is that what she said? That she was checking me out?"

"Close enough."

Meaning he was operating on gut instinct. It was what he did, why he could do deep-cover work. Emma took a more measured, analytical approach. Both, she told herself, had their place.

"Do you know her?" Colin asked.

"We only met today."

He leaned against the counter, then stood straight again. "My back doesn't like that position. I have some nice bruises where two Russians pounded me last night. Imagine that. I also investigated a Russian arms merchant now in federal custody. And here I come home to a Russian jeweler down the road. What are the odds?"

Emma shut off the faucet. "Tatiana wants me to stop a Russian Art Nouveau collection from being stolen. She says it's arriving in Heron's Cove soon."

"Who has it?"

"A woman from Phoenix. She's American. This all goes back to a former Sharpe client."

"The former client is Russian?"

"That's right."

"When you say 'Sharpe,' do you mean you, your grand-father, your parents, your brother or all of the above?"

Emma grabbed two pot holders off the counter by the stove. "It doesn't matter." She glanced back at him, felt his intensity, his restless fatigue. "Yank said you need to rest."

"A wise man, our fearless senior agent in charge." Colin shrugged off his jacket and hung it on a hook by the door. "And your tip about me? Was that from a Sharpe client?"

"No."

"Another Russian?"

Emma didn't want to lie to him. Couldn't lie to him. "I'm glad you're safe, Colin. That's what counts."

"You didn't answer the question."

"No, I didn't. I'm not going to talk about my source."

"Does this source have any connection to this Russian collection?"

She tucked her hand into one of the pot holders. "I came here to do something with the bag of apples. Tatiana Pavlova isn't your problem. I'll deal with her. I've emailed my grand-father and brother already. I'll talk to them in the morning. Tatiana was emotional, and she had no facts to back up her suspicions about the collection."

"All right. For now." Colin touched a finger to her cheek. "How long before the pie's out of the oven?"

"Maybe five minutes."

"Five minutes," he said as if it were an eternity.

"It's basically done now. I can turn off the oven and it'll be fine."

"Excellent plan."

She yanked open the oven door, the burst of heat enough to remind her to think, take her time, be sensible. She lifted the glass pie plate off the rack and set it on top of the stove, then switched off the timer and the oven heat.

"I meant to go straight back to Heron's Cove," she said quietly. "I wanted to give you a chance to get some rest, but I can still go."

"Isn't the Sharpe house gutted by now?"

"Mostly gutted."

"You slept here last night."

"Because of the whiskey," she said.

Colin took the pot holders from her and set them on the counter. "Thank you for the pie." He slipped his arms around her. "We can talk about your new Russian friend later. Let me decide if I need rest. I slept some on my flights."

"But not last night—"

"Not much in recent days."

Steam rose from the pie, sweet juice from the cooked apples, sugar and cinnamon oozing over the crimped edges of the browned crust. Emma eased her arms along his sides and around to his back, her physical attraction to him as strong, as immediate, as the first time he had touched her a little more than a month ago.

"It's been a long month," she said. "If you want to talk, I can put on coffee and cut the pie."

"I'm good with Fin's whiskey and warming up my cold bed

with you. We can save the pie for tomorrow." Colin drew her closer to him. "I don't need to talk about what happened. I'm here. I'm with you. The rest can wait."

"I'm not hiding anything from you. I just can't talk about everything that involves my family's work."

He touched his lips to hers, just a breath of a kiss. "No talking, no thinking. Not tonight." He ran his fingers into her hair and smiled. "No sleeping on a mat in Heron's Cove, either."

She smiled back at him. "Where, then?"

"With me."

"You're in pain, aren't you? These bastards—"

"I don't want to think about them. I want to think about you."

Her heartbeat quickened. "I should carry you upstairs tonight."

He gave a small laugh. "Sweetheart, the day I can't carry you up to bed…"

"You rugged undercover types," Emma said, slipping from his embrace. "I'll finish up here and meet you upstairs. Don't fall asleep on me."

She reached for the faucet, but in one swift move, he swept an arm around her and lifted her off her feet, then up and over his shoulder, potato-sack style. She knew several different maneuvers to get herself back onto the floor in one piece but used none of them as he headed for the stairs. Not that her maneuvers would have worked, anyway. He was strong, in good shape and determined, despite his ordeal.

He didn't put her down at the top of the stairs. In a few more strides, he had her in his bedroom. It was pitch-dark, the shades pulled, not so much as a night-light on. She had hastily made the bed that morning, but Colin kept any remarks to himself as he ripped back the duvet, just as she had pictured, dreamed about, in the weeks since he'd left Rock Point.

"The sheets will be cold," she said.

"Not for long." He wasn't breathing hard at all as he laid her on the bed. He grinned and gave a mock shudder. "Damn. It is cold."

"Are you sure about this? You need time to decompress and reintegrate—"

"Exactly." He fell with her onto the bed, his mouth finding hers. "Nothing's changed, Emma. Nothing. I want you now as much as I did when I carried you up here the first time."

"That's good," she whispered, her throat tight with emotion and a rush of desire.

Her shirt went first, then his, joining the blankets on the floor. Emma inhaled sharply when he skimmed his hands over her bare breasts, then caught a nipple between his lips. She sank deep into the bed, already warm from their presence. He licked, tasted, teased, even as he smoothed his palms down her sides, over her hips.

Her pulse raced; her skin was on fire.

In another two seconds, he had her jeans off, and she raked at his, until finally they, too, were gone, cast onto the floor.

He came to her, as ready as she was. She'd dreamed of this moment, ached for it, hoped for it. He was her soul mate in the only way she understood soul mates.

"Emma," he whispered, "stop thinking."

She could hear the amusement in his tone and drew her arms around him, coursed her palms up his back. "No more thinking. Promise. It's good to have you here."

"Glad you put that pie in the oven?"

The man was irresistible, impossible. She smiled, tried to answer, but he shifted position on top of her, eased himself between her legs, and she found that she couldn't speak. Instead she drew him into her, closing her eyes, lying back, taking in the heat and hardness of him. He thrust deeply and went still, as if to give them both the chance to absorb that this was real, that they were together again, making love on a dark autumn night. Then he drove into her again, and she was lost.

Only later, when her heartbeat had calmed and the cool air chilled her overheated skin, did anything resembling a thought work its way into her consciousness, and it was a good thought. She didn't want to be anywhere else but where she was right now.

She realized there was only one pillow left on the bed, and they were sharing it, facing each other. Colin kissed her on the forehead but didn't say a word.

Colin ended up on the outer edge of the bed, with Emma asleep in the crook of his arm. The milky light of dawn brought out the honey tones of her hair, and he noticed her black lashes against her creamy skin. He'd slept, but not a lot. She was right about the need for decompression and re-integration. They were as important to his work as training, preparation, reports, analysis, experience and instinct. Fatigue bred mistakes. Mental and physical exhaustion put not just his own life in danger but other people's lives, and it jeopardized the mission. It led to burnout and it frayed relationships.

The problem was, he seldom recognized when he was past the point of no return. His ability to push through exhaustion and fear was part of what made him good at undercover work, but he also knew that it made reentry into his home life—his real life—tricky, even difficult.

What made it even harder was his distaste for lies and deception.

His bruises ached, but not as much as before making love

to Emma. Pain wasn't what had awakened him and kept him awake. His instincts had. He trusted them, and they were hammering at him now, telling him that Emma's Russian jeweler and her warning about a Russian collection weren't just some obscure Sharpe matter.

He pictured Pete Horner's supercilious smile. *"I see you're back from the dead."*

Back, but determined to finish the job he had started when he set out from Maine last month. He wanted Horner, Yuri and Boris in custody. He wanted to find out how they planned to get weapons now that Colin's stash was no longer an option. Did they have other contacts in Vladimir Bulgov's old network—access to the same stockpiles of Soviet-era weapons?

When had Horner and his Russian colleagues discovered their turncoat undercover agent had jumped into the Intracoastal? Had they searched for him? Had they tried to go back to the rented house but realized it was crawling with feds?

Had they figured out he wasn't a turncoat after all?

Were they the type to seek revenge? Did they still think they could force him to help them?

Who was their buyer?

Colin had run the same questions over in his mind for hours.

He didn't see himself spending the next two weeks kayaking, drinking whiskey and digging bean holes with Finian Bracken.

Making love to Emma, yes.

She and Matt Yankowski both were holding back on him. Did Yank know about this Tatiana Pavlova?

The wind rattled the windows, reminding Colin that he needed to get the house ready for the winter. He could do that over the next couple weeks, too. Caulk windows, stack wood, clean the chimney.

Dwelling on his frustrations and questions in the middle of the night wasn't helping anything. He looked at the woman lying next to him and put emotion and desire aside. The Sharpes were a family with sixty years of investigations, contacts and secrets behind them. Emma had worked art crimes with her grandfather from childhood—long before she'd become an FBI agent.

Colin didn't expect to know everything about her in the short time they'd been together, but he doubted even Yank knew what all lurked in the Sharpe family vault of secrets.

She shifted slightly, throwing back a slender arm. Colin held her close, and she rolled over, touched her fingertips to a deep purple-and-yellow bruise on his side. "They did this to you?"

"It's not as bad as it looks."

"You could have said something before we—"

"Trust me, sweetheart, I wasn't thinking about my aches and pains while we were making love."

"There are more bruises?"

"A few. I heal fast. Being back here helps."

"They were trying to kill you—"

"Not when they hit me. They were just trying to get me into their car, show me they were in charge. They disagreed on killing me."

"They knew you were a federal agent," Emma said.

"By then, yes. They thought I was playing both sides and was willing to sell them weapons at a cut rate." Colin thought a moment, then said, "Yank is getting the go-ahead to involve the team, but there were three men. Pete Horner, a private pilot out of Florida. He flew planes for Bulgov but wasn't one of his regular pilots. He wanted to wait to kill me."

"The other two?"

"Russians. Yuri and Boris. They wanted to kill me right away. Yuri is in his late forties, with short, thinning gray hair and blue eyes. Boris is younger—maybe thirty. Medium brown hair, brown eyes. Good-looking. Yuri's kind of flat faced."

Emma sat up slightly. "You're describing them to me because you think I might recognize them."

"Do you?"

"No."

"They could be anywhere. They could have split up, or they could still be together. They could have new IDs. Another boat. They could have had a car or a plane waiting for them. I had to bail too soon—"

"It sounds as if you bailed in the nick of time."

"You mean before they fed me to the alligators?"

She gave him a faint smile. "Your sense of humor is a coping mechanism."

He leaned in close to her. "What's funny about alligators?"

"Do they believe they could force you to get them weapons?"

"Hard to say. They want to be arms merchants. They have contacts, resources, funds—seed money, Horner calls it."

"Will their buyer be mad at them for not coming through with weapons?"

"Oh, yes. Very mad." Colin realized suddenly how much he appreciated her approach to a problem. "I made it easy for Horner by turning up with orphaned weapons that I wanted to unload."

"They knew you didn't want a career as an arms merchant," she said. "Just a profit. Everyone has good reason to be mad at you. Horner, the Russians, their buyer. Are they the type to exact revenge?"

Her skin was warm, as soft as anything Colin had touched in a month. "They'd have to find me first," he said.

"And they don't know who you are."

"That's right, they don't—unless your source tipped them off."

"My source isn't one of them. I can tell you that much."

"Did you break rules to find me, Emma?"

She let her fingertips drift over his chest. "I would have." She looked up at him, her eyes as green as he'd ever seen them. "But I didn't need to."

"Why not?"

"You're good at undercover work."

It wasn't an answer. Colin saw that she knew it, too, but he didn't care. Not right now. He kissed her, then let the curve of his hand drift over her smooth, cool skin. "I'm good at this, too."

6

LUCAS SHARPE SLOWED FROM A RUN TO A LIGHT jog as he entered St. Stephen's Green, a welcome oasis in the heart of Dublin. The lush greenery, flowers, statues and fountains were dripping as much as he was, if only from the early-morning rain and not a mixture of rain and sweat. He had pushed himself hard on his five-mile run. Nothing like an enigmatic, irritating email from his one-and-only sister to propel him into the Irish rain in sweats and running shoes:

I need everything you and Granddad have on London jewelry designer Tatiana Pavlova and her interest in the Rusakov collection. I'll call tomorrow.
   Btw, Colin is back.
   Hope you're enjoying Dublin,
   Emma

She had sent the email at 8:00 p.m. Maine time, 1:00 a.m. in Ireland. Lucas had picked it up when he had awakened at seven in the spare bedroom of his grandfather's Dublin apartment. Checking messages first thing, before he even crawled out of bed, was a habit he was trying, with limited success, to break. Given the five-hour time difference, there was even less point to diving onto his iPhone at first light in Ireland than in Maine, where at least he could rationalize that he wanted to stay abreast of what was going on in Europe.

As it was, by the time he read Emma's email, it was the middle of the night on the U.S. East Coast. He would have to wait several hours before he could call his sister for more information.

Was Emma referring to Russian tycoon Dmitri Rusakov?

"Bloody likely," Lucas muttered, jogging past a curving ornamental pond, ducks grooming themselves in the rain-soaked grass.

He slowed to a walk on a meandering path that led to a gate on the east end of the iconic green. The rain had let up but he was already soaked to the bone. Dublin was quiet so early on a drizzly Sunday morning. He crossed the normally busy street and continued into the heart of residential Georgian Dublin where his grandfather had lived for the past fifteen years.

Three days ago, Lucas had seized on the disruption of the renovations at the Sharpe house in Heron's Cove as an excuse to fly to Dublin. He had barely had time to adjust to Irish time and get over jet lag before he had received Emma's urgent message.

Having a sister who was an FBI agent had its drawbacks, but Lucas didn't doubt that she was as concerned about their grandfather as he was. Ostensibly Lucas was in Dublin to check out the status of the Sharpe Fine Art Recovery office there, but he was also checking out the status of his grandfather. His health, his well-being, his plans for the future.

Easier said than done with an independent-minded old codger like Wendell Sharpe, Lucas thought with a sigh of exasperation.

He came to the narrow brick town house where his grandfather had an apartment. Born in Dublin, Wendell Sharpe had been just two when he had left Ireland with his parents for Boston. They soon moved to southern Maine, where his father had worked as a property manager and his mother as a domestic at large summer homes. Wendell had started out as a security guard at a Portland museum, ultimately finding his calling in investigating and recovering missing fine art and antiques.

His decision to open a Dublin office and return to Ireland had been a surprise, but it had also worked out well. At first, his only son—Lucas's father—had run the Heron's Cove office. Then a fall on the ice landed Timothy Sharpe in chronic pain, and bit by bit Lucas took over.

Now in his early eighties, Wendell, a widower for almost two decades, was giving up day-to-day work in the business to which he had devoted his life and edging into retirement, or at least semi-retirement.

Lucas went around back and ducked through a gate onto the terrace and into the kitchen. It was past eight but still no sign that his grandfather had yet rolled out of bed. Lucas was dying for coffee but returned to the small guest room and stripped off his wet clothes, leaving them in a heap on the tile floor. He pulled on a robe and headed for the apartment's only bathroom.

A hot shower, shave and dry clothes didn't ease his tension.

He headed back to the kitchen, filled the electric kettle with tap water and plugged it in. He dumped loose-leaf Irish Breakfast tea into an earthenware pot for his grandfather and fresh-ground beans into a glass coffee press for himself. By the time he had tea and coffee steeping, his host entered the kitchen dressed in dark gray wool trousers, a crisp white shirt, black vest and red bowtie.

"It's Sunday, Granddad," Lucas said.

"I thought I might go to church. Don't worry. The rafters won't cave in. I've been going more frequently in recent months."

Lucas *was* worried, although not about his grandfather's churchgoing habits. "I just don't want you to be depressed," he said, loading the tea, coffee, plates, silverware and a basket of toast onto a tray.

His grandfather looked mystified. "Depressed? Why would I be depressed?"

"Sometimes there's not a reason. It just happens. Come on. The rain's stopped. Let's have breakfast outside."

Lucas carried the tray and Wendell grabbed a towel to dry off the chairs and two-person round table on the small brick terrace. The sun broke through the clouds as they sat across from each other. They were both lanky and blue-eyed, but any resemblance ended there. Except for her green eyes, Emma favored their grandfather more than Lucas did.

He watched his grandfather butter a piece of toast with a steady hand. For all his expertise in fine art, Wendell Sharpe lived simply. The only art he owned was by contemporary artists and craftspeople, mostly Irish, whose work appealed to him for whatever reason. He didn't care about critics, reviews, whether a particular work or particular artist would ever end up in a museum or prized by discerning collectors. He just bought and bartered for what he liked. His lack of snobbery, combined with his knowledge, experience and extensive contacts, made him a formidable, insightful expert in art theft and recovery. He could see, think and feel what others couldn't or overlooked because of their blind spots and prejudices.

Lucas wanted to follow in his grandfather's footsteps, but he knew, too, that he had to carve out his own path. And he was just thirty-four. Wendell did have a few decades on his only grandson.

Wendell took a bite of toast and poured tea. "What's on your mind, Lucas?"

"Do you know a London jeweler named Tatiana Pavlova?"

"No, I don't, but that's a Russian name. Why? Who is she?"

"I don't know. Emma sent an email last night asking about her. She said she'd call today." Lucas poured his coffee, appreciated its heat. "She also wants anything we have on the Rusakov collection."

"The Rusakov collection?" Wendell went still, knife and toast in hand. "You're sure?"

Lucas nodded. "I'm sure. You can read the email if you'd like."

"No. I don't need to read it." He set his toast on his plate and glanced at the sky, the sun back behind the shifting gray clouds. He seemed to give himself a mental shake, then picked up his teacup and focused again on Lucas. "What else did Emma say?"

"Colin Donovan is back."

"I met him in September when he and Emma were in Ireland chasing that killer. Good-looking fellow. All the Donovans are."

"I didn't realize you knew them," Lucas said, already wishing he'd made more coffee.

"They'd come by the waterfront from time to time, mostly in a lobster boat. I'd wave. They'd wave. That was the extent of it. They were teenagers. I was old even back then. Their father was a town police officer."

"Did you think Colin would become an FBI agent?"

"No, I thought he'd become a lobsterman. I'm better at figuring out art thieves than I am at figuring out law enforcement officers. They surprise me every time. Look at Emma. You said Colin's back? Where did he go?"

"Washington, supposedly. I don't think that's the whole story. I think he was in trouble."

Wendell nodded thoughtfully. "I suspect trouble's a way of life for Colin Donovan. As it's becoming for Emma, I fear."

"They're FBI agents, Granddad. It's their job to look for trouble. What about this collection? Does it in fact belong to Dmitri Rusakov?"

Wendell shifted in his chair, a ray of sunlight catching his thinning white hair. "I haven't been back to Maine in far too long. How is life there?"

"It's fine," Lucas said, not hiding his impatience well. "Granddad—"

"I'll recognize the house when you're finished with it?"

"Yes. I've worked with an architect and designer to make sure we keep its character. My main focus is modernizing the offices. You've seen the drawings."

"The apartment will be ready by winter?"

"Yes, but you have a place to stay in Heron's Cove any-time you want to be there. You know you can always stay at my place. And you'll love the apartment when it's done. I promise."

"I know I will, Lucas," Wendell said, pouring himself more tea. "I'm physically and mentally fit for a man my age, but I can't help but feel that moving back to Heron's Cove will mean I'm about to die. People will take it that way, though. Mark my words."

Lucas felt a spray of drizzle and sat back, wishing now he'd stayed inside and turned on the Irish news instead of trying to have a conversation with his grandfather. Coffee first. Then talk of going home to die.

The rain didn't develop, and the sun popped out again.

Finally Lucas said, "Granddad, if you're having second thoughts about retiring, we can work something out. You'll still be a consultant but if you miss going into an office, there are options."

"I know, I know."

"And there's a difference between retirement and death, you know."

His grandfather gave a wry smile. "Yes, I do know, Lucas. What about you? You never thought you'd be running the show at your age. You thought you'd have more time to sow your wild oats."

"Dad's accident changed all that."

"And Emma," Wendell said. "The convent, the FBI. We thought you would share the responsibility of running the business with her."

"It's all worked out. Dad's still a valuable asset to the business even if he can't run it. Mom, too."

With another sigh, Wendell ate his toast, drank more of his tea. "Your father's strength was always research and analysis. He and Emma have that same ability to dig into something and see all the pieces and how they might fit together."

Lucas again reined in his impatience and focused on enjoying his coffee and toast. He could feel his run in the backs of his thighs. He had pushed too hard. He could blame jet lag, but he didn't. He blamed Emma's email, and his grandfather's attempt to deflect the questions about Pavlova and Rusakov—and his melancholy mood. Lucas had hoped that his presence in Dublin would be a boost for his grandfather. Instead, he was just another reminder that Wendell Sharpe had more days behind him than ahead of him. Transferring what he knew—what wasn't in the files—to his grandson drew him into the past and underscored that he was at the end of a long and storied career.

"I don't know what the next chapter will be for me," Wendell said, buttering his last triangle of toast, "but it'll be short."

"Granddad, that's morbid."

He shrugged. "It's true."

"You could live to a hundred-and-five. That's more than twenty years."

"I shudder at the thought." He winked. "It's all right, Lucas. I'm not about to leap off the Cliffs of Moher. In fact, I've decided to take a sort of walkabout on the southwest coast."

"Of Ireland?"

"Yes, of Ireland. Of course."

"It's late October, Granddad."

"The weather's fine. There'll be rain, of course, but the days are getting shorter. I'll just have to find my way to a pub once it gets dark."

"When will you leave?"

"As soon as you do. I presume you'll be going to London to look into this Tatiana Pavlova. Ah, Lucas." His grandfather looked up at the sky again, peeks of blue showing now. "Sometimes it's best not to ask too many questions. Have you learned that yet in your work?"

"I treat every situation individually—"

"That sounds like a line from a Sharpe Fine Art Recovery brochure, or these days its website." Wendell looked across the table, his blue eyes as incisive as ever. "It's against Emma's nature not to ask a question, to dig deeper. She wants to have all the pieces, the whole picture. I'm convinced that's one reason she entered the convent. Asking, probing, analyzing, thinking. Those practices come naturally to her."

"She can also kick ass," Lucas pointed out, if only to lighten the mood.

"And shoot," his grandfather added with a laugh.

Even as teenagers, Lucas had noticed Emma's fascination with the intersection of art crimes and other major crimes—the illegal trafficking of weapons and drugs, human trafficking, extortion, money laundering, murder. That interest coupled with her expertise in art history and preservation had made her an attractive candidate for the FBI.

"I'd see more of both you and Emma if I moved back to Heron's Cove," Wendell said, pensive again. "That would be a good thing."

"We'd like it, Granddad. You know that, I hope."

He nodded. "I do. Lucas..." His grandfather sighed as if in pain. "We do the best we can to influence, to inform, but in the end, we can't control the people who come to us for help. What they want, what they know, what they're willing to tell us."

"Are you talking about Tatiana Pavlova and the Rusakov collection now?"

"I told you I don't know this Tatiana Pavlova." He drank more tea, setting the cup off balance on the saucer, so much so that it tipped off on its side with a clatter; he left it, pressed his cloth napkin to his lips, then put the napkin back in his lap. "Dmitri Rusakov hired us twenty years ago. I met with him in Moscow. Then he hired us again four years ago. And I sent Emma to him in London."

"Granddad," Lucas said, "why don't I know any of this?"

He tapped the tip of his index finger to his temple. "Because it's one of those cases that's in here and not in the files." He got stiffly to his feet and glanced at his watch. "I don't want to be late for church."

"I'll go with you," Lucas said, rising.

Wendell's eyes sparked with sudden humor and energy.

"Now I will have to warn Father O'Leary or the rafters will cave in for sure."

"You can tell me about Dmitri Rusakov on the way."

After sitting impatiently through church with his grandfather, Lucas let himself into the Dublin office of Sharpe Fine Art Recovery on the second floor of a small brick building on a cobblestone street a few blocks off St. Stephen's Green. He shut the door quietly behind him and noticed through the tall windows that the day had gone gray again. He didn't mind. He just needed time to think.

His grandfather was having a postchurch full Irish breakfast with friends. In preparation for his retirement, he had removed all his personal items and personal files from the office where he had worked for the past decade and a half, leaving behind two desks, shelves, a credenza and a computer. There was no hint of the intriguing work that had gone on there. He had never been one for bulking up a staff, instead taking on consultants and temporary assistants as needed. Lucas wanted to keep a Dublin office but needed to identify a role for it now that his grandfather wouldn't be there on a daily basis.

When Emma worked with their grandfather in Dublin the year after she had left the Sisters of the Joyful Heart, Lucas had been in Heron's Cove, devoting every waking hour to learning the complex business he would soon be running on his own. He had already done a year in Dublin with his grandfather. He had soaked up as much of Wendell Sharpe's wisdom and Irish culture as he could, hit nearly every pub in the city, then was happy to return to Heron's Cove.

As much as Emma loved the work and their grandfather, Lucas had never expected his sister would stay with Sharpe

Fine Art Recovery after the convent. It was as if she had been destined for the FBI.

And maybe for Colin Donovan.

Lucas grimaced as he sat at the computer and did a quick internet search.

Tatiana Pavlova was a young, up-and-coming designer of jewelry and high-end decorative arts at the Firebird Boutique in London's Mayfair district. She was mentioned in a BBC piece on the Firebird's opening three years ago that included a photograph of one of her creations—a gleaming red enameled feather pendant, edged in gold, studded with rubies and diamonds. Fittingly enough, it was described as a glowing feather of a mythical firebird.

Neither the BBC article nor the Firebird's website included a picture of her.

His grandfather was right, Lucas thought. He'd be heading to London to look into Tatiana Pavlova himself.

He glanced at his watch—*1:00 p.m.* Emma had to be stirring by now. He dialed her number but his call went straight to her voice mail.

"It's Lucas," he said. "Call me."

7

"OOPS," MIKE DONOVAN SAID AS HE ENTERED Colin's kitchen through the back door, discovering Emma at the table. He grinned, obviously not the least bit awkward. He nodded to the pie on the counter. "I guess you two were up all night peeling apples, huh?"

Emma was relieved she had come downstairs fully dressed in jeans, black sweater and boots. Colin was at the table in a charcoal flannel shirt untucked over jeans, no socks, no shoes. *Sexy,* she thought, slipping into her leather jacket as she rose. "Help yourself to pie," she said.

"Too early," Mike said.

She smiled. "It's never too early for pie."

"Where are you headed?" he asked, opening a cupboard and lifting out a mug.

"Heron's Cove. I promised the carpenters I'd clean out the kitchen."

It wasn't the only reason. Lucas had left her a voice mail and she wanted to return his call away from any Donovan scrutiny. Simpler that way, she told herself. Last night, as she inspected Colin's healing cuts and bruises, each of which he

dismissed as nothing, she had realized how little she knew
about the actual work he did—its dangers, its risks, its pressure. The toll on his family. Rock Point was his refuge, and
he deserved a few days of rest and calm. She would handle
Tatiana Pavlova and whatever was going on with the Rusakov collection.

Mike poured coffee. "I know most of the carpenters working on your place. They say your brother's a decent sort. Not
a jackass like some."

"Good to know," Emma said, heading for the back door.

Colin eyed his older brother. "What's up, Mike?"

Mike sat at the sturdy oak table with his coffee. "The folks
have summoned you to Sunday dinner. I'm the messenger.
Don't shoot."

"What time?" Colin asked.

"Noon arrival. Food on the table at one. All of us will be
there." Mike glanced up at Emma, then back at his brother.
"Emma can come, too. Up to you. She can bring the pie.
The folks like her because she can cook."

Colin touched a fingertip to the rim of his mug. "How do
they know she can cook?"

"They got together when you were off shuffling papers
in D.C."

Emma didn't buy the innocent look Mike gave her. He
knew he was stirring the pot. "They invited me for coffee,"
she said, suddenly self-conscious, as if she had intruded in
Colin's life in his hometown.

"She brought muffins," Mike said. "Apple walnut. Pop
wants the recipe. He's into being Mr. Innkeeper. You'd never
know he was a cop for thirty years. He tried to get you to
tell him where Colin was, didn't he, Emma?"

She debated whether to respond. Mike lived five hours up
the coast but had been down to Rock Point for most of the

past week. As an independent wilderness guide, he kept his own hours. It was a life that apparently suited him, and it wasn't lost on Emma that the two eldest Donovan brothers were a lot alike.

She had met Rosemary and Frank Donovan briefly with Colin before he left to pursue the remnants of Vladimir Bulgov's arms trafficking network. She hadn't thought anything of popping in with muffins. She certainly hadn't expected Colin's parents to grill her about him.

No way was she going to Sunday dinner with the entire Donovan clan.

"I enjoyed my visit with your parents," she said carefully. "They understand that I can't discuss Colin's work."

Mike pushed back his chair and stretched out his long legs as he addressed Colin. "This woman. Emma." He glanced back at her and winked. "Wouldn't want me talking behind your back, right, Special Agent Sharpe?"

Emma refused to let him get to her. "Not that it would matter," she said half under her breath. "You'll say whatever you have to say regardless of who's around."

"Yep." Mike drank some of his coffee and turned his attention back to his brother. "Emma's great. Really. She's just complicated. Sharpe, ex-nun, FBI. That's a lot of baggage for one person." He shrugged his big shoulders. "Not that it's any of my business."

"You got that right," Colin said.

Mike frowned at the two empty plates. "You had apple pie for breakfast?"

"It was that or beer," Colin said.

"Tough choice." Mike nodded at Emma. "Call if you need help cleaning out the kitchen. Think your Russian friend will show up? The one who asked Father Bracken about you?

What's her name, Colin? Tatiana…" He eyed his brother. "Emma tell you Tatiana's last name?"

"Pavlova," Emma said calmly.

"Ah," Mike said. "Is Tatiana Pavlova a Sharpe client?"

"No." Emma turned to Colin. "I'll see you later?"

"You bet," he said.

Mike grinned. "Hey, don't let me run you off, Special Agent Sharpe."

She ignored him as she pulled open the door and shut it behind her, welcoming the bright morning sun and brisk air. She needed to keep a clear head when dealing with any of the Donovans.

More leaves had fallen overnight from the sugar maple on the corner of the driveway, and she pushed back an image of raking leaves with Colin on a lazy autumn Sunday. It wouldn't happen today. It might not ever happen.

She got in her car, pulled the door shut. She understood that Colin's brothers were sizing her up, but she also suspected that he was, too. He'd had a month on his own to think about how she fit into his life.

If she fit.

Maybe in her own way she'd been doing the same.

She took the coast road, the Atlantic sparkling under a cloudless blue sky, white-crested waves crashing on the rocks and seagulls wheeling overhead. Halfway to Heron's Cove, she pulled over, parking under a gnarled evergreen. She was tempted to sit in her car and watch cormorants dive for food but instead dialed her brother's cell phone.

"Hey, Emma," Lucas said. "Where are you?"

"Watching cormorants. You're missing a beautiful day in southern Maine."

"It's been raining on and off here. I'm at Granddad's apartment. He's packing for his walkabout on the southwest coast."

"Walkabout?"

"Soul work, he calls it. I think he's depressed. That's not why I called. Why is there next to nothing in the files on our work with Dmitri Rusakov? By 'our' I mean the company. He hired us twice—twenty years ago and again four years ago—and the files on the case suck, unless there's more information in Heron's Cove."

"There isn't," Emma said. "I don't know why not. You'll have to ask Granddad."

"I did and he hasn't given me a straight answer. This walk down memory lane he and I have been having seems to have triggered some kind of dark mood. I'm doing the best I can but I don't know how much help I can be."

"Does he know anything about Tatiana Pavlova?"

"He says he's never heard of her. I haven't gotten much out of him on Rusakov, either."

"He told me he was reluctant to take on Dmitri as a client—"

"Dmitri? You two are on a first-name basis?"

"It's nothing like that. Forget what you're thinking. Dmitri Rusakov is one of the original Russian tycoons who made his fortune in early post–Soviet Russia. He's managed to survive the social and economic upheavals and political witch hunts."

"Did you ever see this Rusakov collection for yourself?"

"Only pictures. Granddad saw it when he was in Moscow after it was first discovered. I didn't get involved until it disappeared four years ago."

"'Disappeared' can mean a lot of things," Lucas said.

"So it can. I worked under Granddad's supervision and direction, but he stayed in Dublin while I went to London to meet with Dmitri. He had an apartment there."

A red squirrel chattered at Emma from the branch of the

spruce but her mind was in London four years ago, when she'd walked into Dmitri Rusakov's Mayfair apartment. She had never seen anything like it.

"He had the collection in London?" Lucas asked. "Why?"

"I don't know. He wouldn't say. He refused to involve the police. I told him we couldn't cover up or ignore a crime. He said he understood and just wanted us to figure out what happened to the collection."

"And did you?"

"To my satisfaction, yes. He was in the middle of a divorce. For years, he'd told people he'd never marry, but he finally did. The marriage lasted less than two years. His wife was American—"

"Renee Warren Rusakov," Lucas said. "Granddad remembered her name. She helped herself to the collection?"

Emma nodded as if her brother were in the car with her. "I told Dmitri I suspected she took the collection with her back to Tucson. He said thank you very much for my assessment and sent me back to Dublin."

"And now Renee Rusakov is dead and her daughter is trying to figure out what to do about this collection. Do you think she knows her mother took it against Rusakov's wishes?"

"I've no idea what Renee told Natalie. That's the daughter. Natalie Warren. I met them briefly when I first arrived in London." Emma watched a seagull swoop onto a huge granite boulder above the glistening cove. "We don't even know if Natalie is on her way to Heron's Cove. What are your plans, Lucas?"

"I'm booked on a flight to London in the morning," Lucas said.

"Will Granddad go with you?"

Her brother hesitated, then said, "No. He's heading

off to Killarney to start his walkabout." Lucas's tone was neutral, as if he were simply reporting their grandfather's words.

Emma's seagull flew off as a large, white-capped swell crashed onto the rocks, spraying salt water in the clear air. "But he's okay, isn't he?"

"Yes and no. I think something about this Rusakov thing got to him. Did Granddad ever meet Renee Rusakov?"

"Not that I'm aware of. She wasn't involved with Dmitri twenty years ago."

"What was she like?"

"Renee Rusakov was…" Emma pictured the attractive American with her perfectly highlighted hair, her barely detectable facelift, her manicured toes and fingernails and expensive clothes and jewelry. "She was lovely, and she was toxic."

"How lovely and how toxic?"

"Enough for Dmitri Rusakov to fall for her and regret it. As I said, I only met her for a few minutes. Most of what I learned about her was from Dmitri, and from our investigation into the disappearance of the collection."

"And the daughter? Natalie? What's she like?"

"Even prettier than her mother and much nicer." The seagull flew off, and Emma sat up straight, turning on the car's ignition. "Let me know what you find out in London."

"Emma, is the FBI involved in this thing?"

"I'm involved, Lucas, and I'm an FBI agent twenty-four hours a day. I can't flip a switch and turn it on and off."

Her brother was silent a moment. "All right. I'll call you from London. Keep me in the loop on what's going on there, okay?"

"I will. Thanks, Lucas."

★ ★ ★

When Emma arrived in Heron's Cove, a small crowd had gathered at the marina next to the Sharpe house. As she crossed the yard to the retaining wall above the docks, she saw why. A luxury yacht, as big and as expensive as Heron's Cove had ever seen, had arrived at the yacht club. Even with a halt to two-way boat traffic, it must have just barely fit through the narrow channel from the Atlantic into the tidal Heron River.

Emma squinted in the bright sun at the name on the stern. The *Nightingale*.

She took in a quick breath and jumped down to the waterfront for a closer look.

A bejeweled nightingale pendant had been Dmitri Rusakov's favorite piece in his missing collection.

This had to be his yacht.

Tatiana Pavlova hadn't chosen the fable of the cat and the nightingale at random, and not just because of its moral. She must have known the *Nightingale* was on its way to Heron's Cove. Where was she now? Her cottage was on the other side of the yacht club, out of Emma's view.

Emma stepped onto the wooden pier and noticed two men walking in her direction. They might have been ordinary yachtsmen enjoying a brisk autumn day, but she recognized Russian billionaire Dmitri Rusakov and, next to him, his friend, security expert Ivan Alexander.

Why tell her they were coming when they could just show up in her backyard?

Dmitri waved, his wild graying hair whipping in the stiff breeze off the Atlantic a hundred yards behind her. He was compact and stocky, dressed in red pants and a dove-gray windbreaker and moving with his usual purpose and energy.

"Emma," he called. "Emma Sharpe."

Ivan said nothing. He was tall, at least ten years younger than Dmitri, with fierce dark eyes and dark, close-cropped hair. He wore black, his long stride at once unhurried and powerful.

Pushing back any hint of irritation, Emma smiled as she intercepted them by a post, a small dinghy banging against it in the wind. "Dmitri, Ivan," she said, deliberately using their first names. "This is a surprise. Welcome to Heron's Cove."

"Home of the Sharpes." Dmitri gave her a wide smile and took her hands into his, then kissed her on each cheek. "Ah, Emma. It's good to see you. You look well." His English was flawless, if heavily accented. He stood back, letting go of her hands. "You're as beautiful as ever."

"Thanks, Dmitri. It's good to see you, too." She glanced at Ivan, nothing in his expression suggesting that just over twenty-four hours ago he had given her information about an FBI agent in serious trouble. "And you, Ivan."

He inclined his head in a slight nod. "Emma."

His dark eyes settled on her a half beat longer than was comfortable. She turned back to Dmitri. "When did you arrive?"

"In Heron's Cove? Early this morning. We had to come in at high tide or anchor off-shore given the size of the *Nightingale.*" He gestured back toward his yacht. "She's on the upper end of what the harbor can accommodate. I flew into Boston last night. Ivan met me there and now here we are. He and I haven't seen each other in months. This is good. All good. Our own little reunion."

Reunion, Emma thought, but kept any skepticism to herself. "Where do you go from here?"

"We'll sail down the East Coast to the Caribbean," Dmitri said. "I've wanted to do that for several years but just haven't taken the time. Of course, I've wanted to see Maine since meeting your grandfather. How is he, Emma?"

"He's doing well. Thanks for asking. My brother's with him in Dublin, if you're here on Sharpe business. As I'm sure you know, I no longer work for Sharpe Fine Art Recovery."

"You're an FBI agent now." Dmitri sighed with satisfaction as he looked past her toward the ocean just beyond the channel. "Wendell told me all those years ago in Moscow that Heron's Cove was blessed with natural beauty. He didn't exaggerate. It's as beautiful here as I imagined."

"It's one of my favorite places," Emma said.

"It's home for you."

She nodded. "Yes, it is."

Dmitri Rusakov's cheerful, open manner belied his worldliness and vast wealth, even a certain ruthlessness. "Renee died a few months ago. Did you hear?"

From Tatiana Pavlova, whom Emma had no intention of bringing up. "I'm sorry."

"She had cancer. Melanoma, discovered late. She went downhill fast. That's something, at least. She was too young but it's not a surprise that she died so young. She wasn't yet fifty. I tried to help her curb her excesses. She refused my help. Anyone's help." He took in a deep breath, his pale brown eyes shining with tears. "She was a difficult woman, Emma. I saw through her too late."

"I hope you can remember the good times you had together and put aside the bad ones."

"Yes, I hope so, too." He paused, watching the dinghy bang against the post. "You were right, you know. Renee had the collection."

Emma noticed that Ivan had moved a few steps down the pier, obviously giving Dmitri a chance to talk to her in private.

Dmitri sighed again. "You're not going to say you told me so?"

She shook her head. "No, I'm not."

"Renee must have taken the collection because she realized it was very special to me. She left it to her daughter. The poor girl doesn't know the collection belongs to me. She doesn't know its history."

"Is this why you're here, Dmitri?" Emma asked.

He touched a thick finger to the rope tying the dinghy to the post. "You don't know that Natalie is coming to Heron's Cove?"

"I haven't heard from her."

"She'll be here this afternoon. She got in touch with my people a few days ago." He waved a hand. "Not Ivan. My personal assistant. Natalie said she'd discovered some interesting pieces in her mother's possessions and thought they might be Russian, perhaps worth something, then said she was heading to Heron's Cove to talk to the Sharpes."

"Why didn't she make an appointment?"

"She's impulsive but I also know she wants to be discreet. For many reasons."

Including the Internal Revenue Service, Emma suspected. "You were a Sharpe client, Dmitri. My grandfather and brother won't talk to Natalie about your business without your permission."

"Ivan said the same thing. Eh, Ivan?"

Ivan, who had kept silent, observant, turned from whatever he was pretending to watch just down the pier and acknowledged Dmitri's words with another slight nod.

Dmitri grinned. "A man of few words, as always. Ivan has told me for years I talk too much." He laughed, clearly not bothered by his friend's criticism. "I persuaded Natalie to stay on board the *Nightingale*. It's best I tell her about the collection myself, in person. I've no doubt she'll return it once she learns the truth."

"And if she doesn't?" Emma asked.

Dmitri again took her hands into his. "Now you're talking like an FBI agent," he said cheerfully. "Join us aboard the *Nightingale* later. I want you to meet Natalie. Come for dinner, or at least for drinks."

It didn't seem to occur to him that she might have something else to do. "Thanks, Dmitri, but—"

"We'll look forward to seeing you whenever you can get there."

He abruptly started back down the pier toward his yacht. Ivan met Emma's eyes but he said nothing before he turned and followed Dmitri. She watched the two men. Dmitri Rusakov and Ivan Alexander couldn't have been more different, but they'd been friends for at least twenty years. They'd had their army careers and plans for their future shattered by the breakup of the Soviet Union. Barely out of his teens, Ivan had taken a job working security for Dmitri, a natural entrepreneur who had capitalized on his military contacts to gain a foothold in Russia's oil and gas business. As Dmitri's company grew into an international energy giant, Ivan's fortunes, too, rose. Now he was on his own, an independent consultant wealthy in his own right—and free to do as he pleased.

Emma returned to the Sharpe house. The sheet with her watercolor washes and Tatiana's great blue heron was still clipped to the easel on the back porch. Tatiana would be able to see the *Nightingale* from her cottage. Emma had no intention of exposing the Russian designer to Dmitri Rusakov's scrutiny.

Or to Ivan Alexander's.

What about to Colin Donovan's scrutiny?

Emma dug out her cell phone. She'd let him know about

the arrival of the *Nightingale*. Then she'd call Yank and let him know. Yank would give her room to maneuver. He would trust her judgment. It was one reason she was on his team in Boston.

Colin?

He would want answers, and he would want them now.

8

COLIN DRAGGED HIS KAYAK UP FROM THE
water and threw it into the back of his truck parked behind
the old captain's house that Frank and Rosemary Donovan
had transformed into an inn. They had painted the rambling
Victorian a fresh white, with black shutters, a yellow door
and flower and vegetable gardens that kept them busy even
when guests were few and far between. Colin had promised
to join Mike in helping to get the place ready for winter.
His mother had made a crack about expecting him to head
off to Washington again at any moment, but he let it go. His
father had kept silent.

An hour on the water had cleared his head and worked
out any remaining stiffness from his fun and games in Fort
Lauderdale. His night with Emma had done most of the job.

Emma, Emma.

Just as well she hadn't come to Sunday lunch with his family. Over roast chicken, acorn squash and the last of the garden spinach, he had learned that she had volunteered to bake
pies for St. Patrick's bean-hole supper. Two apple pies and
one Irish-style rhubarb crumble.

"Volunteered" could mean she'd been asked and had said yes, but Colin had to acknowledge his mixed feelings about what she had been up to while he was away. On the one hand, he hadn't wanted her to be alone. He wanted her to feel welcome in Rock Point. On the other hand…muffins for his folks? Pies for the church?

It all felt a little too fast.

Either that, or his family and friends in Rock Point were sucking her in, checking her out, testing her, using her to push him out of the undercover work they all knew he did.

He checked his cell phone and saw Emma and Yank both had called.

Her late-night tip from her unnamed source and now this Russian jeweler.

No wonder he was unsettled, questioned what was going on with her—what he had gotten into when he had fallen for her.

And what he had gotten her into. The men he had escaped when he dropped into the dark, warm waters of the Fort Lauderdale Intracoastal wouldn't hesitate to kill him on sight if they found him again.

He had to find them first.

Kevin wandered out from the inn. "Don't worry, I'm not going to make you plant tulip bulbs. Mike's got that covered. Mom bought five hundred bulbs. That has to be more than the deer can eat."

"Mike's going crazy, isn't he?"

"He needs to get back to the Bold Coast. He doesn't mind helping out, but you know how he is. He can only take so much civilization. He came down here because he was worried. We all were. Even Pop was getting nuts."

Colin grabbed his dry pack and tossed it into the back of his truck with the kayak. "I know," he said, abandoning any pretense with his youngest brother of a desk job in Washington.

Kevin looked out at the small inlet, yellowed marsh grasses giving way to a tumble of rocks, then rippling blue water. "You can't do this again. We know what you do. Next time—"

"No guarantees there'll be a next time, Kevin." Colin went around to the front of his truck. "Matt Yankowski has me on his team in Boston now. I could be at a desk for real."

"It wouldn't be such a bad thing," Kevin muttered, turning from the view. "I just got a call. A luxury yacht arrived in Heron's Cove this morning. The owner is a Russian tycoon. Dmitri Rusakov. Know him?"

Colin went still. "The name. I don't know him personally."

"What about Emma? Is Rusakov a Sharpe client?"

"No idea."

Kevin paused as if he were assessing Colin's response and the slight edge in his voice. "Rusakov's yacht is sitting about fifty yards from the Sharpe place. Thought you'd want to know."

Colin opened the driver's side door of his truck. "Thanks, Kevin."

His brother narrowed his eyes. "Keep me in the loop."

"As soon as I get in it myself," Colin said.

He climbed into his truck and pulled the door shut. Dmitri Rusakov's arrival in Heron's Cove no doubt had prompted the calls from Emma and Yank, as well as helped explain the presence of the Russian jeweler, Tatiana Pavlova.

What were the odds they had nothing to do with Emma's tip about Pete Horner's Fort Lauderdale house?

Lousy, Colin thought. *Damn lousy.*

He skipped dropping off his kayak at his house and drove straight to Heron's Cove, trying Emma on her cell phone.

His call went to her voice mail. He didn't leave a message. In a few more minutes, he would be on her doorstep.

He called Yank next. "Dmitri Rusakov's in Heron's Cove," Colin said.

Silence.

He gripped his phone. "You didn't know, or you're surprised I know?"

"I'm never surprised by what you know. That's why I called. To tell you about Rusakov."

"Emma's been in touch with you?"

"Yeah," Yank said. "She didn't tell you?"

"Nope. She's in Heron's Cove. I'm in Rock Point."

"Ah."

"Don't get excited. We're not splitting up." Colin navigated a curve that took him close to the rocks and water, a sailboat on the horizon, about to disappear from view. He loosened his grip on his phone. "Talk to me, Yank."

"Rusakov is apparently here to see about a collection of Russian jewelry and decorative arts that he owns. It disappeared a few years ago and now it's turned up in his dead ex-wife's belongings. She left it to her daughter."

"He brought in the Sharpes to investigate?"

"Right. Emma was working for her grandfather then. He sent her to London to talk to Rusakov. Rusakov discovered the collection himself in the walls of his Moscow house twenty years ago. Wendell Sharpe helped him out back then."

"How long have you known about the Sharpes and Rusakov?" Colin asked.

"Since the beginning."

"'Beginning' as in before you ventured to the Sisters of the Joyful Heart four years ago and met Emma as Sister Brigid, or after she quit the sisters and went to work with her grandfather, or when she applied to become an agent—"

Yank cut him off. "It's all in her file. Where are you now?"

"Pulling in front of the Sharpe house. 'In her file' is a vague answer. What else is in Emma's file?"

"Consider it an expression," he said. "Keep an eye on things up there."

Colin came to a stop. "I keep an eye on Emma. Emma keeps an eye on me. Your idea of a perfect world, Yank. Anything else I need to know?"

"Talk to her. Tell her to tell you everything."

As if that would do any good, Colin thought as he disconnected. Emma wasn't one to act first and think later. She would hold her fire until she knew what she was dealing with. She tended not to operate on impulse and instinct, especially when the situation involved her family and their work as art detectives.

Colin turned off the engine and got out of his truck. The small restaurant across the street was busy, drawing a decent crowd even late in the season. He'd had their lobster rolls himself.

He headed up the Sharpe's short, paved driveway, a carpentry sign and a Dumpster the only obvious indications the house was under renovation. He eased past Emma's car and a one-car garage to the backyard. The afternoon had turned still and cool, daylight leaking out of the sky earlier now that it was late October. He'd missed October in Maine and the best of the fall foliage last year, too.

He didn't see Emma in the backyard or on the porch and walked across the yard to the retaining wall. Down on the stony beach, a white-haired man tossed a yellow Frisbee into the water. His golden retriever leaped in and swam out to it, snatched it up in his mouth. Colin wondered if he and Emma were ever destined for such normalcy as an afternoon out on the water with a Frisbee and a dog.

He looked upriver at the sleek luxury yacht that dominated the waterfront. It had multiple decks and no doubt all the amenities a Russian billionaire would expect.

Colin spotted two men on the top deck. They looked relaxed, held drinks.

A woman joined them. He recognized her honey hair, the tilt of her head as she laughed.

Emma.

"Well, well," he said aloud.

He heard a movement behind him and turned as a woman squeezed through the tall hydrangeas that served as a border between the Sharpe property and the adjacent marina and yacht club. She wore a pumpkin-colored jacket and had long brown hair pulled back in a loose ponytail.

He started to say something, but she put a finger to her lips and shook her head. "Pretend you don't see me. Please." She spoke in a Russian accent and flicked long, slender fingers toward the *Nightingale*. "I don't want them to see me."

"All right." Colin stood on the retaining wall as if he were taking in the sight of the truly amazing yacht and responded without looking at the woman. "Hiding behind a bush will only draw attention to yourself."

She plopped down on the grass, staying close to the hydrangeas, and stretched out slim legs encased in tight-fitting black pants. "I have picnic," she said.

"A picnic requires at least some cheese and crackers, don't you think?"

She shrugged. "Maybe I ate them."

The woman was feisty, Colin thought, and very pretty. "You're Tatiana Pavlova. You met a friend of mine yesterday out at the Sisters of the Joyful Heart. A priest."

"Father Bracken," she said, with a bit of a smile. "He's sweet man. You're not a priest."

"No, I'm not a priest. My name's Colin Donovan."

"You and Emma also are friends?"

He nodded. "We are."

"Are you FBI agent? Like Emma?"

"Yes, but I'm just in Heron's Cove visiting," Colin said. Up on the yacht, the two men had backed out of sight, but Emma was still visible, drink in hand. She didn't wave but he had no doubt she'd seen him. He didn't wave, either, instead addressing Tatiana. "Why are you here?"

"I wanted a closer look at the yacht." She peeked around the edges of the hydrangea, a large burgundy-colored blossom touching her cheek. "Can you see him? Can you see Dmitri Rusakov?"

"Which one is he?"

"He's in the red pants. Terrible, aren't they?"

"Not everyone's color," Colin said.

"Men should not wear red pants." Tatiana gave him a frank once-over. "You don't."

He smiled, trying to keep her at ease. "I had red waterproofs once. Who's the other man?"

She pursed her lips. "Ivan Alexander. He does Rusakov's bidding."

"As in he mops the floors or he doctors the books?"

"He's security expert. Very dangerous. I don't want them to see me."

"Would they recognize you? Do you all know each other?"

"No, no." Tatiana sprang up, no taller than the hydrangea, which she obviously had already calculated. She was pale now, her nostrils flared as she took in deep breaths. "No, Colin Donovan. I know them. They don't know me. If they see me spying on them, they'll find out who I am."

"Then what?"

She shuddered. "I don't want to find out."

"Ms. Pavlova, are you concerned for your safety?"

"It's not like that. I don't need police. I need..." She thought a moment. "I need nothing. I'm calm now. Do you know the Russian fable of the cat and the mouse?"

"I don't," Colin said, no idea where she was going with this.

Tatiana didn't look at him, her gaze focused on the waterfront. "The mouse comes to his neighbor, the rat. He's very excited to tell his friend that their great enemy, the cat, has been caught by a ferocious lion. For the mouse, this is tremendous news. Most excellent news. The rat isn't so impressed. He believes that the lion cannot possibly survive a battle with the cat." Tatiana turned to Colin, her dark eyes shimmering with emotion in the fading afternoon light. "Do you understand the moral of this tale, Colin Donovan?"

"The mouse is kind of dumb?"

She smiled but only a little. "This fable cautions us against letting our own fears cloud our judgment. We tend to think that what we fear, all the world fears."

"Ah. It's a good fable. Are you alone here, Ms. Pavlova?"

Her smile brightened. "You must call me Tatiana. Yes, I'm here alone. My little cottage is perfect for solitude. I'm using this time as a personal artistic retreat."

"When did you decide to come to Heron's Cove?"

His question obviously caught her by surprise. Her eyes widened. "What?"

Colin repeated the question.

"Oh. I bought my ticket—" she counted out fingers "—four days ago."

"And you booked your cottage then, too?"

She nodded. "It wouldn't have been possible in August but now it is late in the season." She lowered her hand and pulled it up into the sleeves of her oversize jacket. "I must go back to my cottage now. I have a sketch I want to finish. I will stay out of sight of the *Nightingale*."

"Hold on," Colin said, not harshly. "Did you know Rusakov would be in Heron's Cove?"

"No. Only his ex-wife's daughter. Natalie—Natalie Warren. She just arrived. She boarded the *Nightingale* and then unboarded again. Unboarded? Is that the right word?"

"Close enough. You know her?"

Tatiana's brow furrowed as if she didn't understand him, which, of course, she did. "Know her? She lives in Phoenix. I live in London."

"That doesn't answer my question, does it, Tatiana?"

Her chin snapped up as if she were insulted. "I don't know Natalie Warren, no. Or Dmitri Rusakov, or Ivan Alexander. Not personally." She waved a hand vaguely toward the street. "I'm going now."

Colin decided to let her go without further questions. It was Emma he needed to talk to now. "Have a good evening," he said.

Tatiana mumbled a goodbye and marched off, staying close to the hydrangea border and out of view of Dmitri Rusakov's yacht. Once she disappeared on the other side of the Sharpe garage, Colin jumped from the retaining wall onto the pier. He could think of several ways he could get on board the *Nightingale,* not all of which involved a gun and a badge—or even one Emma Sharpe, friend of Russian tycoons.

Another woman approached him from the opposite direction on the pier. She had short, white-blond hair that framed a heart-shaped face and very blue eyes, and she was dressed in flowing white pants and a navy-and-white top, with simple silver jewelry. "I wonder what possessed me to wear open-toed heels in Maine," she said cheerfully. "Honestly, my feet are freezing, and one wrong step and I'll be headfirst in the water." She nodded to the yacht. "Are you joining us for drinks?"

"My friend Emma Sharpe is," Colin said.

"Emma's on board already? Perfect. I haven't seen her yet. I only just arrived and unpacked. I'm from Phoenix," she said, then put out a small hand. "Natalie Warren."

He took her hand briefly and said, "Colin Donovan," leaving it at that.

She breathed in deeply, beamed him a smile. "I love the cool air. I don't want to be here in January, though. I can only imagine the icy wind off the water. I had a room booked at a charming Heron's Cove inn, but Dmitri insisted I stay aboard the *Nightingale*. Who was I to argue?"

"It's a big boat."

She laughed. "Yes, it is. I have no desire to go for a spin out in the Atlantic, though. There's a reason I live in a sun-drenched, landlocked state. Now," she added, pointing at him, "since you and Emma are friends, you must join us. Come. You can be my guest. I'll get you past Dmitri's security."

Following Natalie Warren aboard the *Nightingale* was much easier than any of the options Colin had had in mind. He smiled at her. "Lead the way, Ms. Warren."

"It's Natalie. Please." With another bright laugh, she hooked her arm into his. "You can keep me from tripping in these blasted shoes."

9

THE FALLING TEMPERATURE FORCED DMITRI Rusakov to move his gathering to an enclosed lounge, its large windows overlooking the quaint Heron's Cove water-front with its inns, summer homes and clusters of shingled cottages and small shops. Emma fixed her gaze on a battered lobster boat, a yellow, dirty raincoat hanging just inside its pilothouse. A uniformed crewmember had exchanged her iced tea for a glass of champagne, but she had yet to take a sip. In the hour she had been aboard the *Nightingale,* she had paced herself with small talk with Dmitri, Ivan and the crew.

She had spotted Colin on the retaining wall and knew he had to be curious about what she was up to. She had left him a voice mail, but he hadn't returned her call, probably assuming he would talk to her in Heron's Cove—or because he had talked to Matt Yankowski first.

Yank hadn't been happy about the *Nightingale.* *"Dmitri Rusakov is in Heron's Cove? Emma? Did you just say that?"*

She turned from the windows as Natalie Warren arrived with Colin on her arm. Natalie was attractive, even more so than her mother had been. Colin seemed at ease at her side, but he would, Emma thought as she sipped her expensive champagne. For months, he had pretended to be someone else in his undercover work. He could handle himself aboard the *Nightingale*.

Ivan edged next to Emma. "So this is your man."

"My man? What do you know about Colin?"

"He's an FBI agent. He works at FBI headquarters in Washington." Ivan's voice was almost toneless, with no trace of sarcasm; his English was excellent and Emma noticed he'd had little to drink since her arrival on board. "It's good that he has a safe assignment since you two see each other. I would hate for you to be unhappy."

If Emma hadn't been sure whether Ivan knew the identity of the undercover agent in trouble in Fort Lauderdale, she was now. She hadn't spoken to Ivan in months. Then came his call out of the blue when she was in Colin's bed, wondering what she could do to find him.

However Ivan had learned about Colin's undercover status, it wasn't from her.

"Colin wouldn't be on board without your approval," Emma said.

Ivan shrugged. "Dmitri has his own security team. I'm here only as a friend."

Emma tasted more of her champagne. "We need to talk, Ivan."

His eyes held hers. "Anytime."

Dmitri spotted Natalie from behind the curved bar where he was mixing his own drink and surged toward her. *"Moya sladkaya,"* he murmured, kissing her on each cheek. "My sweet Natalie. It's been far too long."

"Dmitri," she whispered, then stood back and smiled. "You're as handsome as ever. My heavens. I can't believe it's been four years."

"I'm sorry I missed you earlier."

"It was good to have a chance to settle in. I went up to the yacht club for a few things. Oh, Dmitri. My stateroom is fabulous. I'm so happy to be here with you."

"We're happy to have you." His expression softened. "I'm sorry about your mother."

"Thank you. That's decent of you to say." Natalie took Colin's arm again, as if she were looking for an excuse to change the subject. "Forgive me, I almost forgot. Dmitri, this is Colin Donovan. He and Emma are friends. Colin, Dmitri Rusakov. Emma, I don't know if you remember me. We met in London a few years ago."

"Of course I remember you, Natalie," Emma said, aware of Ivan still at her side. "Welcome to Heron's Cove."

"I know my visit is a surprise. I understand your brother isn't here. I'd love to meet him, and your grandfather, too, but maybe you can help me. Well, there's time for all that. First things first, as we say." She smiled, no sign of awkwardness as she surveyed the elegant lounge with its understated, neutral decor. "It's very cool here compared to Phoenix. We're still sweltering at home."

"You came straight here?" Emma asked, noticing that Ivan had yet to say a word.

"I was among the cacti this morning." Natalie laughed in obvious delight when a crew member handed her a cosmopolitan. "Oh, Dmitri. How sweet. You remembered."

He gave a slight bow. "Of course."

She held up the drink to Emma and Colin. "I was into cosmopolitans when I last saw Dmitri. I was in London for a few days with my mother. She was—well, being my mother." Her eyes shone with sudden tears as she sipped her drink and smiled through them. "Dmitri, you gave up your London apartment, didn't you?"

"I was never there after I bought the *Nightingale*," he said.

"I wouldn't be, either. I could live on the *Nightingale* even if it stayed anchored right here and never went anywhere. It's elegant without being stuffy or intimidating. Thank you for having me."

Dmitri kissed her on the cheek. "Anytime, my dear. You know that."

"I do. I've always known. It was just easier not to stay in touch when my mother was alive." Natalie shook her head, swallowed more of her drink. "Let's not talk about her, although she's the reason I'm in Heron's Cove, really."

Dmitri nodded toward a small, gleaming brass elevator. "Why don't you show Emma what you brought with you?"

Natalie looked tentative. "Are you sure? I just got here—"

"It'll ease your mind. Please. I've released Emma from any client privilege. She can tell you what she knows." He motioned toward the circular bar with his champagne glass. "Ivan and I will have a drink with Colin here. Colin, what would you like? Beer, vodka, whiskey? You don't look as if you drink champagne or cosmopolitans."

"Beer would be fine," Colin said.

Dmitri grinned, clapped a hand on his shoulder. "Excellent."

They went to the bar, crafted of dark wood and edged in chrome, with swivel chairs covered in neutral-colored leather. Ivan glanced at Emma, then Natalie. "Let me know if you need anything," he said, then joined Colin and Dmitri at the bar.

Natalie seemed a bit nonplussed as she sighed at Emma. "You don't mind?" she asked quietly.

Emma smiled. "Not at all."

"Dmitri can be hard to refuse. It amazes me sometimes that he and my mother ever got together, never mind lasted two years. He sees through everything and everyone, but he didn't see through her. At least not at first." Natalie waved a hand. "I'm sorry. I don't want to go down that road. This'll only take a few minutes. If you're sure—"

"I'm sure."

Natalie smiled, looking less tentative. "Then let's go."

They took the elevator down one deck, and Emma followed Natalie into a guest stateroom. Its built-in queen-size bed, nightstands and dressers had the feel of free-standing furniture, and the decorative pillows, linens and upholstery were in more soothing neutrals. A lush painting of white roses hung on the wall opposite the windows. The shades were pulled, the recessed lighting on a dim setting.

"I don't live like this, in case you were wondering," Natalie said. "I actually don't know that I'd want to. Would you, Emma?"

"It's not something I think about."

"An FBI agent's salary—but you must do the work because you love it. I do retail marketing for upscale boutique shops near where I live. I can't say that I love it, but I'm good at it." She kicked off her open-toed heels and stood barefoot on the cream-colored carpet. "That feels better, I think. The *Nightingale* was Dmitri's gift to himself after getting my mother out of his life. I can't blame him. He was so misled by her. It had to sting once he figured her out. You met her, Emma. She was charming, wasn't she? You don't have to answer. I know she was. Narcissists are often very charming at first."

Emma glanced around the elegant guest stateroom. Natalie had, indeed, unpacked, even setting up her toiletries in the en suite bathroom. The door was open, cosmetics neatly lined up on the sink, a dark pink bathrobe hanging from a hook on the door.

With a stifled yawn, Natalie walked between the bed and the closet. "My mother was a master at charming people when it suited her. If she thought someone could be of use to her, she'd pull out all the stops. That's how she lured Dmitri into her little web."

"I gather you and your mother didn't get along," Emma said.

"It's not a question of getting along. I've had lots of therapy. I've learned to accept her. Dmitri is one of the few people who cut her out of his life instead of the other way around. My mother was very tactical in her relationships. Once some-one was no longer of use to her, that was it. They were gone. She'd make up or exaggerate an offense and snip, snip. Out went that friend, lover, husband."

Emma sat on a soft, built-in couch along a paneled wall. "We don't have to talk about your mother, Natalie. I know this must be difficult for you."

"Not as difficult as you might think. As I said, years of therapy have helped. Trust me, this apple fell far, far from her mother's tree." Natalie took a quick, shallow breath, as if controlling her emotions. "I'm not like her. I've made a point of not being like her, but I now realize I didn't have to. I'm just not wired the same way she was, for whatever reason."

From what she had seen of Renee Warren Rusakov herself, and learned about her during her work on the disappearance of the Rusakov collection, Emma could understand Natalie's complex feelings about her mother.

"What can I do for you, Natalie?" Emma asked.

"I probably should have called but I was so determined to be discreet. Now here I am, on the biggest damn boat in Heron's Cove. You should see all the people coming out of the woodwork to check it out." Natalie paused, yanked open one of the closet's double doors. "My mother's estate was a mess, as you can imagine. She was so young, and she was in denial about how sick she was. Although I suspect if she'd lived to a hundred she'd still have left things in a mess."

"Sometimes people can't face their own mortality," Emma said.

"I didn't expect to inherit anything of value from her. She burned through money. I was surprised when I discovered she owned some rather gorgeous pieces of Russian jewelry and fancy knickknacks."

Emma leaned back against velvety cream-colored throw pillows. "You brought them with you?"

Natalie lifted a large black case out of the closet and plopped it onto the bed. "I did indeed." She waved a hand. "Don't worry. It's fine. I haven't told anyone except Dmitri and now you. Well, and Ivan, of course. To tell Dmitri is to tell Ivan. But can you imagine anyone trying to steal anything with him around?"

"I thought he and Dmitri were just friends these days."

"Ivan owes Dmitri his start. He'll always have his back." Natalie unlatched the case and opened the top. "He checked in with me after my mother's death. That was decent of him. She never liked him. I think she was jealous of his friendship with Dmitri. They go way back. Dmitri sent flowers for her funeral. My mother at the end of their marriage—well, you know. You were in London then."

"For a few days only, Natalie," Emma said. "I wouldn't presume to judge your mother or her relationship with Dmitri or anyone else."

"I appreciate that. I really do, but I've found that I do best when I don't pretend my mother was a nice, sweet, gentle soul. She wasn't. She was mean." Natalie rubbed her fingertips across the soft black velvety interior of the case. "I did hope at first that maybe Dmitri could change her. He's such a forceful personality, as well as incredibly wealthy—not that I cared about that, but my mother did. He and I got along well. I was already in my twenties when they met. I had my own life. I never wanted anything from him. He doesn't have children. I think for a while I was like the daughter he never had."

"Do you have any siblings?"

Natalie shook her head. "Just me. I suppose my father might have other kids but I don't have any contact with him. He was one of my mother's flings. She threw him away before I was even born. I'm sorry if I sound harsh, but it's easier if I face the truth. I'm happier as a result." She withdrew a deep purple velvet bag from the case. "I don't hate her, though. I never have."

Emma remained on the couch as Natalie gently removed a brooch from the velvet bag—a delicate, intricate red flower edged in gold, its petals gleaming with tiny rubies.

She held the brooch up to the dim light. "It's gorgeous, isn't it? Does it look familiar to you?"

It did, Emma thought. She remembered photographs of a flower brooch, one of the most interesting works in the Rusakov collection. She rose and took a closer look at the brooch and its perfect red flower. "There's a folktale called 'The Crimson Flower,'" she said. "Do you know it?"

Natalie frowned. "I'm afraid I don't."

"A father is getting ready to leave for a trip and asks his three daughters what they'd like him to bring home for them. One daughter wants a gold crown, one wants a crystal mirror and one wants—"

"A crimson flower," Natalie finished with a smile. "How cool."

"The father finds one on the property of a beast."

"Ah. Of course. And this beast turns into a handsome prince?"

"Eventually. The daughter is forced to live with the beast, but he allows her to go home to visit her father, who is sick. She promises to return by a certain time. Her sisters trick her and she doesn't keep her promise and returns to the beast late."

"Oh, dear. He died?"

Emma nodded. "She's overcome with grief and falls on his body, finally realizing that she loves him. Her genuine love breaks the spell that turned him into a beast. He comes to life as the handsome prince he really is."

"And they live happily ever after," Natalie said with a satisfied sigh, then returned the brooch to the velvet bag. "I'd rather fall in love without tricks and evil spells, wouldn't you?"

"Most definitely," Emma said with a laugh.

"It might take a little magic, though," Natalie added lightly. "All the pieces in the collection have some kind of Russian folk or fairy-tale theme. There are two pendants, the brooch, a bracelet, a ring, a decorative hand mirror, a cigarette case— you get the idea. Do they sound familiar?"

"Natalie..."

"They're from Dmitri, aren't they?"

"I think you should talk to him," Emma said.

"He said you could tell me."

"I know he did, but I'd prefer you two sort this out yourselves. Your mother never said anything to you about this collection?"

"No. Nothing. She didn't want me to have anything to do with Dmitri after the divorce. I could have told her to go to blazes, but I didn't. I respected her wishes." Natalie sank onto the edge of the bed. "Emma, he gave this collection to my mother, didn't he?"

"Is that what you think?"

"Yes, of course. What else? My mother was a lot of things but she wasn't a thief." Natalie snapped the case shut. "I just want to know if Dmitri gave my mother some or all of these pieces, or if someone else did, or if she bought them herself. Provenance won't be an issue, right? I own the collection. I inherited it."

"I suggest you talk to Dmitri about those details."

Natalie slipped back into her heels. "My mother manipulated and used people but I swear to you she wasn't a thief. I don't want to keep what's not mine, but things were so bad between Dmitri and my mother at the end, who knows what happened. What he agreed to in the heat of the moment and regretted later. What she got out of him in exchange for keeping her mouth shut after they split."

"Do you have plans for the collection?" Emma asked.

"Sell it. Give it away. I don't know. Can you at least tell me where these pieces came from? I mean, what they are—when they were made, who crafted them?"

Emma debated a moment before answering. "The crimson flower brooch looks like it could be Russian Art Nouveau. If it's genuine, it was probably crafted in the late nineteenth-century. Beyond that..."

"I know, I know. Talk to Dmitri." Natalie gave a small, sad laugh. "He's sweet in his own way, but he can be quite ruthless. I can't imagine that he'd just let this collection go without a fight if he didn't mean for my mother to have it. Can you?"

"It doesn't matter what either of us can or can't imagine."

Natalie fingered a silver latch on the case. "I wish I'd been brave enough to stand up to my mother and stay in touch with

Dmitri in spite of her, but he knows what she was like." She jumped up and returned the case to the closet, shutting the door firmly. "Were you in London four years ago because of this collection? Did Dmitri hire Sharpe Fine Art Recovery because it disappeared?"

"Dmitri was a client, yes—"

"Did he tell you my mother took the collection?"

"My grandfather always conducts an independent investigation. He doesn't take anyone's word for anything."

"Maybe the collection was part of the divorce. The spoils of war. My mother had a passion for Russian art. She and Dmitri actually met at the Tretyakov Gallery. She loved Russia." Natalie smiled, visibly less tense. "I preferred Dmitri's apartment in London to that mansion he refurbished in Moscow."

"I've never seen Dmitri's Moscow house," Emma said.

"I was only there once. It felt like a big old dungeon to me." Natalie moved to the door, her pale hair a few tones darker in the dim light. "Time for a fresh cosmopolitan."

Emma followed her back out to the elevator and up to the lounge. Colin, Dmitri and Ivan were laughing together at the bar. It was dark now, village lights sparkling in the clear night air, stars out over the ocean. As she crossed over to the men, Emma was aware of Colin's smoky eyes on her. She had no idea what Dmitri and Ivan had been telling him, what he might have guessed about what she was doing aboard the *Nightingale* herself.

Natalie inhaled, then smiled widely and slipped in between Ivan and Dmitri. Dmitri kissed her on the cheek, then went back behind the bar to fix her another cosmopolitan.

Emma stood next to Colin. He watched her over the rim of his glass. "Another glass of champagne?" he asked.

"No, thanks."

"I didn't know you liked champagne."

"It was what was offered," she said.

"Your friend Ivan is armed."

"I'm sure he has any required permits. He's careful that way."

Colin set his beer glass on the gleaming bar. "I'm armed, too. I'm an FBI agent. You are, too."

"Think I need reminding?"

"You tell me."

She ignored him and shifted her attention to Dmitri as he measured vodka for the cosmopolitan. "I should go, Dmitri, and give you and Natalie a chance to get reacquainted."

"Did she show you the collection?"

"Just a brooch. It's lovely."

"But you didn't tell her where it came from," he said, dumping the vodka in a martini glass.

"It's not up to me, even if I have your permission."

He reached for fresh-cut limes. "I understand." He glanced at Natalie, who was talking with Ivan, either not paying attention to Dmitri or pretending she wasn't. He squeezed lime into the glass. "I'd hoped you might make this easier for me. Are you sure you can't stay for dinner?"

"Not tonight. Another time, I hope. It's good to see you again. Thanks for having me on board. It's quite a yacht."

"When will your grandfather and your brother return from Ireland?"

"Lucas should be back any day. My grandfather..." Emma smiled. "He's heading to the southwest Irish coast to do some hiking. He's starting in Killarney. Doesn't that sound like the thing to do at eighty-one?"

Dmitri handed the drink to Natalie. She took a quick sip and smiled. "I think at eighty-one I'd want to be drinking cosmopolitans on the beach."

"Or here," Dmitri said, splashing vodka into a clean glass.

"Such a spot, Emma. Wendell has a good life to return to in Heron's Cove. What about you? Do you like the FBI?"

"It suits me."

"More so than Sharpe Fine Art Recovery, or than being a nun?"

"Each had its own time in my life."

"A sensible answer." He set his drink on the bar and took her hands, kissed her on both cheeks. "We'll see you tomorrow?"

"I hope so," Emma said, then thanked him, said goodnight to Natalie and Ivan and started to leave.

She heard Dmitri offer Colin another beer. "A Coke would be great," he said, making no move to follow her.

Emma continued on out.

Colin could find his own way home.

Not for one second had she forgotten she was an FBI agent, or, she thought, a Sharpe. She was both, and he had just gotten a full dose of what that meant.

And so had she.

10

EMMA PAUSED ON A SMALL BRIDGE THAT
spanned a shallow cove next to the yacht club and marina.
The cottage Tatiana Pavlova had rented was down on the
water, tucked among a half-dozen small, shingled waterfront
cottages and shops. The *Nightingale* was just out of sight from
where Emma stood, but Tatiana would be able to see it from
her cottage.

And anyone on board would be able to see her.

The lights inside the cottage were on but the blinds and
curtains were pulled, as if she didn't want to have anything
to do with the world outside. Maybe she was sketching great
blue herons, Emma thought, deciding against walking down
to the cottage and knocking on the front door. Dmitri or Ivan
could be watching her, or even Natalie. Emma didn't want
to draw attention to Tatiana for no good reason.

She crossed the bridge and continued down the quiet street
toward the Sharpe house and the ocean. On a summer night,
Heron's Cove would be filled with people—tourists, second-
home owners, locals. Most of the inns and restaurants were
still open, but the high season was winding down.

The Sharpe house was dark except for a solitary light on in the kitchen. Emma went around back, and as she mounted the steps onto the porch, she saw that the kitchen door was open, as if it were a warm midsummer evening.

Colin materialized in the screen door and pushed it open. Emma smiled. "You rugged undercover types do like to live dangerously. What if I'd thought you were an intruder? I could have shot you."

"You have more self-control than to shoot me." He stepped back, letting her pass him into the kitchen. "I thought you'd stay for dinner with your Russian friends."

"Natalie Warren isn't Russian."

"Dmitri Rusakov is. Ivan Alexander is. Most of the crew is. And Tatiana Pavlova. She is, too, even if she lives in London. I found her hiding in the hydrangeas in your backyard." Colin shut the door; it was original to the house but would go in the renovations. "Is she safe?"

"From who, Colin? You, me, Dmitri, Ivan, one of the crew? Herself?"

"You tell me."

"If Tatiana were afraid for her safety, would she stay alone in a cottage within sight of Dmitri's yacht? Would she stay alone at all?"

"She didn't want to be seen."

Emma nodded. "I understand that."

Colin went to the sink, pulled an empty pottery sugar pot and cream pitcher off an open shelf and placed them on the counter. "You're going to need more boxes for all this kitchen stuff."

"We got most of the food out already. My grandfather gave us a list of what items he wants to keep. The rest can go. We'll donate whatever looks decent to a church yard sale." Feeling chilly now, if only because of Colin's mood, Emma crossed her arms over her chest. "I called you so that you wouldn't have to come down here and walk into this situation without warning."

"Situation?" He assessed her with those smoky eyes. "Finding you drinking expensive champagne on a Russian luxury yacht is a situation?"

She pulled open an upper cupboard filled with mismatched juice glasses, wineglasses and dessert bowls. She lifted out a stack of bowls and set them on the counter, quickly straightening them as they tilted and nearly toppled over. She could feel Colin's eyes still on her.

"I can't be in the dark, Emma," he said. "About anything."

She reached for more dishes. "You know most of what I know."

"I don't know who your source is."

"I haven't told you who my source is." She grabbed three wineglasses by the stems. "There's a difference, isn't there?"

Edging closer to her, Colin took a stack of bowls from a high shelf and set them next to the wineglasses. "Did this same source tip you off about Vladimir Bulgov's interest in Picasso?"

She grabbed more glasses. "No."

"Do Bulgov and Dmitri Rusakov know each other?"

"I have no information one way or the other."

"Meaning you don't know," he said, reaching for an old casserole dish.

"Do you know?" Emma asked.

"Rusakov wasn't on my radar until his yacht turned up outside your back door. What about Ivan Alexander?" Colin set the casserole on the edge of the sink, his movements deliberate, controlled; the bruise on his forearm had deepened to shades of dark purple and blue. "Tell me about you and Ivan."

"You two had yourselves a good chat," she said coolly. "You probably know more about him than I do."

"He says he got his start with Dmitri but he's out on his own now. Works as a consultant when and if he feels like it. He's loyal to Dmitri."

"They're friends," Emma said.

With one hand, Colin took a half-dozen small, flowered dessert bowls from the shelf and set them next to hers. "Do you trust them?"

"Trust them in what way?"

He gave her a slight smile. "Spoken like an analyst. Dmitri's the former Sharpe client you mentioned last night. When you said Tatiana Pavlova was worried about a collection that involved a former Sharpe client, I wasn't thinking Russian tycoon."

"It's not unusual for a Sharpe Art Recovery client to be someone of means."

"There's 'means' and there's billions."

Emma raised an arm for more glassware, but her elbow struck Colin's flowered dessert bowls and sent them clattering into the porcelain sink. None broke but she managed to startle herself. She took a deep breath, aware of Colin standing close to her, perhaps not quite trusting her—or at least her ability to handle Dmitri Rusakov and his reasons for being in Heron's Cove.

And knowing, she thought, that she hadn't told him everything.

She ignored the dishes in the sink and shut the cupboard door. "After I left the sisters and before I joined the FBI, I worked with my grandfather in Dublin. You know that. During that time, Dmitri Rusakov hired Sharpe Fine Art Recovery to help him figure out what happened to this collection. He'd had it with him in London. I flew there to meet with him."

"Granddad's idea, or yours?"

"His. I stayed in London for a few days—in a hotel."

"As opposed to…"

"Dmitri's London apartment."

"He invited you to stay there?"

"It's bigger than most houses. Dmitri's a huge flirt, but there was never anything romantic between us."

"What about you and Ivan?"

Emma pretended not to hear the question. "Dmitri's main residence is in Moscow. It had been abandoned for years when he bought it. He was making a fortune in post–Soviet Russia but he wanted to do some of the renovation work himself. He took a crowbar to a wall and uncovered a wooden box filled with jewelry and decorative arts, each work inspired by some aspect of Russian folk tradition."

"Some people have all the luck," Colin said.

Emma held back a smile. "Dmitri wanted an outsider—a non-Russian—to have a look at his find. He hired Sharpe Fine Art Recovery. My grandfather went to Moscow. He was there for about a week. He says the collection is amazing. That it's as if someone had stashed away bits and pieces of the Russian soul."

"And it ended up with Dmitri Rusakov's ex-wife in Arizona?"

"Apparently," Emma said.

Colin lifted a small, misshapen dish Emma had made for her grandparents in a pottery class in fifth grade. Her grandfather had given specific instructions that the dish wasn't to go into the garbage or off to a yard sale. Colin seemed to guess, and put it to one side on the counter.

"I gather that Renee Rusakov was quite a character," he said. "What did she do, just walk off with this collection?"

"Basically, or at least that was my assessment when Dmitri asked us to look into its disappearance four years ago. I think Renee took it a piece or two at a time with her back to Tucson. She never gave up her house there. Dmitri didn't believe it and sent me back to Dublin." Emma shivered in a sudden cold draft. "Colin, this isn't your problem."

He didn't seem to hear her. "Why did your grandfather send you to London? Why didn't he go himself?"

"I was learning the business. It made sense for me to go. It's not as if there were any danger."

Colin frowned. "You're cold." He adjusted the collar on her jacket, touched the back of his hand to her jaw. "Even your skin is cool."

"No red nose, I hope."

He smiled. "No red nose."

"There's no heat with the renovations."

"It was hotter than hell in Florida. Unseasonably so, they tell me. I swore I wouldn't complain about the cold until it's at least ten below." He threaded his fingers into her hair, then cupped the back of her head. "I have a lot of questions about you and your Russian friends, Emma."

"I understand that. Give me time. Let me deal with them. You're decompressing after a difficult experience."

"A difficult experience?" He gave a short laugh and lowered his hand back to her side. "Sweetheart, kayaking against the wind in choppy water is a difficult experience. Escaping arms traffickers out to kill me was one hell of a tough night." He walked over to the kitchen door and pulled his jacket off a peg. "How much of this does Yank know?"

"I called him the same time I called you. I told him all I know."

"Did you tell him about you and Ivan?"

"There is no me and Ivan." Emma stood back from the sink, warmer now. "Lucas is flying to London in the morning to see what he can learn about Tatiana Pavlova. He didn't recognize her name. Neither did my grandfather."

"Who does she think will steal the collection?"

"She didn't say."

"Rusakov wants it back?"

"He seems to, yes. I don't think he wants to upset Natalie, though."

"And Ivan?"

"I haven't talked to him enough to know why he's here, but I imagine it's because Dmitri wants him here."

"Ivan told me he's here because of you."

Emma rolled her eyes. "He did not. Go home, Colin. I'll finish up here. We can talk tomorrow."

"Where do you plan to sleep?"

"I'll make a bed on the floor here. There are enough blankets lying around. I'll be fine."

"You could stay in a guest cabin on the *Nightingale*."

She gave him a cool look. "Maybe I could, but I won't."

He glanced out at the dark waterfront. "Do you Sharpes have any normal friends?"

"I wouldn't call Dmitri a friend."

"Ivan?"

Emma sighed. "You're relentless, Special Agent Donovan."

He winked at her. "Might keep that in mind."

She said nothing.

He shrugged on his jacket, left it unbuttoned. "Even if Vladimir Bulgov were a Russian schoolteacher and not an arms trafficker, I wouldn't like having a Russian tycoon with a history with your family on a big damn yacht within spitting distance of your back porch."

"I get that, Colin, but I'm a fully qualified, experienced federal agent. I can take care of myself."

"Didn't say you couldn't. You and I don't operate in the same circles, Emma. We didn't as kids, either, with you growing up here in Heron's Cove, me in Rock Point."

"Our lives have more in common than many people's lives do."

"When's the last time you caught a lobster?"

"Never," she said. "That's not my point."

He grinned. "Your point's probably way too complicated for my simple mind. I think in straight lines. You think in mazes." He took her by the shoulders, no humor in his smoky eyes now. "I can handle whatever trouble you cause for me."

"I'm not trying to cause you trouble."

"I know." He tightened his hold on her. "What about you, Emma? Can you handle whatever trouble I cause for you?"

"I can. And I can handle you."

"Think so, huh?" He took a few strands of her windblown hair and tucked them behind her ear. "Sister Brigid, Wendell Sharpe's granddaughter, Special Agent Sharpe. Who are you, Emma?"

"I'm not confused about who I am."

"Maybe so. Maybe with your background you've had to think about who you are more than the rest of us. I've had to pretend to be someone I'm not."

"I don't know anything about your undercover identity. I suppose it's unsavory."

"Unsavory." His eyes again sparked with humor. "Yeah. You could say that."

"One day maybe you'll be able to tell me more about who you were, what you did. The kind of things that won't be in any briefing on your mission."

"There was no other woman in my undercover life. You're

it, Emma." He let go of her shoulders but kept his gaze steady on her. "Does that scare you?"

"Not even a little."

He kissed her on the forehead. "I didn't think so."

She caught his hand into hers. "I need to figure out what's going on here."

"I know. Sleep well, Sister Brigid." He squeezed her hand, then opened the door, looking back at her. "Call me if your Russians give you any trouble."

"Where are you going?"

"To become one with a bottle of Bracken's finest."

When the door shut behind him, Emma opened another cupboard and cleaned out plastic containers and tops, heaping them into the sink. She had no illusions that Colin was just off to drink whiskey with his brothers and Finian Bracken. He would be looking into those aboard the *Nightingale*.

He clearly wasn't concerned about leaving her on her own in Heron's Cove.

She lasted two minutes before she abandoned her cupboard cleaning. She had eaten little aboard the yacht but she wasn't hungry. She wasn't used to being in Heron's Cove alone. Most often, her parents, her brother or even her grandfather would be there—or she would be at the convent visiting with the sisters.

Of course, she didn't have to stay in Heron's Cove. She could always follow Colin to Rock Point.

She flipped on the porch light and went outside. It was cool, but there was no wind.

She could take another crack at a watercolor flat wash and give herself a chance to think.

The evening had turned downright cold, and Emma blamed that for her three attempts at flat washes in a row turning to mush. Too much water, or too much paint. She wasn't frustrated, just mystified that it could be so hard to make a simple flat wash work the way she wanted it to. The work itself was restful, and she loved the rich shade of burgundy she had chosen. It reminded her of the late-autumn oak leaves, and the colors of the hydrangea blossoms in the yard.

The fourth wash turning to mush she blamed on Ivan Alexander. She had watched him cross the yard against the backdrop of the village lights and the tidal river and ocean against the dark sky.

He walked slowly up the porch steps and then to the corner where she had set up her easel. "Did you learn to paint when you were a nun?"

She swished her brush in a mason jar of water. "I can't say I know how to paint now. I only painted walls as a sister. I am taking lessons, though."

"Is it relaxing to paint?"

"Sometimes. I get frustrated when it all turns to mud."

He studied her flat wash, which she had tried again with the cerulean-blue. "How are you, Emma?" he asked quietly.

"Just fine, thanks."

"You speak with clenched jaw," he said with a slight smile.

"You must know Dmitri's presence—your presence—here is provocative."

"Dmitri was already planning to take the yacht to the Bahamas when he found out Natalie was on her way here. I told him it was unwise to come but he insisted. He never believed Renee took this collection."

"Who did he think did, then? Has he ever told you?"

Ivan shrugged. "Does it matter now? The Sharpes can't help at this point."

"I hope Dmitri and Natalie will talk and work out a solution." Emma set the brush on the edge of the dresser, as Tatiana Pavlova had instructed her, and gave Ivan a pleasant smile. "At least it's never a waste of time to come to Heron's Cove."

"Or to visit you." Ivan nodded to the fresh sheet of heavy watercolor paper she had clipped to the easel. "Is that supposed to be…what? The ocean?"

"Nothing. I'm practicing flat washes. I managed to keep them from running into each other this time." Relieved she had put Tatiana's great blue heron into a dresser drawer, out of Ivan's sight, Emma turned from the easel and sat on the porch rail. "Why didn't you warn me you were on your way here?"

He stood at the rail next to her, facing the water. "I was still trying to talk Dmitri out of coming, and I hadn't decided if it would be wise for me to join him."

"I could bring you in," Emma said.

"Holding me as a witness would do you no good."

She felt a breeze stir behind her, off the water. "I can't lie about you, Ivan. I can't pretend I don't know you when you turn up on my doorstep with a Russian tycoon."

"You will do the right thing, Emma. You always do, even when it's difficult."

"I try to, but that doesn't mean I always succeed. You help the FBI for your own reasons."

"I help you. No one else."

She doubted her look was casual just then. "Were you in Fort Lauderdale?"

"The men who grabbed your agent continue to elude capture."

"Is that a statement or a question?"

"I've done what I can to help you. Dmitri is here about expensive trinkets from the past. He isn't involved in the illegal weapons trade, and none of the *Nightingale* crew is, either."

"Are you involved, Ivan?"

"I have broken none of your laws."

"Not quite a direct answer, is it?" Emma pushed her hands through her hair. "Ivan..."

"You trust me, Emma."

She didn't respond at once. Ivan had been the first to suspect Renee had taken the collection. Emma didn't have to understand his friendship with Dmitri to appreciate their loyalty to each other. When she was in London four years ago, Dmitri had let Ivan explain to her the difficulties of his marriage and divorce, the varied nature of his enemies and the importance of the collection to him, and of her discretion.

That didn't mean she knew everything. Dmitri, through Ivan, had told her only as much as he wanted her to know. But she suspected that her grandfather had done the same, and there was so much left unsaid. She remembered when she flew back to Dublin, she had felt both a sense of relief and frustration. Relief that she didn't have to peel back the layers of all that lay behind the mysterious and intriguing Rusakov collection. Frustration that she didn't have the whole story.

"I have trusted you, Ivan, yes," she said finally, "but if you have anything to do with arms trafficking, I'll find out and arrest you myself. If you've so much as had a beer with Vladimir Bulgov and haven't told me—"

"Vodka," Ivan said. "Once, long before his arrest."

"How long ago was that?"

His eyes were flat, without emotion. "A couple of months."

"You know the exact date, Ivan."

"April fifth. We ran into each other in London. We were both there on business. We had a drink together. Grey Goose Vodka."

"Where?"

"My hotel."

"What did you and Bulgov talk about?"

"Russia." Ivan stood back from the porch rail. "Anything else, Special Agent Sharpe?"

"What do you know about the address you gave me in Fort Lauderdale?"

"The house is rented by a private pilot who once flew planes for Bulgov. Pete Horner. It's a big house. He lives above his means."

"Do you do business with him?"

"No."

It was a curt answer even for Ivan.

"Security is my business, Emma. It's what I do. It allowed me to help you."

Ivan wasn't rattled by her questions. Not even close. He didn't rattle easily. He stood straight, the porch light catching the lines in his face. He knew how to create a threatening presence with his posture, his expression. His eyes alone suggested he was a man with lethal capabilities. Emma couldn't imagine anyone thinking he was in Heron's Cove for a whale watch or fried clams.

She deliberately didn't mention Tatiana Pavlova.

"How is your FBI agent?" he asked. "He is good to you?"

"Colin's good."

"He wants to know everything about Dmitri, about me," Ivan said without making it a question. "About your relationship with us."

Emma wasn't going there and jumped lightly from the rail. "You do what you have to do, Ivan, but if you cross the line, I'm coming after you."

"The dilemma of a badge. Sometimes one has to break rules to do right."

"That might be the world you live in—"

"It's the world you live in, too, Emma. Are you sure you belong with the FBI? Can you stay in that box?"

"We're not discussing me."

"Perhaps you don't belong with the FBI any more than you belonged with the nuns. Are you running from being a Sharpe?"

"I'm not running from anything."

"You investigate art crimes. Be careful, my friend."

"Threatening me, Ivan?"

Again came that near-imperceptible smile. "I would never threaten an FBI agent."

"I'm not afraid of you. I never have been."

"I take your position with the FBI seriously, Special Agent Sharpe. Emma, Dmitri asked me to invite you to stay aboard the *Nightingale*."

"I can't, Ivan."

"You would have your own cabin," Ivan added, a spark of warmth in his dark eyes.

Emma felt her throat tighten. "Please thank Dmitri for me, but I'll be staying here tonight."

"Not in Rock Point?" he asked, shifting, his eyes suddenly lost in the shadows.

"None of your business. And for the record, you'd be well advised to stay out of Rock Point. You've caused enough problems showing up here in Heron's Cove."

Ivan kissed her on the cheek. "Be safe, Emma. Keep your man safe."

He descended the porch steps without making a sound. Emma waited until he disappeared down on the pier before she returned to the kitchen. A sleeping mat was doable, and she'd be fine with no heat. Fine another night without Colin. He needed this time to himself, she told herself. It wasn't rejection.

No, she thought. The real reason she wanted to stay put was having the *Nightingale* on her doorstep.

She found an empty cardboard box in a side hall.

Might as well get busy, she thought, and started packing dishes.

11

COLIN RESISTED OPENING HIS BOTTLE OF
Bracken Distillers 15 year old and instead settled on a beer.
He took it into his living room, where the only sound was
the ticking of the old cuckoo clock his grandmother had
given him. Hurley's was deserted on a Sunday night, even
Finian Bracken nowhere to be found, so Colin had walked
back home.

Not a good night for whiskey, he had decided.

Just as well, since Matt Yankowski had been waiting for
him in the driveway.

"I hate cuckoo clocks," Yank said from his chair by the
fireplace.

"You get used to them."

"Not me. I'd shoot it."

The house smelled closed up, dusty. Colin figured he probably should have gotten out the mop and bucket today instead of messing with Emma and her Russians. He needed
to regroup, clear his head, trust that his colleagues in Washington and Boston were on the trail of Pete Horner and his
Russian accomplices.

He stood by the small white-painted brick fireplace with its brass-trimmed glass front. Even if he had spent the day cleaning house, Yank would still likely be here, in his crisp suit and polished shoes. Colin imagined Emma there instead, stretched out in front of a crackling fire, her cheeks flushed, her green eyes warm with laughter. His house could be her refuge, too.

"Hell," he muttered, drinking some of his beer.

Yank sighed. "You must be thinking about Emma."

"I'm becoming a romantic sap, Yank."

"It's the adrenaline dump from escaping sharks, snakes and thugs."

"Alligators. No sharks."

"Sharks were next. Drinking beer out of a bottle will help. If you came in here with a glass, I'd worry."

Colin sank into a chair across from his friend and senior agent. "It's time I take the blinders off and see what's in front of me. The Sharpes are renowned art crime experts with contacts all over the world—including Russia. And Emma's one of them."

"Most days that's a plus. It's probably what got us to you before those bastards in Florida could come back and finish what they started." Yank settled back, thoughtful. "Our work isn't easy on relationships. You'd think it'd be easier with another agent, but I don't know. I think it's even more complicated."

"How's Lucy's trip to Paris with her sister going?"

"She called on my drive up here. They'd just come back to their hotel after a late night and a little too much to drink. Lucy's homesick."

"For northern Virginia," Colin said.

"For me, you jerk," Yank muttered good-naturedly.

"She'd like you better if you'd set up your team in Washington instead of Boston."

"Wasn't an option."

"It was, and Lucy knows it. You should quit being so stubborn and just admit you wanted to get out of Washington and do your thing away from the close scrutiny of the higher-ups at headquarters, and you didn't care that she wanted to stay."

"I did care."

"All right. You put aside the fact that she wanted to stay and did what you wanted instead."

Yank just shook his head. "When I want career and relationship advice from you, I'll ask. Tell me about the *Nightingale*."

Colin drank more of his beer. He was glad now he had skipped his Irish whiskey. He gave Yank a quick but thorough rundown of his visit aboard Dmitri Rusakov's yacht.

"What are the dynamics between him and Emma?" Yank asked.

"He's a ladies' man. He assumes she's half in love with him."

"Is she?"

Colin shrugged. "It's a hell of a yacht. You and I could combine our salaries and still not afford the *Nightingale* after a hundred lifetimes."

"You're talking about an ex-nun who once took a vow of poverty."

"First vows. Not final vows."

"Whatever. What about her and Ivan Alexander?"

"That's a different story," Colin said, now wishing for whiskey. "There's an undercurrent there. More than an undercurrent. What do you know?"

"I know Alexander's not a former Sharpe client or an art collector. He got rich working with Rusakov in the early days. He was just a kid out of the Soviet army. He took care of security. Now he does things on his own."

"Like what?"

"He still keeps an eye on Rusakov's enemies."

"What's Vladimir Bulgov to Rusakov—friend or enemy?"

"Maybe just the snake Alexander doesn't want to bite his tycoon friend."

Colin felt the cool night air seep through a window. *That's what I could do tomorrow,* he thought. *Caulk windows.*

"Donovan? You with me?"

"Yeah, sorry. What do you know about Renee Warren Rusakov, Natalie Warren and Tatiana Pavlova?"

"Mostly blanks," Yank said. "Renee's the crazy ex-wife, Natalie's the ignored, pretty daughter and I've never heard of Tatiana Pavlova."

Colin stood and set his beer on the mantel, next to a framed picture of his first lobster boat. What would Emma have on a mantel? Framed pictures of the Sharpes with rich clients?

He pushed aside such thinking and watched Yank get stiffly to his feet, as if he'd been the one beat up by thugs two nights ago. "You should check out Rusakov's yacht before you head back to Boston," Colin said. "The Sharpes might not be anywhere near as rich as Dmitri Rusakov, but they sure know rich people."

"That's one aspect of who Emma is and what she brings to her job. Gas up your truck, Donovan. I want you in Boston in the morning. I'm headed back now. "

"I thought I was supposed to rest up after my close call in Florida."

"You can meet with your new team, then go back to kayaking, drinking whiskey and doing whatever else you do up here." Yank headed for the front door, then turned, adding, "Bring some of Hurley's doughnuts."

He shut the door quietly behind him, but Colin could feel Yank's tension. It was understandable given the past forty-eight hours. Colin was feeling tense himself. He took his beer bottle back to the kitchen and set it in the sink, his bruises aching now. Boris, the younger of the two Russians, had dealt the first blow in the South Florida heat. He'd just been getting Colin's attention, reminding him that his life was hanging by a thread and that thread could be cut anytime they chose.

Colin caught his reflection in the dark window above the sink. He looked like hell. No wonder Emma had sent him back to Rock Point.

Should have had whiskey.

He tore open the back door and headed out to his truck. Was Emma camped out on the floor of the Sharpe house? Settled into an elegant guest stateroom aboard the *Nightingale?*

Wherever she was, he wasn't leaving her alone with the Russians.

When Colin arrived in Heron's Cove, he parked in the lot next to the Sharpe house and walked around to the back, staying out of sight of the *Nightingale.*

Emma had left the kitchen door unlocked.

He went in, calling her name.

"I was about to lock up," she said from the small back bedroom.

Colin leaned against what was left of the doorjamb. The room was gutted to the studs, but she was settled onto neatly folded blankets and quilts. "You don't look as if you're about to lock the door," he said.

She raised her eyes to him. "Intruders aren't usually a big problem in Heron's Cove."

"You look cozy," he said, amused. "Floor's hard?"

"Not too bad with the quilts."

He noticed she had a book in her lap and had plugged in a carpenter's lamp for light. "What are you reading?"

She held up the book. "Russian fables. I found it in one of the boxes in the attic I promised to go through."

"The one marked Russian Tycoons the Sharpes Know."

"Something like that."

The light caught the ends of her honey-colored hair and brought out the green of her eyes. Her cheeks were rosy, as if she'd been caught up in her Russian fables, but it was probably due to the cold room. "I'll lock up," Colin said. "I'm not leaving you here alone. I don't care if I have to make a mat for myself—"

"I can share mine," she offered quietly.

He grinned. "That's the spirit."

He ducked back to the kitchen and flipped the flimsy lock on the back door. Not that he was worried about intruders in Heron's Cove. He returned to the bedroom and settled in next to Emma, stretching out his legs. The floor was damn hard, even through the layers of blankets and quilts, which smelled like mothballs and had holes. Except for Emma, the Sharpes, Colin had discovered, were natural pack rats.

"I'm not sure how I feel about you choosing the floor over me," he said. "We have a few things to work out, don't we?"

She laid her Russian fables in her lap. "I'm glad you're here."

"I parked in the lot next door and sneaked in through the back. Your reputation is safe with the Russians."

She leaned against his upper arm and placed a hand on his upper thigh. "Colin…"

"It's okay. We don't have to talk about us, or your friends aboard the *Nightingale*," he said. "Read your fables. I'll sleep."

"I love you, Colin," she said, sharing her blanket with him.

"I know, babe." He slipped an arm around her and kissed the top of her head. "I love you, too."

12

LUCAS SHARPE SLUNG HIS SOFT LEATHER BAG over one shoulder as his grandfather got behind the wheel of his little Ford, which he'd had since he had arrived in Ireland fifteen years ago. He wasn't big on driving, which only added to Lucas's misgivings about this hiking-in-the-Irish-hills adventure. Wendell adjusted the seat. Lucas, who was taller, had insisted on driving to the airport. He left the door open when they switched seats.

"Do you have everything?" Wendell asked.

Lucas nodded. "I'm good."

"Then go on. I'll be fine. I had espresso this morning to keep me awake on the road."

The image of his grandfather dozing off behind the wheel was just what Lucas needed to envision before he boarded his flight to London. "Granddad, are you sure you don't want to take the train?"

"The drive will do me good. I'll be able to think without you badgering me."

"I'm not badgering you. You know, you're too old to rent a car in Ireland. The cutoff is seventy-five."

"Then it's a bloody good thing I own my own car, isn't it?"

"Just be careful," Lucas said.

Wendell's look reminded Lucas of his younger sister. It was the look that suggested that she was being tolerant, but barely so. Annoyed, but unwilling to say so.

The two were so damn alike.

"I will be careful, Lucas," his grandfather said. "I always am."

"Enjoy this walkabout of yours."

"I intend to."

"Let me know if you remember anything else about the Rusakov collection," Lucas said. "That's why I write things down. I'm lucky I can remember the details of a case two weeks later, never mind twenty years."

"I remember some things from twenty years ago—hell, sixty years ago—better than I remember what happened yesterday. Don't think I'm senile."

"I don't, Granddad." Lucas hoisted his bag higher onto his shoulder. "I should be as sharp as you are when I'm fifty let alone eighty-one. I think you're stonewalling me is what I think."

"Think what you want."

It had always been that way between them, Lucas thought. They trusted each other and yet often butted heads. Not so with Wendell and Emma, but Lucas suspected that whatever their grandfather wasn't saying about the Rusakov collection would be news to her, too.

"When will you get back to Dublin?" Lucas asked.

"When I'm done."

"That leaves a lot of room—"

"Yes, it does. That's the idea." Wendell grunted. "The cops are giving us the hairy eyeball. I'll be on my way. Let me know what happens in London."

Lucas promised he would and shut the car door, then stood back as his grandfather pulled out into traffic. He really wasn't that worried about Wendell driving across Ireland by himself. He had a good mind, decent reflexes, and he would be on a motorway most of the time.

No, Lucas thought, what worried him was his grandfather's overall mood. The idea of him traipsing about the Irish hills on his own for an open-ended amount of time didn't sit well, and neither did his evasiveness about Dmitri Rusakov and this collection that had resurfaced. Wendell Sharpe damn well remembered more than he was admitting.

Nothing to be done about it now.

Lucas headed into the airport. He had no trouble with security, and his flight for London took off on time. With his FBI agent sister asking, he felt compelled to look into Tatiana Pavlova himself, without involving his staff.

When he landed at Heathrow, he sprang for the expensive cab ride into the city. He'd opted to check into a hotel instead of bunking with his parents at the London apartment they'd rented for the year. He preferred to be on his own when he was working.

According to their website, the Firebird Boutique where Tatiana Pavlova worked was just a few blocks from his hotel in Mayfair. Emma would have chosen a small boutique hotel, but Lucas wanted the anonymity of the large, efficient chain hotel with its great location on Park Lane. He unpacked, freshened up and downed a bottle of water.

He was tempted to call his grandfather and see how he was getting on with his trip west but decided not to risk putting the old man over the edge by annoying the hell out of him. Emma had reacted more calmly to the idea of a personal retreat. Maybe it was the former nun in her. Lucas found the whole notion unnerving. Who would want to bang around all alone in the Irish hills for days on end? *Any* hills, for that matter? And at eighty-plus?

He glanced at his watch—*11:00 a.m.* If Emma had any pertinent new information, she would have emailed him overnight or left a voice mail. No point in calling her now. It was only six in Heron's Cove.

Restless, fighting a vague but real sense of frustration and uneasiness, he set out on foot into the attractive streets of up-scale Mayfair, crowded with Londoners and tourists on a perfect autumn late morning. He walked past expensive shops, embassies, homes and banks before turning onto a short, narrow shaded street and arriving at the small, ivy-colored stone building that housed the Firebird Boutique.

An understated, yet elegant, sign indicated that entry was by appointment only.

Lucas had an appointment.

A woman around his age opened the door. She had long, straight dark hair pulled off her angular face and wore a black suit with a white silk blouse and diamond earrings. "Welcome, Mr. Sharpe," she said with a warm smile. "If you don't mind my saying so, you're younger than I expected."

"You must have expected my grandfather, Wendell Sharpe. I'm Lucas Sharpe."

"I see. Please, come in. My name is Ursula Finch. I'm the manager and creative director here at the Firebird. Did you just arrive in London?"

"This morning, from Dublin," he said, keeping his background story simple.

"I hope you enjoy your stay, then."

He entered the small showroom, at once sophisticated, high-end, artistic and charming. Two oval-shaped white tables with white leather-cushioned chairs were on opposite sides of the room, with a wood-and-glass cabinet on the back wall. He had already learned that the boutique's signature works were inspired by fairy tales, folklore and legends. That by itself could explain Tatiana Pavlova's interest in the Rusakov collection.

The walls were painted stark white, the only artwork a large oil painting on one wall, depicting a beautiful woman on a golden horse, a handsome man with a gray wolf and a firebird.

"It's a scene from *Ivan Tsarevich, The Firebird and Gray Wolf,* a popular Russian fairy tale," Ursula said when she noticed Lucas eyeing the painting. "Russian fairy tales and European fairy tales often have many similarities, but, of course, instead of kings, princes and princesses, Russian tales have tsars, tsareviches and tsarevnas. This painting is done with watercolor and ink on paper, modeled after the fairy-tale illustrations of the great nineteenth-century Russian artist Ivan Bilibin."

"Whose work is it?" Lucas asked.

"One of our designers, Tatiana Pavlova, painted it. She's multitalented." Ursula smiled as she led him to one of the tables. "Tatiana can do anything she sets her mind to. Can I get you anything? Coffee, tea, water?"

"Nothing, thanks."

She gestured with one hand. "Please, have a seat. Your family business is well-known to us here at the Firebird. The art world is lucky to have you doing such work."

Lucas sat in one of the cushioned chairs. "I learned all I know from my grandfather."

"That's decent of you to say."

"And true," he added.

"Tatiana is in America right now." Ursula sat across from him; she looked uneasy if not exactly nervous. "She said she needed to go off on her own for a week or two to do some pure creative work. The timing's not perfect, but it never is."

"Do you know where in the U.S. she is?"

"New England, I think. It'll be interesting to see what effect being in America has on her. I'd love to attract more American clients." Ursula spread a black felt cloth on the white tabletop. "I thought you might like to start by seeing some of Tatiana's work."

Ursula showed him a perfume bottle, a picture frame and a pendant, each unique and yet each in a highly individual, distinctive style.

"Tatiana's style is in the tradition of the great Russian designers of the nineteenth and early twentieth century," Ursula said. "They're her inspiration, but her artistry, creativity and craftsmanship are uniquely her own and, as you can see, nothing short of amazing. She is truly gifted. Right now she's into birds that are popular in folklore. Firebirds, swans, nightingales."

Lucas lifted the bejeweled perfume bottle. "Quite the luxury, isn't it?"

"It's a true marriage of art and craft, of the everyday and the extraordinary. Something as simple as a perfume bottle becomes a work of art that stands next to the finest in painting and sculpture." Ursula touched a fingertip to the pendant, in the shape of a mythical firebird. "We're all fond of Fabergé's cigarette cases, but they really are of another era, don't you think?"

Lucas laughed. "I suppose you're right."

"But perfume never goes out of style," she said, visibly relaxing. "Tatiana does all kinds of little boxes. They're so clever. She always includes a surprise, much as Fabergé did with his legendary Imperial Easter eggs. She's gained quite a following here in Great Britain. There's a Russian spirit in her work that crosses over and is becoming very, very popular. It's mystical, fanciful and quite beautiful."

"How did you two connect?"

"We met at a show in Switzerland a little over three years ago. She was already working in London. Her talents and my ambitions were a perfect match. We started the Firebird together. She never wanted to get involved in the business. That's what I do."

"Does she ever go back to Russia?"

"Not since I've known her. Would you like to see her work studio?"

"That'd be great," Lucas said, getting to his feet.

"She'll have put away anything she doesn't want seen yet. She's careful about protecting work in progress. She doesn't like to let it out into the world until she's ready for it to be seen by someone besides herself. Some artists like to keep their work close to them until just the right moment. Others like input throughout the process."

A slender, fair-haired young man came out from a back room, and Ursula left him with the perfume bottle, pendant and picture frame and led Lucas up an open flight of stairs to a small workroom, surprisingly simple and incredibly messy.

Ursula sighed. "Needless to say, no one touches a thing in here."

Tatiana's main workbench was chest-high and positioned so that when she was standing at it, or seated on her tall swivel chair, she would be able to see out the two windows that overlooked the street. Carts, pegs and shelves were filled with the tools of her trade, everything she needed to bring a work from inspiration to design to final product. Sketch pads, newspapers, books, magazines, computer printouts and who-knew-what-else were crammed into cubbies and stacked haphazardly on the floor.

Lucas noticed several sketches of swans cast off under the workbench. "She does best with her stuff at hand?"

"She says she'd spend all her time sorting and cleaning if she had to keep her studio downstairs, within sight of clients. I'd go mad trying to work in here."

"Where did she train?"

"In Russia and Switzerland, but she's continued her study here in London, too." Ursula ran her fingertips over a three-inch square black onyx box. "As with Fabergé before her, it's not just the precious metals and gems that make Tatiana's work special. It's her vision and artistry, her marriage of high art and the everyday. One can find gaudier necklaces and bracelets than anything she's done."

Lucas didn't notice any pictures of family, friends—of Tatiana Pavlova herself.

Ursula Finch frowned next to him, her arms crossed on her chest. "You aren't investigating a theft, are you?"

"No, not at all." He gave her a reassuring smile. "Although I wouldn't mind recovering the missing Fabergé Imperial Easter eggs."

"Who wouldn't? The House of Fabergé crafted fifty jeweled Easter eggs for Alexander III and Nicholas II. Forty-two survive. One does wonder what happened to the other eight. Malcolm Forbes collected nine of the Imperial Eggs but after his death his family sold them privately to a Russian tycoon. They're masterpieces." Ursula unfolded her arms. "Is there anything else I can do for you, Mr. Sharpe?"

"Has Tatiana mentioned other collections of Russian jewelry and precious objects?"

"Not that I know of," Ursula said. "Do you have anything particular in mind?"

Lucas dodged her question. "Does she have any Russian friends here in London?"

"We're both always so busy with work, but she has many

friends. I can't think if any are Russian. I'm sure there must be but I don't really know. Why? Does it matter?"

"I've taken up enough of your time," Lucas said with a smile. "Thank you."

Ursula hesitated, as if she were considering pressing him for more details. Then she, too, smiled. "Anytime. If you think of anything else, please call or stop by. Tatiana's a treasure. I hope you'll come back when she's here."

They returned to the showroom. Lucas thanked Ursula Finch and headed out of the elegant, almost otherworldly Firebird Boutique back into vibrant, bustling London.

He walked back to his hotel and ordered coffee delivered to his room. Once it arrived, he called Emma. "Is it too early for you?"

"I've been up for over an hour," she said.

"Are you in Boston?"

"Heron's Cove. I slept on a mat on the floor. The carpenters haven't shut off the water yet, but there's no heat. It wasn't too bad."

"You know you can stay at my house," Lucas said.

"Thanks, I do know that. It's fine here. I'm picking out kitchen cabinets before I head to Boston. You didn't tell me you hadn't picked them out yet."

"I did. You just don't like what I picked and are pretending I dropped the ball."

She laughed. "I didn't want to hurt your feelings. There's contemporary, Lucas, and there's ugly. What you picked is ugly. Not that I'm an artist. Have you been to the Firebird Boutique?"

"Just got back."

"Is Tatiana Pavlova's work as impressive in person as it is on the Firebird website?"

"It's fantastic. What about her? Is she as pretty in person?"

"You know I don't notice such things," Emma said.

Lucas stood in front of a large window that looked out across Hyde Park toward Buckingham Palace. "How's Colin?"

He heard his sister take a quick breath.

Lucas felt a twinge of guilt at his teasing tone. "Everything okay? He was gone for a while. You guys met under stressful conditions. You know, adrenaline—"

"Tell me about the Firebird Boutique."

He didn't push. He poured more coffee, then sat on the cushioned window seat and told his sister what he had learned about Tatiana Pavlova, as well as his impressions of her, her work and her upscale jewelry and decorative arts boutique.

When he finished, Emma was silent for a few moments. Finally, she said, "You didn't ask about Dmitri Rusakov, then?"

"Not specifically, no."

"Lucas..." She took in another audible breath. "Be careful, will you?"

"Always," he said.

Lucas met his parents for a late lunch at a pub near his hotel. He sat across from them at a booth, under photographs of nineteenth-century London and beer posters. A television above the bar had on a soccer match. He and his father ordered beer and fish-and-chips. His mother, frowning at them, ordered poached salmon. Timothy and Faye Sharpe were in their late fifties, well liked, interested in other people and down to earth, and Lucas generally enjoyed their company. Years of chronic back and neck pain often made his father restless, but meditation, exercise and a positive outlook helped. He worked as a consultant with Sharpe Fine Art Recovery, focusing on analysis and research, always his strengths. Faye Sharpe was a former elementary art teacher, a quiet, cheerful woman who was ambivalent about her son and daughter specializing in art crimes. Lucas sometimes wondered which kept her awake more nights—Emma as a nun, or Emma as an FBI agent.

She hadn't even met Colin Donovan yet, unless she had bought lobster from him when he was a teenager or had a run-in with him as a Maine marine patrol officer.

Lucas decided not to bring him up. He chatted with them about generalities and pleasantries—the Dublin weather, his flight to London, the ongoing renovations of the Sharpe house in Heron's Cove—and waited for his beer to arrive before getting into the substance of his visit, or even mentioning his grandfather or his sister.

He let his father drink some of his beer. His mother, he noted, had ordered white wine, but she didn't touch it, her eyes narrowed on him as if she knew what was next. He found himself half hoping that whatever she was imagining was worse than what he had to say. Finally, he said, "You remember Emma the year after she left the convent, before she joined the FBI. She worked for Granddad in Dublin."

"Of course," his mother said. "She was figuring out what to do with her life, who she wanted to be after she'd given up being Sister Brigid. Working with her grandfather was the perfect opportunity to sort things out."

His father nodded. "It was a busy year. My dear father worked her so hard she didn't have time to dwell too much on her situation, overthink things."

"At one point, Granddad sent her to London to meet with a client, one of the early post–Soviet era Russian tycoons."

"Dmitri Rusakov," Timothy Sharpe said with a sigh.

Lucas hadn't expected such an immediate response. "Anything I should know?"

His mother picked up her wine. "We met Rusakov once at a charity function here in London, about ten years ago. It was several years after Wendell had worked with him on the Russian Art Nouveau collection he discovered in Moscow. I assume you know about that?"

"Some."

"He's told us very little." She tried her wine. "Odd, isn't it? How someone already so rich and about to become even richer ends up finding a fabulous collection of jewelry and precious objects in his walls."

His father welcomed the arrival of the two plates of fish-and-chips and dug right in. "Rusakov was embroiled in the Wild West, no-holds-barred mentality of Russian politics and economics. He lives a chaotic, exciting life."

"I remember at the time wondering if Emma was attracted to him," Faye Sharpe said.

Lucas leaned forward. "Romantically, you mean? Are we talking about some kind of an affair between her and Rusakov?"

"I don't know as I'd go that far," his father said. "Rusakov is a lot older. He's amassed vast wealth and the responsibilities, influence and problems that come with it, especially in Russia."

His mother swiped one of her husband's fries. "He had a security expert with him that night," she said. "I don't remember his name. He was with Rusakov when we met him. Very sexy."

Timothy Sharpe rolled his eyes. "I didn't notice."

"Emma must have. She was coming from a near-cloistered existence. She was figuring out who she was, what she wanted in life. Security, excitement, work. Romance, too, I'm sure."

"Wait," Lucas said. "What? I thought Emma was attracted to Rusakov. She and this security guy were an item?"

His father looked uncomfortable. "If there was ever anything between Emma and either one of these men, it didn't go anywhere, at least on her part."

Lucas thought back four years. Had he missed anything between Emma and the Russians—romantic or otherwise? He had been focused on work in the U.S. and hadn't had the time or interest to keep tabs on what his sister and their grandfather were up to in Dublin. At the time, he hadn't even known if Emma would stay with Sharpe Fine Art Recovery after her year in Dublin, although he had always suspected she wouldn't.

Emma, he was quite sure, had paid equally little attention to his love life.

He was surprised his parents were aware of her possible romantic interest in the Russians. Usually they were oblivious to that sort of thing, or at least pretended to be. Lucas could remember only a handful of conversations with either of his parents on the possibilities and perils of falling in love. He doubted Emma could remember any more, either.

Just as well, he thought, happy to abandon the subject of his sister's love interests. "Have you heard of a Russian jewelry designer here in London named Tatiana Pavlova? She's with the Firebird Boutique. It's relatively new—it's a few blocks from here."

That piqued his father's interest. "I don't know the name, no, or the Firebird. Is this why you're in London?"

Lucas nodded. "Tatiana's in Heron's Cove." He tried some of his fish but didn't go near the mushy peas on the side of his plate. "She warned Emma that the Rusakov collection has resurfaced and someone's going to steal it."

Faye Sharpe frowned. "Steal it? Who would steal it? Someone would have to know about it first. Rusakov never publicized his discovery. Personally, I thought he should have donated it to a museum. It's not as if he went out and bought the pieces because he loved them."

"Still," her husband said, "the collection does belong to him."

"Maybe not," Lucas interjected, then related what he'd learned from Emma about the arrival of Dmitri Rusakov, Ivan Alexander and Natalie Warren—and the collection— in Heron's Cove.

"Sounds like a royal mess," his father said when Lucas had finished. "I hear Colin Donovan's back in Maine. How well do you know him, Lucas?"

"Not well. We met a few times after Sister Joan's death. Then he took off for D.C."

"That's where he works," Faye Sharpe said, her tone neutral. "Another FBI agent. Nothing to be done about it. Of course, we just want both you and Emma to be happy."

Lucas gave her a quick grin to break some of the tension. "Hell of a burden to put on us, Mom. I figure Colin's either the best thing to happen to Emma or the worst. I just don't know which. Maybe she doesn't, either."

His father drank the last of his beer. "Oh, she knows. Emma may have changed her path in life a few times, but she always knows her own mind. The Donovans are a solid family. I think I got a speeding ticket or two from the father back in the day."

Lucas smiled. "Have you been doing any driving in London?"

"Not if I can help it," he said with a grunt. "Traffic's terrible. We're enjoying our year in London but look forward to going home."

"It'll be good to have you back when the time comes." Lucas started to order another beer but decided against it.

"Were you aware that Matt Yankowski talked to Emma four years ago when she was still at the convent?"

His mother sighed, shaking her head. "She never said. That's not unusual for Emma. We weren't convinced she would ever make her final vows but we tried not to pressure her one way or the other. We would have respected her choice if she had. The FBI..." She grimaced. "The FBI was a surprise in its own way almost as much as the convent was. But that's in the past. I'm just glad she's based in Boston now, closer to home."

Lucas had long suspected that his father's pain was worse in Heron's Cove. He would never admit it, but his hometown was a reminder of what he had lost, the costs of his injury to himself and his family. Timothy Sharpe, Lucas knew, blamed himself, at least in part, for Emma's decision to enter the convent. It was too simplistic to think that she had embraced a religious life because she couldn't face the reality of their father's injury and rehabilitation. Her time with the Sisters of the Joyful Heart had been a journey of faith for her, deeply personal...and it was over.

She was Special Agent Sharpe now.

His mother changed the subject. "How's your grandfather?" she asked.

"He should be settling into a pub in Killarney by now."

"Killarney?" His father frowned in surprise. "What's he doing there?"

So Wendell Sharpe hadn't told his son and daughter-in-law about his "walkabout" and instead had left the job to Lucas.

He decided to order that second beer after all.

His parents took the news of Wendell's solo trip into the southwest Irish hills better than Lucas had expected. They were more amused and pleased than worried. He felt like a wet blanket.

"You wait, Lucas," his father said. "When you're eighty and can go off on a hike on your own, you won't want your grandson fretting you've sunk into a depression."

"What if he has?"

"Then the Irish hills are just what he needs."

They headed out together, Lucas noticing his father's limp, the ashen color around his mouth, the dark circles under his eyes and the pinched look that he got whenever his pain was flaring up. No one mentioned it. They had all learned a long time ago to let him take the lead and define what he needed.

"We'll take a cab back," his father said in a low voice.

Once they were on their way, Lucas walked back to his hotel. The perfect day had turned gray, with a fine mist falling. He didn't mind. He buttoned his jacket, enjoying the scenery and the chance to process what he'd learned from Emma, Ursula Finch and his parents.

As he turned onto busy Park Lane, he glanced back and saw a man making his way down to the subway station on the corner. Tall, fair, shaved head, dark sweater and trousers. Lucas had noticed him outside the pub and slowed as he arrived at his hotel.

The man disappeared down the subway steps.

The doorman asked Lucas if he needed anything.

Lucas shook his head and went into the hotel lobby. Maybe it was lunch with his parents and the talk about Emma and their grandfather's melancholy—or just the mention of Colin Donovan—but he couldn't shake the feeling that the man with the shaved head had followed him.

Maybe it was none of the above, Lucas thought as he got into the elevator. Maybe it was having two beers at lunch.

13

AFTER A THOROUGHLY UNSATISFYING VISIT
with Julianne Maroney's grandmother, Finian Bracken took
his BMW for a spin along the southern Maine coast. He
rolled down the windows and let in the autumn air. How
had he landed up in this blasted place, so far from home and
the people he knew and loved?

Starchy Franny Maroney had all but chased him out of her
kitchen with a broom. "Mad at God, indeed," he muttered,
slowing the BMW, his one indulgence.

Mrs. Maroney had said she would keep her promise to
help with the bean-hole supper. She was on the cleanup detail, and was bringing coleslaw, made from the recipe her
now-departed mother had provided St. Patrick's; it was in
the bean-hole supper folder.

Finian thought she had softened slightly as he left, but she
plunged out her front door and followed him to his car.

*"Don't waste your time visiting me again unless I'm in the hos-
pital about to take my last breath,"* she told him in no uncertain
terms. *"Visit the sick and dying."*

He had resisted a number of quick retorts and said a prayer

for her through gritted teeth as he climbed back into his car. Now he wondered if his family and friends had felt much the same when he had been raging after the deaths of his wife and daughters. They were taken from him so young—thirty-three, seven and five. Yet he knew not to compare his loss with that of Franny Maroney. It wasn't a competition, and her rage—her crisis of faith—was her own and had nothing to do with him.

By the time he parked in the pretty village of Heron's Cove, Finian had hold of his temper and his frustration with not being able to help an elderly woman so filled with pain. What had he been thinking when he decided on parish work—on thrusting himself upon a small American fishing village?

He found his way to the shop the Sisters of the Joyful Heart ran on a narrow side street in the village. Sister Cecilia greeted him with her usual pleasant smile. "How nice of you to stop by, Father Bracken."

"Lovely to see you, Sister Cecilia," Finian said, struggling to return her good cheer.

Sister Cecilia wore the order's modified habit with a wide white headband holding back her medium-brown hair, an oversize hand-knit sweater, dark-colored tights and black clogs. She lifted a pottery pitcher, painted with a cluster of wild blueberries, from a shelf and dusted underneath it. "Everyone's buzzing about the fancy yacht that arrived here over the weekend. Have you seen it?"

He nodded. "It's impossible to miss."

"It's owned by a Russian billionaire. I wonder if he's a Sharpe client. I heard that Emma was on board yesterday, but I haven't seen her—I think she's gone to Boston. I've been giving her painting lessons."

"So I've heard," Finian said. "How are the lessons going?"

"Well…they're going."

He laughed, relieved to be in the company of the cheerful young sister. Sister Cecilia and Emma had become friends after the terrible events at the convent in September. The Sisters of the Joyful Heart were still grappling with the aftermath of the murder of one of their own, as well as the discovery of a genuine Rembrandt hidden in the convent. The killer had tortured Sister Cecilia, cutting her so that she would bleed to death, but she had prevailed, with the help of Emma and Colin. Her wounds—psychological, physical and spiritual—were healing. She found comfort and purpose in the mission and the charism of her order, and her calling to their work. In a few weeks, she would profess her final vows of chastity, poverty and obedience. Finian had been asked to participate in the ceremony.

He watched as she wiped down the rest of the shelf, which already looked spotless to him. "You keep track of what's going on in town," he said.

"It's not hard when people tell me things. It's interesting to know an FBI agent. Two FBI agents, really. Colin Donovan is back. He and Emma are from such different worlds, even if they both are FBI agents."

"Same world as I see it."

She smiled, blushing. "I hope I'm not being a busybody."

"Not at all. They're your friends. You care about them."

"I do," she said. "I haven't seen Colin yet. He's well?"

Finian was spared answering by the arrival of the dark-haired woman he had met at the convent the other day—Tatiana, the London-based Russian jewelry designer. She looked flushed, as if in a dilemma, but she managed a bright smile at Sister Cecilia. "What beautiful work, and what an adorable shop," she said in her pronounced Russian-British accent. "I had to stop by and see for myself."

Sister Cecelia thanked her but withdrew to the back room when Tatiana gave a tentative look at Finian, as if she might want to talk to a priest. Tatiana watched her, wincing as she turned to Finian. "I went for coffee this morning and someone mentioned the nun who was killed here last month. An awful thing, yes?"

"Very much so," Finian said without elaboration.

Tatiana seemed momentarily embarrassed. "That's not why I'm here. I don't want to remind anyone of a painful time." She motioned with a slender hand in the general direction of the waterfront. "I walked here from my cottage. I'm sketching seabirds for my work. I won't use all of them, but some. The herons. Perhaps a gull. Do you paint or sketch, Father?"

"No. In a previous life, I made whiskey."

She smiled. "Ah, yes. *Aqua vitae.* 'The water of life,' as they say. And now here you are in Heron's Cove. We're both strangers in a strange land, yes?"

"I have faith that I am where I should be."

"I wish I had such faith. I stopped by the Sharpe house but Emma's not there. I ran into carpenters. No one else. They said she's gone to Boston. She works there, yes? And Colin Donovan, also?"

Finian was reluctant to give many details on his FBI agent friends. "Perhaps you should talk to them."

"Oh, of course." Her smile widened. "I'm nosy, yes?"

Finian smiled back at her. "They're FBI agents and we're not."

She laughed out loud this time. She took a quick walk around the shop, eyeing the displays of pottery and other handmade goods. Finian wanted to ask her about the Russian yacht but a group of women came in for a drawing class with Sister Cecelia, and Tatiana left quickly. After a few moments of uncertainty, he went outside himself. Was her visit to the sisters' shop worth reporting to Colin?

Finian gave an inward groan at his own sense of drama. As he opened his car door, he saw Tatiana walking unhurriedly down the narrow street. She turned toward the waterfront and disappeared from his view.

A man in a black jacket crossed the street from another shop and quickly dipped out of sight, down the same street as the young Russian.

Finian stood motionless. Was this the same man who had spoken to him the other night in Rock Point? Was he following Tatiana?

He shut his car door and walked down to the corner. He hadn't seen the man's face, or even the color of his hair.

He saw no sign of either the Russian designer or the man in the black jacket on the quiet, narrow street. Finian paused, feeling foolish. How many men on the Maine coast wore black jackets? And even if this were the same man who had followed him out from Hurley's, did his presence in the village of Heron's Cove mean anything? He could just be waiting for his wife to finish shopping, or be off for a lobster roll at one of the popular hole-in-the-wall restaurants on the waterfront.

Still, Finian decided he would feel better if he checked on Tatiana. He had only a vague idea where her cottage might be, but there weren't that many choices.

And what if he ran into the man in the black jacket and he was, in fact, following her?

Well, Finian thought, he'd been in a few bar fights back in the day. He could defend himself.

He could also call 911.

He returned to his car and drove a little too fast out Ocean Avenue, toward the Sharpe house, slowing as he came to the knot of cottages and shops where he suspected Tatiana was staying. He spotted her approaching a tiny cottage with weathered cedar shingles trimmed in marine-blue. She started up the stairs to a deck that overhung the water, her dark hair shining in the sunlight.

The man in the black jacket was nowhere in sight.

The massive luxury yacht, however, was very much in sight. Even in his freewheeling entrepreneurial days, Finian had never imagined owning such a yacht, not that he could ever have afforded one. Since the sailing accident that had claimed his family, he didn't want to step foot on another boat.

Interesting that he had taken a parish in a fishing village. Why not in Colorado or Idaho if he'd wanted a temporary assignment at an American church?

Still uneasy, he continued out past large summer houses and spectacular Atlantic views, and on to Rock Point.

All was quiet at St. Patrick's rectory and church.

He sighed, wishing he had stayed in his office after mass that morning and studied, or gone back to the rectory and read a book. For one, Franny Maroney might have been in a better mood on a Tuesday morning than a Monday morning.

I might have been in a better mood, he thought, chastened, and as he pulled his BMW into the rectory driveway, he noticed a dark gray truck park on the street in front of the church.

Mike Donovan climbed out. "Hey, Father," he said in greeting as he joined Finian on the driveway.

"Hello, Mike," Finian said. "And how are you this gorgeous Monday?"

Mike grinned. "Bored and irritable. You?"

Finian laughed. "The same, I'm afraid."

The eldest Donovan brother cocked his head. "What's up, Fin? You look a little shaken."

"Nothing. Nothing's up. Thank you for asking."

"Nothing usually means something."

Finian felt even more ridiculous but he could see that Mike wasn't going to give up. "I had another encounter with the Russian woman. The one I told you about."

"Tatiana Pavlova."

"I didn't know her last name."

Mike shoved his truck keys into the pocket of his canvas jacket. "What kind of encounter?"

"I ran into her at the Sisters of the Joyful Heart's shop in Heron's Cove."

"And?"

Finian regretted opening his mouth now. "It's not worth mentioning."

"This Tatiana is attractive, though, right? Just because you're a priest doesn't mean you didn't notice."

Finian cleared his throat. "She's very pretty, yes. Colin must have noticed, too. Of course, she isn't Emma. There's only one Emma Sharpe."

"Damn good thing," Mike muttered, but he looked unsatisfied. "Do you want to talk to Colin about this encounter of yours?"

"'Encounter' is the wrong word. It was an innocent conversation." One Finian now regretted bringing up; the Donovans were a suspicious lot. "Did Emma return to Boston this morning? I forgot to ask Colin."

"I don't know. She stayed in Heron's Cove. Sleeping on a hard floor. The nun in her."

"She's a complex woman with simple needs."

"Not that simple," Mike said. "And you're changing the subject. Why was Tatiana Pavlova in the nuns' shop?"

"She was curious, she said. Mike, if you had any information about her and the Russian who owns the fancy yacht in Heron's Cove, would you tell me?"

"Probably. If I wasn't told to keep my mouth shut."

"You Donovans are all good at confidences?"

Mike nodded without hesitation. "Yep. Wired that way."

"I'm a bit on edge today. Miss Pavlova and I had a pleasant, innocuous exchange, and she returned to her cottage. She said she's sketching birds. I'm sure all is well, and I'm sure you didn't stop by to listen to me. What can I do for you?"

"Colin told me he ran into you at Hurley's this morning before he headed to Boston and you seemed preoccupied. That was before you saw this Russian jewelry designer in Heron's Cove." Mike eyed Finian as if debating whether to get out the thumbscrews. "Everything okay, Fin?"

Finian decided the Donovans didn't need to worry about him. And he didn't need them worrying about him. He had little breathing room as it was in Rock Point, where everyone knew everyone else.

"Yes, everything is fine," he said. "I admit this church supper is hanging over my head. It's a first for me. We're digging new bean holes this year. Have you ever dug a bean hole, Mike?"

He looked pained. "Many times."

Finian grinned at him. "Now why isn't that a surprise? We'll need several. I'm told that each must be about a meter deep, lined with rocks. The beans go into them in pots and cook for hours—at least a day."

"Nothing like a bean-hole supper, Fin."

"Yes. So I've heard. This will be my first."

"You don't sound that thrilled," Mike said, obviously amused.

"To be honest, I'm not." Finian pictured cranky Franny Maroney and her blasted coleslaw recipe, but he immediately regretted his uncharitable thoughts. "I don't want to insult anyone, though. I was going to start on digging bean holes. Would you like to help?"

Mike gave a nearly imperceptible shudder. "Bean holes. Yeah, sure, Father."

"I don't want to inconvenience you."

"Are you kidding? I've been planting tulip bulbs and mulching flower beds. Bean holes are right up my alley these days. Got a shovel?"

"There must be one here somewhere. I'll go put on work clothes. You look for a shovel."

14

MATT YANKOWSKI STOOD SILENTLY AT THE windows overlooking Boston Harbor in the conference room on the second floor of the discreet brick building that housed his hand-selected team. The harbor was gray in the late-afternoon light. Emma, as tight and tense as she'd been all day, stayed behind at Yank's request as eight of her colleagues began to file out.

The intense, ninety-minute meeting had focused on the search for Pete Horner and his Russian colleagues and the investigation into their activities. With Colin safe, no longer operating undercover, Yank had pushed Washington hard for a role for his team.

Having Dmitri Rusakov up the road in Maine had added weight to Yank's insistence that HIT, as his team was known, get involved.

Emma had maintained a neutral posture throughout the meeting, with the hope that none of her fellow agents would guess how uncomfortable she was with their scrutiny. They had just gotten used to the idea that she had been a novice with the Sisters of the Joyful Heart. Now they were getting used to the idea that she knew Dmitri Rusakov. But did his presence in Heron's Cove mean he had anything to do with Vladimir Bulgov and his illegal arms trafficking?

Colin's initial undercover mission to get inside Bulgov's network predated Yank getting him onto his team in Boston. Not one for close oversight, Colin had nonetheless agreed to have Yank as his contact agent when he went back undercover a month ago to look into anyone trying to pick up the threads of Bulgov's network.

Yank had briefed the team on some of the details of Colin's work the past month. The constant danger. The risks. The vigilance and the need for the days of silence to protect the mission—to stop Pete Horner and to identify and locate his buyer.

A month in hell.

As the door shut behind the last agent to exit the room, Emma subtly took in a breath, held it, then let it out, slowly, with control. Her colleagues included experts in everything from big business and taxes to cyber-security and profiling. They were accustomed to going after well-connected, well-resourced individuals whose illegal activities were often transnational in nature.

When she first arrived in Boston in the spring, Emma had felt as if she would fit right in.

Now she wasn't so sure.

Yank continued to stare out the door windows. He had chosen Boston for HIT because he'd worked there as a young agent and liked the city, and, Emma had come to suspect, because it was close enough to FBI headquarters in Washington but not too close. His wife hadn't yet moved up from northern Virginia to join him. Yank said she was selling their house but Emma had heard she was in Paris, shopping with her sister. She didn't ask. Yank didn't invite that kind of personal question or intimacy, at least not from her.

She remained seated at the conference table. "What did you tell Colin?"

"About what? The apples you brought to the office while he was away?"

"Trying to be funny, Yank?"

He glanced back at her with a grudging smile. "It doesn't suit me, does it?"

"I'd like to know what you told Colin about Dmitri Rusakov, Ivan Alexander and Tatiana Pavlova."

"He knows what I know."

Emma took note of Yank's slightly critical tone. "If you have any questions, ask me," she said tightly.

He turned from the window. He had on a dark charcoal suit with a red tie but he looked as if he hadn't slept well. "I haven't done all the paperwork on making Colin an official member of this unit."

"Are you having second thoughts?"

"You two…" He bit off a sigh and plopped down in a chair across from her. "I warned you he's independent. Straightforward. Doesn't like games. He has a sense of humor but you can't let that fool you. He's a serious, experienced agent."

"I figured out he wasn't a pushover the day we met."

"Right. You wouldn't want some guy who didn't want to drown you once in a while, or who couldn't pull it off."

"That's politically incorrect even for you, Yank."

He shrugged, not at all defensive or apologetic. "It's a metaphor. Not literal. Donovan's a go-it-alone type with a tight-knit family behind him. He couldn't do what he does without that foundation."

"Which you don't want me to screw up," Emma said.

"You Sharpes live in a big world compared to Rock Point."

Yank placed his elbows on the table, folded his hands and leaned toward her, his gaze unflinching. "Talk to me, Emma. Walk me through this. Twenty years ago, Dmitri Rusakov hires your grandfather to sort out this collection of baubles and perfume bottles and such that turned up in his Moscow house after the fall of Communism. How'd he know to call Wendell Sharpe?"

"Sharpe Fine Art Recovery was recommended to him."

"Who did the recommending?"

Emma glanced past him at the view of the harbor. "Ivan Alexander."

"He was a kid then. How did he know about Sharpe Fine Art Recovery?"

"Ivan was ambitious and my grandfather has an international reputation in his field."

"Art theft and recovery. This collection was a discovery."

"It could have been stolen decades ago and hidden in the walls of Dmitri's house," Emma said. "He didn't know anything about it."

"Dmitri." Yank grimaced. "It kills me that you're on a first-name basis with one of the richest men in the world. One of the richest Russians. I knew he'd been a Sharpe client…" He stopped himself. "Never mind. Had your grandfather had any dealings with Alexander before Rusakov?"

"I don't know. I'll ask him, but he's not easy to reach right now."

"He's in Dublin?"

"He's on a personal retreat. Walking the Irish hills."

Yank stared at her as if he couldn't imagine such a thing. "On his own?"

"Yes, on his own."

"Hell, he's eighty."

"He has his full faculties, and he's in great shape. Don't you want to hike in the Irish hills in your eighties?"

"I don't want to now. I'll probably be watching television in my undershorts in my eighties. If something does happen to him, at least you'll have the consolation of knowing he was doing something he loved. If I keel over at my desk, you'll know I died miserable." Yank grinned at her. "Kidding."

"It's been a difficult autumn," Emma said.

"Yes, it has. Back to Rusakov. He's managed to stay out of prison, unlike some of the other Russian tycoons who made their fortunes at the same time. Those were freewheeling days. Optimists, pessimists, opportunists, idealists, scum. Former KGB operatives. They were all at work. Still are. Even a good man has to be touched by that level of chaos."

Emma didn't respond at once. "I had a job to do when I met Dmitri in London four years ago. My only focus was the whereabouts of the collection. My grandfather had briefed me. I reported to him—not to Dmitri."

"You were in London a week?"

"Less than a week. It became clear early on, at least to me, that Renee Rusakov had taken the collection."

Yank sat back in his chair. "Messy divorce?"

"Not really. It wasn't amicable but it wasn't messy. Renee clearly wasn't entitled to the collection."

"But Rusakov didn't do anything about it. Now she's dead." Yank drummed his fingers on the table. "As far as we know he doesn't have any ties to Russian organized crime syndicates. I still don't like it that he's had two of my agents on board his damn yacht. This Tatiana Pavlova didn't tell you he was on his way to Heron's Cove?"

"Not specifically, no."

"Think she knew?"

"I'd be speculating—"

"Speculate, then."

Emma resisted an urge to get up, pace, work off the tension that had been building since she arrived in Boston a few hours ago. *Best just to get through this.* Let Yank ask and re-ask his questions so that he could clarify and solidify his thinking.

Finally she took a breath and said, "Tatiana told me a Russian fable about a nightingale, which is the name of his yacht, so I think she suspected it was a possibility Dmitri would come to Heron's Cove."

Yank frowned. "A fable?"

"You know. An ultrashort story with a moral."

"I know what a fable is. Don't you think it's odd she told you one?"

"She draws on Russian folk tradition in her work, and she's—" Emma searched for the right word "—passionate."

Yank pushed back his chair and rose. "She obviously thinks Rusakov will steal this collection from his stepdaughter rather than go through a protracted legal process to prove he didn't give it to her mother."

"I agree, but I don't know for sure."

"We don't care about a spat about this collection. We care if Dmitri Rusakov and Ivan Alexander have anything to do with the men who just tried to kill one of my agents. Even without that, I'd want to know why a Russian tycoon has parked his yacht on your doorstep." Yank glared at her. "Damn, Emma."

She burst to her feet and walked over to the windows. She pictured herself spending a quiet afternoon wandering around Boston. She was still getting to know the city, make new friends, settle on her favorite spots. After three years largely in Washington, she had looked forward to being closer to home in southern Maine.

She hadn't imagined a man like Colin Donovan swooping into her life.

Yank stood next to her. "We don't know much about Rusakov's early life." His tone was softer, more reflective. "That's not unusual since he grew up in the Soviet Union and wasn't a big player in the Soviet military, plus he guards his privacy. Renee Rusakov was quite the black widow, wasn't she?"

"She had her demons," Emma said. "She was beautiful, compelling—narcissistic."

"Think she was aware she used and manipulated people?"

"I think she just wanted what she wanted and felt so entitled to it that the rest didn't matter. Imagine being inside her skin."

Yank squinted out at the harbor, the water as gray as the sky. "Rusakov didn't have anything to do with her or her daughter after the divorce?"

"Not as far as I know. Renee had already moved back to Tucson when I arrived in London. Natalie had been living in Phoenix since college."

"But you met them," Yank said.

Emma nodded. "Briefly. They were in London right as I got there. They stopped to pick up some things from Dmitri's apartment. I think she'd already made off with the collection by then. I don't know why Dmitri had it with him in London."

"Think Ivan Alexander approved?"

"I didn't get that far before Dmitri sent me back to Dublin. I haven't seen either one of them since then."

Yank thought a moment. "And now they turn up in Maine before Colin's bruises have had a chance to heal."

"Dmitri is there because Natalie told him she wanted to talk to us—my grandfather, Lucas, me—about the collection." Emma tried not to sound defensive. "I know the timing raises questions."

"A ton of questions," Yank said half under his breath, then sighed. "If I were this Natalie, I'd give the collection back to Rusakov and forget him and the mother. Go live my life."

"That still could happen." Emma turned from the window, grabbed a notepad she had brought to the meeting but hadn't touched. Her throat tightened as she thought of Colin. The timing of the *Nightingale*'s arrival in Heron's Cove was lousy for both of them. "You knew all about my involvement with Dmitri Rusakov before I stepped foot at the academy."

"Not all."

But it was Colin, not Yank, who had answered. He entered the conference room. He wasn't wearing a suit. He had on dark canvas pants, a dark sweater and a worn leather jacket that added to his air of rugged masculinity.

He leaned against the open door. "Yank doesn't know what all your grandfather knows about Rusakov, about this collection."

Emma kept silent, her heartbeat quickening. Yank, she noticed, didn't say a word.

"Then there's Ivan Alexander," Colin said. "Bet Yank doesn't know everything about your involvement with him. He's a ghost. An independent security consultant. No footprints, no fingerprints. He has a place in Moscow but he's never there."

"Ivan operates according to his own set of rules." She turned to Yank. "I'll let you two talk."

"Is he playing you, Emma?" Colin asked as if she hadn't spoken. "What's his relationship with your grandfather and brother?"

She moved toward the door, controlling her breathing, refusing to let him see that he was getting to her. "You'd have to ask them. You're thinking this is a Sharpe can of worms, but what if it's something else? What if it's a Special Agent Donovan can of worms?"

Yank glared at her, then at Colin. "It's the two of you together. A can of worms on steroids."

Colin pulled out a chair, dropped into it, deceptively casual. His attention was still on Emma. "Where are your grandfather's records on the Sharpe dealings with Rusakov?"

"Even if I knew," Emma said coolly, "they're not mine to hand over."

"What about your personal records?"

"I don't have any personal records. I wasn't with Dmitri in London for weeks and weeks. I was there for one week. One frustrating week with little to show for it."

"Ivan's your source," Colin said abruptly, tipping back in his chair.

Emma felt heat rush to her face but addressed Yank. "Anything else you need from me?"

Colin didn't give Yank a chance to respond. "I've been doing some checking. Let's put aside the Sharpes and this collection for now. Our friend Vladimir Bulgov was in London in April. You know who else was there? Dmitri Rusakov." Colin's voice was low, controlled. "So was Ivan Alexander."

Emma kept any reaction to herself as she met his eyes. "Guilt by association, Colin?"

His gaze bored into her. "You tell me."

"Ivan had a drink with Bulgov in London on April fifth," she said.

Yank sat at the conference table. "And you know this how?"

"Because Ivan told me."

"When?" Colin asked.

"Last night. He stopped by the house."

Yank sighed. "Lovely," he said through clenched teeth.

"Ivan's everywhere," Colin said. "He's that kind of guy."

"Did Rusakov and Bulgov meet?" Yank asked.

"Ivan didn't mention that Dmitri was in London then," Emma said. "I didn't ask. It wasn't that kind of conversation."

"Maybe it should have been," Colin muttered.

She gave him a cool look. "What was Bulgov doing in London? Might want to find that out."

She brushed past him out of the conference room and went down the hall into her own office. As she sat at her neat desk, calming herself, her gaze rested on notes she had jotted down that morning. She had brainstormed everything she could remember about Dmitri and Renee Rusakov, Natalie Warren, Ivan Alexander, the Rusakov collection.

The divorce was Dmitri's first but not Renee's. It hadn't been pleasant but as far as Emma knew there hadn't been any serious issues. Now Renee was dead. She'd gone downhill fast, with little chance to get her affairs in order.

Lucas had said that Tatiana Pavlova was a superb designer, just untidy. So far, he'd had little luck finding out much about her personal life in London, or about her past in Russia.

"Maybe she created a new life for herself in London and put Russia behind her," her brother had suggested.

Lucas had also noted that all kinds of rich people went in and out of the Firebird.

Who did Tatiana know?

Emma sank back into her chair. She had a photo of Ivan Alexander up on her computer screen. She knew a fair amount on him, but not everything.

Not nearly everything, she thought, studying his ever-impassive face.

She had taken the photo herself, surreptitiously, in London four years ago but had always felt he had known and didn't care. She admitted that she was defensive where he was concerned, but she had no reason to be.

Or maybe you do.

She pushed back such thinking. Yank hadn't asked her the identity of her confidential source, and she hadn't volunteered Ivan's name. It was understood that it was someone from her pre-FBI days.

Nonetheless, she was positive Yank knew.

"Yank always knows," she said under her breath, managing a smile as she shut down her computer and headed out.

Colin was still holed up with Yank in the conference room. Everyone was working hard on the investigation. They had all agreed that, with Dmitri Rusakov in Heron's Cove, she should return there.

She would stop at her apartment, pull a few things together, then make the two-hour drive back up to southern Maine.

With any luck, the *Nightingale* would be gone by then, and Pete Horner and his Russian thugs would be in custody, with no troubling connection to Dmitri Rusakov or Ivan Alexander.

15

COLIN WAS READY TO JUMP OUT OF HIS SKIN. "Mike called on my way down here," he said, following Yank out of the conference room into his office. "He'd just come from the rectory with Finian Bracken. Fin ran into the Russian designer, Tatiana Pavlova, at the Sisters of the Joyful Heart's shop in Heron's Cove. She told him she was just checking it out."

"She's an artist. It's an arts-and-crafts store. Makes sense, doesn't it?"

Colin shrugged as he sat on the wide brick windowsill, Boston Harbor spread out before him on a gray afternoon. "She also stopped up at the convent. Mike says Fin was out of sorts. He thinks there's more to it but Fin didn't want to tell him."

"Maybe he'll tell you."

"That's what Mike said, too."

Yank sank onto the tall-backed chair at his desk. Behind him was a credenza with no personal items, not even a picture of his wife. Colin had met Lucy Yankowski, a dark-eyed psychologist with a pixie haircut and a pixie face. She was a lot cuter than her husband of ten years, and at least as smart.

"Does Lucy know you don't have any pictures of her on your desk?"

Yank scowled. "I don't like distractions. I've got pictures at home."

"At home in Virginia or—"

"None of your damn business, Donovan." Yank pushed back his chair, thought a moment. "What if Rusakov's arrival in Heron's Cove really is Sharpe-related and has nothing to do with you?"

"It does feel personal." Colin returned his gaze to the harbor as he continued. "I don't like having Rusakov, Alexander and Bulgov in London at the same time. We weren't on Bulgov around the clock then. We don't know what he did, who he met with. London's a big city but these three are all rich, well-connected Russians."

"That's why we had the meeting today that you skipped."

Colin ignored the gibe. "Do you still think you know Emma?"

"I know more about the Sharpes and who the Sharpes know than I do about you and who you know."

"I'm a Donovan from Rock Point and I know a bunch of lobstermen, cops, FBI agents and thugs."

"Don't try to pretend you're simple."

"I am simple. Emma isn't. Rusakov and Alexander aren't." Colin watched boats return to the wharf next to Yank's building. "I can do my job, Yank, but I'm not objective. Not where Emma's concerned."

"It's possible Rusakov is just in Heron's Cove to get this collection back, but I want to know why he and Alexander were in London the same time as Vladimir Bulgov."

"So do I," Colin said.

As he eased off the windowsill, he felt an unwelcome twinge of pain in his lower back. He had woken up stiff and sore to his bones, with no Emma. She had already slipped out of her makeshift bed early to make coffee. He had joined her in the kitchen and helped her pick out new cabinets, an act of normalcy that underlined just how abnormal their relationship and the situation with the *Nightingale* were.

"You okay?" Yank asked with obvious concern.

Colin nodded. "Maybe I should have stayed in Rock Point and dug bean holes with Finian Bracken. Has it occurred to you that Emma might be better—more valuable to you—on the outside rather than on the inside?"

Yank's eyes narrowed. "Where she wouldn't be constrained by a badge, you mean?"

"Might be better for you personally. Having a Sharpe on your team has its downside. Who knows what else could come crawling out of the Sharpe family files to bite you in the ass."

"Or you," Yank said.

"I didn't have anything to do with the Sharpes before you and Finian Bracken twisted my arm and got me to look into Emma's involvement with Sister Joan's death in September."

"It didn't take much twisting."

Colin realized he was too restless to sit. He walked over to the door, shut against the cubicles, offices and bustle on the other side. He glanced back at Yank. "My life was just fine before I knew about Special Agent Sharpe down the road in Heron's Cove."

"Your life wasn't fine." Yank swiveled around in his chair and assessed Colin with his usual frankness. "You were a valuable deep-cover operative who was flirting with burnout. You were in danger of hitting the self-destruct button and getting yourself killed or kicked out of the Bureau."

"Comes with the territory." Colin knew that Yank was serious, and that he had a point. He just wasn't going there. "Maybe Emma is asking herself whether she made the right choice. She could go back to Sharpe Fine Art Recovery and you could hire her as a consultant. She has to be wondering if that's on your mind, too."

"You're a worry for me, too, Donovan. A go–it-alone type always is." Yank rubbed the back of his neck and sighed. "How valuable is this collection?"

"You're asking me? The most expensive thing I own is a pair of silver cuff links I never wear. My grandmother gave them to me when I quit the marine patrol. She thought I was getting out of law enforcement and going back to lobstering. Then she found out I was heading to Quantico and she wanted her cuff links back."

"More chance of you wearing cuff links as an FBI agent than a lobsterman," Yank said.

"That wasn't her point. She wanted me to have a safe career."

"And going out on a boat every day is safe?"

Colin grinned. "I'll never convince you to like boats, will I?"

"Not a chance," Yank said, no sign of a grin. "Did you give the cuff links back?"

"Nope. She relented. I wore them to a black-tie event when I was working undercover. Vlad invited me."

"Vlad. Hell, Donovan." Yank grimaced as he stood up, loosened his tie slightly. "We're still digging into everything Bulgov touched. It takes time. His ties go back two decades and involve at least two dozen countries."

"Ivan Alexander's name hasn't turned up?"

Yank sat on the edge of his desk and didn't answer.

"Damn," Colin said. "It has, hasn't it? Talk to me, Yank."

"Pete Horner piloted a plane Alexander chartered eighteen months ago. Aspen to Los Angeles. Turns out Alexander's a big skier. Two days later, Horner was fired from the charter company."

"Alexander's doing?"

Yank shrugged. "Don't know yet. We're on it."

"Emma?"

"The team. Horner banged around for a couple months, then hired on with Vladimir Bulgov and flew chartered cargo humanitarian relief flights for him."

"Smuggling weapons with the rice and beans," Colin said. "He was a relatively new hire with Bulgov. He wasn't on our radar until late in the game. Did Alexander keep tabs on him?"

Yank shook his head. "Don't know. That's all I've got right now."

Colin put his hand on the doorknob but glanced back at Yank. "Ivan Alexander is Emma's source. No doubt in my mind. A bottle of Bracken Distillers' finest on it."

"Too expensive for my blood. A beer instead." Yank's humor evaporated almost as soon as it had appeared. "Not that it's a fair bet. You and I both know he's her source. If we're right, if he's someone she can trust, I'm not mucking things up. Imagine what he knows."

Colin opened the door. "Imagine what Emma and the rest of the Sharpes know."

"Yeah. I wouldn't mind doing a Vulcan mind meld with the grandfather." Yank followed Colin out into the hall. "I don't like this damn yacht in Heron's Cove, Colin. I wouldn't like it on a good week."

"We're on the same wavelength there." Colin nodded toward an open office with a cluster of desks. "Seeing how I always do as you say, I did bring a couple dozen of Hurley's doughnuts. I left them with the team. Told them to save you one."

Yank walked with him to the exit. "See why I keep you and Emma around? She brings me pies, and you bring me doughnuts."

Colin grinned. He felt marginally better as he left than he had when he had arrived.

Let Yank be irritated with Emma for a change.

Emma's apartment was a few blocks away from the HIT offices. Colin had parked nearby, figuring he would end up there. It was small, in one of the renovated old wharf buildings. The first time he was there he searched the place. Even after several months in Boston, she still had little furniture.

Seemed to be a thing with her, he thought as he buzzed the intercom.

She opened the door for him. Colin sensed she was debating telling him to shove off but didn't blame her. She was tight, frustrated and as intensely focused as he had ever seen her.

Then again, so was he.

"You need to talk to me, Emma."

She left the door open for him, giving him the choice to follow her inside or go on his way. He deliberately waited a few seconds, then went in to her little one-bedroom apartment.

"I thought you might have bought more furniture since my last visit," he said.

"I have." She pointed to a coffee table stacked with books. "I bought that."

The place looked less lived-in than a hotel room. It had potential with its single exposed brick wall and windows that looked out on a small marina. *Just like home in Heron's Cove,* he thought. He didn't like to get too far from the water himself. One thing he and Emma had in common, maybe.

That and a fierce physical attraction to each other, he thought as he caught a glimpse of her neatly made bed in the next room.

She was still cool, annoyed. "If you're trying to wear me down, you can give up now," she said, standing in the middle of the hardwood floor. "I don't wear down easily."

"That I already know."

She angled him a look. "Is that meant to remind me that we've slept together?"

He let his gaze drift over her. "Do you need reminding?"

"I don't," she said.

"You're blushing, Special Agent Sharpe."

"I'm not. I walked fast from the office." She motioned toward the adjacent bedroom. "I'm just pulling together a few things before I head back to Heron's Cove. What are you doing?"

He shrugged. "Watching you."

"Yank told you to?"

"He didn't need to."

"I was caught flat-footed by Dmitri's arrival," she admitted, loosening up ever so slightly.

"Did you expect him to notify you that he was on the way?"

"It would have been nice. He didn't have to call me himself. He has a staff." She went into the bedroom, barely big enough for her double bed, and ripped open a closet door. "I just wish I'd known. That's all. Especially given the timing with your ordeal."

His ordeal, he thought, leaning against the white-painted wood doorjamb. "What about your pal Ivan? Couldn't he have called?"

She disappeared into the closet. "He could have."

"Have you talked to him in the past four years?"

No response.

"You have," Colin said, not that he hadn't figured that out already. That and just how hard it was to get Emma Sharpe to talk when she didn't want to.

She reappeared with a folded sweater that she set on the bed. Her hair had picked up some static, but she didn't seem to notice as she raked a hand through it. "Ivan and Dmitri come out of a difficult and turbulent era in Russia." She dipped back into the closet and produced a couple of folded shirts. "They don't look at the world the same way you and I do. If they'd been born at a different time, who knows what they'd have become."

Colin didn't care about any of that. "Ivan knows who I am."

She nodded. "I know. I didn't tell him."

"But he's your source." Colin didn't want to press too hard now that he'd gotten this far with her. "I'm not asking you to give up a confidence. I'm telling you what I know. I assume you trust him."

"Yes."

"You give people the benefit of the doubt, Emma. You don't judge. People feel comfortable with you, and they tell you things. You have a tendency to believe the best about them."

"You're saying I don't have good instincts. That I'm too trusting."

"As a nun, as a Sharpe—you could take people as they are. Maybe you had to. You also didn't have to build a case. You weren't a federal agent. There's a difference between having sources and keeping a toe in your old life. "

"I understand what you're saying." She stood back from

the bed, staring down at the decorative pillows, then looked at Colin, her green eyes warm, clear. "Ivan is the first man I was attracted to after the convent."

Great, he thought.

"Nothing ever happened between us," she added quietly.

"It's none of my business if it did, except as it affects your judgment—and what he's up to."

"It doesn't affect anything. It never did."

"You believe that. Does Ivan?"

She gathered up her sweaters and tops and walked past him back into the living room. "Ask him if you want to," she said finally, setting the clothes atop the books on the coffee table.

"Your Russian friends are a distraction," Colin said. "Tatiana Pavlova believes someone will steal the collection. It doesn't mean she's right but she might have instincts about the players. Rusakov, Alexander, Natalie Warren and her dear departed mother. Your grandfather. Your brother."

He expected her to argue, or at least to take offense, but she remained calm. "Yank's not happy about this."

"Nope. Does he know you have a thing for Ivan?"

Her eyes settled on Colin, cool, hard to read, as sexy as ever. "That's irrelevant. It's also incorrect."

"Ivan still has a thing for you."

"You're assuming he ever did—"

"I am."

"Well, if he does, he won't act on his feelings."

"He's more disciplined than I am," Colin said, slipping an arm around her.

She smiled, no resistance, no doubt, and his mouth found hers as he drew her tight against him. He felt her give herself up to the kiss, clutched his arm as she drew him closer.

"I can't stay," she whispered. "I have to go back to Heron's Cove and talk to Tatiana."

Colin stood back, her hand still on his arm. "What's up?"

"I checked on Tatiana's flight from London. It turns out she didn't come straight here. She flew to Phoenix first. She stayed overnight there, then flew to Boston and headed up to Heron's Cove."

"Natalie Warren is from Phoenix. Does Yank know Tatiana was there?"

Emma shook her head. "I just found out. I'll call him on my way to Maine. Tatiana didn't lie to me but I still want to talk to her. I'll stop at the house and walk over to her cottage.

"Do you want company?"

"You'll need your truck, and she's jumpy as it is—two FBI agents showing up could be counterproductive. I'll meet you back at the house."

"Not a problem," Colin said, a sarcastic edge to his voice. "If I get bored, I can grab a crowbar and tear apart a few walls, see if I can find a fortune in jewelry and such. That'd be something, wouldn't it?"

"It'd be a miracle. You'd be more likely to find mice skeletons." Emma's quick smile didn't soften her tense, uneasy look as she dropped her hand from his arm. "I'll see you soon."

"Drive safe. No speeding."

"If you're annoyed—"

"Not annoyed."

"I'm not shutting you out," she said.

He kissed her on the cheek. "Go," he said softly. "Do what you have to do."

She eyed him. "You don't like this situation, either."

"Not even a little.

She nodded, her smile gone. She stuffed her clothes into a canvas tote bag and headed out with a murmured goodbye. After the door shut behind her, Colin glanced around the small apartment. He would need a place to stay in Boston if he had to go into the HIT offices every day. Emma's apartment was tight quarters for the two of them, and it was her space.

He didn't remember any pictures of her and Ivan Alexander from his quick search of her apartment in September.

Of her and any man.

He decided he would have to get Finian Bracken or one of his brothers to take a few shots of him and Emma together. Laughing together, he thought. Kayaking together. Picking apples. Walking hand in hand on some quiet stretch of rocky coast.

Drinking whiskey at Hurley's, even.

If he was going to work in an office for real, he wanted a picture of Emma on his desk.

Colin found carpenters but no Emma at the Sharpe house when he arrived in Heron's Cove. He didn't know if she'd changed her mind about parking there, or just didn't drive as fast as he did.

Gerald Riegler, a beefy guy Colin had grown up with in Rock Point, was in the front room, packing up for the day. "Hey, Colin. I heard you and Emma Sharpe were an item." He grinned as he returned a tape measure to his toolbox. "Should I read anything into her sleeping on the floor last night?"

"Shut up, Gerald," Colin said good-naturedly, deciding not to mention that he had slept on the floor with her. He had left early, before any of the carpenters had arrived or those aboard the *Nightingale* had stirred. "How's work on the place going?"

"It's going great, especially with Lucas Sharpe in Ireland." Using the toe of his work boot, Gerald shoved his toolbox against the wall. "Emma brought us a pie the other day. We like Emma. Did you bring us anything?"

"No, I didn't bring you anything. Hell, Gerald."

"I wasn't thinking you'd bring pies. Lobster, maybe."

Two more carpenters, also from Rock Point, materialized from other rooms in the house. They greeted Colin, teased him about the mat on the floor. They obviously liked Emma, too. After they left, Colin shut the door behind them and headed to the kitchen. He saw that the blankets and quilts were folded and stacked in the small adjoining bedroom, as if Emma didn't plan to spend another night there.

Good, he thought.

Of course the stacked blankets didn't mean she planned to spend the night with him in Rock Point.

He really could take a crowbar to a wall.

He went out to the back porch and thumped down the steps, slick with the gray mist. He noticed a woman on the small riverfront beach below the inn just past the parking lot. The hood to her rain jacket fell back, and he recognized Natalie Warren's white-blond hair. She seemed to be alone. He walked across the wet grass, through the evergreen bushes that served as a border to that side of the Sharpe yard, then along the retaining wall on the edge of the parking lot.

By the time he jumped down to the beach, Natalie was aware of his presence. "Well, well," she said cheerfully. "Here we are again. I was just up at the Sharpe house. The carpenters said Emma's in Boston."

"She was. She's on her way back here."

"The house looks so shabby and empty right now, but what a romantic spot for Sharpe Fine Art Recovery to have its offices."

Colin tried not to show any of the tension he felt. "Have you ever worked with the Sharpes before?"

"No, I haven't. I wouldn't say that I am now." Natalie inhaled deeply, facing the water. The hem of her flowing pants had dipped into the rising tide, but at least she was wearing lace-up waterproof shoes today. "I love the mist and the taste of salt in the air. I'm such a desert rat, but this is just spectacular." She gave a satisfied smile, even as she seemed to well up with emotion. "How are you today, Special Agent Donovan?"

"Doing just fine. You?"

"I'm still on Phoenix time. I didn't sleep well last night. Tonight should be better." She watched a lobster boat make its way through the channel into the tidal river. "I've had lobster salad but I've never tackled a whole lobster. I'm not sure I'd want to mess with one."

"It's not that hard."

"One of your brothers is a lobsterman, isn't that right?"

Colin felt the cold mist on the back of his neck. "How did you know?"

"Oh, now don't get all suspicious over an innocent comment," she said, teasing him. "I found out from another lobsterman this morning on the docks. We were just chatting."

"And you happened to ask about my family?"

"Actually, I asked about the Sharpes and mentioned that Emma's an FBI agent, and he said he was from Rock Point and knew an FBI agent there. *Then* we got to you and your brother the lobsterman."

"Did you talk to anyone on board the *Nightingale* about my family?"

"No. Heavens. I was just making conversation." Natalie squatted down and picked up one of the small, saltwater-polished stones that covered the beach. "Have you ever caught a lobster?"

"It was my first job," Colin said.

She stood straight and tossed the stone into the shallow water. "But you ended up as an FBI agent." She scooped up another stone. "What an interesting path."

Colin nodded up the river, in the direction of Dmitri Rusakov's massive yacht. "What have you all been up to today?"

"Getting reacquainted. I assume Emma told you about the collection."

"Some."

"My mother never mentioned it to me when she was alive. I wanted to know more about it. That's why I came here."

"Have you showed it to Rusakov?"

She nodded, then let out another breath. "Last night, after you and Emma left."

Colin worked a stone loose from the wet sand with his boot. "How did he react?"

"He wasn't surprised. He'd guessed what it was. He was kind. He didn't make any demands. Since we're both here and the collection's here, we might as well figure out what to do like civilized adults."

Colin picked up the loosened stone, rubbed off some of the mud. "You suspected he knew about the collection, maybe even that it came from him, didn't you? That's why you called him. Did you hope he'd follow you here so that you could precipitate a meeting?"

Her eyes widened with mock surprise. "You are a suspicious type, aren't you, Special Agent Donovan? I don't manipulate people. That, to be honest, was my mother. Although I am pleased to see Dmitri, even more so than I thought I'd be."

"You could have just knocked on his door if you wanted to see him."

"It's not that simple. Well, maybe it is now, with my mother gone, but he could have told me the collection's history when I called. I didn't speak directly to him, but he knew how to reach me. He decided to meet me here, in person, to see the collection for himself—so that he could be sure it's the one he discovered in his Moscow house. I'd never been on board the *Nightingale,* of course. I wouldn't be surprised if it's worth more than Dmitri's other homes combined, would you?"

"I haven't seen his other homes," Colin said.

"Anyway, I learned not to rock the boat with my mother. She didn't want me to have contact with him, and so I didn't. Ask any daughter of a mean, controlling, narcissistic mother and she'll tell you we learn to do what we can to not get hurt."

"Do you think your mother pilfered this collection from Rusakov?"

"As I told Emma last night, and Dmitri this morning, no, I don't." Using both hands, Natalie pulled her hood back over her head, her hair glistening with mist. "I'm just trying to figure this all out the best I can. You have to understand my mother's personality. She had her own way of thinking. Tell me, Agent Donovan. How long have you and Emma been seeing each other?"

He took a few steps closer to the water's edge, with no intention of answering Natalie's question.

"I see you're the closemouthed type. Now there's a surprise." She pointed to his forearm, her fingertip not quite touching his skin. "That's a nasty bruise. Did you get it lobstering with your brother?"

"Something like that. Where are Rusakov and Alexander now?"

"I have no idea. I went out for some air about an hour and a half ago. I don't mind the wet weather—it's a novelty for me. I walked along the ocean, past some gorgeous houses. Frankly, they're more along the lines of what I expected Wendell Sharpe to own."

Colin wondered if she had run into Tatiana Pavlova but didn't ask. A young couple walked down from the inn with two toddlers. One child burst ahead of them, squealing when he saw a seagull.

Natalie smiled, watching the young family. "Dmitri told me this morning that he thinks I should find a good man and get married and have a half-dozen fat babies. Can you imagine? Me? A good man might be in my future but not six babies. Perish the thought." She faked a shudder, laughed. "What about you? A good woman and a bunch of babies in your future? Oh, Emma. Of course. Looks as if you two have a good thing going."

"I should get moving," Colin said, again dodging her curiosity about his relationship with Emma. "Are you going back to the *Nightingale* now?"

She nodded. "Although I'm tempted to take off my shoes and walk in the salt water and rocks. It'd be like a rough-and-ready reflexology pool."

"Can't say I've ever been in a reflexology pool."

"Big surprise." Natalie grinned at him before she continued. "My mother introduced me to reflexology. Please don't think I'm some kind of horrible daughter for talking about her the way I do. I loved her but I also had no illusions. I did enough therapy to accept that she was pretty much a nasty piece of work. Everyone had a turbulent relationship with her. It shouldn't be surprising that I, her only child, had a turbulent relationship with her, too."

"I'm not here to judge you," Colin said. "How did your mother and Dmitri meet?"

"At a museum in Moscow. Isn't that romantic? They were good together for a while. She didn't get bored with him as fast as she did with most of her men."

Colin started across the rocky beach, Natalie joining him. "Why didn't your mother tell you about the collection?" he asked. "Why leave it to you with no details?"

"A very good question. At first I wondered if she'd just forgotten about it, but now I think it was her way of trying to manipulate and control me after her death."

"Did she have a chance to get her affairs in order? She was a relatively young woman. If she was sick—"

"That's a fair point, but only if you didn't know her. She never accepted how sick she was and she was always so competitive with me, her own daughter. Well, it doesn't matter now. She's finally at peace. The collection is spectacular, but I was awake half the night thinking about it. I don't want to keep it. I know that much."

"What will you do with it?" Colin asked.

Natalie turned to him, her very blue eyes sparkling even in the gray late-day light. "I have to sort things out with Dmitri first, before I can do anything. I want to be sure all the pieces are from this Rusakov collection, or if maybe some are from other sources—just pieces that my mother collected that have nothing to do with Dmitri."

When they reached the retaining wall, Natalie continued onto the pier, tilted her head back. "Are you really an FBI agent?"

Colin stepped onto the pier with her. "I really am."

She looked out at the water. "There's something I want to tell you. I'm not even sure why except…" She crossed her arms in front of her. "I thought someone had been in my house in Phoenix the other night."

"What night?"

"Thursday. I called the police but they didn't find anything amiss. It was so weird. I was absolutely convinced I heard someone sneaking out as I got home from a late night at work. The police think I could have heard the air-conditioning kicking on."

"Was it? Were you mistaken?"

"Maybe. I don't know. I don't think so." She sighed again, frowning at Colin now. "My mother had tight security at her home, but she had more to protect than I do. I'd much rather spend my money on a trip than on art and jewelry, if you know what I mean. I have an alarm system, but I'm lax about using it."

"Might want to rethink that."

She blushed, smiling. "I suppose I'll have to."

Colin nodded to the luxury yacht. "How well do you know the *Nightingale*'s crew?"

"I don't know them at all but I have no reason not to trust them. Ivan would never have let me bring the collection here if I couldn't."

"Then you trust him."

"Yes, of course. Shouldn't I?" When Colin didn't answer, Natalie pulled off her hood. "I think the drizzle's stopped, at least for now. Thanks for the chat. Join us later if you can. Bring Emma. I know Dmitri wants to see her again. You, too."

She didn't wait for a response and headed down the pier. Colin waited for her to disappear up the gangway onto Dmitri Rusakov's yacht before he turned back to the Sharpe house.

Emma still wasn't back from her visit with Tatiana Pavlova.

He would give her five more minutes.

Then he would go find her.

16

THE DECK TO TATIANA PAVLOVA'S TINY RENTED cottage jutted out over the water. As Emma mounted the steps, she noticed the tide was in, the late-afternoon air a mix of mist, fog and salt water. Two white-painted Adirondack chairs were positioned on the small deck for the best view. The bow of the *Nightingale* was visible to her left, the marina and yacht club reasonably busy as working and pleasure boats both wound down for the day.

The sliding glass doors that led out to the deck were half-open, the vertical blinds blowing and clacking in the breeze. Emma knocked on the marine-blue wood trim. "Tatiana? It's Emma Sharpe."

There was no answer from inside.

She turned back to the water and touched her fingertips to the raindrops and mist that had collected on the flat arm of one of the Adirondack chairs. It was cold, damp. Not the best weather for sitting outside and watching boats, shore-birds, workers and yachtsman on the docks—or leaving the doors open.

She squinted into the gray. The mist and fog were supposed

to lift, not get socked in. Had Tatiana stepped out to clear her head after working and just hadn't bothered to shut the door?

Emma looked down at the water. A half-dozen ducks had gathered by a rock outcropping, quacking as they swarmed onto some unseen bit of food.

She heard a sound beneath her, as if someone had sucked in a deep breath.

Then a sniffle.

She went still, listening, but heard only the wash of the tide, the chattering ducks and the distant voices of the people on the docks. She walked slowly back down the deck steps, slick and slippery with the mist. The stairs ran along the side of the cottage, toward the street, the tide reaching under the front part of the deck.

She heard a movement and squatted by a bright red wooden canoe that was shoved haphazardly in the wet sand and small stones under the deck, its bow against the front edge of the cottage. High tide pushed water under the stern of the canoe.

"Tatiana?"

There was another sharp intake of breath.

Emma pressed in closer to the canoe. "It's Emma Sharpe, I'm here alone. No one else is with me."

"That man. The Russian bodyguard." It was clearly Tatiana's voice, more angry than frightened, but she remained hidden behind the canoe. "He was here. He knows who I am."

"What Russian bodyguard, Tatiana?"

"Ivan Alexander. He will help Dmitri Rusakov steal the collection from Natalie."

"Where is Ivan now?"

"He left. He walked up to street. I don't know where he went. He came in front door. I ran out back and hid. I heard him come down the steps."

"It's cold and wet down here," Emma said. "Why don't we go upstairs and talk?"

Tatiana rose up from her crouched position behind the canoe, squeezed under the low part of the deck, but remained on her knees in the mud. "Ivan must be back on the *Nightingale*. At Dmitri's side."

"I didn't see him—or anyone else." Emma felt her boot sink into the wet ground. "Tatiana, I'm a federal agent. You know that, right? You can come out."

She thrust her chin up. "Ivan came here to intimidate me."

"Did he say anything to you?"

"No. He said nothing. He knows silence can be more intimidating than words."

"Why would he want to intimidate you?" Emma asked.

"I told you. He will help Dmitri steal the collection. I know it in my bones. Dmitri will say he is taking back what is his. Ivan will go along with him because that is what Ivan does. Then they'll lock the collection in a vault and no one will ever see it."

"Why would Ivan think you believe that?"

Tatiana's jaw set stubbornly. "I don't believe. I know."

"I need more to go on than your gut. What makes you think Natalie wouldn't sell the collection or lock it away herself?"

"She wouldn't. I know she wouldn't."

"What if she and Dmitri work out an arrangement and he buys the collection from her?"

"He will never pay for what he already owns."

"Maybe if it was Renee instead of Natalie." Emma kept any impatience out of her voice. "Come on. Let's go up and make a cup of tea and talk."

Strands of dark, wet hair hung in Tatiana's face, her skin pale, her dark eyes wide with emotion—anger and indignation more than fear. "I'm not police. You have FBI file on Dmitri Rusakov, yes? You know what he did to get where he is now, yes?"

Emma heard the ducks quacking on the other side of the rocks, not far from one of the outer deck posts. She felt the water and mud seep under her boots. "I'm not sure what you're getting at. Did Dmitri or Ivan hurt you or your family back in Russia?"

Tatiana didn't move from behind the battered canoe. "I have no family." She shivered, her pumpkin-colored jacket not adequate in the cold, wet conditions. "I have my work, and my friends in London."

"You've gone to a lot of trouble to be here. If you're afraid of them—"

She thrust up her chin again. "I'm not afraid of them. I don't like them. There's difference."

"How do you know them, then?"

"I know their type."

Emma noticed Colin on the narrow walk, coming toward them from the front of the cottage, but kept her focus on Tatiana. "Here, let me help you. We can go up to your cottage where it's warm and dry and compare notes on Dmitri and Ivan." She put out her hand. "Colin Donovan is here, Tatiana. He's a friend and colleague. You met him at my house."

Colin stood next to Emma as Tatiana peered up at him and inhaled, but she didn't look afraid. He leaned over and took her by the wrist. "Come on. Up you go. You're five minutes from hypothermia. Even a mild case isn't any fun."

Tatiana hesitated, but Colin gave her an encouraging tug and she crawled out from her hiding spot, slipping in the wet, gray mud and rocks as she cleared the bow of the canoe. She had on black leggings, soaked at the ankles and knees, and she was shivering, her lips turning purple.

"I've ruined my shoes," she said, kicking mud off one of her black flats.

"You need a good pair of L.L.Bean boots up here," Colin said. "You're from Russia and you live in England. You must know about staying warm and dry. What were you doing under there?"

She wriggled her wrist free of him and pushed her wet hair off her face. "I was hiding from Ivan Alexander."

"Why?"

"Wouldn't you?"

"I wouldn't," Colin said. "Have you two met before? Has he threatened you?"

Tatiana clamped her mouth shut, but her teeth were chattering. "I'm cold."

Emma stood straight, aware of Colin's smoky eyes on her, as if she were the one who needed to do the explaining. "Ivan wasn't here when I arrived," she said.

Tatiana sniffled, smudges of mud on her nose and forehead. "I go up to my cottage now."

She muttered something in Russian, then ducked past Colin and ran up the deck stairs. He watched her a moment before turning to Emma. "I think that was 'arrogant bastard' in Russian. Should have been, anyway. Meaning Ivan, of course."

"You don't like him," Emma said.

"I don't trust him."

"Even if I do?"

He winked at her. "Now you're catching on."

He followed him up to the deck and through the half-open sliding glass door into the one-room cottage. Tatiana stood shivering on the edge of a marine-blue round rug and surveyed the mess. Sketches, pencils, erasers and clippings of various birds from magazines and guidebooks were scattered on a round table, the floor, the pullout love seat. Clothes were flung on the two side chairs. Canned goods, bread, crackers, an open jar of peanut butter and a bottle of Diet Coke covered the small kitchen counter. The sink was stacked with dirty dishes.

"Did Ivan toss this place, Tatiana?" Emma asked.

The young designer stared at her. "Toss?"

"Search," Colin said.

"I don't know. I don't think so. He wasn't here long. I work..." She waved a hand. "I'm not neat."

"An understatement," Colin said under his breath. "Can you tell if anything is missing?"

She gave a tight shake of the head. "Nothing. I don't think Ivan came inside. I left door in front and door in back open. I have no proof he did anything wrong. You can't arrest him." She shivered, her teeth at least no longer chattering. "I'll be more careful with locks."

"Why don't you want us to arrest him?" Colin asked.

Tatiana frowned as if she didn't understand the question. "It's not Ivan's fault I hid from him. I tell you the truth. That's all."

Colin still looked skeptical, but Emma said, "You should get into dry clothes and warm up. You were crawling around in that cold mud and water for a while."

Tatiana shook her head. "I'll be fine in two minutes."

Colin pulled a throw off the love seat and handed it to her. She took it and set it on a nearby chair. He shrugged. "Suit yourself. Does Ivan know who you are?"

"Who I am? A Russian jewelry designer in London, you mean? I don't know what he knows."

"What about Dmitri Rusakov? Does he know who you are? Would he recognize you if he saw you?"

She tugged off her jacket and let it fall to the floor. "I didn't want him or Ivan to see me. I wanted my interest in the collection to remain anonymous. I didn't want to draw their attention to me. It's too late now."

"Were you doing anything provocative?" Colin asked.

"What do you mean, provocative?"

"Spying on the *Nightingale,* taking pictures, that sort of thing?"

Tatiana's mouth snapped shut, as if she just remembered that she was speaking to a federal agent. "No. I'm just tourist."

Colin remained on his feet in the middle of the small room. "You're being evasive, Tatiana."

"Evasive? I don't know what that means."

Which was more evasiveness, Emma thought, but Colin let it go and moved over to a sketch of a great blue heron that was hanging off the edge of the table. With one finger, he slid it back among other sketches. "You were at the Sisters of the Joyful Heart shop this morning."

His comment seemed to catch Tatiana by surprise. "Yes. I met Emma's friend Sister Cecilia."

"You also met a friend of mine. A priest."

"The Irish priest. Father Bracken. Yes. He's very nice."

"Anything happen while you were there?"

"Happen? No. I wanted to see shop. I heard people talk about it, about the sisters. I told Emma. I listen." She picked up sketches on the floor by the sliding glass door. "Why you ask me questions? I'm one who was hiding under deck."

"We can call the local police if you want to file a complaint," Colin said calmly.

She dumped the sketches on the table. "The wind is stronger here by the water than I expected. Everything blows around, but I'm not always very neat to start. I saw a heron this morning when I sat outside. Such a bird. So ungainly looking and yet so graceful."

"Tatiana," Emma said, "why did you hide from Ivan? Why not just tell him to leave you alone? Are you afraid—"

"I told you I'm not afraid of him. It's easier to hide." Her dark eyes weren't as angry, as indignant. "Please, I only have interest in safety of the Rusakov collection, but it's out of my hands. I warned you. It's all I can do." She smoothed the wrinkles out of a pencil sketch of a seagull. "So now I draw and think."

Colin flipped through some of the other sketches on the table, unearthing one of a bald eagle. "Have you ever done work for Rusakov?"

"No. Never." She seemed offended at the idea.

"Renee Rusakov? Her daughter?"

Tatiana shook her head as she cleared off a spot on the love seat. "I make bed here at night. There's no bedroom. It's cozy. Nice. I like having my work around me when I sleep."

Colin set the eagle aside. "What about a Russian named Vladimir Bulgov? Have you ever done any work for him?"

She made a face as if she'd just eaten something very distasteful. "The criminal."

"Did you do work for him?" Colin asked, repeating his question.

Still shivering, Tatiana sat down and pulled the throw she'd refused over her legs. "I don't want to say yes or no without checking my records."

Colin raised his eyebrows. "You don't remember?"

Emma would have told him anything he wanted to know but Tatiana again thrust her chin up at him. "You can go. I'm not afraid to stay here on my own. I'm accustomed to living alone in London. This place has good locks, and it's obvious I have nothing of value here."

"What if you're of value?" Colin asked.

"I overreacted when I saw this Ivan Alexander," she said, ignoring the question.

Emma picked up a pencil sketch of a fanciful-looking swan that had ended up in a corner by a floor lamp. "You enjoy Russian folklore. What's your favorite Russian story?"

"I don't have one favorite." Tatiana tucked her hands under the throw and drew it up over her chest. "The stories are what they are. Each stands on its own."

"It's such a graceful swan," Emma said. "You draw quickly?"

"Most times. I have image in my head and get it down fast."

"Why do you believe Dmitri will steal the collection from Natalie? Why would it matter? He used to own the collection and may in fact still own it," Emma said casually, keeping her eyes on the swan; she knew Colin was watching Tatiana for any reaction. "Do you have a reason other than you know it in your gut? Do you believe Dmitri will deface or destroy the collection?"

"I work on my sketches. London…Moscow…" Tatiana sighed, slipping off her muddy flats, the throw still around her. "They seem so far away. I have no answers for you, Emma Sharpe. Only more questions."

Emma placed the swan sketch on the table. "You travel on a Russian passport."

"Yes. I told you I have no one left there. I was raised by my grandparents in small village outside Moscow. They're gone now. My grandfather first. Then my grandmother. I left Russia after she died." Tatiana looked out the sliding glass door at the Heron's Cove waterfront. "I sometimes miss Russia."

"Do you want to go back there to live one day?" Emma asked.

"No. Never."

Colin kept silent, pretended to check out Tatiana's food choices. The misty drizzle had stopped and the fog was lifting, the promised clearing underway. Emma turned to the Russian designer. "Why did you fly from London to Phoenix, before you came here?"

Tatiana flung off the throw and rose but didn't seem particularly rattled by the question. "You look up my travels? I suppose it makes sense. I went to Phoenix to see Natalie. She wasn't there. I stayed overnight at airport hotel and flew to Boston the next morning. Then I came here."

Colin moved back from the small kitchen area. "Why are you sticking your nose in this business with the collection?"

"I'm not. I've talked to no one—"

"You've talked to Emma," Colin said. "What dog do you have in this fight?"

She frowned. "Dog?"

"Did you break into Natalie's house while you were in Phoenix?" he asked abruptly.

Tatiana gave him a hot, angry look. "Now you say *I'm* thief?"

"Are you?"

She muttered something in Russian and huffed off to the sliding glass door. "I didn't break into Natalie's house," she said, no longer shivering as she glanced back at Emma. "You go now. Thank you for your help. I call police if I have any problem. Right, Emma? That's what I do, yes?"

Emma nodded. "That's right. That's what you do. Or you can call me."

Tatiana smiled. "I'll do that." She slid the door open and stepped outside in her stocking feet.

Emma sighed at Colin. "Do you see Tatiana breaking into Natalie's house? Because I don't."

He gave a curt nod. "Agreed, but she's holding back."

"I know but there's no crime—"

"Did your brother or grandfather discover any connection to Bulgov? Horner?"

"I'd tell you if he had."

Colin walked past her and went outside, said good-night to Tatiana and headed back down the deck stairs.

Emma swept her gaze over the small room, taking in Tatiana's sketches, her art supplies, her scattered clothes. What could Ivan have wanted here? What did he know about Tatiana, the Firebird Boutique, her interest in the Rusakov collection?

What am I missing?

Stifling her frustration, Emma joined Tatiana on the deck. "We can help you, Tatiana, but only if you tell us everything."

"I know." She didn't look at Emma. "Thank you for getting me out from behind the canoe. Have a good evening, Emma."

"Right. Thanks. You, too."

Emma descended the steps. Colin was waiting for her. The ducks had divided up, some still by the rocks, some by the deck posts. She stood close to him. "Tempting just to watch the ducks, isn't it?"

"We'll have that chance," he said. "In the meantime, we can walk back to your place, and you can tell me again why you trust this Ivan Alexander character."

17

THE WIND PICKED UP ON THE BRIDGE OVER the cove, but Emma welcomed the cooler, drier air as she walked next to Colin. "I'll find out what Ivan wanted with Tatiana," she said.

"I'm glad I didn't walk in and find him trashing the place and have to shoot him."

"I can take care of myself, Colin," Emma said quietly, firmly.

"So you'd have shot him?"

She decided not to answer him. "Why didn't you wait for me at the house?"

Colin shrugged. "I got restless."

"Well, thanks for checking on me," Emma said. "It's good to know you have my back. Let's just remember there's a difference between having my back and protecting me."

"Hair-splitting. When Ivan told you where I was, was that having my back or was that protecting me?"

"I was trying to find you. It wasn't because I lack faith in you."

"If I'd found you and Tatiana in a mess with Ivan and had

to shoot him, it wouldn't have been because I lacked faith in you. It would have been because he needed shooting." Colin paused, winked at her. "Hypothetically."

"Fair enough. Let's leave it at that. How did you find out about the break-in at Natalie's house? Did Yank tell you?"

"Natalie told me," Colin said.

"Ah. Natalie. She's very attractive."

"Bombshell. That blond hair and smile. Tatiana's cute, too."

Emma rolled her eyes.

He slung an arm over her shoulder. "So, what's going on here in little Heron's Cove, Emma? Think Tatiana's setting us up so she can steal the Rusakov collection herself?"

"Why would she?"

"Maybe she's hooked up with Pete Horner, wants to get a foothold in arms trafficking. She could have a buyer in place for the collection, or she could be planning to ransom it back to Rusakov." Colin slowed his pace. "Now I'm in your world, thinking like an art thief."

"I don't know what Tatiana's up to. She seemed genuinely unnerved when I found her under the deck, at least at first."

"Ivan's a scary guy. She's feisty, though."

"The more she thought about him, the angrier she became. Maybe it had to sink in that he was gone and hadn't done anything."

"It'd be easy to get caught up in Tatiana's sense of drama. Maybe it helps her with her work. You're out of sorts, Emma." Colin let his arm drift down her back and settle on her waist. "Sleeping on a hard floor will do that. I know this from experience."

"The floor wasn't that hard. I had a mat."

He grinned. "I could make a lewd comment but I won't."

She bit back a smile. "Do you know what I've learned

about the Donovan brothers since you've been gone? You're all impossible. Mike, Andy, Kevin. You. You know that's your reputation, don't you?"

"Not a bad reputation to have."

"Impossible but also sexy, rugged, tough—"

"All four of us?"

"All four of you. Your father, too."

"Pop? He's planting tulips and trying out muffin recipes these days."

"That doesn't mean he's not impossible, sexy, rugged or tough." Emma slipped from his embrace but caught her fingers in his and noticed the healing bruise on his wrist. "You're not getting much of a break, are you?"

"Not with your Russian friends in town."

"Colin..." She took a few more steps before she continued. "You wouldn't keep me in the dark about anything, would you?"

"That's a two-way street. Did you know that your pal Ivan fired Pete Horner?"

"Only because Yank called on my way up here and told me."

"Has Ivan been keeping tabs on Horner? Is that how he knew about Horner's house in Fort Lauderdale?"

"Ivan doesn't know where Horner and his men are."

"How do you know, because he told you?"

Emma ignored the note of skepticism in Colin's voice. "Tell me about you and Natalie."

"She thinks I'm a stud."

"You are a stud," Emma said with a smile. "But Natalie didn't actually say that, did she?"

"Close enough." He glanced up at the clearing sky. "Front's moving in. The air feels good." He kept his arm around her as he related his conversation with Natalie Warren. "She's something of a lost soul. She won't say so outright, but she wants to keep this collection."

"It's beautiful. I can't say I blame her."

"But her mother stole it?"

"Dmitri says he didn't give it to her. I don't know why he would lie about that." Emma leaned into him, just for a second. "We could pretend we're tourists enjoying a cool, crisp autumn afternoon in Heron's Cove."

"We could."

"I wish you'd had at least a few days to rest before Dmitri showed up."

Colin nodded but didn't respond. Emma appreciated the gusty wind as she walked with him. Whether they were making love or curled up together on the hard floor, being close to him was powerful, enough to push any other thoughts out of her mind. Not a good thing when she had to be on her toes. She couldn't afford to miss a clue, a connection, a memory—anything that might help root out the men who had come so close to murdering him.

They passed a row of small shops in side-by-side cedar-shingled cottages, lit up against the darkening afternoon. The shop doors were brightly painted, with pots of mums in white, yellow and deep gold on their steps. Their windows displayed upscale housewares, watercolors of Maine scenes, handmade jewelry, stationery and warm-looking throws.

A middle-aged woman, a shopkeeper Emma knew, waved from the desk where she spent most days, catering to locals and tourists who loved her eclectic little gift shop.

Emma waved back, knowing the next time they ran into each other she would have to explain the man walking with her. She and Colin had met during the crisis of Sister Joan's murder, and then he took off after the remnants of Vladimir Bulgov's arms network. They hadn't had many quiet days for wandering about Heron's Cove, checking out the shops, eating lobster rolls, meeting people.

Colin patted her hip. "We'll have our chance to laze away an afternoon and do normal things," he said, as if he had read her mind. "The *Nightingale* isn't staying here forever."

As if to underline his point, they found Dmitri Rusakov standing in the Sharpe driveway with Ivan Alexander. They had obviously just arrived. Emma felt Colin tense next to her but then realized she had tensed, too.

"Let me handle this," she said in a low voice.

His smoky eyes settled on her. "Sure, babe."

"I'm not going to mention Tatiana in front of Dmitri."

"Got it."

"Or Pete Horner," she added.

Colin said nothing.

Dmitri saw them and waved. "Hello, hello," he said with a wide smile. He had on a turquoise jacket with sparkling white pants, a contrast to the autumn colors around him. "I couldn't resist. I had to get a closer look at the house where Wendell Sharpe got his start."

Emma returned his smile. "Come in, then. I'll give you the grand tour. The place is mostly gutted for renovations." She stepped ahead of Colin, past Dmitri and Ivan, and then led the three men into the house. "It's not the *Nightingale*— I can tell you that."

"Even better," Dmitri said. "I've always had the impression your grandfather prefers to work in simple surroundings."

"That's Granddad."

Colin positioned himself between her and Ivan, who stayed close to the front door. Dmitri walked through the living room, stopping at the open door to a small room that overlooked the street. He glanced back at Emma. "This is Wendell's office?"

"Not for the past fifteen years, but it's where he worked for many years."

Dmitri placed a hand on the door and peered into the gutted room. "Imagine all the important investigations into ill-gotten and disappeared art that went on in here." After a moment, he gave a deep sigh, then shifted his attention back to Emma. "We must never forget our beginnings, eh? No matter where life takes us."

"I guess that depends," she said.

"Yes. Just so." He moved back into the living room, the small Victorian so different from his luxury yacht. He paused at a tall window. "Natalie and I have discussed the collection. She didn't realize its history. We will sort out what to do. It's so good to see her. She has her mother's best qualities and none of the bad."

"Then you're working things out?" Emma asked.

"I'm hopeful." Dmitri smiled, pulled his gaze from the window. "I want to take the *Nightingale* along the Maine coast and see Atlantic puffins but my crew tells me it's not likely this time of year. Agent Donovan, you were a marine patrol officer. What about puffins?"

"I didn't arrest many puffins in my day," Colin said.

Dmitri grinned. "I like a sense of humor. You have a brother who lives on the..." He turned to Ivan. "What's it called?"

"The Bold Coast," Ivan supplied.

"Such a name. Yes." Dmitri started back toward Ivan. "I understand there are puffins out there."

Colin stood by a fresh stack of two-by-fours that must have been delivered today. "That's right," he said stiffly.

Dmitri paused at the hall to the kitchen and eyed him, no hint of a smile now. "You're concerned that I know about your family. No need to be. Natalie told me—as she told you—that she had an idle conversation with a man on the waterfront about you and your brothers. Why don't you bring them aboard the *Nightingale* for a drink?"

"Thanks, but they're all busy."

"Of course." The billionaire Russian peeked down the short hall that led back to the kitchen. "No wonder Wendell and I got on. We both come from humble origins. He's more erudite and educated than I will ever be, of course. I'm just a businessman. He's quite a brilliant man."

"I'm sure he'd appreciate the compliment," Emma said.

"Heron's Cove is so different from Moscow. Perhaps I will come back one day when Wendell is here, or stop and see him in Dublin—or get him to join me aboard the *Nightingale*." Dmitri smiled. "We can always meet in London. I'm there often, although I gave up my apartment. I understand your parents are in London for the year."

"That's right," Emma said, her tone neutral.

"As it happens, a young jewelry designer who works in London is also in Heron's Cove." Dmitri's smile faded and he steadied his gaze on Emma. "She's Russian. Her name is Tatiana Pavlova. She's a rising star at a London boutique, the Firebird."

Emma didn't look at either Ivan or Colin. "Did Ivan tell you about her?"

Dmitri gave a small shrug, without apology. "Of course. He looked into her after one of the crew saw her sneaking around on the docks. Apparently she is extraordinarily talented. It's a shame Russia lost her to London. She's passionate about Russian folklore." He picked up a crowbar that was leaning against a wall and ran his fingers over the metal. "But you know about her already, don't you, Emma?"

She unbuttoned her jacket, the house suddenly feeling warm, closed in despite the clearing skies and dropping temperature. "It's not incumbent upon me to tell either you or Ivan who I talk to or don't talk to."

Dmitri shook his head. "If the talk involves me..."

"Doesn't matter," Emma said, not backing down.

He didn't seem to take offense. "It wouldn't surprise me if Tatiana Pavlova doesn't trust me, my motives for being here. Many in Russia don't trust me because of my business, my wealth, politics—they all have their reasons. Some are legitimate. Some are fanciful, based on prejudice, gossip and tales told by my enemies."

Forcing herself not to look at Colin, Emma walked over to the stack of two-by-fours, the air thick with the smell of sawdust. "You don't have enemies in Heron's Cove, do you, Dmitri?"

His eyebrows went up in surprise, then he laughed. "I hope not. The only person I know in Heron's Cove is you, Emma, and I consider you a friend. Why don't you join us for dinner aboard the *Nightingale*?" He replaced the crowbar against the wall and kissed her cheek. "At least come for a drink. Bring your man here." He gave Colin a polite nod. "Good to see you, Special Agent Donovan."

After Dmitri and Ivan left, Colin shoved the load of lumber against the wall with the toe of his boot. "Ivan definitely still has the hots for you."

Emma made no comment.

"I'm going back to Rock Point." He stood back from the wood. "I don't know much, Emma, but I know I'm not sleeping on your floor tonight. Neither are you."

"I'm not worried about staying here on my own. I told you, I can handle myself—"

"It's not about that. It's time to get some space between you and whatever is going on here." He moved closer to her, threaded his fingers into her hair. "And a little less space between the two of us."

Before she had a chance to take a breath, he lowered his hand and headed for the kitchen. Emma reminded herself that if she had wanted an easy man, she wouldn't have fallen for Colin Donovan.

Not that she'd had time to think, reflect, analyze before she found herself in bed with him a month ago. She had never thought of herself as a woman who would be swept off her feet by such a man. By any man, really.

She wouldn't change a thing, she thought with a sudden smile.

She went down the short hall to the kitchen, welcomed the cool air as Colin opened the back door. "Are you going to check in on Father Bracken?" she asked.

He nodded. "You'll be right behind me?"

"Thirty minutes, tops."

"I'll be waiting."

"A promise or a warning?"

He didn't smile. "Take your pick."

Emma followed him out to the porch and watched him amble down the steps and across the yard to the parking lot on the other side of the hedges. He moved with his usual strength and determination, but she could feel his dark mood, the seriousness that had come over him since he had arrived at Tatiana's cottage.

When he disappeared from view, she let out a cathartic breath. Stubborn gray clouds remained to the south, toward the sandy beach that was a favorite with tourists to Heron's Cove. The Maine beaches in Ogunquit, York, Wells and Kennebunkport were all close, and she wondered how many people were looking out at the passing storm clouds, debating whether to go for a walk before nightfall.

She saw Ivan down on the pier and checked her iPhone for messages as he walked toward her. She had a few updates from her team and an email from her mother but no further news from Boston or London.

"Your man knows I'm still here," Ivan said as he stood at the bottom of the porch steps. "He has good instincts."

"Does that mean he's right not to trust you?"

Ivan put one foot on the bottom step and looked up at her. There was a softness in his dark eyes that she hadn't noticed—or he hadn't let her see—earlier. "He knows I care what happens to you, and he knows I helped you find him."

Emma sat on the top step. So. No more pretenses. She didn't bother denying or sidestepping that Colin was the agent Ivan had helped. "Why did you call me?" she asked. "Why did you help?"

He came up and sat next to her, not quite touching her. "Because I could." His intense gaze was focused on the waterfront, not her. "The FBI knows Pete Horner, the man who held Special Agent Donovan, once piloted a plane for me."

It was a statement, not a question. Emma leaned back, her leather jacket falling open. Ivan's eyes slid to the Glock 22 in her holster. "Does Horner have any axes to grind with you?" she asked.

"He has axes to grind with everyone."

"And you? An axe to grind with him?"

"If I find him before you and your FBI friends do, I will let you know."

"Don't interfere in FBI business, Ivan. It won't end well for you if you do."

"I don't want my actions to hurt you," he said quietly.

"I appreciate that but I don't need you to protect me. I have a job to do, and I'm not as confused as I was four years ago."

His mouth twitched in what passed for a smile. "You're never confused, Emma."

"You are not telling me everything, Ivan."

"That doesn't mean I'm not doing the right thing."

Emma braced herself against a sudden, stiff wind off the water, as if it meant to clear her head. "What did you want with Tatiana today?"

"To persuade her to return to London where she belongs."

"Is she in danger?"

"Not from me."

"From anyone else?"

He continued to stare out at the water. "I have no reason to believe so."

"Does she pose a danger to the collection?"

"You've met her. Does she look dangerous to you?"

"You know I can't make decisions on that basis. Is she involved with Vladimir Bulgov in any capacity? With Horner, his men?"

"She makes trinkets for rich people. That's all."

"And you, Ivan?" Emma stood and walked down the stairs, the wind whipping her hair into her face as she looked up at him. "Have you or Dimitri ever had Bulgov aboard the *Nightingale* for champagne and cosmopolitans?"

His dark eyes warmed with amusement, even affection, as he rose. "Only vodka for me." He walked down the stairs and kissed her on the forehead, through the hair that had blown into her face. "Good night, Emma. If you need to reach me, you know where to find me." He gave her one of his near-imperceptible smiles, then said, exaggerating his Russian accent. "I be in big boat on water."

She laughed, at least for a moment as he walked back down to the docks.

She glanced at her watch.

Not much time to get on the road before Colin doubled back and tracked her down.

18

COLIN RAPPED HIS KNUCKLES ON THE OPEN door to the parish priest's office in the back of St. Patrick's Church. It was dusk, and there were no lights on the walk outside or in the rectory, and only a desk lamp on in the small office. Finian Bracken, dressed in a black suit and Roman collar, sat behind a massive oak desk facing the door.

"You know, Fin," Colin said, "we have electricity and everything out here on the coast. You can turn on some lights."

Finian pointed the tip of his ballpoint pen at the ancient lamp with its thread of dim light. "It serves its purpose."

"Which is what, comparable to a hair shirt? This place is spooky in the dark."

"As if you're spooked by anything," Finian muttered.

Alligators, Colin thought, trying to lighten his own mood. "Mind if I come in?"

"Of course not. Come." He set the pen on a folded-back yellow pad. "What can I do for you?"

"Mike said you seem preoccupied. Anything going on?"

Finian sighed. He motioned to the chair facing his desk. "Have a seat."

"Not going to try to talk me into confessing my sins, are you?"

"No. As interesting as your sins must be."

It wasn't like Finian Bracken to make that kind of joke, and as Colin sat in the club chair with its leather seat cracked, his Irish friend's mood seemed to darken even more. The office was lined with bookshelves filled with volumes that either belonged to the church or to the priest Finian was replacing for a year. The regular priest, Father Callaghan, was in Ireland, searching out his Irish roots. He was close to retirement and beloved in Rock Point, but Colin didn't know him well.

He noticed a thick book on the history and geology of the Iveragh Peninsula that occupied a corner of the oak-wood desk. He was fairly certain the book belonged to Finian, not Father Callaghan. It was likely a recent purchase. Although Finian was well-off financially and hadn't entered the priesthood until his thirties, he had come to Maine with few personal possessions. He was a priest and committed to a simple life, but it was more than that. He was escaping memories. In his undercover work, Colin would go for long periods without his personal possessions, pretending to be someone else. It was deliberate, his job. He wasn't escaping anything, but in the past few weeks, before Pete Horner and his friends had decided to kill him, he hadn't dared even to think of Rock Point.

But he wasn't here to talk about himself, or about Fin's reasons for coming to St. Patrick's.

"Talk to me, Fin," Colin said.

Finian's eyes seemed almost black in the dark shadows. "No matter that you trust Matt Yankowski and Emma and I assume most of your fellow agents, you'll always be tempted to go it alone. It's who you are. Your close family helps you to do what you do."

"I'm not here for pastoral counseling," Colin said. "Mike's not one to sound false alarms. What's going on?"

Finian brushed his fingertips across the picture of an ancient Irish beehive hut on the front of his thick book on the Iveragh Peninsula. "When we made our first bit of money, Sally and I bought a ruin of a cottage on the Iveragh and fixed it up. We did much of the work ourselves on weekends."

"Sounds idyllic."

"Sally had an eye for color. Now when I go to the cottage, which has been some months since I've been in the States, I can touch what she loved, touch what she touched. I can see our daughters playing by the fire. It's not a sad place. It's charming. We deliberately kept it simple, with no personal mementoes—so that friends and family could stay. One day, perhaps, you'll go there with Emma, and you'll take long walks together in the hills."

"That'd be great, but right now—"

"You have to go easy, my friend," Finian said. "Precipitous action will only lead to mistakes and regrets."

Colin checked his impatience; Finian wasn't going to be rushed. "Think I should do things Emma's way?"

"You can only do things your way." He sighed heavily, looked away from his book. "On Saturday night, after I left Hurley's…" He stopped himself with a small groan. "It sounds ridiculous now that I'm mentioning it aloud. I'm being a fool."

"What happened?"

"A man followed me across the street after our drink at Hurley's."

Colin leaned forward. "He followed you?"

"All right, 'followed' is a bit strong."

"What did he want?"

"He didn't seem to want anything but it was an unusual conversation, at least for me." Finian paused, clearly reluctant to explain further. "He said it was his first time in Rock Point and that he'd asked about you and your brothers at Hurley's. He told me what each of you does for a living."

"Why?"

"I don't know. He didn't say. It was a quick conversation. I asked him if he wanted me to give you a ring, and he said no, he was on his way to Heron's Cove."

"Heron's Cove? Why?"

"He went on his way before I thought to ask." Finian glanced past Colin as if he didn't want to meet his eye. "I didn't ask enough questions. I wanted him to go."

"It wasn't your job to ask questions. It was your job to get home safely." Colin took in a breath, hating the idea that his friend had been upset by someone claiming to know him. "Describe this guy."

"Your height, and fair-skinned. He seemed to be in good condition." Finian patted his own stomach. "No fat at all in the middle. He wore a black fleece jacket and a baseball cap. Those are the only details of his appearance that I remember."

"Did he speak with an accent?"

"American," Finian said with a slight smile. "He called you and your brothers 'tough guys.'"

Tough guys, Colin thought. He didn't like that one. "Did he mention Emma?"

"No. I suggested he come to our bean-hole supper and he moved along. When I went into the rectory, I had the feeling..." Finian sat straight, cleared his throat. "I left the front door unlocked. I'm sure that's all it was."

Colin got to his feet. "You had the feeling what, Fin?"

"That someone had been in the rectory. I attributed it to

my mood, given the worry over your silence. I was on alert, I suppose."

"It's fine to be on alert. It's good. Keeps you on your toes. I'm sorry you all were worried about me." Colin looked down at Finian's book on the Iveragh Peninsula and imagined himself there with Emma and no concerns, no FBI baggage, no Sharpe baggage. Just the two of them. But he pulled himself out of his thoughts and nodded to his friend. "Want me to take a look around the rectory?"

Finian shook his head. "There's no need. Nothing's missing or out of place. I'm sure my reaction is out of proportion to the offense, if there even was an offense." He rose stiffly. "Whiskey and adrenaline talking."

It was possible, Colin thought, but Finian Bracken wasn't one to overreact. "This guy hasn't turned up again?"

"I can't say for certain..." Finian hesitated, flipped the pages on his yellow pad so that the cover was back on top. "I might have seen him in the village this morning. As I told Mike, I ran into the Russian girl, Tatiana, at the sisters' shop. We chatted a bit, and she left. Then I left, and I saw a man in a black jacket. For a moment I thought he might be following her, but I don't know—I don't even know if it was the same man from the other night."

"Did you see him speak to Tatiana?"

"No, no. I didn't see them together. Perhaps I just reacted to the black jacket."

"Would you recognize this man if you saw him again?"

Finian stared at the ancient Irish stone hut on the cover of his book, then looked at Colin. "I think so, yes. I'm sorry I can't provide a better description. But this man's done nothing wrong, has he? Tatiana..."

"I saw her earlier. She's fine."

"Thank God," Finian said, visibly relieved. He came

around from behind his desk and started across the shabby but comfortable office. "I'm allowing myself to be influenced far too much by you Donovans. Especially Mike and you, but even your father. I imagine only Andy doesn't keep a gun under his pillow—and I don't know for a fact that he doesn't, too."

Colin ignored his friend's rant. "Anything unusual—anything at all—you call me, right? Or call my father or one of my brothers. Any one of us will help. Understood?"

Finian nodded. "Yes. Thank you."

"Don't hesitate," Colin added, hoping he'd gotten through to him.

"I won't. Of course, I could just be naturally embellishing a good story."

"Is that what you think?"

He shrugged. "Does it matter? I'll clean up and head to Hurley's in a bit."

"I'll meet you there."

"Good man," his friend said, the spark back in his expression.

Colin swung by his house but Emma wasn't there yet. He texted her to meet him at Hurley's instead but drove first to his parents' inn. When he got out of his truck, he saw that she hadn't responded. For all he knew she was back aboard the *Nightingale,* drinking champagne with her family's Russian billionaire client and her Russian source.

Ivan Alexander, the first man she was interested in after she gave up being Sister Brigid.

Colin gritted his teeth. He had fallen for one hell of a complicated woman.

He found Mike planting tulip bulbs out front in the light from the porch. "Tell me you're not bringing me another hundred bulbs," his brother grumbled, getting to his feet with trowel in hand.

"I'm not bringing you more bulbs."

"You came to help then? Ground's soft. Full of worms, which I know you don't like, but no snakes. A big, tough FBI agent should be able to handle a few worms."

"Worm, yes. Planting tulips, no. At least not right now. I'd go out of my mind."

Mike cast him a dark look. "What do you think I'm doing?"

"You're contributing to the economic and emotional welfare of our folks. People love tulips. Guests will be raving about them in their reviews on TripAdvisor." But Colin heard the edge in his voice and gave up on any attempt at normal conversation. "I talked to Finian Bracken."

Mike set his trowel atop a burlap bag of Dutch-grown tulip bulbs. He wasn't wearing garden gloves, and his hands were crusted with mud. "Something happened, right?"

Colin told his older brother what he knew. "If this guy turns up again, I don't want Fin dealing with him on his own. Think you can check on him from time to time?"

"Not a problem."

"If you see this guy, call the police, Mike. I just want Fin to have a friend nearby. It's not just that he's a priest and an outsider. I've gotten to know him, and he's a risk-taker at heart."

"Since he wasn't on board that boat with his family," Mike said, not making it a question.

"Even more so since then. He and his twin brother started a whiskey distillery at twenty-two. The odds of success were against them. Fin's wired for taking risks."

"No wonder you two get along."

Colin looked up at the inn's wide front porch, decorated with pumpkins and pots of mums. His parents were enjoying working on the place, giving it a charm and a level of sophistication that people liked. Word was getting out about the breakfasts. It would do fine.

His brother wasn't finished. "This woman. Emma. Hell, Colin. Are you sure you can think straight where she's concerned?"

"You don't like her," Colin said, matter-of-fact.

"I don't have a reason to like or not like her. I just don't think we get her world."

"Can't argue with that. Everything's good here?"

Mike narrowed his eyes, studied Colin a moment, then sighed. "Everything's fine. Only four hundred tulip bulbs to go. I won't finish tonight. I'll do a few more and see you at Hurley's in a little while."

Colin returned to his truck. Still nothing from Emma. He drove back to his house and walked down to the harbor. He was crossing the street to the waterfront when he got a text message from Emma: I'm at Hurley's with your brothers and whiskey. HELP.

He grinned, his tension lifting as he slid his phone back into his jacket and went to join her.

Finian had settled into his favorite table by the back window. Hurley's was reasonably populated for a Monday and what had turned into the coldest night yet that fall. Emma, Mike, Andy and Kevin Donovan had arrived ahead of Colin and were finishing off an order of steamed clams. Not one of Finian's favorites.

Colin didn't look thrilled with them, either, as he joined them and took off his jacket. "Perfect timing," he said, pulling out a chair by the window. "Clams are gone, and there's whiskey left."

As he sat down, Julianne Maroney swept over to them and

set a plastic pitcher on the table so hard water splashed out. Andy Donovan calmly blotted the spill with the callused palm of his hand. "A lot of energy there, Jules," he said.

"It's Julianne. Or Ms. Maroney." She addressed Finian with a controlled smile. "No ice in the water, as requested, Father."

"Thank you, Julianne," Finian said.

"You're welcome." She seemed to want to get away from them as fast as possible but stood there, adjusting her half apron. "I wanted to thank you for visiting my grandmother this morning. She said it did her a world of good to talk with you."

"She did?" Finian was mystified. "She all but ran me out with a pitchfork."

Julianne laughed. "That's my granny." Her smile vanished as she glared at Andy, then spun back to the kitchen.

Andy watched her with a wince. "She's got a temper like her grandmother."

"What'd you do to her?" Mike asked.

"Why did I have to do anything?"

"Because she's Julianne Maroney, a hardworking marine biologist, and you're Andy Donovan, the rake of Rock Point."

Andy shrugged, as accustomed to the eldest Donovan's bluntness as the rest of his brothers—and, by now, Emma. "Julianne's decided I cheated her father out of his boat." He glanced at Finian and Emma then filled them in. "The *Julianne* is a classic wooden lobster boat I'm restoring and using as a backup. It's a heap. The Maroneys are lucky I took it off their hands and have managed to keep it afloat. It'd be rotting in their shed if they'd had to deal with it."

"It's named after Julianne?" Emma asked.

"Yeah, her father named it in her honor when she was a baby. Crazy thing to do but that's how he is. They figured

I'd give it another name but I haven't gotten around to it. The whole thing's a thorn in Julianne's side."

"I'll bet it's not the only thorn in her side when it comes to you," Mike muttered.

Andy ignored him. Julianne returned with a basket of crackers, warm rolls and butter. Finian noticed that she was flushed, more so than she should have been even with the running back and forth from Hurley's kitchen to their table. "Let me know if you need anything else," she said, crisp, marginally controlled.

"I'll see you tomorrow on the docks?" Andy asked.

"Bright and early. You'll be there with my boat?"

"I'll be there with the *Julianne*." Andy tilted his chair onto two legs. "Bright and early for me is four."

"Good, you won't keep me waiting," she said and spun off again.

Finian poured the whiskey as Mike, Colin and Kevin grinned at their lobsterman brother. Andy didn't look at all embarrassed. "Jules and I go way back. She'll get over whatever's eating her."

"What are you doing with the boat?" Emma asked him, nibbling on a cracker.

"Showing her the progress I've made on restoring it."

Mike reached for a cracker, too. "And that's supposed to calm her down?"

"She'll see I'm treating it with respect and calm down. What chance would it have had if her father had kept it? So," Andy said, obviously looking to change the subject, "what's the story with this Russian yacht in Heron's Cove? I was down there today. Wow. Emma, you know the owner? I hear he's a Sharpe client."

"Former," she amended.

"Colin had a drink on board," Kevin said.

He pushed aside a plate of clamshells. "Think I've arrived?"

"Yeah, Colin, you've arrived," Andy said. "Rusakov invite you to the Bahamas?"

"Not yet. There's time."

Mike ate his cracker in two bites. "I don't know if it's the whiskey but I don't have a good feeling about what's going on."

Kevin Donovan sat forward, out of uniform but looking every inch the Maine state marine patrol officer he was. "I don't, either." His gray-eyed gaze leveled on Emma, then Colin. "We don't have anything on Rusakov."

"Pop and I talked while we planted tulip bulbs," Mike said. "It was the Russian mob who gave you those bruises, wasn't it, Colin? You don't have to answer, but if any of those bastards show up around here—"

"You'll call Kevin or me," Colin said.

"Or Emma," Mike added with a devilish grin.

Finian held up his bottle of Bracken 15 year old before the battle was on. "Shall we retaste my favorite Irish whiskey?"

The early risers Andy and Kevin said good-night and left after a modest amount of whiskey. In another few minutes, Mike and Colin excused themselves and headed outside and down to the pier in the dark, for reasons Finian couldn't fathom. Emma stayed at her place at the table. When he saw her troubled look, he got up and went behind the empty bar, returning with a bottle of Auchentoshan.

He uncorked the Scotch and splashed a little in a glass. "A *taoscán* of Auchentoshan will put the color back in your cheeks," he said. "This is Auchentoshan 12 year old. You've had it before. It's a delicate yet complex single-malt Scotch whisky, made without a trace of peat, triple-distilled and matured in oak casks. It's a gorgeous whisky."

"I remember I liked it." She took the glass from Finian and

gestured with it toward the silhouette of the two men down on the pier. "Colin and Mike are thick as thieves."

"The Donovans are quite a clan."

"Mike's right. I don't belong here."

"Don't think about belonging, perhaps, and think instead about making a place for yourself."

Emma didn't seem to hear him. "I found Sister Joan. I was at the convent when she was killed. Now Dmitri Rusakov is in Heron's Cove. Maybe I should go back there." She kept her gaze fixed on the starlit docks. "Colin needs a chance to decompress."

"What if he's saying the same about you?"

"I don't need to decompress."

"Don't you, Emma? You went straight from your ordeal with Sister Joan's death to Colin's...situation." Finian corked the Auchentoshan. "You've had a fair amount of stress in recent weeks."

"I'm an FBI agent, Fin. I'm trained to deal with stress."

"And Colin isn't?"

"He is, but it's different. Trust me when I say he needs to decompress."

"He thinks you're hiding something about your relationship with the Russians aboard this yacht in Heron's Cove. He didn't tell me as much, but I can see it."

She took a roll from the basket and broke it open. "I don't know, I might wish my secrets were as juicy as all that. I'm an ex-nun, remember?"

"You have work secrets, personal secrets, family secrets. I came to the priesthood already in my thirties, a widower, a man who'd known love. You were just a teenager when you became a postulant."

"I was in college, living at home. I didn't move into the convent until I made my first vows as a novice."

"You were drawn to the focus and containment of convent life. I suspect you were drawn to the FBI for similar reasons. You know who you are in each of those environments. You know what's expected of you. Life with Colin…" Finian shrugged, half smiled. "I expect it's messier."

Emma smiled back at him. "You could say that." She poured some water and drank it down. "I'm not driving after even just a few sips of this stuff."

"I see that Mike's left Colin alone on the docks. I'll clean up here."

"Fin…Father Bracken…"

He patted her hand. "Fin is perfect. I'm your friend, Emma. That's all."

"It's a lot. Thank you."

He finished the small amount of whiskey he had poured for himself as Emma left for the evening. Then he cleaned up and said good-night to the Hurley's staff. He didn't see Julianne Maroney. Diners had dwindled to just a few watching a football match at the bar. Finian had concluded early on that he would never follow American football. The game made little sense to him. He preferred Irish hurling and Gaelic football.

The cold air took him by surprise, but he appreciated it after the clams, whiskey, Donovans and Emma, not to mention Julianne Maroney. He descended the steps from the rustic restaurant to the small parking lot. He had allowed himself to overdramatize his brief conversation with the man the other night and then his supposed sighting of him that morning. Finian knew it wasn't just Colin's work, his absence, the days of worry among his family and friends that had him on edge. To place blame solely on the Donovans—and Emma—was a disservice to them, and ultimately, he thought, dishonest.

The truth was, his doubts about his role in Rock Point had also contributed to his reaction to the man in the black jacket

the other night and again that morning. The newness of life
in a small Maine fishing village and his work in the parish
had worn off since his arrival in June. He felt foreign and out
of place, and more than that, he felt useless. He could never
belong in Rock Point the way the Donovans did. He could
never follow his own advice to Emma and make a place for
himself there. He would always stand apart.

"Bean holes," he muttered.

But he reminded himself that he wasn't in Rock Point to
belong. He looked up at the sky and saw scattered stars, as
sparkling and as bright as any wish he had ever had, and he
remembered his faith and his purpose. He laughed to himself,
welcoming the prospect of the cold walk back to the rectory.

Mike Donovan rolled up out of the shadows by his truck.
"Come on, Father. I'll give you a ride home."

Home. Finian never referred to the rectory as home. It was
always "back to the rectory" or "back to St. Patrick's" for
him. Home was Ireland. Home was his and Sally's cottage
in the Iveragh hills.

Perhaps that was another part of why he had latched onto
the FBI dramas.

He smiled at Mike. "Are you keeping watch on me, my
friend?"

"Yep." He motioned to the truck. "Climb in."

"One does always know where one stands with a Donovan." Finian got into the truck, as spotless as he would have
expected of a man as intentional and controlled as Mike
Donovan. "I noticed you didn't overimbibe this evening."

"Never do," Mike said, starting the old truck. "You
wouldn't have these whiskey tastings if any of us did. Although if I were Colin, I might curl up with a bottle for a
few days. You saw his bruises?"

"I did see them," Finian said.

"He didn't get them running into a desk in Washington. I think these Russian gangsters got hold of him. You read about the arrest of Vladimir Bulgov? He ran an international arms trafficking network. I think Colin was in on that."

Mike pulled out onto the quiet street and drove up to St. Patrick's with more speed and twists and turns than Finian believed was necessary. The rattling truck didn't inspire confidence, either.

He held on to the door handle. "Colin hasn't told you the real nature of his work with the FBI, has he?"

"Nope. He won't. He's loosening up some, seeing how we've figured it out on our own, but not much. I guess it's good he can talk to Emma about what happened." Mike paused, then said, "Think I'm too hard on her, Father?"

"What matters is what you think," Finian said, dodging that one.

"She's tougher than she looks. Tougher than you might think, given her background."

"As a religious sister or as a Sharpe?"

Mike didn't hesitate. "Both."

"You might consider the strength it takes to embrace the life of a religious sister."

"Poverty, chastity and obedience? Poverty I could do. The other two? Nope. Not for me."

"You're thinking of these vows in narrow terms."

"I'm sure I am," Mike said with a grin.

When Mike pulled in front of the dark church and rectory, Finian suddenly wished he had left on more lights. Any lights, for that matter.

"Thank you for the lift," he said, opening the truck door. "And thank you again for your help digging bean holes earlier today."

"Bean holes and tulips." Mike gave a mock shudder. "I gotta get back up north."

Finian laughed as he climbed out of the truck, expecting Mike to go on his way. Instead, he got out, too.

He nodded to the small church and rectory. "I'll take a look around."

"That's not necessary. I'm sure I exaggerated—"

"I'll feel better," Mike said.

Finian realized further protest would get him nowhere and went with Mike, checking all the doors to the church and both the front and back door to the rectory. They discovered nothing more treacherous than a note from a parishioner with a list of pies being donated for the bean-hole supper. Finian had no idea what the eldest Donovan would do if they had found something amiss, or an intruder hiding in the shrubs, but suspected he was in good hands. In any event, all was well.

"Keep a light on at the front door and back door," Mike said as they returned to his truck. "And lock up."

"I will. Thank you, Mike."

"Anytime." The dark night brought out the angles of his face so that he looked even more ferocious. "If you get spooked, give a yell. My folks put me up in a room with cross-stitch samplers and rose wallpaper. The other rooms are either occupied or they're working on them. I wouldn't mind camping out on your sofa."

Finian bit back a smile and nodded. "I'll keep that in mind. Thank you again."

"No worries."

Mike got back in his truck and drove off. Finian shivered in the chilly air and went into the rectory, realizing he was in much better spirits than when the evening had started. He thought of his visit with elderly Franny Maroney and smiled, marveling at how two people could look at something with such different eyes. He had convinced himself he had done more harm than good in visiting her, but she had been satisfied, perhaps now on the road to reconciliation with God over her husband's death.

Then again, Julianne Maroney could have told him what he wanted to hear. But he thought of her banging the water pitcher on the table and scowling at Andy Donovan, and he doubted that it was in her nature to do anything but call things as she saw them.

Finian took a mystery by an Irish writer upstairs with him. He wanted a touch of home. He would take a bath and read into the evening, putting aside any thought of an intruder wandering the streets of Rock Point and Heron's Cove.

19

EMMA SAT ON A COMFORTABLE CHAIR AT AN angle in front of Colin's fireplace. His house was warmer, already felt lived-in again. On the walk up from the harbor, he had told her about Finian Bracken's stranger. Even if Finian had called the local police immediately, they would have needed some luck to find the man who'd approached him, given the vague description. And what would they have done if they had found him? He had merely talked to a priest on a public street.

The description didn't fit Ivan, at least. Less certain was whether it fit any of the men who had tried to kill Colin in Fort Lauderdale.

Emma could feel his tension as he built a fire, down on one knee. Withdrawing from an undercover mission under the best of circumstances was difficult. In September, he had come home to Sister Joan's murder. Now, he had come home to more complications from Emma's past.

"Horner, Yuri and Boris didn't just disappear," she said. "We'll find them. They know you're not getting them weapons. They know the FBI's looking for them."

He struck a wooden match to the kindling. "Are they more afraid of us or of a disappointed buyer? I was taking them to a garage we had under surveillance, playing what came next by ear—"

"You wouldn't have arrested them until you had their buyer."

"Not a chance. And I want to know who's bankrolling them. Their operation is amateurish, opportunistic."

"That doesn't make it less lethal," Emma said.

Colin glanced up at her. "They're killers. I got away but the next poor bastard they want to shoot and throw overboard might not."

"I know. We all want the same thing." She heard a crackle as the fire took hold. "Pete Horner and his men know you're a federal agent, but they don't know your name, where you live."

Colin stood and shut the brass-edged glass fireplace doors. "Would your friend Ivan tell them?"

Emma gave up any pretense with him, too. "Ivan doesn't tell anyone much."

"Did he break into Natalie Warren's house?"

"We should focus on Pete Horner."

"I am." Colin watched the fire spread from the rolled-up newspapers to the kindling sticks, the flames reflected in the brass trim of the doors. "I don't like leaving a mission unfinished."

"No one's left anything unfinished. We're making progress. It just feels slow."

"You didn't come across Bulgov's name when you investigated the disappearance of the Rusakov collection four years ago?"

Emma shook her head. "My grandfather and I were convinced Renee Rusakov had taken it from Dmitri. It was up to Dmitri to decide what to do about it."

"A personal matter," Colin said.

"Exactly."

She eased off the chair and sat on the floor in front of the fire. She stretched out her legs, her boots still on. She was tempted to take them off but wasn't sure she would be staying.

Colin remained on his feet, staring at the fire.

"I love this time of year," she said. "The leaves falling, the nights turning cool. It'll be Thanksgiving before we know it."

He pulled his gaze from the fire, as if he were making a conscious effort to focus on something besides the missing arms traffickers. "Where are you spending Thanksgiving?" he asked, sitting next to her on the floor.

"I don't know yet. We used to always spend Thanksgiving in Heron's Cove. If it wasn't too icy, we'd walk on the rocks together, check out tide pools and watch the birds. My father can't do that anymore, with his back. He and my mother are in London for the year, and Granddad's in Dublin. He hasn't been back to Heron's Cove in ages." Emma realized Colin had moved very close to her, their hips almost touching. "What about you?"

"I've spent every Thanksgiving in Rock Point."

"You were piecing together Bulgov's network last year."

"We didn't zero in on him as our primary target until spring. I was on the outer fringes of his network at Thanksgiving." Colin studied the fire a moment. "Bulgov's a charmer. A lethal, amoral charmer."

"But he's talking," Emma said, half speculating.

"Not enough."

"What's Pete Horner like?"

"He's a devil-may-care pilot who's bounced around for

years and saw his chance at the brass ring when Bulgov was arrested."

"He thought you were an easy route to weapons." Emma, too, found herself staring at the flames. "He and his Russian friends decide it's too risky to trust a turncoat FBI agent and try to kill you. Instead you escape, and then you come home to Dmitri Rusakov and this wild tale about a Russian Art Nouveau collection."

"That's it in a nutshell."

Emma felt the heat from the fire. "Colin...I don't want to complicate your life because I'm a Sharpe."

"Too late," he said lightly, then glanced around the small room with its dark wood ceiling beams, white walls and deep neutral furnishings. "My folks will have us all to the inn for Thanksgiving, but I could do a decent gathering here. This isn't a bad room."

"It's a great room," Emma said.

"How would you decorate it? What color would you paint the walls?"

"You know that sort of thing doesn't matter to me—"

"It matters to me. What you want. Who you are." He turned to her, the fire reflected in the smoke-gray of his eyes. "You won't be able to stay in Heron's Cove once renovations pick up. It's hard enough to stay there now. You know the house won't be the same once it's finished."

"I have my apartment in Boston."

"Good location but it's not much bigger than your room at the convent."

Emma had forgotten that he had seen the novice quarters at the Sisters of the Joyful Heart during the investigation into Sister Joan's murder. She supposed it was a good thing. Colin didn't have to imagine her day-to-day life as a novice.

He crossed his ankles, the fire blazing now. "Do you ever think about buying your own place in Heron's Cove?"

"I can stay with them anytime." She glanced around the quiet living room, the crackle of the fire and the ticking of the cuckoo clock the only sounds. "As for here…a soft white on the walls would be nice."

"They're white now."

"It's not a soft white, and I'd add some color. You know the decorators' rule of thumb. Sixty percent the main color, thirty percent a secondary color and ten percent an accent color."

"Nope. Didn't know the decorators' rule of thumb."

"You don't really have an accent color. But it's a good room, Colin. Solid, like you."

"Solid and serviceable, huh?"

She smiled. "Historic? Classic? Intense?" She shifted back to the fire. "Do you ever wonder what your life would be like if you'd stayed a lobsterman?"

"I could be Andy, breaking hearts up and down the Maine coast."

"That's not what I meant."

"I know it's not." He stood, stared at the fire a moment, then looked at her. "Here's the thing, Emma. I want to know everything about you. No holding back. You're all in with me."

She leaned back, taking him in from his boots up the full length of his body to his eyes, her breath catching in her throat at just how sexy he was. And how intense.

"And you?" She met his gaze as she got to her feet. "Do I get to know everything about you?"

"What else is there to know?" He left it at that as he eyed her. "So tell me, Sister Brigid. Do you ever lose your temper and throw things?"

"Why do you ask? Are you about to test my patience?"

"You have a personal connection to this case."

"Yes," she said. "Pete Horner and his men almost killed you."

Colin tilted his head back, studied her. "That's not what I'm talking about. You've been in touch with your brother and grandfather. You sent Lucas to London to research Tatiana Pavlova."

"It makes sense. She's here because she's worried about a collection that involves a former Sharpe Fine Art Recovery client."

"Rusakov, Alexander and Tatiana Pavlova are Russian. Alexander tipped you off about me. Now they're here in Maine with you." Colin's voice was low, controlled, his eyes unwavering. "And, not incidentally, you and I are sleeping together."

"Ah. Is that so?"

"Getting annoyed, Emma? Looking for a vase or something to throw?"

"I'm not hiding anything from you."

"You did."

"You mean Ivan," she said. "You have confidential sources, don't you? You disappear for weeks at a time with hardly a word to anyone. Even I know next to nothing about your undercover life."

"For good reason," he said.

"And for good reason I didn't tell you about Ivan."

"Emma, even if your Russian friends have nothing to do with arms trafficking, I don't need them checking me out."

She took in a breath. "Fair enough. I've kept Yank and the team informed. And you." She reined in a sudden mix of emotions. "Trust me or not, Colin. It's your choice."

He didn't relent. "You have to straighten this out. Decide who you are. A Sharpe, an FBI agent, an ex-nun. My lover."

"I'm all of those things."

"Maybe that's the problem."

"I didn't think there was a problem." She was cool, angry, hurt. She whirled across the room to the front door, half expecting, half hoping Colin would stop her, but he didn't. She pulled open the door and looked back at him. "I'll figure this out. Rest. Be with your family."

He almost smiled. "You do want to throw something."

She walked out of the house before she did just that.

The cold air jolted Emma out of her anger, and she shivered on the front walk, feeling strangely alone, with Colin frustrated with her, her entire family in London and Ireland. She reminded herself that she had friends, including several sisters at the convent, and a team behind her in Boston.

She glanced back at Colin's house, regretting that she let him get to her. That had been his intention, she realized. He didn't like Finian Bracken's story of the man who approached him across from Hurley's and had possibly followed Tatiana Pavlova in Heron's Cove. He didn't like feeling as if his friends and family were potential targets, even if just of the thoroughness and curiosity of a wealthy Russian who liked, as the saying went, to keep his friends close and his enemies closer.

Steamed clams, crackers, a roll and whiskey didn't make for the greatest dinner. She could go to Lucas's house and raid his refrigerator, but she wasn't particularly hungry.

Colin's questions, his prodding, seeing Dmitri and Ivan again, talking with Natalie and even Tatiana about the collection and the events of four years ago had all, Emma realized, dragged her back to that uneasy time between the convent and the FBI. They raised questions, if not doubts. Had she chosen the right path in leaving Sharpe Fine Art Recovery?

Mike Donovan's truck rattled around the corner, its headlights on as it pulled over next to her. He rolled down his window. "Hey, Emma. What're you doing out in the cold?"

"I'm just—" She stopped, manufactured a smile. "I'm heading back to Heron's Cove."

Mike sighed, one hand still on the wheel. "Colin's doing his caged-lion thing. I could see it when we were at Hurley's. You wouldn't want a perfect guy, I hope."

She shoved her hands into her jacket pockets, wished she could feel warm. "I'm not sure he and I will make it." The words were out before she could pull them back. "Never mind. He's your brother. Forget it."

"Yeah. He's my brother. That's how I know he can be a jerk sometimes. Takes time for us Donovans to let anyone in. Not every woman's up to that."

Emma smiled. "You guys are all so different and yet—"

"And yet we all can kick ass when we need to." Mike nodded toward the house. "Before you go back to Heron's Cove, tell my rock-headed brother that I saw Father Bracken back to the rectory. All's quiet at Saint Pat's."

"That's good, but maybe you should tell him yourself."

His dark gray eyes narrowed on her. "I'm not one for giving romantic advice since I live alone in the woods, but I have one thing to say. Stop keeping score."

"We're not keeping score."

"Yeah, you are."

Her mouth snapped shut. "You can be a jerk sometimes, too, Mike."

He grinned. "You've got backbone, I'll say that, Special Agent Sharpe. Hang in there. You can handle Colin." Mike winked at her. "I have a feeling he can handle you, too."

He rolled up his window and drove off, leaving Emma to give Colin the message. Maybe it would reassure Colin to know his friend was home safe. Maybe it would ease his intense mood just to know that his eldest brother was fine, too—that all was well in Rock Point.

"And maybe you're just looking for an excuse to go back in there," she muttered to herself.

Her anger dissipated. Colin was a straightforward, no-nonsense man who also had a sense of humor. He was loyal, grounded, with a good feel for people—and himself. He was back from a difficult ordeal, his exit from his mission unsatisfying, at least in his own mind. It wouldn't occur to him that not getting killed on Friday night in Fort Lauderdale had been a positive outcome.

He hadn't come home to a quiet few days kayaking and drinking whiskey. He was still on alert when what he really needed was to decompress.

Emma headed back up the walk and front steps. He had left the door unlocked. She went in, the living room warm, cozy with the fire. Colin wasn't there. She walked back to the kitchen and found him opening a bottle of Smithwick's at the sink.

"It tastes better in Ireland," he said.

"I just saw Mike."

"He texted me. Told me to be nice."

"Big brother," she said with a smile.

Colin drank some of his beer, then set the bottle on the counter and stood close to her. He touched her hair. "You're worried Yank's lost faith in you. I can tell, Emma. I remember when I worried about the same thing."

"If I am, it's the least of my worries."

"If Yank had lost faith in you, you'd be talking to your grandfather about a job right now. He wouldn't just boot you off his team. He'd have your badge. This isn't about faith, or trust—"

"Skill? Competence?"

"It's about who you are."

"A Sharpe," she said.

"Even if Yank knew about Rusakov and Alexander, he didn't necessarily expect them to show up in Heron's Cove. If they're up to something—if anything goes wrong because they're up here—then Yank's in a mess, too."

"I understand that. At the same time, if I hadn't found out where you were, you'd be dead, Horner and his men would still be who they are, involved in whatever they're involved with and we wouldn't know as much as we do now."

"Hold on." Colin tapped a finger on her chin. "A correction, Special Agent Sharpe. I wouldn't be dead. I got away from those bastards. The tac team just saved me from having to fend them off again if they doubled back and came after me."

She couldn't resist a smile. "So cocky."

"The facts are the facts," he said with a grin that didn't last. "Was Ivan there, Emma?"

"If he had been, he wouldn't have let those men kill you. You could have spared yourself jumping overboard."

"Just what I want, your old flame saving my damn life. I'd rather jump and take my chances with the snakes and alligators." He was half teasing, half serious. He threaded his fingers into her hair. "Did you make a mistake trusting him?"

"You're alive. That's not a mistake. I doubt the timing of your situation and Ivan turning up in Heron's Cove is likely not a coincidence."

"It was just another day on the job for me." His hand eased to the back of her neck, and he drew her close, no humor in his eyes now. "Do you ever see yourself with kids, doing the work you do?"

His question caught her off guard. "In the abstract, sure, why not? I'm an analyst most days. I'm not a field agent. In terms of kids...well, I'd have to have a man in my life for starters."

"Which you do."

His mouth was close to hers. "Which I do. Do you think about having a family?"

"Maybe. I know what I'm doing in the field, but I'm still learning the ropes with you. Was it fear of having a man in your life, having kids that drove you to the convent, Sister Brigid?"

"It wasn't fear. I wasn't running from the world. I was embracing a life." She brought her hand up, touched her fingertips to the hard line of his jaw. "I thought I was. That's part of what the novitiate process helped me figure out."

He caught her fingers in his, his eyes dusky, intent on her. "I think I might want to sweep you off your feet again."

"That'd be good. In fact, that'd be perfect."

"Done," he said, and caught an arm around her middle.

But Emma whispered, "Let's walk up together." She smiled. "Save your energy for other things."

"Looking out for me, Emma?"

"And maybe for myself, too," she said with a laugh.

His room was chilly when they reached it, but their skin was already heated by the time they slipped between the sheets. Colin gave an exaggerated, entirely fake shiver and drew her close to him. "Can't think of a better way to warm up."

Emma wrapped her arms around him, felt the taut muscles in his back, along his hips. "Me, either," she managed to say.

"From wanting to throw something at me to this." His eyes sparked with amusement as he settled on top of her, held her in the near-darkness. "Be yourself with me, Emma. You think a lot. You can always tell me what you're thinking."

"And what about you? What are you thinking right now?"

He smiled. "I'm a simple man," he said, lowering his mouth to hers. "I'm just thinking about making love to you."

20

LUCAS SPOTTED URSULA FINCH ACROSS THE busy hotel lobby. He was at his table in the adjoining restaurant, his breakfast of eggs, scones and jam finished but his plans for the day in flux. *Looks as if it'll start with a chat with Ms. Finch,* he thought, heading out to the lobby. He passed a trio of businessmen, his khakis, dark sweater and scuffed shoes a contrast to their expensive suits and ties. Ursula, he noticed, wore another black suit, the skirt coming just to her knees, but she had on killer red heels. She carried a black leather tote, and he wondered if she had tucked a pair of walking shoes in there and changed into the heels as she entered the hotel. He really didn't have a good feel for her, he decided.

"Sorry I didn't call ahead," she said as he approached her. "I'm on my way to work."

"It's fine. Good to see you. What's up?"

"I checked our records."

She lowered her tote to a chair, out of the way of the main bustle of the lobby. Her hair was carefully pulled back, everything about her visibly under control, despite the current of tension Lucas felt from her. "Would you like to sit down?" he asked.

She shook her head. "I can't stay long. I just wanted to let you know that Tatiana has done a number of commissions for our Russian clients, but no one stands out. It's not as if every Russian is a criminal, you know."

"Of course," Lucas said, calm. "Would all her commissions be in your records?"

Ursula hesitated, then said, "I have no reason to think otherwise."

"Ursula," Lucas said, glancing past her for a moment, then meeting her eye again. "I think you know more about what's going on with Tatiana than you've said—or you at least suspect more. It's time to say what's on your mind. For her sake as well as your own."

"She's a sweet soul. She has heart. She's a fighter, too, though. She has such spirit but she's up against so much." Ursula lowered her eyes. "I don't want to see her hurt."

"What is she up against?"

"Her past." Ursula fingered the strap on her bag, clearly uncomfortable. "At least that's what I think. She seldom talks about her life in Russia and then only in generalities. She was raised by her grandparents. Her mother was an artist who died in a car accident when Tatiana was small. That sort of thing."

"What about her father?"

"She never knew him. That's what she told me, anyway." Ursula straightened, as if she had just made up her mind to say what she came to say and get it over with. "There was this one incident. It was a few months ago—late June or early July. A man was here. He was Russian. Tall, very fit. I mean, you and I are fit but this guy…" She gave a little shudder. "He must have been some kind of bodyguard, a soldier. Something."

"A police officer, maybe?"

"No. I don't know that, of course, since I have no idea who he was, but—no. He wasn't a police officer. Tatiana knew him. She seemed happy to see him, but surprised, even awkward."

"She didn't introduce him to you?" Lucas asked.

Ursula shook her head. "I was in the back room. I started to come out when I saw him, and I immediately realized it was a private, personal meeting and stayed in back. He was only there a few minutes. I didn't tell you until now because I didn't think of it, and because—well, frankly, I didn't think it was any of your business. I'm still not sure it is. Sorry."

"Not a problem. So why did you tell me?"

"I spoke to Tatiana last night. I called. She didn't call me." Ursula grabbed her bag, hoisted it back onto her shoulder. "She wasn't herself. I'm worried about her."

"Did you tell her about me?"

"Yes, but I was already worried. She's not telling me something. To be honest, I've felt that ever since she decided to make this trip to the U.S. I know her, Lucas. I get that she doesn't want to talk about her past, that it's complicated—that she was a child at an exciting but turbulent time in Russia. She's built a good life for herself here in London."

"I understand," Lucas said.

Ursula seemed calmer. "She left London in such haste. She gave me a key to her apartment, in case she needed me to get in while she was away. To water her plants or check on things. You know." Ursula glanced toward the busy hotel entrance, as if the doormen might call the police on her, then reached into a side pocket of her bag, pulled out a set of keys and handed them to Lucas. "I have a packed schedule today. Perhaps you could check on Tatiana's apartment for me."

He folded the keys into his palm. "Happy to."

"I'm trusting you, Lucas."

"For good reason. I'm trustworthy." When she didn't smile at his remark, he added, "I'll return the keys to the Firebird when I've finished."

"Give them to me personally." She attempted a smile. "Well. I'll see you, then."

Ursula seemed marginally reassured as she crossed the lobby and left the hotel. Lucas took the elevator back up to his room. He checked his map of London. Tatiana's apartment was within reasonable walking distance, and it was another beautiful day in London. He packed his bag but didn't check out, and in a few minutes was on his way.

It wasn't even dawn yet in Heron's Cove. He would call Emma later. Ursula's description of the Russian who visited Tatiana Pavlova at the Firebird was worth noting but not worth getting his sister out of bed.

Regardless of whose bed she was in, Lucas thought with a wince.

He found Tatiana's quiet residential street without making a wrong turn or, he was reasonably certain, without being followed. He wasn't an expert at spotting a tail but once he moved off busy Park Lane, he would have noticed anyone— thug or otherwise—taking the same route he was. Tatiana's apartment was located on the second floor of a town house on the corner, with window boxes trailing ivy and a glossy red-painted door.

There was no doorman, and Lucas let himself into the vestibule with one of the keys, then walked up the stairs. He didn't run into anyone before he unlocked Tatiana's door and went in.

Tatiana Pavlova, he noticed right away, was not a neat freak at home, either.

The apartment was small, with decent natural light and a

whimsical flair to the furnishings. The wood floor was almost entirely covered with an off-white rug and a gold-edged mirror hung above a low, off-white sofa. The sofa was overflowing with throw pillows, their owner's artistic eye in the mix of bright colors, patterns and textures. A painted dropfront desk was stacked with books on Russian fairy tales, fables, folktales, legends and mythology.

Above the desk hung large framed black-and-white photographs of Paris 1900, the world's fair that celebrated the turn-of-the-century and was dominated by Art Nouveau. The City of Light illuminated its famous landmarks with electric lights, including, for the first time, the Eiffel Tower. The exhibition was also known for bringing together the luxury artists and craftsmen of the day, including legends Carl Fabergé, Louis Comfort Tiffany, René Lalique, Henri Vever and Siegfried Bing, who gave the short-lived but influential Art Nouveau movement its name with his Paris shop, *L'Art Nouveau*. Tatiana undoubtedly would have studied their work in developing her own vision and style.

Given how messy she was, Lucas couldn't tell if the place had been ransacked, but he saw no indication of a break-in or intruder. He supposed Ursula Finch could have slipped the keys to someone else, or had a look around before giving them to him, but he didn't really think so. She seemed torn between wanting to help Tatiana and wanting to keep anything she was into from harming their upscale boutique.

He lowered the desk's drop-front, sketch pads, loose papers and envelopes falling out, as if she'd had them out and shut them up inside without putting them away first. The open cubbies were all likewise stuffed and overflowing.

Lucas grimaced. It would take hours to go through everything just in the desk.

He closed it and checked the bedroom, big enough for

a small lamp table and a double bed with a slender, white-painted four-poster iron frame. The bed, surprisingly, was neatly made. The coverlet was white, with white lace-edged pillows and one decorative pillow with a cheerful red heart stitched against a white background. Chubby Russian nesting dolls were lined up in a row on the windowsill.

Lucas noted the stack of magazines and books on the small table, the heap of laundry on the floor at the foot of the bed. He peeked in the closet—lots of oranges, rusts, deep blues and turquoise, almost no black, and a gigantic mess.

He shut the door and checked the bathroom. A pedestal sink was covered in bottles and tubes, white towels hung haphazardly from a single bar and a family of rubber ducks was lined up on the edge of the tub.

How could a woman who had rubber ducks be a danger to anyone?

Lucas returned to the living room and crossed into the separate kitchen. Sunlight streamed through a filmy curtain on a double window overlooking the street. The cabinets, countertops and walls were white, the towels and pot holders were red, complemented by framed illustrations of Russian fairy tales next to copper-bottomed pots on hooks.

The top of the farmhouse table was buried under computer printouts of internet articles. Lucas flipped through them, stiffening as he saw they were all on either Dmitri Rusakov or Vladimir Bulgov, including one from the *Los Angeles Times* on Bulgov's arrest in June on multiple charges.

Lucas thought of the visit from the Russian that Ursula Finch had mentioned. Had one of Vladimir Bulgov's men come to warn Tatiana? Talk to her about his arrest? Threaten her?

Who the hell was she? Bulgov's ex-lover, a friend, a relative—one of the Russian arms trafficker's many enemies?

Where did Dmitri Rusakov fit in? The printouts on him were mostly about his energy businesses and lifestyle. As far as Lucas could see, the Russian tycoon hadn't been arrested and wasn't under suspicion for any criminal conduct. Some of his business decisions were controversial, and he was often at odds with Russian politicians.

Lucas dug through more of the papers on the table. Maybe Tatiana had her own axes to grind with her compatriots.

He came to a sketch pad and opened it, discovering pencil drawings of Russian nesting dolls in Tatiana's unique style. She had jotted notes about colors and materials, but it was the scrawl at the bottom of one of the drawings, underlined several times, that caught Lucas's attention: *Vladimir Bulgov wants them by July 1!!!!!*

It was as if she were giving herself a little goose to make sure she finished the nesting dolls on time.

Vladimir Bulgov was under arrest in the U.S. and living in a federal cell on July 1.

So when had he commissioned Tatiana Pavlova to create a set of Russian nesting dolls?

Damn good question, Lucas thought as he shut the sketch pad.

He locked up and took the stairs back down to the main floor, then walked toward his hotel. Did Ursula Finch know about Tatiana's work for Bulgov? Had Ursula given Lucas the key to her apartment hoping that he would find out on his own, without her having to tell him?

He decided to make a detour to the Firebird Boutique. He was so preoccupied with what he found in Tatiana's apartment that he forgot to check to make sure he wasn't being followed. He paused at a busy corner and looked around him.

Just down the street, a man with a shaved head stopped and crouched down, as if to check a loose shoelace. He was in a suit and looked more like a banker than a thug, but Lucas was convinced it was the same man he had seen outside the pub and then at his hotel. He couldn't get a good look at the man's face without drawing attention to himself.

Lucas put his hand on his phone, ready to call the London police if he needed to, and abruptly crossed the street, dodging a cab, the driver swearing at him through an open window.

Maintaining his brisk pace, Lucas zigzagged through a small park, then ducked down another street. He glanced behind him but didn't see the man he had spotted—or anyone else—following him.

He passed upscale Mayfair shops he didn't recognize. He hoped he wasn't getting himself lost, but he had a decent sense of direction and ended up at the Firebird—without, he was fairly certain, a tail.

Ursula Finch opened the door herself but didn't seem that happy to see him. "I didn't expect to see you again so soon," she said. "Have you been to Tatiana's apartment?"

"Just coming from there." He handed her the keys as he followed her into the elegant showroom. "Vladimir Bulgov commissioned Tatiana to do a set of Russian nesting dolls. Did you know?"

"Yes," Ursula said, her voice clipped.

"Is he a Firebird client?"

"No. Absolutely not." She was emphatic as she stood behind the desk. "It was a onetime private arrangement between him and Tatiana."

"You okayed it?"

Ursula gave a tight nod. "I'm sure Tatiana had no idea at the time that he was—well, a gangster. I didn't, but I didn't like him from the start. People say he's charming but he rubbed me the wrong way. He came here with bodyguards. Not unusual among our very wealthy clients, but they were…" She hesitated, working a simple silver ring on her finger. "I don't think they wanted to be here, or wanted him here. It wasn't anything they said. Just a feeling."

"Why nesting dolls?"

"I don't know. Tatiana never explained and I didn't ask. It wasn't any of my business."

"Did she work on them here? Did she finish them?"

Ursula exhaled, avoiding Lucas's eye as she traced a finger across the gleaming desktop, obviously just to have something to do. "Yes. Tatiana worked on them here, and she finished them. They're incredible—some of her best work. Mr. Bulgov never came for them, of course, since he was arrested."

"Had Tatiana finished the dolls before his arrest?"

"I think so, yes. They're locked away in her studio."

"When was he last here?" Lucas asked.

"In April. I looked up the date last night." She raised her gaze to him. "In case you asked."

"You had to let me find out on my own."

"It's unsettling. Telling you myself would make me feel more involved, and I'm not. Not really." She straightened, getting some of her starchy demeanor back. "I'm sure you understand."

Lucas thought he did. "I know this is difficult for you, Ursula, but I need to understand what's going on."

She seemed slightly less uncomfortable and defensive. "You'd like to think you'd sniff out a dog like that, wouldn't you? Tatiana is a designer, Lucas. She's not mixed up with Russian or any other organized crime. I can't imagine she even knows anything about weapons, except maybe Russian medieval swords and such."

From his quick search of Tatiana's apartment, Lucas couldn't imagine she was criminally involved with arms traffickers, either.

Ursula scowled, took a step back from the desk. "One would think the FBI is more concerned with Bulgov's interest in shoulder-fired missiles than in Russian nesting dolls."

"What about Dmitri Rusakov?" Lucas asked. "Did Tatiana have anything to do with him?"

"I know nothing about him, I'm afraid. Except who he is. He's not a client, and he wasn't with Mr. Bulgov when he came to see Tatiana, at least not that I know of."

Lucas nodded toward the back room. "I'd like to go up and take another look at her studio," he said, not making it a question.

Ursula sighed, then reluctantly led him up to the messy creative room where Tatiana Pavlova spent much of her time.

"I'm going to take a closer look," Lucas said, a hand on the edge of her main worktable.

"Do what you have to do." Ursula crossed her arms and paced, clearly impatient, even nervous—and annoyed. "I believe in Tatiana. I hope that whatever you find will help ease your suspicion of her."

"I'm not suspicious. I just need to know what's going on."

"I don't like feeling like a snitch."

"Understood."

Lucas glanced at the messy worktable, no idea of where to begin. Then he noticed a pendant in the shape of a nightingale on top of a small lacquered box, as if it were perched there. It sparkled with clusters of gleaming gems.

He lifted the nightingale between two fingers and turned to Ursula. "Is this genuine?"

Ursula lowered her arms to her sides as she frowned at the pendant. "I've always assumed it's a replica."

"It'd be worth quite a lot if it's real," he said.

"More than Tatiana could afford on her own," Ursula added.

"Did you ever talk to her about it?"

"No. It didn't occur to me, and she never mentioned it. We both have our interests, and fortunately we're always very busy with our work. Why? Is the nightingale significant for some reason?"

Nightingale was the name of Dmitri Rusakov's yacht, Lucas thought as he carefully set the pendant aside. The lacquered box had a removable rather than a hinged lid. It was stuck, but he managed to get it off without breaking it and set it next to the nightingale.

Inside the box was a single, faded color photograph.

Using the pads of his fingers, Lucas lifted out the photograph, held it in the light by the window for a better look.

A man, a woman and a small child were standing in front of a black-iron fence in the snow, all three of them bundled up against a cold winter, smiling at the camera.

Lucas showed the photograph to Ursula. "Do you recognize these people?"

She shook her head. "Not straight off. It's not a recent picture, is it?"

"I don't think so, no. Could the girl be Tatiana?"

Ursula seemed reluctant to take a closer look. "It must be her, wouldn't you say?"

Lucas didn't push her and placed the photograph flat on the table, next to the nightingale. He took out his iPhone and snapped several shots of both items.

He slipped his iPhone in his jacket and turned to Ursula. "I don't know what's going on here, Ursula, but you need to take extra safety precautions until you hear back from me with an all clear. If you even think you're being followed or watched, call the police."

She went pale but nodded. "All right. Don't worry about me. Worry about Tatiana. What are you going to do?"

"I'm sending the pictures I just took to my sister. She's with the FBI. She's in Heron's Cove with Tatiana."

"Are you staying in London?"

"I'm catching the first flight I can back to Ireland."

"You want to talk to your grandfather," Ursula said.

Lucas managed a smile. "You have good instincts."

They returned to the showroom and she walked to the door with him. "I'll call Tatiana later," she said, then managed a small smile. "Thank you for looking after her."

"If you remember anything else—"

"I'll call you."

He was positive no one followed him back to his hotel, but he made sure he wasn't alone on the elevator up to his room. He collected his bag, checked out and grabbed a cab.

His first call was to his parents. He told them to look out for themselves. "One wrong look from anyone," he said, "and you call the police."

"Lucas?" his father asked. "What's wrong?"

"I think Granddad knows something he's not supposed to know."

"He knows a lot of things he's not supposed to know. It's the nature of the work he does."

Lucas immediately regretted the urgency in his voice. Stress always made his father's pain worse. "I know, Dad. Don't worry."

"Have you talked to him?"

"I've got a call in to him." The truth was he had only a vague idea of where his grandfather was. "Emma and I will figure out what's going on. Stay in touch."

He disconnected, glanced at his watch. Still early in Maine. He emailed Emma the photos he'd taken in Tatiana's studio and a note about the nesting dolls. After he hit Send, he gripped his phone, stifling a surge of anxiety. If the nightingale pendant was part of the Rusakov collection, how the hell had Tatiana Pavlova ended up with it?

Lucas sat back, impatient, hating the long drive to Heathrow. He'd get there just in time for his flight to Cork.

21

KEVIN DONOVAN STOOD AT HURLEY'S BACK window, pointing his coffee mug. "What's Julianne doing down there?"

Colin and Mike both got to their feet and went to the window, standing on either side of their youngest brother, in his Maine marine patrol uniform. Directly below them, Julianne Maroney was marching through the mud, her hair flying with the early-morning breeze, the incoming tide oozing under her L.L.Bean boots.

"She looks pissed," Mike said.

Kevin nodded. "I'll bet Andy stood her up."

The three brothers had met for breakfast, assuming Andy was either out with his lobster boat or with Julianne. Colin still had no food in the house. He was on his way to Heron's Cove. Emma was already there. When he left his house, she was picking fallen orange maple leaves off the dew-soaked windshield of her car. For a fleeting moment, he felt as if they were an ordinary couple heading to work. Colin wasn't sure what a normal life looked like for him anymore. He wasn't sure "normal life" and Emma Sharpe fit in the same sentence, but he couldn't imagine not having her as a part of whatever came next for him.

Not that "normal life" and Colin Donovan fit in the same sentence, either.

Julianne disappeared out of view. He took a last sip of his coffee and set the mug back on the table. "I'll go talk to her."

"You're the risk-taker of the family," Mike said with a grin.

Colin started to reach for his wallet but Kevin shook his head. "Go. Least we can do is buy you breakfast since you chose the short straw." He grinned, too. "Good luck."

Colin headed out, pulling on his canvas jacket. The light morning fog had cleared, the bright, brisk October day just the sort he had dreamed about the past month. He noticed Andy's lobster boat at its mooring thirty yards out from the main pier in the small, horseshoe-shaped harbor.

So his brother wasn't out checking his traps.

Julianne's boot prints trailed across the gray mud still exposed by the tide, which hadn't yet reached under Hurley's floorboards. Colin stepped into the mud, keeping to the right of Julianne's trail and out of the incoming tide. He figured Mike and Kevin were watching. He continued past the restaurant, then out of its view as he angled back above the tide line.

Hurley's was at his back now. Up ahead, just at the natural curve of the harbor, a small dock jutted into the water next to a boathouse that John Hurley used for his prized Boston whaler. The weathered-shingle exterior was covered with old lobster buoys.

Julianne stood at the end of the dock, next to a stack of lobster pots. She was leaning over, hands on her hips as she peered at several pots that had fallen into the shallow water. Out past the boathouse, bobbing in the rising tide, was the *Julianne,* the bone of contention between her and Andy Donovan—if not the only bone of contention.

Colin waved to her. "Hey, Julianne, how's it going?"

She didn't seem to hear him. He had noticed his brother's truck in Hurley's parking lot. Andy could have gone off with a friend on another boat, or he could have gotten distracted and was off helping someone. He had to see to any lobsters he had caught but he didn't punch a time clock.

Colin debated leaving Julianne to her mood, but she shifted, leaning even more over the edge of the dock, then yelled. "Andy!" She jerked upright. "Colin, help!"

He was already bolting across the mud, stones and threads of wet seaweed. "Hang on, Julianne," he called to her. "Don't move."

She ignored him and jumped into the water at the tip of the dock. An incoming swell hit her at the knees, but she stayed on her feet. She grabbed one of the fallen lobster pots, tossed it into the mud so that the tide wouldn't drag it back to her.

"It's Andy," she yelled. "He's not moving."

Colin charged into the water, taking in a breath at the jolt of cold as a wave rolled past his calves, then out again, sucking sand and tiny stones with it. Julianne shifted, and he saw Andy, wedged facedown between the lobster pots and one of the dock mooring posts. His arms were splayed out at his shoulders, his head turned so that his right cheek was in the mud. The dark blue shirt he wore was soaked through, his lower body already partially submerged in the tide.

His legs appeared to be hung up under the dock.

Julianne dropped onto her knees in the rising water. "He's breathing. He's got a big bump behind his ear."

"Go," Colin said. "Kevin's at Hurley's. He can get an ambulance out here."

"We can't wait. The tide's coming in. He'll drown. And

he has hypothermia. You can see his lips are purple. We need to get him out of the water."

"I know." Colin took her by the shoulders. "Julianne. Get Kevin. Now."

She nodded, stood. Water had soaked into her baggy, hip-length wool sweater, its pale gray matching the color of her face. "He moved our meeting later. He texted me last night. When I got down here and didn't see him, I was so mad—" She broke off. "I'll be right back."

Colin squatted down by Andy's shoulders and saw that Julianne was right and his brother was suffering from at least mild hypothermia. He was semiconscious, trying to speak. Colin placed a hand on his brother's arm. "It's okay, Andy. We'll get you warm and dry. How're your legs? Can you move them for me?"

He tried to push himself up, then sank back into the mud. "Julianne?"

"She's fine. Screaming your name, brother."

Andy swore at him and Colin figured that was a good sign. He heard men's voices and glanced behind him, saw Julianne with Mike and Kevin. Colin started to wave to his brothers, but they raced into the water, Julianne sprinting back onto the dock.

Mike fell in opposite Colin, on Andy's right side, Kevin at his head. They got up under him, lifting him, then waited as another swell rolled in. As the wave motion raised the dock, they freed Andy's legs.

"Let's get him up onto the dock," Mike said.

Moving in unison, they heaved him up onto the, dock, laying him flat on the dry wood. He shivered, moaned, swore some more, but Julianne was there, pulling off her sweater, only the lower edge wet. She draped it over Andy, not waiting for one of his three brothers to tell her what to do as they climbed onto the dock.

She raised her eyes to them. "I helped with beached dolphins. It's not that different."

"Ambulance is on the way," Kevin said, then squatted down and took a look at the lump behind Andy's ear. "How'd that happen?"

"Blindsided," Andy said, his teeth chattering as he clutched Julianne's sweater to him.

Mike frowned down at him. "Bad spot to get hit. You probably went right out. Took a few lobster pots with you, got caught under the dock."

"You're lucky Julianne came over here when she did," Colin said. "What were you doing?"

"I was stacking traps, waiting for Jules." Andy shivered, then moaned, as if his shivering made him hurt worse; his speech was slightly slurred with the onset of hypothermia. "Damn, my head feels like it's going to explode."

"Go easy," Mike said.

"I wasn't paying attention. Next thing, you're pulling me out from under the damn dock and I'm freezing my ass off."

Kevin stood up. "Where were you stacking the traps?"

Andy shut his eyes, his lips still purple. "By Hurley's boathouse. I don't…"

"You ended up in the water by the dock," Colin said.

"I must have… Hell." Andy tried to sit up, cursed in pain and stayed down on his back. "I think I heard something. I can't remember."

"Warm up," Mike said. "You'll remember more when your body temperature is back to normal."

Julianne sprang to her feet and frowned at Kevin, then Colin. "We need to check with anyone who was on the docks, at Hurley's, in the parking lot. Someone must have seen something, right?" She caught herself. "Sorry. You guys know what to do."

Kevin, always the most patient Donovan, touched her shoulder. "What about you, Julianne?"

"Me? I didn't see anything. And I didn't hit him. I swear."

Mike grinned at her. "You were just muttering about drowning him from one end of the harbor to the other."

"What were you doing, watching me?"

Mike nodded back toward the waterfront restaurant. "We saw you."

Kevin tried to intercede. "Julianne—"

"Bastards," she said. "Every damn one of you. You're all bastards."

Mike shrugged off his jacket and put it over her shoulders. "Andy'll be okay. You did good today, kid."

She fought back tears, then pulled off Mike's coat and added it to her sweater atop Andy. He unearthed a hand from under the layers and placed it on her muddy ankle. "Thanks, Jules. Who knows what would have happened if you hadn't found me."

"You'd have drowned," she said, sniffling back more tears.

An ambulance and town cruiser arrived on the boat launch.

"I'll check on Father Bracken," Mike said.

Kevin glanced at Colin. "You're getting in touch with Emma?"

He nodded. "On my way to Heron's Cove now."

Apple cider was as quintessentially Maine as bean-hole suppers, Finian thought as he set a plastic jug of cider on the kitchen table in the rectory. But what an odd thing. He'd walked over to the rectory after morning mass, and there was the cider on his back doorstep, along with a sheet of thick white sketch paper rolled up and tied with a purple velvet ribbon. A note card was clipped to it: "Compliments of Tatiana Pavlova, Firebird Boutique, London."

Finian was about to untie the ribbon when Mike Donovan materialized in the screen door. "Thought you were going to keep your doors locked," the eldest Donovan said, entering the kitchen.

"At night," Finian said, "and I refuse to lock my church office when I'm there, so don't even ask."

Mike frowned at the note. "What's that?"

Finian could tell something was wrong, given Mike's grim look and his sodden jeans. "It can wait. You—"

"Just tell me," Mike said, glancing at the note card.

Finian explained, and when he finished his tale, Mike withdrew a small jackknife from a pocket and cut the ribbon on the sketch. "Let's have a look," he said, unrolling it on the table. He grabbed the salt and pepper shakers and set them on corners diagonally across from each other, then eyed the pencil sketch. "A falcon? A guy?"

"So it appears." The sketch took up the entire page and wasn't elaborate but was beyond anything Finian knew that he could accomplish. "It looks as if the falcon transforms into a handsome man. A prince, possibly."

"Is the prince supposed to be you?" Mike asked.

Finian sighed, mystified. "I have no idea."

"Why would this Tatiana Pavlova leave you a sketch and a jug of cider?"

"Again, Mike, I have no idea."

He gave a curt nod. "All right. I'll call Kevin and Colin. Tell them. Did you see her?"

"No."

"Anyone else?"

"Just a handful of people at mass." Finian shifted his attention from the sketch to the man next to him. "What's happened?"

"Andy was attacked down by Hurley's," Mike said. "He'll be okay."

Finian waited for him to continue, but Mike Donovan was nothing if not succinct. "Shall I pour us some cider and you can tell me—"

"Don't touch the cider."

The intensity of his words, his tight look, reminded Finian of Colin during his hunt for Sister Joan's killer. Finian felt his heartbeat quicken, his palms sweat. "Is there anything I can do?"

"Loan me your cell phone. Mine got wet."

"When Andy was attacked?"

"After. We weren't there when he got hit."

"He was in the water, then," Finian said, handing over his cell phone.

Mike nodded but didn't elaborate as he punched in a number. In another moment, he spoke to Kevin Donovan, the marine patrol officer. "Finian's okay. We need to find out if Emma's Russian friend Tatiana Pavlova had cider and a sketch delivered to Saint Patrick's rectory or if she delivered them herself. And why."

As Mike explained the situation in more detail to his youngest brother, Finian sank into a chair at the table, looking at the lovely sketch and the cider with its charming, distinctive label from a local cider press.

What was this life he had embraced when a gift from a young artist could provoke such suspicion and fear, not just in Mike Donovan, Finian thought, but in himself, too?

Mike disconnected, in no better spirits. "Kevin found cider, sketches and notes from Tatiana for him, Andy and me in the back of his truck."

"Not for Colin?"

"He's checking Colin's house now. If you rated a personal delivery, maybe he did, too."

"But Tatiana has only met Colin and me," Finian said thoughtfully. "Not that you and your youngest brothers aren't deserving of a gift."

"But it's odd," Mike said, dialing his phone again.

"You're calling Colin?"

"He's on his way to Heron's Cove. He can check with Tatiana and figure this out."

Finian hoped so. Parishioners sometimes dropped off gifts for him. Homemade breads and cakes, the occasional stew, fresh vegetables from their gardens. He had never thought twice about anything they offered.

He sighed, even as he noticed that the cider looked as if it had already been opened.

When Mike didn't get through to Colin, he left a curt message and disconnected, impatient. "There's no cell service for a stretch along the coast above Heron's Cove. He's probably there."

"What do we do now?" Finian asked.

"We wait."

Colin left a message for Emma and texted her before he hit a dead zone with his cell phone. When he came out of it just above Heron's Cove, she still hadn't responded. He saw that Mike, Kevin and Matt Yankowski had all called during the ten minutes he had no service. He didn't check his voice mail, just hit Yank's number.

Yank answered on the first ring. "Where are you?"

"A mile out of Heron's Cove. Have you talked to Emma this morning?"

"Not yet. What—"

"You first."

"We've been looking into Vladimir Bulgov's activity in London in April. We checked his financial records. He bought a little something for himself at the Firebird Boutique. By itself, it's not earth-shattering. He's Russian, and the Firebird's premier designer is Russian-born and does work inspired by Russian folklore and fairy tales and such. Only now she's in Heron's Cove."

"Tatiana Pavlova has met my friend Vlad."

"Almost certainly," Yank said. Colin noticed a sailboat, its white sails sparkling against the blue water and clear blue sky. "My brother Andy was attacked in Rock Point this morning."

Yank remained silent as Colin filled him in, then said, "You're sure your brother didn't just trip over a lobster pot?"

"Whoever hit him knew what he was doing."

"You didn't see anything?"

"Not a thing. It happened before Kevin, Mike and I met for breakfast. We're lucky Julianne found Andy when she did. Cold water, high tide, a hit on the head—"

"Not a good combination. Keep me posted. You're okay?"

"All set. I got my feet wet but I'll dry out. No alligators and poisonous snakes in Rock Point."

He disconnected, and as he pulled in front of the Sharpe house, Mike called again. "I'm with Finian Bracken. We're good. This Russian designer is either eccentric as hell, or something's up."

Colin was ready to jump through the phone but managed not to interrupt Mike's explanation. Cider? Falcons? What was Tatiana Pavlova thinking?

"I thought it was weird," Mike said as he wrapped up, "especially so soon after Andy got bashed in the head."

"And Kevin says we all got cider and a sketch?"

"Yeah. Yours is on your back doorstep. I don't want any-one touching the cider. Call me paranoid if you want."

"Not today," Colin said.

He hung up with Mike and climbed out of his truck. The carpenters had left the front door to the Sharpe house open as they hauled out old kitchen cabinets, wallboard, insulation and whatever else one would expect to find in the walls of a hundred-year-old house. Colin headed up the walk as he returned Kevin's call.

His youngest brother gave a quick update. The local police were going over every inch of the Rock Point waterfront, every boat, every lobster pot, every damn rock, for any evidence of who had attacked Andy and why. He was getting checked out at the emergency room, but Kevin was confident he wouldn't be admitted.

"He's arguing with Julianne," Kevin said. "She still wants her boat back. You've talked to Mike?"

"Yeah," Colin said.

Kevin didn't like the gifts, either. Why wouldn't Tatiana at least have said a quick hello? From what Colin had seen of her, she wasn't shy.

He disconnected and went into the house but Emma wasn't there. He stifled an edge of worry as he choked on the stirred-up dust and debris and ducked out to the back porch.

The *Nightingale* was still moored next door.

He could drive over to Lucas Sharpe's house in the village, bust in its door and see what he could find on the Sharpes and Dmitri Rusakov. Same with the parents' house, which was serving as the temporary offices of Sharpe Fine Art Recovery while they were in London and Wendell Sharpe's home was under renovation. Bust in its door, see what was what.

Emma probably wouldn't like that.

Colin walked down to the yard. Hydrangea petals had

blown off and were scattered over the grass like burgundy-colored snowflakes. Heron's Cove was a pretty place, and he did fine at the docks and in a few of the regular places—a couple of bars, a clam shack—but he had never been comfortable there the way he was in Rock Point. He wondered if the reverse was true for Emma. He had liked having her at his house last night, and not just because of the sex, although that was a big part of it. He had liked talking to her about what color to paint the walls, and watching her roll her eyes when she discovered he still more-or-less only had beer in his refrigerator.

He wanted to know more about her family, what it was like growing up as a Sharpe. They couldn't have just sat around talking art heists all the time.

Then again, maybe they had, Colin thought, heading down to the docks to see if Emma was with her Russian friends, and if any of them knew about falcon sketches, cider and the attack on his brother.

22

"WATCH YOURSELF, LUCAS," EMMA SAID AS SHE paused on the pier where the *Nightingale* was moored. "Tatiana had a chance to tell us Vladimir Bulgov had commissioned those nesting dolls from her, and she didn't."

"The man in the picture is Dmitri Rusakov?"

"Definitely." She had received his email with the pictures when she arrived in Heron's Cove. "I don't recognize the woman with him. It must have been twenty years ago, at least."

"Around the time that Granddad was in Moscow, then." Lucas sounded calm but also intensely focused. "I'll ask him about her."

"Where are you now?"

"Almost to Killarney. Don't worry. I'll find him."

Emma gripped her phone as she approached the gangway onto the *Nightingale*. She didn't see anyone up on the sky deck, or in the lounge. Were Dmitri and Ivan watching her, wondering who she was talking to, what she was learning about them and their real reasons for being in Heron's Cove?

She envisioned Lucas driving on the twisting road to

Killarney in southwest Ireland and heard his tense sigh. "Is the girl in the picture Tatiana Pavlova?" he asked.

"I can't tell for sure but that's my guess."

"If the woman's her mother and she was involved with the Rusakov collection somehow, that could explain Tatiana's interest."

"Yes, it could," Emma said half to herself. "The original collection that Granddad investigated included a nightingale pendant. I don't know if Natalie ended up with it and what you saw in Tatiana's workroom is a different nightingale. If it's not—if it's part of the Rusakov collection—then how and when did she get it?"

"Good question. I hope Granddad can help with an answer."

"If you're being followed—"

"I'd know it on this damn road," he said.

"Just be careful. Don't take any chances."

"You, too, Emma. Sorry. I forgot for a second that you're an FBI agent."

Lucas promised to stay in touch but when he disconnected, Emma had to push back a surge of worry for her brother and grandfather. She mounted the gangway, losing her already weak cell-phone signal as she walked onto the cool main deck. She expected a crewmember to turn up but saw no one in the dimly lit corridor.

The door to Natalie Warren's guest cabin was open. Emma stood in the doorway. Natalie was zipping up a suitcase on her bed and jumped, startled, before Emma had a chance to announce her presence. "Oh, it's you," she said, grabbing at her chest even as she smiled. "I didn't hear you. Please, come in."

Emma entered the elegant stateroom but stayed by the door. "Where is everyone? I just walked right on board."

"The crew's getting the boat ready to sail. Is *sail* even the right word? Dmitri invited me to sail with him down to the Bahamas, but I have to get back home. I think he's up on the top deck somewhere."

"Is Ivan on board?"

"I haven't seen him, but I'm sure he's around. We had a visit earlier this morning from Tatiana Pavlova. I...um..." Natalie faltered, as if she weren't quite sure what to say. "I guess you two have met already."

"She came here on her own?"

Natalie nodded. "Of course, what else? Dmitri or Ivan dragged her on board?"

"Invited her," Emma said.

"Oh, right. It was your tone—or maybe I'm just out of sorts. This trip hasn't gone the way I thought it would. Tatiana had her back up about the collection. She'd heard I was bringing it here, to discuss it with you and your family. She didn't say how she heard, but her work brings her into contact with appraisers, auction houses, other designers. I'd been asking around but I thought I'd been discreet. I guess not that discreet."

"Who all was here—you, Dmitri, Ivan?"

"Not Ivan," Natalie said. "I don't know where he was. I think Tatiana's a bit of a character. Of course, now I want to see the Firebird Boutique."

"You've never been there?"

"No, never."

"I see you're packed," Emma said, nodding to the suitcase still on the bed. "When are you leaving?"

"Any minute. I've said goodbye to Dmitri already. I don't think he was that serious about inviting me to join him in the Bahamas." Natalie grabbed a brush off the dresser and ran it quickly through her pale hair, which she then deftly pulled back with a tortoise-shell clip. She added in a mock conspiratorial whisper, "I think he has a girlfriend down there."

"And the collection?"

Her eyes misted almost immediately. "It stays here."

"Then you and Dmitri…"

"I believe him when he says he didn't give it to my mother himself."

"Then why did she take it?" Emma asked. "Do you have any idea?"

"My guess is spite. Pure, unadulterated spite. That, Emma, was my mother. I'm sure in her mind she believed she wasn't stealing it. She would have convinced herself she was entitled to it. She must have known it was special to Dmitri. Some people can only feel better by making someone else feel bad, too. I get that Dmitri never meant for her to have it—or me. It's not as if I'm his daughter."

"He obviously cares about you."

"Which I appreciate. I think he feels bad about this whole situation. He says he wants to help me out." Natalie lifted her suitcase off the bed and set it on the floor. "That's up to him. I'd never ask, and I'm doing fine on my own, really."

"Where is the collection now?" Emma asked.

"Still in its case in the closet. It's not my problem any longer. Tatiana Pavlova says she wants to see it back in Russia, in a museum for everyone to enjoy. Dmitri didn't look too keen on the idea." Natalie gave a small laugh. "That was a moment, I have to say. This billionaire Russian tycoon scoffing at this pretty little Russian jewelry designer."

"How did Tatiana react?"

"Scoffed right back. Called him a gangster. It was more amusing than offensive. Tatiana is a passionate, talented designer who will go back to her life in London and no doubt on to a stellar career." Natalie picked up a bright turquoise tote bag off the floor and set it atop her suitcase. "This was all fun while it lasted. Well, mostly fun. At least I knew not to get my hopes up too high. After all, the collection came from my mother." She pulled up the handle to her suitcase. "Now, if you'll excuse me, I have a car waiting to take me to the airport."

With a mumbled farewell, she wheeled the suitcase out of the stateroom. Emma followed her out but didn't go with her to the gangway, instead heading up to the lounge.

No one was there, either.

A pencil sketch lay on the bar, held in place by a half-gallon jug of cider from a local press. Emma recognized Tatiana's style and saw that the sketch depicted a soaring falcon, with a good-looking man in medieval Russian garb in the background, standing against a gnarled tree.

Emma didn't remember any falcons among the sketches she'd seen at the cottage yesterday, but Tatiana worked fast.

Still, why the sketch? Was it a peace offering somehow?

She stood straight, felt a cool breeze and heard the distant cry of seagulls.

Not a peace offering.

Two empty glasses stood next to each other on the bar.

Why only two? Had Tatiana not joined in drinking cider? Natalie? Dmitri?

Did it even matter?

Emma left the sketch and the glasses where they were and headed back down to the main deck. She didn't see Natalie or anyone else.

Where was Dmitri? Why wasn't he there to see Natalie off?

And where was Ivan?

Tatiana…why the sketch? Why the visit?

Why falcons?

Emma stood in the doorway of the cool, quiet guest stateroom. The Russian fairy tale of Olga was similar to the Western European tale of Snow White, except in the Russian version, instead of seven dwarves, there were twelve falcons that turned into handsome men. Olga still had to contend with the vain, jealous stepmother, the magic mirror and the poisoned apple.

A jealous stepmother…a beautiful stepdaughter…a poisoned apple.

Was Tatiana's choice of a falcon transforming into a handsome man—of that particular fairy tale—as deliberate as her choices of the fables she had told?

Emma went through the stateroom to the closet and opened the double doors.

Natalie's hard-sided black case sat at an angle on the floor where she had left it.

Wouldn't Dmitri want to store a collection potentially worth millions in a vault?

A luxury yacht like the *Nightingale* had to have a vault.

Probably more than one, Emma thought as she got down on one knee, flipped the latches on the case and opened the lid.

The case was empty.

The Rusakov collection was gone.

23

WENDELL SHARPE THREW OFF A THICK RED tarp that he'd had over his lap and climbed out of a small, flat-bottomed wooden boat onto the concrete pier. Lucas waited for him, knowing better than to offer a hand. His grandfather had already ignored help from the boat's operator. It was just the two of them, a private trip in Lough Leane, the largest of the lakes in the Killarney National Park, a popular tourist destination that was quiet now, so late in October. Even in the light mist, the area was stunningly beautiful, the lakes nestled at the base of forested hills.

Lucas appreciated the energy with which Wendell moved. He had on an open rain jacket over a wool sweater vest and looked pleased with himself, even as he frowned at his only grandson. "Lucas, what're you doing here? How did you find me?"

"I called Declan Bracken. You mentioned you'd see him and I hoped he'd have an idea of where you'd gotten off to. He told me he dropped you off here this morning."

"Good, good."

"I'm glad you decided to let someone know where you are."

"Yes, I thought about that. If anything happened to me, I'd hate for a hiker to have to stumble across my bones. Best a trained search team find them." He nodded across the choppy water, toward a small island visible from the shore. "I've been to the Innisfallen ruins. Ah, Lucas. They stir the soul."

Lucas had never visited the ruins of the sixth-century monastery founded by Saint Finian, where monks wrote down tales of pre-Christian Ireland. Emma had been out there during her year working in Dublin. Lucas was relieved to see that his grandfather's melancholy had lifted. Yet his own worries had gripped him, given his trip to London and the anxiety he'd heard in his sister's voice when they'd talked earlier.

Wendell frowned. "Why the glum look, Lucas?"

"I'll tell you back at—where are you staying? Not in a tent, I hope?"

"Declan insisted I stay with him and his family. I'll meet him at Bracken Distillers. It's not far from here."

Lucas felt a ripple of uneasiness. He hadn't been followed from London. He was sure of it, but he put a hand on his grandfather's thin shoulders. "I've a car, Granddad. Let's get over to the distillery."

Wendell Sharpe's decades of experience showed in his narrowed blue eyes. "Lucas?"

He started up a grassy bank. His grandfather bit off a sigh and followed him. The storied fifteenth-century Ross Castle, stronghold of the O'Donoghue clan, now open to tourists, loomed above them. Lucas wouldn't mind wandering through a stone castle, losing himself on the hiking trails, heading out for a boat ride on the lakes, but he had Tatiana Pavlova on his mind.

And his sister, he thought. Emma's troubles back in Heron's Cove.

He glanced at his grandfather as he caught up with him. "I need to know what's not in the files about your work with Dmitri Rusakov twenty years ago."

"What's going on?"

As they walked to where he had parked his rented car, Lucas handed his grandfather his iPhone. "I took several photos in London. Have a look at them while I navigate the Irish roads."

Once belted into his seat in the tiny car, Wendell thumbed through the photos, at eighty-plus having no trouble with the iPhone.

"Do you remember the woman and the little girl?" Lucas asked as he drove back out to the main road.

His grandfather folded his hand around the iPhone and sighed out his window. "The woman said she was a curator at the Tretyakov but I always believed there was more to it. She was frequently at Dmitri's Moscow house."

"Where he discovered the collection?"

"Yes. He wasn't living there yet. She had an infectious passion for Russian folk traditions. I only knew her as Katya."

"And the girl?"

"Her daughter."

"Did you meet her?"

"Oh, yes. A little charmer. Feisty."

Lucas navigated a curve. The pensiveness he had observed in his grandfather in Dublin had returned. He stared out the window as they wound their way away from the main town of Killarney, toward the Iveragh Peninsula.

When Wendell didn't go on, Lucas prodded him. "Granddad? Did something happen to this Katya and her daughter?"

"I only heard rumors after I left Moscow."

"What rumors?"

He sighed heavily. "Katya is the reason I sent Emma to London instead of going myself. I thought it would be interesting for Emma to go, easier for me if I didn't. I've seen it all, Lucas, but Katya was a special woman." He turned from the window, his skin gray as he added, his voice barely audible, "She was killed in a car crash a few weeks after I left Moscow."

"That's a tough one. I'm sorry." Lucas concentrated on a tight, rather harrowing turn even by Irish standards. He would prefer to look at the scenery than to drive—or consider what went on in Moscow twenty years ago. "The crash wasn't a rumor? It happened?"

"Unfortunately, no, it wasn't a rumor. It happened. It's the circumstances..." Wendell turned away from Lucas and gazed back out the passenger window. "My Russian has never been terribly good and I was focused on my work, not Dmitri Rusakov's personal life, but I always felt that there was something between him and Katya."

"An affair? Was he married then?"

"I don't know, Lucas. I never asked. I had no reason to. I was only in Moscow a short time. When I heard about Katya's death, I tried to contact Dmitri to ask him to give my condolences to her family. And to ask about her daughter. He never responded, and I left it at that."

Lucas slowed for another curve. "What were the rumors about the circumstances?"

"That the car crash that killed Katya wasn't an accident."

"She was murdered?"

His grandfather didn't answer at once. "It was just talk, or so I thought at the time. Dmitri Rusakov was already wealthy, and he was still on the rise. He's a tough businessman, and he has his share of enemies. If Katya was in his way somehow...

or if his enemies believed eliminating her could be to their advantage…" Wendell sank back against his seat and stared straight out the windshield at the mist and Irish green. "The rumors never took hold. I always assumed it was because they were false and the crash was in fact an accident. Now…it's as if Katya never existed."

Lucas slowed, turned onto a paved lane that would take them to Bracken Distillers. "Did you look into the rumors?" he asked his grandfather.

He shook his head. "They just faded away and I was in Heron's Cove, not Moscow."

"And we're not homicide detectives," Lucas added.

"I don't believe Dmitri Rusakov is a killer, Lucas. I never would have sent Emma to London if I did." Wendell sighed again, making it almost a moan. "That doesn't mean I'm right. I've been wrong many times."

"Don't worry about that right now, Granddad. It's not our job to conduct death investigations. Do you think this Tatiana Pavlova could be Katya's daughter?"

"I suppose it's possible. She could have created a new identity for herself and left Russia. I'm sure you've discovered by now that the toughest aspect of our work is when we see how its limitations can touch the innocent."

"Do you think Tatiana blames Rusakov for her mother's death, assuming for the moment Katya was her mother?"

"Dmitri Rusakov is one of the most thorough people I've ever encountered, and you know I've encountered many thorough people. If he's in Heron's Cove and Tatiana Pavlova is in Heron's Cove, trust me, Lucas, he knows whatever there is to know about her."

"He could have his own reasons for wanting to keep Tatiana's identity a secret," Lucas said, noticing a discreet sign for Bracken Distillers. What he wouldn't give for an evening

in an Irish pub, nursing a glass of Irish whiskey and listening to traditional Irish music. Instead, here he was, talking
about a potential twenty-year-old murder. "What if Tatiana
is a threat? What if she's after revenge, or wants the Rusakov
collection for herself?"

"She could blame Dmitri for her mother's death."

Lucas thought of Tatiana's messy apartment, its cheerful,
whimsical atmosphere and couldn't believe she would hurt
anyone. "I was followed in London. I'd be surprised if it was
Tatiana's doing."

"Dmitri's?"

"Could he think you have more information about Katya's
death than you've said?"

"He must know that I would never cover up a murder."

"Maybe it's just having met Katya and her daughter all
those years ago."

"There are so many possibilities," Wendell said, sounding
tired now. "When I was in Moscow with Dmitri Rusakov, I
was thinking about Russian Art Nouveau and this fascinat-
ing, newly discovered collection. There wasn't even a whisper of any criminal activity involving its discovery. It was
just as Dmitri said. He swung a crowbar, and there it was."

Lucas drove along a hedgerow, sheep feeding on the rock-
strewn hillside. "But he's never publicized the collection or
done anything with it."

"Until London four years ago," Wendell said. "And look
what it got him."

"He didn't go to the authorities when he realized the collection was missing. He called you. He had to know you
wouldn't cover up a theft. Do you think he really didn't believe Emma when she told him it was Renee?"

"It's hard to say. He pulled us off the case once Emma told

him. Our work was done, anyway. The disappearance of the collection was a personal matter."

"Why did he have it in London in the first place?"

"At the time he said he was considering talking to a Russian art expert in London about his options for what he could do with it—whether he should put it on display or loan it to a museum. Renee had found out about it a few months earlier and wanted him to introduce it to the public in a big, splashy way."

Lucas slowed as the narrow, snaking road rose into the hills overlooking some body of water—a lake, a bay—in the distant mist. He wanted nothing more than to park the car, get out and walk until nightfall. For the first time, he could understand his grandfather's desire to be here.

"We need to find out what's going on in Heron's Cove," Wendell said. "This is one of those times I hate not being there to help. I'm worried about Emma."

"She carries a semiautomatic pistol, Granddad."

He grunted. "Don't remind me."

But Lucas could see his grandfather's worry, his fear for Emma. Never mind that she had been an FBI agent for three years and had worked with him in Dublin for a year, he still on some level thought of her as a nun, locking herself away in a convent. Lucas understood, because he had to fight the same impulse himself. She had explained dozens of times that her life as a religious sister hadn't removed her from the world, but it was drastically different from being an FBI agent.

He wondered if being Sister Brigid and now Special Agent Sharpe had prepared Emma at all for falling for a guy like Colin Donovan.

Probably not, Lucas thought as Bracken Distillers finally came into view. Declan Bracken had gone into the whiskey business with his twin brother, now the temporary parish priest in Rock Point, Maine. Lucas had met Finian Bracken briefly in Heron's Cove but hadn't yet met Declan, who lived with his wife and three children not far from the distillery.

Lucas turned in at an iron gate, which he suspected was there more to keep local sheep out of the landscaped grounds than intruders. The stone buildings were visible down a curving drive with a lush border of late-autumn flowers and shrubs glistening in a sudden ray of sunlight.

"I'll get the gate," Wendell said.

But Lucas noticed it was unlatched, and he shook his head at his grandfather. "No, wait."

"I'm not so old I can't—"

"That's not it." Then he saw a small black van parked among the trees just up the road. "Granddad."

"I see. It could be a delivery." He held up the phone. "I'll call the police just in case."

Lucas nodded. "Do it."

A man stepped out from behind a thick palm tree.

Shaved head...dark sweater...

It was the same man Lucas had spotted in London yesterday and again that morning, on his way back to the Firebird Boutique from Tatiana Pavlova's apartment.

"He has a gun," Wendell said in a hoarse whisper.

Lucas saw the weapon. Saw the man raise it, ready to fire. He reached for his grandfather. "Get down!"

Wendell had already ducked, and Lucas sped straight into the swinging gate, smashing it into the man. He fell backward, his gun skittering across the pavement.

Lucas leaped out of the car, grabbed the gun and pointed it at the man. "Don't move."

The man glared up at him, silent.

"Granddad, are you all right?"

"Never better. I'll make that call to the police now."

24

THE SLIDING GLASS DOOR THAT LED OUT TO the deck to Tatiana Pavlova's rented cottage was partially open, the vertical blinds clattering in the breeze. Colin pushed the blinds aside. He had spotted Ivan Alexander headed in that direction and hoped to find Emma there, too. Either way, it was time to talk to one London-based, Russian-born jewelry designer.

Seagulls squawked down by a lobster boat puttering toward the channel. If he were a visiting artist on such a perfect late-autumn day in Maine, he would be in an Adirondack chair on the deck with his feet up, watching the boats and the birds.

Not that he had a clue how Tatiana's mind worked.

The cozy one-room cottage was tidy, her personal belongings packed up, her sketches gathered and stacked on the love seat, a deep rust-colored tapestry bag holding them in place.

He didn't see their owner.

He rapped on the metal door casing. "Tatiana, it's Special Agent Colin Donovan. May I come in?"

She emerged from the bathroom and walked unsteadily to the door. She seemed to have trouble focusing on him.

"Yes, please come in, Agent Donovan. I'm sorry. I'm a bit under the weather."

As he stepped inside, Tatiana backed into the middle of the room. She had on her pumpkin-colored jacket, both arms holding her abdomen as if she were in pain. Her skin was pale, almost waxen. She looked tiny, vulnerable.

Colin frowned at her. "Are you all right?" he asked.

"I have terrible cramps. Nausea. It's my own fault. I fear that I've turned Dmitri Rusakov into a monster in my mind."

"You went to see him?"

She nodded, sank onto the love seat next to the stack of sketches and her tapestry bag.

"When?" Colin asked.

"Early this morning. I was up, pacing. I saw he was, too. We are alike in that way. I wasn't sure he would let me on board the *Nightingale,* but he did."

"Was Ivan Alexander there?"

"No. At least I didn't see him. I saw Natalie. She is so gentle. So sweet." Tatiana's shoulders slumped; her jacket looked gigantic on her. "You FBI people always find out everything about everybody, yes?"

Colin narrowed his eyes on her. "Is there something about you we should know?"

"Much, yes. Much." She tried to smile, then moaned, tightening her arms against her abdomen. "Such cramps."

"Tatiana, how sick are you?"

She seemed confused. "Sick?"

"Are you running a fever?"

"No."

"Are you having difficulty breathing?"

"A little. I think it's nerves. My stomach…" She shuddered, gave him a meek smile. "You don't want to know."

"Have you been vomiting?"

She nodded, obviously embarrassed. "It's nothing." She seemed to make an effort to square her shoulders and give him a stubborn, dramatic look. "Ask your questions, Special Agent Colin Donovan."

"Your speech is slurred. What have you had to eat or drink?"

"It doesn't matter—"

"Cider?" Colin asked sharply.

Tatiana paled even more. "Yes. With Dmitri. How do you know?"

"Where did you get the cider?"

"I brought it."

"And sketches?"

"No. I did the sketches there. On the *Nightingale.* I drew falcons. They're from the story of Olga. The falcons protect her from her wicked stepmother." Tatiana wriggled out of her jacket and let it fall onto the love seat. "My first visit to Maine hasn't gone well. Heron's Cove is very beautiful. Life here must be nice but I feel as if I have poisoned this place with my selfish fears. The Rusakov collection isn't worth bad things happening to innocent people."

Colin moved closer to her. "What bad things, Tatiana?"

She shoved the tapestry bag off the sketches, then pointed a shaking finger at the top sketch. "Do you know what this is?"

"Looks like a kite and—what, a butterfly?"

"A moth. A simple moth."

Colin didn't give a damn about moths and butterflies.

"I will tell you another fable," Tatiana said, her dark eyes fixed on the sketch. "A moth sees a kite flying high in the sky, above everyone else. The kite thinks the moth—so tiny in the valley below—must be envious. But the moth isn't envious, for the kite is on a string that is controlled by someone else. The moth might never attain such heights as the kite, but she is free to go and to do as she pleases."

She moaned, and Colin got out his cell phone. "I'm calling an ambulance."

She looked up from the sketch, tears glistening in her eyes, on the lashes. "I like to be tiny moth." Her arm fell away from her abdomen, as if she didn't have the strength to hold it there. "I should have stayed in London. I was wrong to interfere, but I return today. I'll be inconsequential again soon. A speck, like moth." Tears spilled down her waxen cheeks. "I've always believed the worst about Dmitri Rusakov."

"It's true," Ivan Alexander said as he entered the cottage from the deck. "She has from the time she was a small child."

Colin hit Kevin's number on his cell phone even as he took in Ivan's words, his presence—Tatiana's reaction to him. Not just acceptance. Expectance. She had known he would be there for her.

"A small child?" Colin sighed. "She's Dmitri's daughter?"

Ivan nodded.

"I want nothing from Dmitri Rusakov," Tatiana mumbled, sobbing silently.

Ivan said something to her in Russian, then switched to English as he addressed Colin. "She convinced herself that her father was involved in arms trafficking with Vladimir Bulgov. She wanted to save the collection from him and help Natalie understand that she needs to stay away from him."

Tatiana looked up at Ivan, her eyes wide with fear and whatever was making her sick. "Ivan...I'm a mere moth. I can't fly as high as the kite but I am free."

But she was fading.

"She needs to get to a hospital," Ivan said.

Colin nodded as Kevin answered. He spoke to his brother.

"I'm at Tatiana Pavlova's cottage in Heron's Cove. She needs an ambulance. I think she's been poisoned."

"The cider?" Kevin asked.

"That's my guess."

Kevin swore. "There's more. Now that he's warmed up and fully conscious, Andy remembers seeing two men by Hurley's boathouse. Julianne says she saw a dinghy but didn't see the men. One was in his mid-thirties. Medium brown hair. Scary-looking, according to Andy. The other was older. Gray hair. Andy started over to them when he was hit from behind."

Colin sucked in a breath.

"Colin?"

He gave Kevin Yank's number. "Tell him that Horner, Boris and Yuri are here."

"These are the guys that tried to kill you?" Kevin asked.

Colin didn't sidestep his brother's question. "Yes. Tell Yank to fill you in. Then meet me at the *Nightingale*." He disconnected and turned to Ivan. "The cider. Did you drink any?"

"No."

"Who did?"

"Dmitri," Ivan said, focused, any emotion banked down.

"Tell the ambulance crew you suspect deliberate poisoning. My guess is botulism. It's soon for symptoms to appear if she drank the cider this morning, but it's not impossible—and she could have ingested the botulism sooner, another way."

Ivan glanced at Tatiana, then leveled his gaze at Colin. "Agreed. You'll find Emma?"

"She trusts you."

"She should."

"And I trust Emma. I don't know if that's an algebraic equation, but yes, I'll find her. The ambulance is only minutes out." Colin started for the sliding glass door, looked back at the Russian. "Can you handle this situation?"

"I'll keep Tatiana safe."

"You always do, don't you?"

Ivan didn't answer, and Colin headed out, dialing Emma again. She still didn't pick up. By the time he reached the street, he was running.

His guys from Florida were there.

A Russian billionaire...a collection worth a fortune...

An anxious, dangerous buyer who wanted the promised weapons.

Pete Horner and his Russian thugs wouldn't hesitate this time.

They would kill whoever they had to kill.

25

EMMA RACED OUT THE GANGWAY. SHE EXPECTED
Natalie to be on her way by now, but she was still on the pier,
a man in a car service uniform with her, taking her suitcase.
Natalie gave an exaggerated shiver as she slung her tote bag
over one shoulder. "It's chilly," she said to the driver. "Just as
well I'm going back to Arizona. Thanks for waiting for me.
Shall we be off?"

"Hold on, Natalie," Emma said. "I need to talk to you."
She showed her badge to the driver. "Move back, please."

Natalie turned to him. "It's okay. I'll only be a minute. I'll
pay extra for your wait." She smiled at Emma, a little impatiently. "What can I do for you?"

"I want you to come back on board the *Nightingale* with
me and clear up a few things."

"Why? Is something wrong?"

"The Rusakov collection isn't in the case in the guest
cabin."

"It's not? Well, I wouldn't know where it is. Ivan or Dmitri must have collected it."

Emma cut her off. "I'm a federal agent, Natalie. You don't want to lie to me. Were you in London in April?"

"London? I don't see what that has to do with anything. You're checking up on me? The FBI? You can do that for no good reason?" Natalie gave a hollow laugh. "This is absurd. I'm leaving."

"Not until I'm sure Dmitri, Ivan and the collection are all safe. It's for your safety, too." The driver stepped forward and started to reach for Natalie's tote bag. Emma shook her head at him. "Hold on."

He ignored her. As he shifted to take the bag, Emma noticed a scar under his left eye, remembered that Yuri, the older of the two Russian thugs who had attacked Colin, had a scar under his left eye.

It was enough for her. She reached for her Glock in its holster on her belt, but he reacted immediately, swinging around and nailing her in the midsection with his elbow. She shifted, avoiding the worst impact of the blow, but it was still enough to bring her to her knees. She drew her weapon just as Colin jumped onto the pier from the yacht club.

He already had his weapon in his hand. "Don't move, Yuri. Not even a twitch. You, too, Natalie. Keep your hands where Agent Sharpe and I can see them."

"I will." Natalie was pale, shivering. "You two just do your thing."

Colin focused on Yuri. "Where's Horner?"

The Russian didn't answer.

"Who poisoned the cider? Him? Boris? You?"

Still no answer.

"Where's Dmitri Rusakov?" Emma asked.

Yuri muttered something in Russian that she took to be a curse. Colin turned him around, cuffed him and sat him down on the gangway. "Emma," he said, his eyes still on Yuri, "did you touch any cider?"

The cider. She shook her head. "No."

"It's poisoned. Tatiana's sick. An ambulance is on the way. Ivan Alexander is with her."

Natalie gasped. "Poison? What on earth—"

Emma steadied her Glock on her. "Keep your hands where we can see them."

"Of course. I don't want any trouble. I don't have a gun hidden up my sleeve."

"What about poison?" Emma asked. "What did you put in the cider?"

"Me?" Natalie looked shocked. "What are you talking about? Why would I want to poison anyone?" She blinked back tears. "You're scaring me."

"You should be scared," Colin said without sympathy. "You're in the middle of a volatile, dangerous situation. Your only good option is to cooperate."

"I'm sure you're both good at what you do, but the only volatile, dangerous situation I'm in the middle of is the one you two are creating." Tears streaming down her cheeks, Natalie pointed at Yuri. "I don't know who this man is. All I did was hire a car service to take me to the airport."

Colin was unrelenting. "You had your Russian friends deliver poisoned cider and sketches to Finian Bracken and my family and pretend they were from Tatiana."

"I did no such thing!"

"Yes, you did," Emma said, the pieces of what Colin was saying falling into place with what she had seen up in the lounge. "What did you do, slip poison into cider Tatiana brought on board? Was the sketch of the falcon your idea?"

"Fin got a falcon, too," Colin said, tight.

Natalie was pale, her lower lip trembling. "Tatiana wanted

to show Dmitri how good she was, how clever. Why? What's wrong with the sketches?"

"Tatiana is Dmitri's daughter," Emma said. "But you know that already. Did your mother know? Was she jealous of Tatiana? Are you jealous, Natalie?"

She snapped up straight. "I have no idea what you're talking about."

"I'll bet we're going to find out you were in London in April," Emma said, still addressing Natalie. "You met Pete Horner then. Got swept up in that world. Made promises you couldn't keep. Now you and Horner and his Russian friends owe weapons to some very bad people."

"You're in a mess, Natalie," Colin said. "Rusakov's not buying the collection from you. There's not going to be any quick cash. You've got all you're going to get from him."

"Colin and I haven't touched your poisoned cider," Emma said. "Tatiana is still alive. She's getting medical help."

Colin nodded. "My family and Finian Bracken are fine. No one's dead, Natalie. You can still walk back from the precipice. Tell us where Dmitri is before it's too late. There's an effective antitoxin to botulism poisoning. It needs to be administered as soon as possible after ingestion. Symptoms typically start appearing in eight to twelve hours, but it can be sooner—as apparently is the case with Tatiana. Left untreated, botulism poisoning is lethal."

"People won't just get sick," Emma added. "They'll die. Dmitri and anyone else who drank the cider need immediate medical help."

Natalie put her hands in front of her, palms down, defiant now, insulted. "If you think I tried to kill anyone, put me in handcuffs. Arrest me."

Colin shrugged. "Sounds like a good idea to me."

Kevin Donovan and his colleagues in the state and local police swarmed the pier.

Yuri glared up at Colin. "I should have killed you when I had the chance."

"Yeah. You should have." He turned to Emma. "Let's go find Dmitri and anyone else who had a taste of the cider."

They located Dmitri Rusakov in a small study next to the master stateroom, slumped on the floor amid a pool of fresh vomit. Emma had heard his moan, and she and Colin smashed in the locked door.

She knelt next to the Russian billionaire. He was having difficulty breathing and was clearly weak, in pain. "Tatiana," he mumbled. "My sweet girl."

"She's safe," Emma said. "Ivan's with her. Are you alone?"

Colin checked the room, nodded to her. "It's clear."

"He needs a hospital, fast," she said.

Dmitri fumbled for her hand. "Tatiana is not responsible for this. She didn't try to kill me, herself. Anyone."

"I know, Dmitri. Hang on, okay? Help is on the way."

Tears ran down his cheeks but he was too weak to answer. Colin squatted down next to him. "I bet Natalie and her friends managed to get botulism into him and Tatiana last night. Damn. The sick bastards."

They made Dmitri as comfortable as possible as the state and local police checked the yacht, discovering sick crewmembers but no Pete Horner or Boris, then let in the paramedics.

"Boris and Pete are waiting for Yuri and Natalie to join them," Colin said as he followed Emma out into the sprawling master stateroom. "Boris and Yuri stopped in Rock Point early this morning in a dinghy."

Emma paused at the foot of the king-size bed. "So they have a bigger boat."

"Yep."

He was already on his way out of the stateroom. Emma followed him to the gangway and disembarked the *Nightingale* with him.

Natalie was on the pier, handcuffed, screaming. "You all think you're so smart, don't you? Damn you! Damn you to hell. I want you all out of my brain. I want you all dead. Dmitri, Ivan, Tatiana, Emma, Colin, his family, her family. All suffering. All dead."

Colin grimaced next to Emma. "I guess that's the real Natalie," he said. "Glad I showed up?"

"Yuri should be. I was about to lose my temper. I don't like getting hit."

"I don't like you getting hit, either," Colin said in a low voice, close to her. "You had everything under control."

"More or less. You saved Tatiana."

"Ivan would have found her in time," he said.

She touched his arm. "We're not keeping score, right?"

"Right. A jug of poisoned cider was meant for us, too, Emma."

"I love cider, just without botulism."

Kevin Donovan approached his older brother. "We think we know where Pete Horner's boat is. Want to come with me?"

Colin glanced at Emma. "I used to be with the marine patrol."

"That much I do know about you. Go, Colin." With more local and state police descending, and Matt Yankowski en route, she resisted kissing him. "Get the bastards who tried to kill you."

Kevin grinned at her, then clapped his brother on the shoulder. "See why we all like Emma?"

"My turn," Colin said an hour later as he sat across from Pete Horner at a table in the *Nightingale's* lounge. A cool breeze that tasted of salt and smelled of home floated off the water, but Colin stayed focused on what he was there to do. Emma stood by the bar. He liked having her there and knew she liked being there, seeing into a corner of his world as an undercover operative.

Matt Yankowski was in the vicinity but hadn't yet come aboard the luxury yacht. Colin had reported that he, Kevin and a contingent from the Maine State Police had found Horner, Boris and a stash of illegal weapons on a boat about to cruise out of Heron's Cove into the open ocean. The use of overwhelming force had convinced Horner and Boris to surrender without a fight.

Now Colin hoped he could convince Horner to talk, too.

"Going to feed me to the alligators?" Horner asked with a smirk that was half bravado, half for real.

Colin shook his head. "Nope. We don't have alligators up here in Maine."

"Water's cold, though. How long would I last?"

"A beefy guy like you? Longer than you deserve." Colin sat back against the cushioned, elegant chair. "You look tired, Pete. Rough few days, huh?"

The pilot's watery, bloodshot eyes leveled on Colin from across the table. "You have no idea."

Colin was unsympathetic. "My baby brother and I probably just saved your life. Yuri's and Boris's, too. You've got some pissed-off bad guys on your tail. Now you're going to tell me who they are." He leaned forward. "Who's your buyer, Pete?"

"Why should I tell you?"

"Well, if saving your life isn't enough, then because I'm a federal agent and it'll be better for you if you do."

He coughed, then yawned as if he didn't have a care in the world. "Natalie and these crazy Russians went after your family. I didn't."

"Emma talked to her brother in Ireland. Your guy there is under arrest. He's talking."

"I don't have a guy in Ireland."

"Yeah, you do. Another Russian. One of Yuri's and Boris's friends. We have their real names now. We're learning more by the second. By 'we' I mean the FBI and my friends in the Maine State Police."

"You don't have to remind me you're a fed." Horner's eyes were hard now, despite his obvious fatigue, his obvious disgust with himself. He hadn't shaved since he had tried to kill Colin, or probably showered, either.

Colin glanced at Emma, but she didn't give away anything she might be feeling. She would still be processing just how close her brother and grandfather had come to getting killed that day, too. Colin knew it would take time for him to process having poisoned cider delivered to his family.

In the call from Lucas Sharpe, Emma had also learned about Katya Rusakov and her tragic death.

Something Yank's Vulcan mind meld with old Wendell Sharpe would have turned up.

Colin shifted back to Horner.

"My friend Finian Bracken will recognize you from the other night when you followed him."

"So? I talked to a priest. I didn't do anything wrong."

Colin supposed he had a point. "You went into the wrong business and you fell for the wrong woman."

"Natalie was in Paris in April," Emma said, as if on cue.

"We figure she drove to London when you were there with Vladimir Bulgov. Is that when you two met?"

Horner gave Emma a strained smile. "Love at first sight."

"She found out Dmitri Rusakov was in London and drove over," Colin said. "You can do that now. Did she see him?"

"No. Ivan Alexander headed her off at the pass, so to speak, and persuaded her that wouldn't be a good idea. I ran into her crying into her champagne at the hotel bar."

"Sucked you right in," Colin said.

"Oh, yeah. I fly planes. Your basic nobody. Natalie made me feel… Hell." Horner coughed, fatalistic. "After Bulgov's arrest, Natalie got the idea about picking up some of his loose ends, making a few bucks. I told her we had to wait for things to cool down."

Colin stretched out his legs but there was nothing casual or nonchalant about how he felt. "You got the cart before the horse and started spending too much money. An expensive house in Florida. A woman with expensive tastes and big ideas."

"I make good money flying planes."

"Maybe, but with Bulgov's arrest, you were out of a job. Maybe you missed the action of working for him."

"Doesn't mean I knew what all he was into. I thought I was flying rice and beans to feed the hungry and medicines to heal the sick."

"Right," Colin said, not bothering to hide his sarcasm. "You found out about my alter ego's orphaned weapons."

"Yeah. That lying bastard." Horner grinned but there was no humor in his eyes. "It felt like everything was starting to fall into place. Natalie says you're the devil. I think she's right."

"You flew up here to meet her after I cleared out. Was that always your plan?"

He nodded. "Get the weapons from you. Meet her here."

"She promised you money."

"She thought she could get a bundle for the collection," Horner said, matter-of-fact.

"Boris and Yuri believed her, too?"

"Sure. Why not? Her mother used to be married to Rusakov. She was a piece of work but he liked Natalie. What was the worst that could happen? He'd tell her to take a hike. She'd sell it to someone else. You and I had a deal. We weren't in any big hurry."

"Then our deal fell apart and suddenly you needed money fast," Colin said. "There you were with no weapons and an anxious, impatient, dangerous buyer who wasn't going to let you fail without consequences."

Horner grimaced as if he were in physical pain. "I'd have been happy with whatever we could get for the collection, maybe bleeding Rusakov a little more, but Natalie wanted it all. She liked to think big, she said. She liked the action." He sat back in his chair, as if they were discussing golf handicaps. "She'd tell me people often make the mistake of assuming she's stupid and weak. That's what her mother thought. Natalie sees herself as sensitive and intuitive."

"Turns out she's just like her mother," Colin said.

"Yep. Obsessive, envious. She didn't like it when I told her you weren't a turncoat FBI agent and there were no weapons, that we'd have to start over. Then when you turned up here…" Horner shrugged. "Small world, huh?"

"I'd never met Natalie. You told her who I was."

"She asked me to check into Emma Sharpe's FBI guy. She went nuts when I told her who you were. Then she talked to you on the beach. Man, that was it. She wanted you to suffer. Nothing went her way once she got here. The collection, the Sharpes, Rusakov, Tatiana. You. She wanted revenge."

"And you just went along with her," Colin said.

"You've seen her. It's like I drank poison myself. Like she put a spell on me."

Colin gave no hint of the skepticism he felt. Pete Horner was an experienced pilot who had played a dangerous game for a long time. He knew what he was doing. He just hadn't wanted to stop. He wanted it all: money, weapons, danger, adrenaline and Natalie.

"Could you think straight with her?" Horner asked ruefully. "I've never had a woman like that. I wanted to score, then retire to Florida with her…." He trailed off with a moan and blew out a breath. "She had other ideas. Spiraled out of control—"

"Bullshit, Horner." Colin bolted up out of his chair. "You were thinking just fine when you tried to buy weapons from me at a cut rate and then decided to kill me. I'll bet you were thinking just fine when you decided to help her kill Lucas and Wendell Sharpe and poison Finian Bracken and my family. What did you hope to gain?"

"Boris, Yuri and I had to go along with her or we got nothing, except maybe a bullet in the head from our unhappy buyer. Natalie…" Horner sighed, philosophical, his anger and entitlement turning into acceptance that he had grabbed for the brass ring and missed. "What does anyone gain by revenge? I told you, Natalie was in a rage. You turn out to be a federal agent. You escape. Then you show up here, sleeping with Emma Sharpe, who, come to find out, told Rusakov that his ex-wife stole the collection. Natalie was so sure she could get him to buy it from her."

"She knew all along it came from him?" Colin asked.

"Suspected. Maybe more than suspected."

"She'd charm him," Emma said.

Horner directed a cool gaze at her. "Yeah. Like her mother

had. Then Tatiana Pavlova shows up and your brother goes
to London to check her out. Renee Rusakov always suspected there was a daughter, but Dmitri never would tell
her the truth. Tatiana rejected her Rusakov inheritance—
everything Natalie wants." Horner, his cheeks red now with
emotion, turned back to Colin. "Wouldn't that get to you,
Agent Donovan?"

Colin tried to wrap his head around that one. "Why would
Natalie feel entitled to anything from Dmitri Rusakov? She
was an adult when he and her mother married. He set her up
financially. It's not his fault she spent all the money."

"You have to understand how she thinks."

"No," Colin said, "I really don't. How did Natalie find
out Tatiana was in Heron's Cove?"

"I told her," Horner said quietly. "Words I'd like to take
back."

"You recognized Tatiana from when you were in London
in April," Emma said. "Vladimir Bulgov stopped at the Firebird Boutique and commissioned the nesting dolls from her."

"Yeah. I knew Bulgov met with a Russian jeweler. I didn't
think anything of it until I came up here and saw her sneaking around. Natalie insisted I get Yuri to have one of his guys
in London keep tabs on Lucas Sharpe and find out what he
knew about Tatiana."

"She already suspected Tatiana was Rusakov's daughter,"
Colin said.

Horner nodded. "I think so, too."

Emma walked over to the table. "We found botulism in
Tatiana's cottage. You all planted it there."

"Prove it," Horner said.

Colin shrugged. "I'm sure we will."

"A little botulism goes a long way," Emma said, her eyes on
Horner. "Did you get it for her, or did one of the Russians?"

Horner crossed his arms on his chest. "I'm not talking to you about botulism."

Emma stood straight, and Colin noticed how the sunlight played on the honey highlights in her hair, caught the green of her eyes. But he turned to Horner. "Natalie must have had the botulism with her when she arrived in Heron's Cove. That suggests she was planning to kill someone before she knew I was in the area."

"Once she unraveled..." Horner sighed heavily. "There was no reasoning with her. I figured just let her do it, then move on."

Colin shook his head. "Even if she'd succeeded in killing everyone who pissed her off, she still wouldn't be satisfied."

"No argument from me. She used to tell me her mother would draw in men, chew them up and spit them out when she had no more use for them. Rusakov was the first man to throw her out first. Natalie will never be free of her mother. She is her mother."

Horner looked as if he could bang his head against a wall. Colin didn't blame him.

"I want a deal. The guys you're after are badasses. Why do you think Yuri, Boris and I went along with Natalie's crazy scheme? We needed to keep these bastards happy. They want their weapons."

"You should have stayed a pilot, Horner."

"I know." He gave another hollow, fatalistic laugh. "I don't even like guns."

26

"CLOSTRIDIUM BOTULINUM BACTERIA," MATT Yankowski said as he swallowed some of the Talisker 18 year old that Finian Bracken had dropped off at Colin's house in Rock Point, on the assumption that he would be having company. Yank stood in front of the cold fireplace. "It produces the deadliest toxins nature has to offer. A little over a pound is enough to kill every human being on the planet." He glanced at Colin, also standing, also with a glass of Talisker. "It's a good thing you Donovans are suspicious types. You're rubbing off on Father Bracken. How did he take his near-poisoning?"

"Reasonably well. He wasn't keen on the attack on Wendell and Lucas Sharpe at Bracken Distillers. Fin's brother, Declan, was there. He doesn't like thinking Declan could have been caught in the crossfire or dispatched as an unacceptable loose end."

"'Dispatched'? He said that?"

Colin almost smiled. "Fin's word choice."

After dropping off the Talisker, Finian had returned to

St. Patrick's for a church meeting but planned to be at Hurley's later.

Colin didn't know yet if he'd be there.

Yank seemed to sense his mood. "You're a Donovan and Emma's a Sharpe," he said, splashing more Talisker in his glass. "That's not going to change. It won't matter if you go behind a desk or if you go on another deep-cover mission. Your worlds will collide again."

Colin shook his head. "They won't. I'm out."

He polished off the last of his Scotch. It was smoky, spicy, with notes of burned heather and the taste of sea salt—at least according to Finian. Colin's palate wasn't that discerning yet. He didn't know if it ever would be. He just liked what he liked.

And it beat thinking about his situation...how damn close his family, his Irish priest friend, Emma and her Russian friends had all come to dying earlier that day.

Because of him. His work.

It was late afternoon, already dark. Emma was still in Heron's Cove with the FBI and Maine state police.

Horner had continued to talk. He was hoping to cut a deal, or he just didn't care anymore now that the brass ring had slipped from his grasp. Boris and Yuri were in custody, not talking. They had served as fill-in bodyguards for Vladimir Bulgov from time to time but had never been part of his inner circle.

Their buyer was a violent paramilitary group based in the Southwest, primarily composed of mercenaries for drug cartels. Vladimir Bulgov had never done business with them. Yank had already pointed out that there would have been no finding them or stopping Horner if Colin hadn't gone undercover again in October.

Mission accomplished. Time to move on.

"You need a break," Yank said. "You've been overdue for a while."

"I need a new life." Colin lifted a duffel bag he'd packed in haste before Finian had arrived with the Talisker. "Help yourself to more Scotch and whatever's in the fridge."

"What are you going to do in Ireland?"

"I didn't say—"

Yank nodded toward the kitchen. "I saw the ticket print-out on the counter."

"I have to get my head screwed on straight. The past few days…" Colin cleared his throat. "I should have leveled with my brothers."

"You weren't cleared to provide the kind of leveling you're talking about, and they weren't cleared to hear it. Hindsight can be a great teacher, but it can also be misleading, make us harder on ourselves than we need to be. Still…" Yank helped himself to more of the Talisker. "Makes sense to put an ocean between you and the Donovan clan after this mess. Not that they blame you for the attack on Andy, the poisoned cider, almost getting killed yourself."

"I know that. It doesn't mean I'm not responsible."

"Take a break, then. Go to Ireland and drink whiskey and look for leprechauns. I said on Saturday morning before you even got back here that you need time." Yank set his Scotch glass on the coffee table and stood straight, leveled his dark gaze on Colin. "Emma?"

Just hearing her name made Colin's throat tighten. "She's a Sharpe. You knew that when you recruited her." He managed a smile. "Good luck with that."

"We'll see what's what when you get back."

"Mike's got a boat on the Bold Coast. Captain Colin tours. Nice ring to it, isn't there? Come up sometime. I'll take you out to see the puffins."

"What the hell's a puffin?"

"It's a bird, Yank."

"And I'd have to take a boat ride to see one? Forget it. Crawling through the *Nightingale,* as fancy as it is, didn't make me like boats any better." He corked the bottle of Talisker. "I used to think Lucy and I were lifers. I don't know that we are. Our marriage has always been conditional, and right now, she doesn't like the conditions."

"Give her time."

"How much time?"

"As much as she needs."

"You and Emma are lifers, Colin. You just don't know it yet."

"Lifers, Yank? Sounds like a prison sentence."

"It means that you belong together. You'll be together until you're both sitting here by the fire drinking Bracken Distillers' finest and recounting what happened the past few days as if it were yesterday."

Colin walked over to the front door. It wasn't like Matt Yankowski to get philosophical, to comment on one of his agents' romantic life. But they'd been through a lot together over the past four years, and they'd become friends.

"I'm right," Yank said.

He was, Colin realized. He and Emma belonged together. He just didn't know if it was the right thing—for her.

There was no question in his mind that it was right for him.

Yank sighed. "It's been a rough couple of months, with Sister Joan's murder and now this mess with Dmitri Rusakov, this collection, arms trafficking. See what happens after you've cleansed your soul or whatever it is you plan to do in Ireland."

"Cleansed my soul?"

"You're the one who's friends with an Irish priest and sleeping with an ex-nun."

Colin grinned and left. It was dusk, the air still and colder than he had expected.

Finian Bracken eased in next to him halfway to Hurley's and walked with him the rest of the way. Yank, Colin knew, would go on to Heron's Cove.

"I brought danger here," Colin said without looking at Finian. "It wasn't Emma. She was dealing with a spat over a Russian Art Nouveau collection. I was the one dealing with killers."

Finian's eyebrows went up. "Isn't Natalie Warren the one who came here with the collection, and isn't she under arrest for poisoning those jugs of apple cider?"

"Only because she was mixed up with my killers."

"You're in no mood for a logical argument. I've emailed you directions to the cottage Sally and I renovated. The key is under the purple flowerpot."

Colin slowed his pace and glanced at his Irish friend. "Why are you telling me this?"

"Because you need somewhere quiet and beautiful to stay while you're in Ireland." Finian smiled. "I recognized the Aer Lingus shamrock when I dropped off the Talisker."

"No secrets in this town."

"So I've discovered. You're welcome to stay at the cottage however long you'd like. If you get bored, there's some work you could do around the place—"

"What kind of work?"

"Painting, tightening this and that. I've a short list. When's your flight?"

"Tonight. If I don't go now..." He looked up at the starlit sky, pictured himself on the southwest Irish coast. "Then I won't go, and that's not a good idea."

"You haven't told Emma?"

Colin shook his head without comment.

"She will find you, Colin, but not through me," Finian said. "I will keep your confidence."

When they reached the waterfront, Finian went into Hurley's alone while Colin walked down to the docks, the tide rising but barely making a sound. He could hear his brothers' laughter. Andy wasn't cleared to drink whiskey yet but he was there.

Colin felt the pressure in his chest, the tightness of emotion. He had a great family. He was damn lucky.

He walked out to the end of the pier and dialed Emma. She didn't pick up. She was still holed up with her colleagues, or maybe Yank had arrived. He waited for her voice mail, shut his eyes at the sound of her voice.

"I have to go away for a while," he said. "I'll be in touch. I love you, babe."

He didn't know what else to say.

When he walked back to Hurley's, Mike was waiting by the steps. "Come on. I've got my truck. I'll give you a ride to wherever you're going."

"Ireland."

His older brother's mouth twitched in something like a smile. "To the airport, then."

"You hate the city."

"I'll be back on the Bold Coast soon. Let's go, brother." As they started across the parking lot, Mike glanced at Colin. "We don't have to talk on the way."

"Suits me."

"I thought it might."

Matt Yankowski was waiting on the back porch of the Sharpe house when Emma walked up from the pier where she had been looking at the stars sprinkling a dark, clear sky. The *Nightingale* was still moored at the yacht club, its owner and crew recovering in the hospital.

"I like the cabinets you picked out," Yank said, nodding toward the kitchen.

She sank onto the rail. "Don't try to make me laugh."

"I'm not. I'm serious. I figure I have a stake in how this place turns out now that I've had a tac team go through here searching for poisons and such." He stood at the rail next to her, facing the water. "How are your brother and grandfather?"

"I called again a couple of hours ago. They were in the middle of a whiskey tasting with Declan Bracken. They're okay." She took a breath. "How are things in Rock Point?"

"Does anything ever change there?"

"You have to know what to look for," she said with a smile.

"Colin sometimes makes quick decisions," Yank said without looking at her. "He goes with his gut, which doesn't usually let him down."

Emma eased off the rail. Her side ached where Yuri had hit her, and she flashed on running her fingertips along Colin's much-worse bruises. She felt heat rush to her cheeks and was glad for the cool air and darkness, especially with Yank watching her.

"Colin's trying to make it to Boston in time to catch a flight to Ireland," she said.

Yank raised his eyebrows. "He called you?"

"Well, yes and no, but I have my sources." She smiled. "Mike Donovan texted me."

"Not Father Bracken?"

"He's sworn to secrecy."

"No guilt in that grin of yours, Emma. I think you have these Donovan brothers beat."

"Or vice versa, maybe."

Yank looked down toward the *Nightingale,* partially lit against the dark night. "Your pal Ivan took off before the police and ambulance arrived at Tatiana Pavlova's cottage." Yank shifted his gaze back to Emma. "He made sure she would be okay first."

"He hadn't drunk any of the poisoned cider."

"Either that or he keeps botulism antitoxin in his wallet."

Emma wouldn't be surprised if he did. "I've been going over everything in my mind, and we both know that none of this would have happened if the arts crimes expert on your team wasn't a Sharpe."

"Colin said the same thing about himself. You knew Dmitri Rusakov before Colin ever went undercover. Colin would have been killed or rounded up smaller players or taken longer and more arms would have ended up in the wrong hands if I hadn't gone to the Sisters of the Joyful Heart and met you that day four years ago."

"Did you know back then that there was a Sharpe-Rusakov connection?"

"I don't remember if I knew then or found out, but I knew before you went to London to look into the disappearance of this Rusakov collection. I don't have a crystal ball, Emma. I just pick good people. Your connections coupled with your knowledge, experience and temperament make you a valuable agent."

"I appreciate the vote of confidence."

"A lot of fish in the Sharpe sea," he said.

"You put in a line—through me—and see what you catch."

He sighed. "I wish it were that simple, or that easy. Don't start turning into a cynic, Emma. It's not your nature. Your fresh, open look at the world—at your work—is an asset, not a liability."

She angled him a smile. "Does that mean I'm not fired?"

"Why would I fire you?"

"For being a Sharpe," she said without hesitation.

He shook his head as if he had no clue what she was talking about.

Emma crossed her arms against a cool breeze off the water. "What about Colin? What's next for him?"

Yank grimaced. "That's what he needs to decide on this trip to Ireland. He needs to get his head screwed on straight. It's hard to do with you around."

"Is that a compliment or an insult?"

"It's the way it is."

She didn't argue with him. "Natalie hooked up with some dangerous men. At first she thought she was just falling for a sexy pilot. After Bulgov's arrest, when she realized Pete Horner and his Russian friends could pick up the pieces of their boss's arms trafficking network, she couldn't resist."

"She thought she could handle them," Yank said.

"The real question was whether they could handle her. They wanted Colin's orphaned weapons—"

"Which didn't exist."

Emma nodded. "And they'd have killed him either way." She paused, but Yank made no comment; she felt another breeze as she continued. "Natalie wanted Dmitri to buy the collection back from her, but that money became essential once Colin escaped. They needed it to buy weapons and keep their buyers happy, get their foothold as illegal arms merchants."

"She was drawn to the danger, glamor and sexiness of her idea of arms trafficking," Yank said, thoughtful. "She wanted to be a player and she used what leverage she had available to her."

"Horner's attraction to her. The collection. Her relationship with a Russian billionaire." Emma paused, listened to the wash of the tide down on the stony beach. "Do you think they'd have killed Natalie when they no longer had any use for her?"

"Tried to, maybe. The Russians, especially. Horner was all-in with her."

"She didn't want to kill us all for any sensible, strategic reason. She wanted to kill us to make herself feel better. We didn't drive her into Vladimir Bulgov's world, and we didn't drive her into hating herself."

Yank nodded. "It all came together in an outburst of violence and revenge," he said.

"Natalie's fears about herself were justified. She is like her mother. She's as mean, selfish and unfeeling. Worse, since her mother never resorted to poisoning people."

"Another *baba yaga,*" Yank said. "An evil Russian witch."

"I didn't realize you knew Russian folklore."

"A few things you still don't know about me, Agent Sharpe." He stood straight and eyed her in the dim light from the kitchen window. "Colin isn't the only one who has some thinking to do. You do, too. You need to decide where you belong, who you are. I can't have someone on my team with doubts."

"Yank—"

"You can always go back to Sharpe Fine Art Recovery but once you cross that threshold, you can't go back to the FBI, at least not to my team."

Emma nodded. "I understand."

"As smart as you are, I'll bet the hell you do." Yank walked over to the back door, pulled it open as he glanced at her. "Think about taking a break yourself. You're due."

He went inside, heading out through the front door to his car. Emma stayed on the porch. She was tempted to paint, but it was too cold. Instead she sat on the steps and stared out at the water, listening to the tide and wind, clearing her mind, centering herself. Meditation had been an important aspect of her life as a novice.

After a while—she didn't know how long, exactly—Mike Donovan walked across the yard from the parking lot on the other side of the hedges.

Emma walked down the steps and joined him on the cool, dew-soaked grass.

"I was in here once as a teenager," Mike said. "I'd done something wrong. I forget what, but your grandfather had me sweeping floors to make amends. You'll notice I'm not one of the law enforcement Donovan brothers."

"Did a few years in the military straighten you out?"

"Not really." He grinned at her, but his deep gray eyes remained serious as he turned and faced the water. "Finian Bracken owns a cottage in the Kerry hills."

"How do you know?'

He shrugged. "Big brother Mike knows all."

"Why are you telling me?" Emma asked.

"My brothers and I have broken enough hearts." Mike shoved his hands into the pockets of his canvas jacket. "Colin's being a rock head. He probably knows it by now."

Emma smiled. "Mike, you're a romantic."

"That's why I live alone in the woods." He winked at her. "Give Colin a few days to get good and miserable before you go find him."

27

EMMA STOPPED IN HERON'S COVE TO CHECK with the carpenters before her evening flight to Ireland. She had lasted three days. She couldn't wait any longer. Matt Yankowski had all but shoved her out of her office in Boston, insisting she finally take time off. She hadn't since Sister Joan's death.

The *Nightingale* was still at its mooring, but preparations were under way for its departure. Dmitri Rusakov and Tatiana Pavlova—his daughter—had been released from the hospital that morning and were spending time together on board.

Ivan Alexander mounted the steps to the back porch. He smiled at Emma's latest attempt at watercolor, clipped to the easel in the corner. "A great blue heron?"

"My version, anyway." She pointed with her brush at another watercolor heron, beautifully rendered, on the dresser where she kept her supplies. "Tatiana gave me that one. I'll treasure it. She's truly gifted."

"She's done everything on her own." He studied Tatiana's watercolor. "Her mother and Dmitri fell in love as teenagers. Katya was—is—the love of his life. It's hard to believe she's been gone twenty years. Dmitri let his work consume him after her death. He told me it was best Tatiana stay with her mother's family while he tended business. She had a quiet life, people who loved her. She was safe. He got caught up in money, his enemies—women."

"Tatiana wanted nothing to do with him, and he did nothing to correct her view of him."

"Nor did I," Ivan said. "She was always artistic, like her mother."

"And feisty," Emma said with a smile.

Ivan didn't return her smile. "Yes." He picked up a pencil, checked its tip with his thumb. "I warned Dmitri about Vladimir Bulgov."

"In April?"

"Then, too."

Emma digested his words. "You mean twenty years ago," she said.

"Dmitri didn't listen until it was too late."

"You suspect Bulgov killed Katya."

"He wanted Dmitri to help him get started in business and Dmitri refused. He didn't like Vladimir. I didn't like him." Ivan set the pencil down again. "I couldn't prove that he killed Katya."

Emma rinsed her brush in a jar of water and set it to dry on the edge of the dresser, as Tatiana had taught her. "Was it revenge for not helping him?"

"I think he believed Dmitri was in the car, too."

"So he didn't target Katya," Emma said. "What did he want with Dmitri in April?"

"He wanted him to know that he'd found Tatiana. It was quite by accident, he said. He'd heard about the Firebird, that a young Russian designer was getting a lot of attention. When he saw her..." Ivan steadied his gaze on Emma. "He knew."

"But he never had a chance to use what he knew against him. Did you have anything to do with luring Bulgov to Los Angeles, Ivan? With helping me find out about his interest in Picasso?"

He shook his head. "I would have helped you, but no."

Emma looked at her great blue heron, remembered Tatiana arriving at the Sharpe house. Was it only a week ago? "You're Tatiana's falcon," Emma said. "Her protector. You have been since she was a little girl."

"She doesn't always make that easy."

"Ivan—"

"She's like a baby sister to me," he said, as if guessing what Emma meant to ask. "When Vladimir came to the Firebird and commissioned the nesting dolls, Tatiana let her imagination get carried away."

"She convinced herself you and Dmitri were in cahoots with him," Emma said.

He smiled, just a twitch of his straight mouth. "'Cahoots.' I like that word." His smile faded as quickly as it had appeared. "When I learned Natalie was bringing the collection here to Heron's Cove, I thought Tatiana might find out, too."

"Dmitri knew you would put her first. He would protect her."

"It didn't mean she would listen."

"No," Emma said. "She knows now that she should never have hid from you, or from her father. She'll make a full recovery. You got to her in time."

"And your man," Ivan said quietly.

She smiled. "Yes."

"He's decisive. He acts on instinct but that's good." Ivan's gaze didn't waver. "He loves you very much."

"Ivan—"

"I'm seeing Tatiana and Dmitri to the Bahamas. They will

need weeks more of rest. They can get to know each other again, as father and daughter. They've made mistakes but it's time to put the past behind them."

"The police found the collection in Natalie's tote bag."

"It will be returned to Dmitri. There's no question that he is the rightful owner." Ivan turned and looked out at the water, not even glancing toward the *Nightingale*. "I didn't see through Renee, or Natalie."

"You tried with both of them. It was you who broke into Natalie's house in Phoenix?"

"I knew Tatiana was there. I wanted to know what she would find."

"Nothing," Emma said. "Natalie hid her affair with Pete Horner well. She knew what she was doing, just as her mother did when she made off with Dmitri's collection. She'd found out about Tatiana, hadn't she?"

Ivan didn't answer.

"She didn't like not being the fairest of them all," Emma said, remembering Tatiana's sketch. "And Tatiana knew."

"Renee sought her out. Dmitri found out. It was the last straw. At first she seemed like a beautiful woman who wanted to enjoy life."

"She and Natalie excelled at keeping their true natures hidden," Emma said. "They knew how to make themselves irresistible when they wanted to ensnare people, capture them in their webs to use for their own needs and wants." Emma was silent a moment, picturing the two women together in London four years ago, then Natalie just a few days ago, screaming in a rage. "They're the sort who manipulate and use people—even the people who love them—and then discard them."

"Maybe most especially the people who love them," Ivan said.

"Renee's gone, and Natalie and Vladimir are under arrest here in America. It's time to heal."

Ivan turned to her, his eyes suddenly lost in the shadows. "Thank you, Emma, for all you've done. You were an excellent Sharpe. Now you're an excellent FBI agent."

"I still am a Sharpe. I just don't work for my family's business."

"Dmitri asked me to invite you aboard the *Nightingale* for a drink before he and Tatiana depart. He doesn't want you to have any problems because of him."

"I won't. I'll stop by, but only for a minute. He and Tatiana both need to rest."

"And you have a plane to catch," Ivan said with a small smile. "Give my best to your grandfather, and your agent."

"What makes you think—"

"You're here alone, and you don't want to be."

She swallowed through a sudden surge of uncertainty. "Colin and I have complicated each other's lives. I don't know what's next."

Ivan caught her fingers into his and squeezed them gently as he kissed her on the cheek. "I do," he whispered.

In the next moment, he was gone.

By midmorning, Emma was walking with her brother and grandfather on a lane that ran along a green ridge above Kenmare Bay and Declan Bracken's house. She could hear sheep and cows, the rush of water in a nearby stream, and nothing else.

"Walking's the best cure for jet lag," she said.

"And for all that ails the soul." Her grandfather slung an arm over her shoulders and hugged her close. "It's good to have you here in one piece, Special Agent Sharpe."

But Lucas didn't smile. He stayed along the hedgerow, the

tangles of greenery dripping after an early-morning shower. The sun was out now, sparkling in the fields and down on the bay.

Emma slipped out from her grandfather's embrace and moved in closer to her brother. "I know you're concerned that my job with the FBI endangers you, Granddad, the work you do. You dispatched your thug with no trouble, but I never should have sent you to London."

"It's a damn good thing you did," Lucas said with a grunt. "I don't have to worry about the red tape that the FBI or Scotland Yard would have required."

"That's true, but it doesn't change the fact that what happened in Heron's Cove with Dmitri Rusakov proves your concerns about my role with the FBI aren't unfounded."

"Does it, Emma?" her brother asked, not waiting for an answer. "Maybe there's another way to look at this. Maybe being a Sharpe endangered a sensitive FBI mission. The thug that came after Granddad and me was a result of Sharpe work as much as of FBI work. That's just the way it is."

"Maybe so," Emma said quietly.

Her grandfather caught up with them and paused at a barbed-wire fence, several brown cows coming up to him. "To think that my folks could have become farmers instead of moving to Boston when I was a little tyke. How different my life would have been."

Lucas took in a quick breath, impatient, concerned, but Emma hadn't spent the past few days with their grandfather, and smiled at him. "No regrets, Granddad?"

He patted one of the cows. "I don't know that I'd have made a good farmer, but I've done all right as an art detective. Now as I retire, I have to decide what needs to be said and what doesn't need to be said. I thought the tragic story of the young artist who helped me in Moscow twenty years ago was one that I would take to the grave with me."

"I need to know everything, Granddad," Lucas said without hesitation, then added, "And so does Emma. Sixty years is a long time, but I'm willing to listen. I want to, and if I'm to carry on your work, I need to."

Wendell Sharpe stood back from the cow and motioned with one hand at the surrounding hills. "This area is filled with ancient Celtic sites. The Celts had no written language. They passed on stories, poems, history and knowledge orally. Nothing was written down."

"The key word is 'oral,'" Lucas said. "That means they talked. They didn't die with the knowledge in their heads. Sorry, Granddad. I don't mean to be so blunt."

"I prefer blunt. You kids were always more polite than I ever was."

The cows wandered off into the field, and he continued down the lane. Emma and Lucas glanced at each other, then followed their grandfather. The lane dipped down a hill and they crossed a small bridge, the air cool with the stream flowing under them. A holly tree branched out over a clear pool, and Emma stopped to take in the sight.

"I don't know if I can do this anymore," she said, half to herself. "It's too messy, being an FBI agent and a Sharpe. That's why Colin's not here. He's figured that out. He's pushing me to figuring it out, too. He didn't just go away for himself. He went away for me."

Her grandfather eased in next to her. "Your experience as a Sharpe is one reason you're as valuable to the FBI as you are. The people you work with, including Colin, must see that."

Lucas, she noted, made no comment.

They followed the lane down the hill, then back along another lane below the ridge and up to Declan Bracken's house overlooking the bay. Then it was on to a pub in his small village.

"My poor brother is digging bean holes in America," Declan said cheerfully, sounding so much like his twin brother, "and here we are, enjoying ourselves. Then again, Fin does sound content when I talk to him."

"The bean holes are all dug," Emma said.

"Ah. Good to know."

Emma smiled. "The supper's on Saturday. I volunteered to bring pies, but my friend Sister Cecilia is making them for me. She says I can repay her by exercising patience the next time I try my hand at watercolor. Maybe you can come for a visit one day."

Declan obviously liked that idea. "Perhaps at Christmas. I'd love to experience a New England winter, at least for a few days." He leaned closer to Emma, as if he were about to tell a secret. "Finian says that he's alive now because of you and Colin Donovan."

"Your brother has good instincts. I bet he'd have dumped that cider down the drain."

"What if he'd shared it with parishioners instead? Thank God he didn't, and all's well with Saint Patrick's of Rock Point, Maine."

Emma drank some of her Guinness. "And how is Colin?"

Declan sat up straight. "Why ask me?"

She peered at him over the rim of her glass. "Why, indeed?"

Her grandfather laughed. "She's a Sharpe, an ex-nun *and* an FBI agent, Declan. You didn't stand a chance."

Declan was clearly amused. "Special Agent Donovan and I had a *taoscán* of Bracken 15 year old together this afternoon. I promised not to give away his location." The Irishman poured a clear, caramel-colored whiskey from a debut "expression" of Bracken Distillers. "Finian oversaw it going into the casks before Sally and little Kathleen and Mary went to God. I believe you'll taste their love."

Emma held back tears as she, Lucas and her grandfather raised their glasses. *"Sláinte."*

Finian Bracken noticed Julianne Maroney edge closer to the simmering bean holes behind St. Patrick's Church. The supper had ended and the last of the sizable crowd had left. "Father, do you have a minute?" she asked, unusually tentative. She had her hair pulled back and wore a sweatshirt over jeans, and her L.L.Bean boots.

Finian smiled. "Of course."

She hesitated, as if debating whether she should do an about-face and flee. It was a pleasant evening, the air dry, the stars twinkling above them as Finian waited for the bean-hole fires to die down. Then he would take a long walk in the village to burn off the meal, including two slices of Sister Cecilia's apple pie. She had laughed, telling him he was in danger of becoming a true Mainer.

Julianne took a breath and said, "I came to tell you that I've accepted a marine biology internship in Cork next semester."

"Cork?"

"Yes. Cork, Ireland. I'm a little nervous. I've never been so far from home, even for a vacation. But I'm excited, too."

"Cork's a lovely town. I have friends there."

"Good to know." She stamped out an ember that had escaped, then zipped up her jacket, although it wasn't a terribly cold evening. "It wasn't healthy. What I was doing with Andy. Not letting go."

"A broken heart heals in time," Finian said.

She raised her eyes to him. "Has yours healed, Father? I know it's different, losing your family compared to a stubborn rake like Andy Donovan and me going our separate ways." She paused, looking embarrassed. "I just wondered."

Except for the Donovans, no one in Rock Point had ever asked him about his family, the depth of his loss. "I know my family is with God. Beyond that..." Finian searched for the appropriate words. "Some breaks don't heal. Instead we learn to live with them, and trust in God's plan for us."

"I think that's why my grandmother connected with you. You didn't try to tell her how she should feel." Julianne smiled suddenly. "She wants to come visit me in Cork. Ireland's going to be great on so many levels."

The note of defiance in Julianne's tone suggested she wasn't as over Andy Donovan as she thought, or wanted to be. Maybe in showing him what she could do and be without him, she'd show herself.

"I'm glad Andy wasn't killed, though," she added. "Rat bastard that he is. Sorry, Father."

"No worries," he said with a laugh.

Julianne thanked him, although precisely for what he didn't know, and left Finian to his bean-hole fires. It was markedly colder when he was satisfied that the fires for his first bean-hole supper were out. He went into the rectory, and he sat in the kitchen. He had an email from Declan with a picture of him and the Sharpes, an Irish rainbow in the background.

Finian smiled, then poured himself a *taoscán* of Bracken 15, thinking not of the past but what was next for his little church in Rock Point, Maine.

28

THE COTTAGE WAS TUCKED ON A HILL ABOVE an inlet on an isolated stretch of the Iveragh Peninsula, far from any tour buses. Not that tourists were an issue so late in the season. Emma noticed that she wasn't at all nervous or self-conscious when she climbed out of her rented car.

The wind blew across the water, straight from the Atlantic, with the promise of rain by nightfall. She had dressed for the conditions in her lined trench coat, her boots, wool socks, a wool scarf, a wool sweater and hiking pants.

She wasn't sure how long she'd stay. A few minutes? A few days?

There was no car in the gravel driveway, but Declan Bracken had already told her—or at least hinted—that Colin hadn't bothered with one. The cottage was just a three-mile walk to the nearest pub and a short walk to the water. It was equipped with two kayaks, paddles and life jackets and two bicycles. On the drive down the peninsula and its twisting roads, Emma would catch peeks of glistening Kenmare Bay and picture kayaking with Colin along the shore.

The cottage was tiny, constructed of gray stones collected long ago from the surrounding lands. Its front door was painted a cheerful, glossy blue that she suspected Sally Bracken had chosen, along with the collection of colorful flowerpots on the step.

The door was cracked open, and as Emma raised her hand to knock, she recognized the smell of peat smoke.

A perfect afternoon and evening for a fire, she thought with a smile.

She heard the crunch of gravel behind her and turned just as Colin materialized from around back, carrying a bucket filled with small chunks of peat. He hadn't shaved in several days and his face and corduroy shirt were smudged with black soot, his jeans hanging low on his hips.

Her breath caught in her throat.

The man was so damn sexy.

"I had to let the smoke get out of the house," he said, his voice husky. "Took a bit to get the hang of the stove and managing a turf fire, but I've got it now." He grinned. "More or less."

"Nothing more romantic than a cozy fire."

"Especially when it's not blowing smoke in your face." He pushed the door farther open with his foot. "It's safe to go in."

She angled him a look. "Is it?"

He winked at her. "For the moment."

The cottage consisted of an open room with a loft, its thick stone walls painted white and a small cast-iron peat-burning stove the main source of heat.

Colin set his bucket by the stove. "We have to make good use of our time before Yank sends in a tac team to bring us back to work."

"We complicate his life," Emma said.

"He wouldn't have it any other way. Lucy's back from Paris. He's marginally less cranky."

"So you've talked to him."

Colin opened the door to the stove, layered in some of the peat. "There's no not talking to Matt Yankowski." He shut the stove door and stood back from the fire. "We had to go over a few things."

"Another undercover mission?"

His smoky gaze steadied on her. "No." Then he winked at her. "Yank wants me to bring him back a bottle of Inish Turk Beg whiskey."

"You're not kidding, are you?"

"Nope. I'm making him pay. Damn stuff's expensive."

Emma stepped closer to the fire but she wasn't remotely cold, nor could she imagine anywhere else she would rather be. "Finian wasn't exaggerating when he said it's a small cottage. There's not much room in here."

Colin slipped his arms around her, brushed his lips against hers. "There's enough."

★ ★ ★ ★ ★

Author's Note

Thank you for reading *Heron's Cove*. It was great fun to write, and now I'm deep into *Declan's Cross,* which is next up in my Sharpe & Donovan series. *Saint's Gate,* where we first meet Emma and Colin, is out now in paperback. If, like me, you're fascinated by Art Nouveau and Russian art and folk traditions, you might be interested in some of the books I consulted in researching *Heron's Cove*. They include *Artistic Luxury* by Stephen Harrison, Emmanuel Ducamp and Jeannine Falino; *Russian Fairy Tales,* a collection by Aleksandr Afanasev (translated by Norbert Guterman); and *The Frogs Who Begged for a Tsar (and 61 other Russian fables)* by Ivan Krylov.

A huge thank-you to my editor, Margaret Marbury, and everyone at Harlequin MIRA, as well as to my agent, Jodi Reamer at Writers House, to Nancy Berland and her incredible team and to my friend Jennifer McCord.

Special thanks to my husband, Joe, to our wonderful family, and to our friend John Moriarty—our Inish Turk Beg Single Malt Irish Whiskey awaits us.

For all my latest news, please visit my website and sign up

for my eNewsletter at www.carlaneggers.com. I'm also on Facebook and Twitter. I love to hear from readers!

Many thanks, and happy reading,

Carla Neggers